HER
GILDED
VOICE

HER GILDED VOICE

K.C. AEGIS

Elsewhen Press

Her Gilded Voice

First published in Great Britain by Elsewhen Press, 2024
An imprint of Alnpete Limited

Elsewhen Press, PO Box 757, Dartford, Kent DA2 7TQ
www.elsewhen.press

British Library Cataloguing in Publication Data.
A catalogue record for this book is available from the British Library.

ISBN 978-1-915304-44-5 Print edition
ISBN 978-1-915304-54-4 eBook edition

Designed and formatted by Elsewhen Press

Contents

For Kylie

Part 1

Lacey Clarke

Chapter 1

I'll start with a riddle. What must you lose in order to find?

I like riddles because they're honest. They ask questions while also giving the answer. The solution hides between the words…like a rabbit buried in weeds. It sits quiet, not moving until someone scares it from cover.

I confess, auditor, when this riddle first found me, I had no interest in the answer. But now that it's here, I can feel it sitting on my chest, pushing the air from my lungs. Some riddles are like that. Some questions have answers that change everything.

So what is it? Have you figured it out yet? What must you lose in order to find? Since you're reading my story, I imagine you've already encountered the answer. Unless you're *not* reading. Maybe you're only listening while someone else reads it to you. If that's the case, how can you be sure the words they're saying are the same ones that're written in the book? Maybe they changed things. What're they taking out, and what're they adding of their own? Either way, how would you know?

In the meantime, I'm thinking of another riddle my sister Yadi told me one day walking home from the skin market. She knew how much I liked riddles and would sometimes ask her clients if they knew any.

She put her arm around me and began,

"Turn me on, and I go off.
I can't dream, but *lords,* I scream.
When I cry, my tears will fry.
What am I?"

Her perfume failed to conceal her clients' sour stench. Like frosting on top of a rotting pot roast. Her true smell, if she still had one, had been buried beneath the others. In this way, I supposed, Yadi had become a riddle herself. Her true self hiding beneath foreign fragrances and dazzling makeup.

"Hmm, let me think." I knew the answer, but wanted to

draw it out. I put my hand over my chin, feeling the cloth mask and ragged scar underneath.

The smile that broke out on Yadi's face was enough to make me forget the smell clinging to the air around her.

"Are you stumped?" She rocked back and forth in quiet celebration, long black hair flipping from side to side.

"It's a tea kettle," I said, then laughed when the smile wilted from my sister's face. Her sparkling gray eyes turned accusatory.

"You *knew*." She pushed away, but there was no anger in her touch. "Either that or your voyce told you."

"I'm not cheating," I said. "That was an easy one."

Yadi's disappointment turned into a frown, and her eyes glazed over. I figured her inner voyce was speaking to her, and I wondered – not for the first time – if that was how I looked whenever mine spoke to me.

After a few seconds, Yadi's eyes cleared and her smile returned.

"Okay, I've got another one. I have eyes but can't see a dang thing. What am I?"

I knew this one, too. Or thought I did. But there was more than one possible answer.

<Would you like a hint?> my voyce asked.

"No," I said, shaking my head. "I'll figure it out."

"Hey," cried Yadi. "No help allowed."

"I don't need any help, Yadi. The answer's obvious."

"You think so?" An impish smirk curved her pink lip gloss.

"Yeah, but there's more than one answer. What has eyes but can't see…that could be a needle, a potato, or a storm. Any one of those works."

"And yet, none of them are the answer I'm looking for." She gestured up the street at the pair of muties walking toward us. I felt a sickening jolt as my heart lurched in my chest. This was often the case whenever I happened upon a mutie without fair warning. The throng of pedestrians parted around them like how a river curved around a submerged boulder. Or like how people avoided someone with the latest virus.

"What has eyes but can't see? Give up? A *mutie*!" Yadi cried cheerfully, pointing at the approaching couple. "They can't see."

"But they also don't have eyes," I corrected her. "Plucked right out of their heads for misbehaving." And not just their eyes. I shuddered as the pair grew nearer. It could have been an elderly couple, but it was hard to tell. Obsidian marbles had been pressed in where eyes should have been. Instead of ears, milky white domes stuck out from the sides of their heads. Their tongues had also been clipped off, I've been told, but any sign of this was covered by the dark red masks they wore; the color of blood, or that wine the cellies and wolves drank by the gallon.

"I wish they'd put those masks over their entire face," said Yadi, "not just their mouths and noses. That way, we wouldn't have to see those blank stares. *Creepy*."

The mutie couple made their way down the street, walking hand in hand. I had a hard time imagining what crime could have been so terrible that deemed it necessary to strip them of their sight, sound, taste, and ability to speak...but it must have been bad. Why else would anyone do that to a person?

<Whatever it was, they must have deserved it,> my voyce would usually say.

She was right, but still, a part of me was relieved the pair still had at least the ability to feel physical touch. Without that, how would they even know they were still alive?

The mutie couple held tightly to each other. Their hands locked. The woman put her free hand on the man's wrist. He responded by reaching across his own body and doing the same to her. It was like one set of hands wasn't enough for this mutie couple. They needed both to show the world and themselves how much they meant to each other.

"You asked it wrong," I said. Yadi blinked in confusion so I went on. "Your riddle. You asked it in reverse. Instead of saying 'I have eyes but can't see,' you should say, 'I have no eyes but still can see.'" I wondered if this was one of those unfair riddles. Because even though muties could see, in the technical sense, it wasn't the kind of seeing I'd wish on anyone.

Yadi made no indication she'd heard me. She kept watching the muties with morbid fascination. They shambled over the sidewalk, seemingly unaware of the stares and disgusted grunts of all those around them granting a wide berth.

<Leave them alone, Lacey. They have it hard enough without you gawking.>

So I looked down at the pavement. I meant to stay that way until they passed. But to my dismay, they didn't.

Yadi dug her fingernails into my arm and gasped.

I was so annoyed with her that I didn't notice at first that the pair had stopped directly in front of us.

A violent chill scurried along my spine as I gazed up into their black, sightless eyes. They had stopped less than three feet away. The skin around the domes on their heads was pink with old scar tissue. This close, I could see the freckles and wrinkles that had belonged to people who no longer existed. Their faces were like road maps pointing toward a place that had been torn down a long time ago. The muties before me now were only husks of who they once had been. Like sunken ships, their original selves had slipped beneath the surface and had been lost in some forgotten chasm.

Not entirely lost, I guessed. I imagined it was someone's job to keep track of them. Somewhere – perhaps in a cardboard box in some darkened storage facility – the muties' former lives had been catalogued, archived, and filed away. All that remained of who they'd been now imprisoned on a few eight-by-eleven sheets of multiuse printing paper. It was a depressing end to a life…but a necessary one.

Knowing this, it was strange to see the little hints of identity these muties still displayed. A pink clip hung in the woman's short, curly hair. The man's hair, dotted with flecks of gray, had a neat part and was combed into an elaborate, high wave. I had barely enough time to think who would do a mutie's hair, and for what purpose, when my voyce interrupted my thoughts.

<This one wants to ask you a question.>

"I'm sorry?"

<You don't have to answer them, Lacey. I can send them away if you want.>

"No...no. It's okay." I couldn't deny that these muties unnerved me. They always did. But also, I couldn't deny that I was curious. What on earth could they want to ask *me*?

<This one wants to know if you've seen their cat.>

I told Yadi what they were asking and she frowned.

"Probably want to eat it. Sick weirdos. Tell them to get their food from *Charity House* with the rest of their lot."

The couple gave no sign they'd heard Yadi's words, and I couldn't bring myself to repeat them. Instead, I asked, "What does the cat look like?"

They both shrugged.

<This one says they don't know. They've never seen her, only felt that she has a small hole in her right ear.>

"Does the cat have a name?"

<This one says the cat does indeed have a name, but they've never said it out loud. They can't.>

"Then how do they call her?"

Acting in sync, the man and woman held out a hand and snapped their fingers. It made me think of all the times I had fallen asleep in Loyalty classes. The teacher, Ms. Parks, would waddle up and down the aisle between desks and snap her bright green fingernails in the faces of anyone she felt wasn't paying the proper attention. Once, after staying up all night shelling and deveining shrimp for my job at the wet market, I had been extra sleepy. After dozing off a couple of times, I suddenly felt a cold hand on the back of my neck. I jerked up in my seat only to find Ms. Parks glaring at me from across the classroom. She had been nowhere near me, but I could still feel her hand tightening on my neck. Her green fingernails burrowed into my skin. And when her voyce told me to sit up and pay attention, I winced at the skull cracking volume of it.

The muties were still snapping their fingers at me.

<This one says this is how they call her. They snap three times. Most days, it is enough to bring their cat to them. She's usually waiting when they get home, but she hasn't come in three days. They are afraid something has happened to her.>

The muties snapped a final time, then they both opened their hands, and turned their palms up in a pleading gesture. It looked as if they expected me to hand them something. But all they really wanted was my help.

"I…uh…I haven't seen her. But I'll let you know if I do. Where do you live?"

My voyce let me know she'd recorded the muties' contact information. Then she scolded me.

<You really shouldn't talk to muties, Lacey. People might get the wrong idea.>

The mutie couple bowed their heads – a surprising sign of gratitude – before they turned away and continued down the street.

"I think I need a shower," Yadi said beside me.

"That makes two of us," I said. It wasn't how I really felt, though. It was just something I was supposed to say. Whenever confronted with muties on the street, you were *supposed* to feel disgust. And I usually did. But this time, watching that couple walk away, occasionally stopping in an attempt to ask someone else for help, *disgust* was not a word that came to mind.

"Out of curiosity," I said, "what is their cat's name?"

<They said they never say it out loud.>

"Right, I know that. But they still have a name for her, right? A name they keep in their heads."

<Yes,> my voyce responded. <They do have a name, but it doesn't make any sense.>

"How come? What is it?"

<They call her, *Daughter*. Isn't that a funny name to give a cat? Honestly, we should just pretend we didn't talk to them.>

"Yes," I agreed, "you're probably right." Privately, I promised myself to keep my eyes open. I wanted to help if I could. As Yadi and I walked the remaining six blocks home, I scanned the trash-ridden alleys and cracked sidewalks for any sign of the cat called Daughter.

*   *   *

In case you were wondering, auditor, the cat had nothing to do with the riddle I first asked you about. *What must you lose in order to find?* It's true, the cat *was* indeed lost, and you wouldn't need to find it if it wasn't. It may seem like the cat would fit, but no. Riddles can have more than one solution after all. In this case, the cat was not the answer, only the start to an even bigger problem.

Chapter 2

Another riddle.

<I only move if I *keep* moving,
Sit too long and I'll *keep* sitting.
So weak I am, a child's touch leaves lifelong scars.
So strong I am, I hold cities up toward the stars.
What am I?>

My voyce said this to me as I was stepping off the subway.

"Hmm, I don't know this one," I said.

<Oh, goodie.> My voyce sounded pleased with herself. <Would you like a hint?>

"No, Alina." That was my voyce's name: *Alina*. Yadi said I had picked the name when I was little, although I don't remember when exactly. It had been the name of another little girl who had lived across the hall from us. She'd disappeared when her folks were picked up by some flexer boys. But before then, Yadi said, Alina and I used to play all the time. I only remember bits and pieces of her. Like how she had really big, black eyes and a loud, jack-hammer laugh. But more importantly, I remember how she didn't laugh or make a fuss whenever I took off my mask. It was something I wasn't used to and, all this time later, still appreciated. So, I liked the name and had never changed it.

"No hints, Alina. I wanna sort it out on my own."

<Suit yourself. But it's a *hard* one.> She put heavy emphasis on 'hard'.

"Is that a hint? Dang you, Alina. I said *no hints*."

She chuckled in response.

I was still thinking about the riddle as I climbed the steps up to Jay Street. A flock of coffee drones buzzed overhead. The mermaid logo beamed from the sides as they flitted about like a bunch of morbidly obese humming birds. Each drone carried six to eight cups in thermos containers. All, no doubt, were destined for some cellie or wolf up in the high rises.

Below the drones, the streets were slick with the rain that had passed through an hour earlier. A line of city transports crept along at a walker's pace while the White Line – the upper crest's fleet of autonomous SUVs – hissed by in their own private lane. The penalties for using the White Line were terribly stiff. Even pedestrians, if they were unfortunate enough to step in front of an oncoming White Line vehicle, would have their identity transmitted over to the police. If you were lucky, a cop or two would show up a few days later and demand payment. If you were *unlucky*, a group of flexer boys would do the collecting. Nobody wanted to do business with a flexer. That's why most people did all they could to pay their fines *before* they came knocking.

Just last month, right here on Jay Street, I'd seen them in action. I had been on my way to work when a couple of teenagers came sprinting around the corner. A boy and a girl. Both looked to be about my age, seventeen. They were string thin and dressed in those long, green fabrics I so often see with kids from across the river. The boy was holding a couple of water bottles, while the girl clutched a paper sack with what looked like several large pretzels crammed inside. They wore face masks like me, but the wide-eyed panic was clear for anyone to see. Fear pulsed around them like a horn blast.

<Get out of the way,> said Alina.

I stepped back and pressed against the building.

As they drew nearer, I could see that the girl was crying, and the boy looked to be near collapse. He flung one of the water bottles aside and reached for the girl's hand.

"Come on!" he shouted. "We could lose 'em!"

To this, the girl screamed and dragged the boy to a skidding halt. Her eyes were fixed on something up the street. I turned to follow her gaze and felt the heat rush out of my body.

Two men in dark purple coats, each with crisscrossed red stripes on their arms, were standing on the street corner. *Flexer boys*. They all looked the same to me. If not for the purple coats, they could all pass for professional football players. Tall, burly guys swimming in an aura of violence. At the moment, mercifully, they were looking in the opposite direction.

The teenagers were deathly still for several heartbeats. Their cloth masks puffed in and out as they gasped for breath. I thought maybe they'd already been *iced* until the boy gently but firmly gripped the girl's shoulder and turned her back the way they'd come. It was no use, though. Another flexer had stepped into view. This one was looking directly at them.

"Don't run," I pleaded. "You'll only make it worse."

The boy gave me a fleeting glance, but it was enough to see the world of desperation screaming inside him.

"We jus' wanted somethin' to eat."

He tugged the girl's hand and led her out into the street.

There was no point. Once a flexer set his eyes on you, it was over.

The flexer didn't move as the teenagers slipped past the city transports. In fact, it almost looked like he was going to let them go. But then the boy and girl stepped out into the private lane of the White Line. The flexer raised his arm and made a fist. In an instant, both teenagers crumpled to the ground. The girl's momentum threw her into an awkward, painful-looking summersault up onto the adjacent sidewalk. The boy however had been pushing the girl along, so he collapsed right where he was – right in the middle of the White Line.

One of those SUVs was speeding toward them, but there was still plenty of time to stop.

The boy was sprawled out in the road. Still wide-eyed and conscious but lacking any control over his own body. The SUV did indeed slow down, but it never stopped.

A city car rolled between us and obscured what happened next. All I could see was the top of the White Line SUV. The hood of the vehicle lifted into the air, fell, then the back did the same. Bump-bump. Bump-bump. Once it was clear, the SUV's electric engine whined as it picked up speed and hissed down the road.

<Don't look, Lacey. It's terrible.>

I knew she was right, but part of me wanted…no, *needed* to see.

The city car moved out of the way, and I stared, unblinking at the spot where the boy had been killed. I couldn't see him. That spot in the road was a blurred mirage. Sort of like that heat haze you see in the desert or on the tops of cars in the middle of summer. My voyce was protecting me from what must have been a traumatic sight. The shimmer pulsed with my own heartbeat. I never liked it when Alina shut off parts of my vision, but it was usually for the best.

<Sorry, Lacey. But you really don't want to see this.>

My eyes watered, and my head began to throb. Trying to look through a shimmer always gave me such terrible headaches. So, my attention turned toward the girl. She was still crumpled up on the sidewalk. Her arms and legs thrashed by her sides. The bag of pretzels she'd been carrying were strewn all over the sidewalk.

We jus' wanted somethin' to eat. That had been the boy's last words.

The flexer boys stomped on the pretzels as they formed a box around her. There were five of them now. The one who'd iced the teenagers still had his fist raised. He had it pointed at the girl like she was still a threat. Two of the others knelt to fasten the girl's ankles, then pinned her arms behind her back so they could bind her wrists with zip ties. While this was going on, another flexer reached down into the shimmer. The blurred spot slid toward the side of the road.

I can't say how long it was that I stood there, anchored to the spot. Eventually, a red van pulled up beside them. The flexer with his fist raised lowered his arm and released his control over the girl. She immediately began to scream. Huge, whooping sobs and cries of pain ricocheted up and down the street. All five flexers gripped a part of her and lifted her into the air. She seemed so light in their hold, like a piece of litter getting picked up off the street. Her mask had come loose and I could see a child's face underneath. Tears poured down her cheeks. A dark stain covered the front of her pants, and I realized with some embarrassment that the rumors were true. I'd heard that's what happened when the flexers got you. They'd turn on every muscle in your body at once, making your insides into a vice.

They tossed the girl into the van and clambered in behind her.

A moment later, the van sped away. All that remained of what had happened was the crushed pretzels laid out on the sidewalk…that and the blurred mirage they'd left behind in the gutter.

I tried one last time to look through the shimmer – to see the boy – but I turned away when a migraine began thumping behind my eyes.

So, I looked down at the sidewalk and watched my steps as I made my way over cracked concrete.

I asked Alina about it later.

"How come they were allowed to steal?" I asked. "Didn't their voyces try to stop them?"

<Everyone is given a chance,> said Alina. <People can follow the rules and live their best lives, or they can try to cheat. It is not the place of voyces to stop all bad choices.>

"Why not?"

<Well, look around, Lacey. The streets and buildings. Everything we need in the city. It sure can't build itself. A healthy society needs muties and dead-heads to do important work. And if some people have a hard time using their freedom in responsible ways, well…those people *lose* their freedom. Allowing people to misbehave helps us separate the bad ones from the good ones.>

"So, what am I?"

<Lacey.> There was laughter in her voyce. <You're a good one.>

* * *

I was still thinking about Alina's riddle when an alert flashed along the edges of my vision.

<Incoming challenge,> said Alina. <Feeling up for it?>

"You know I am." A glance up and down the street showed several people stepping out of the main flow of foot traffic. They stood at attention, hands by their sides.

Like good little soldiers, I thought. At any rate, I was glad I wouldn't be the only one accepting today. I found a small spot beside a trashcan that reeked of rotting meat. No sooner had I placed my hands by my sides when the air in front of me started to shimmer.

I blinked, and my eyes watered as a rent in reality tore open right in the middle of the sidewalk. None of the passing pedestrians seemed to notice it. A few even walked straight through the floating gap without so much as a shrug.

But that was normal. Challenges were only for those who'd signed up for them. Alina had convinced me to give it a go shortly after my seventeenth birthday. I hadn't yet cracked the leaderboards, but I was getting better. A few more decent routines and I could crack the lower tiers.

That was the plan at least.

The tear in reality widened to reveal the most handsome man on the planet. Ogden Oliver. His blond hair and blazing, blue eyes glimmered in the midday sun. And when he flashed that world famous grin, I felt a rush of sensations that was somewhere between elation and nausea.

"Are you ready for today's dance-up?" he asked. "Just follow my lead. And like always, remember to have fun."

"Yes, Ogden," I whispered. I liked to pretend he could hear me. That the real Ogden Oliver watched my routines and took pleasure in them.

"Here we go," he said, then began leading me through a series of steps that seemed to be an odd mix between hip hop and fox trot. He slumped his shoulders, elbows flared. Then, he'd stand up tall and click his heels.

It was complicated footwork, but I was getting the hang of it.

"That's it, Lacey. You're a maniac." Ogden's

encouragement was intoxicating and I was getting lost in the movement. It felt as if I could take a step back from my life and let my body take over.

Wham! Something struck me in the side and sent me sprawling onto the sidewalk. The cement tore at my knees and palms as I climbed back up into a sitting position.

<Watch it!> a man's voyce – not Alina's – shouted in my head.

I looked up at the man towering over me. The first thing I noticed were his fingernails. They'd been painted black all except his thumbs which were blood red. Something glowed from their edges…orange like a lit cigarette. The man's pinstriped suit was unbuttoned in the front to reveal a slim figure underneath. I tried to look up into his face, but Alina stopped me.

<Don't look at him!> she cried. <He doesn't want to be looked at.>

"I'm sorry," I said. "Please forgive me."

<Just be more careful next time,> his voyce demanded. Then, before I could do anything else, he stepped over me and hurried down the street. Everyone cleared a path for the man. Men, women, and children all stepped out of his way and averted their eyes. This was the way of wolves. They wished to pass through the city, unbothered and unseen.

<Stop looking,> said Alina. <You're gonna get us both in trouble.>

"Right, sorry."

I looked down at the sidewalk. Ogden Oliver was gone. He'd vanished the moment I'd bumped into that wolf. My hands and knees ached from a few mild scrapes. Not far away, a smear of blood decorated the sidewalk.

I must have fallen hard, I thought. *Either that or the sidewalk is –*

I gasped.

<What is it, Lacey? What's wrong?>

The answer to Alina's riddle slammed into my head.

"Cement!" I cried. "The answer's 'cement'."

Alina laughed. <Is that your final answer?>

"Yes. I'm sure of it. Cement can only move if you keep stirring it. Once it stops moving, it hardens. When it's still wet, a child can write in it, leaving a lifelong scar. And the city's made of the stuff. *Cement*. That's my answer."

A bell sounded.

<Aw shucks, Lacey. I thought I had you this time.>

Chapter 3

Spend enough time anywhere and you start thinking you know a place. Like how you know an old song or family recipe. It's true. I've walked up and down these streets enough times to know what smells to expect. What shadows are empty and which ones aren't. Which restaurants give away their scraps and which ones soak 'em in bleach.

I work at one of the bleach restaurants. They never give anything away, and I should know. In the morning, a truck delivers boxes and boxes of fresh greens. Carrots so orange they glow. Peppers as bright as Christmas lights. And big leafy romaine, greener than green. Greener than my Loyalty teacher's fingernails even.

At the end of the day, after the dinner rush, any of the veggies left over get doused in bleach and tossed in the trash.

<Nobody'd pay for food if the restaurant gave it away for free.> That's what my voyce tells me. And I understood that. Giving away food was no way to run a business. And I also understood why the managers tossed mis-prepared orders in the trash rather than let me or anyone else on the wait staff have a bite.

Still, I couldn't help feeling a bit disappointed whenever the managers tossed out a simmering roast chicken just because the cellie who ordered it suddenly remembered that garlic gave 'em a "tummy ache." They seemed to remember only *after* the plate was on the table. Whenever this happened, the manager would put on a little performance. We had a few managers at *Stratus*, but Greg – a mid-thirties killjoy with white-blond hair sculpted into complicated swirls – was the best at this sort of thing. He'd hunch his shoulders and shuffle up to the cellie's table like a wounded puppy. Next, he'd apologize to the cellie for the inconvenience and explain how this could in no way be *their* fault. "The waitress is a little slow," he'd say. "Her neuro net is on the fritz." He'd say anything as long as it diverted the blame away from the restaurant.

After reassuring the cellies, Greg would return to the slide, and any hint of apology would be gone from his face. Using his voyce, he'd yell at the cooks, yell at me and the other waitresses, and then he'd slam some plates around for good measure. Of the two kinds of manager – apologetic or furious – Greg was more convincing as a furious one. Sometimes, he'd get so worked up playing the part, that he'd need to take a break. He'd disappear into his office – usually with a steaming rack of ribs and mashed potatoes – and we wouldn't see him again until end of shift.

<Being the manager's hard work,> Alina would tell me. <He deserves the food. Work hard enough, and someday you'll have your own office and can eat whatever you want.>

In the meantime, I had to be content with the rice cakes I had stashed behind the coffee filters. They weren't enough to fill my appetite, but at least they kept me going through the dinner rush.

I'm not the only server with snacks hidden around the restaurant. We're like squirrels. We all got a hidden stash somewhere. Behind the jelly baskets. Under the to-go boxes. Buried in dry storage. It was silly, but having a spot to keep snacks was better than being so starved that you gave in to temptation and stole a bite of food from the kitchen. I don't know how, but management always knew when someone cheated. And Greg relished making examples of people.

I despised him. The way he lorded over us servers, treating us like dirt.

<That's part of the job,> Alina said. <The customers want to feel special. It's part of what they pay for. Don't fight it. Accept it. Take pleasure in your part. You're providing them with a service. And they pay you for it. *Cash tips*. Do you have any idea how lucky you are?>

I understood this, but Greg wasn't a customer. He was

my boss, sure, but still a coworker. The way he treated us felt different, more personal. I think it was because of the way he acted like he knew us.

Greg liked to say I'd never amount to much. And the longer I worked at *Stratus*, the more and more I believed him. I hated him for it.

Some people, when they think they know you, it makes 'em feel like they deserve a say in who you are. Like they got some sort of power over you.

<Don't worry about them,> Alina would say. <*I* know you. Isn't that what matters? They don't see what I see. If they did, they'd know – like how I know – that you're a gift.>

"Thanks," I'd say, and most days I meant it. Alina had a way with cheering me up.

* * *

The night I met Ogden Oliver and the rest of his cellie friends started like most others. I arrived on the ground floor twenty minutes before my shift started. After a quick temperature check, security gestured for me to take the staff elevator up to the roof. The doors opened near the breakroom, a small alcove tucked in next to the garbage shoot. I needed a place to change into my work clothes and the small storage closet in there usually worked fine.

I squeezed in between the stacks of plastic wrapped cloth napkins and started to undress. There was no way I'd wear my work clothes outside the restaurant. I did it once, and it had been a terrible mistake. The whole time, Alina kept me posted on all the incoming stares from leering strangers. Several of them guessed wrong that I worked in the skin market. To my horror, Alina forwarded some of their lewd solicitations, to which I politely declined.

The latex pants had long slits cut into the sides from shin to hipbone and were held together by a lattice work of crisscrossing ribbon. It was a real pain getting on.

Even if I wasn't crammed into a closet, keeping my toes from getting caught required loads of concentration. It helped to sprinkle in some baby powder, but I didn't have any with me. The top wasn't as hard to get on but no less revealing. A leather crop top with more ribbons down the front. I didn't quite have the chest to pull it off, but Management still said it was mandatory.

"Get used to it, or find another job." That was the standard response for most complaints. What they really meant was, "*You're expendable.*"

Three loose ribbons finished the uniform. I tied one around each wrist then used the third to pull my long hair up into a ponytail.

The breakroom was still empty when I stepped out of the closet. I used this last bit of privacy to lace up my shoes and switch facemasks.

I examined myself in the wall mounted mirror. It always surprised me how much I looked like my sister. She and I had similar physiques. We could pass for twins – and sometimes did – even though she was two years older. In the clothes *Stratus* made me wear, it was easy to see how I could be mistaken for a skin market employee. Part of me liked people making this mistake. It meant they thought I was attractive. That's why I embraced all the facemask rules imposed in the wake of the current pandemic. As long as I kept on my mask, people made all sorts of flattering assumptions about what I looked like underneath. Most men saw my body, decided they liked what they saw, and pretended my face was just as pretty. I knew this because Alina would tell me so. I kept my mask on as much as possible because I didn't want to ruin the illusion. It was good for tips.

Changing masks, to me, was like changing into a bathing suit. Something to be done in private. I looked around to make sure I was alone, then took off the mask. Catching my reflection in the mirror, the pink scar was always the first thing I saw. It hung beneath my nose and distorted the shape of my upper lip. It was the remnant of the botched surgery I'd had as a child.

I had been born with a cleft lip. Mom saved up for years before finally spending all she had on the operation to fix it. That's why she didn't have anything left when she had gotten sick herself.

<The doctors did their best,> Alina said whenever she talked about either my mom or my face. <Doing more would have been too costly.>

My face was a reminder of who my mother was. I could still see her whenever I looked in the mirror. She had had the same hazel brown eyes and soft angled face I had now. My face was her memory. My scars were her sacrifice.

I heard someone approaching, so I put on my work mask. A moment later, one of the bartenders stepped into the breakroom.

"Have you seen – ah – *there* it is." He snatched a tie off the back of the breakroom's only chair. Then, he turned to look at me. "Oh, hi Lacey. I didn't know you were here yet." Cadence Greene was one of *Stratus'* many bartenders. He nudged in beside me so he could look into the mirror and started fastening his tie. His uniform was not nearly as revealing as mine. He wore a classic button up shirt with black tie.

"Just got here," I said. "How're things going tonight?"

"From what I hear, it's going to be busy. We're booked up on reservations, and Greg says we've got a couple of big cellie groups coming in."

"When?"

"They're putting the first table together now on the East balcony. It'll most likely be yours." He finished his tie, then buttoned the collar. "And word from Greg says it's Ogden Oliver."

I took a step away from Cadence, and tried to gauge whether or not he was joking. It was hard to tell with his face mask on. Come to think of it, I didn't think I'd ever seen him without one. He was a lot like me in that way. Besides that, I hardly ever spoke to Cadence. He seemed nice enough, but our shifts were always so busy we didn't have much time for socializing. Any conversations we had during work were usually brief and related to my tables' drink orders.

He was fixing his hair, pushing loose strands up into a side sweeping undercut. His eyes were a deep brown with a hint of gold flickering near the irises. This close, he smelled like coffee and something mechanical, like engine oil.

"Are you serious?" I asked. "Ogden Oliver? That lifeliner? *Here*?" We were used to cellies coming into *Stratus*, but most were low level stars with limited fame or influence. Ogden Oliver was a different story. His influence was powerful and far reaching. Advertising companies poured fortunes at his feet because most knew how a word from Oliver could save your company or destroy it. Loads of people figured that if Ogden Oliver wanted to buy his way into being a wolf, he could do it. Easily. Still, the guy seemed to enjoy his life as a cellie. I for one looked forward to the days when he hosted the dance-ups. Something about his blinding suits, infectious smile, and turquoise eyes made me feel all funny whenever I saw him. I liked dancing for him. Sometimes, it was the best part of my day.

"Word is, Oliver's working on a new project in town," said Cadence. I thought he might say more until his eyes pointed toward the ceiling. I got the feeling he was listening to his voyce. A second later, my assumption was confirmed. His eyes refocused on mine, and he tapped the side of his head. "Bartleby tells me it's time to sign in."

"Bartleby?" I asked. "That's your voyce's name?"

He shrugged before giving a little salute then backed out of the room.

<Are you ready to sign in?> asked Alina, speaking up for the first time in several minutes.

"Did you know about Oliver?" I asked.

<No,> she said. <Nobody tells me these things. But don't worry. I'll sync up with the other servers and we'll make sure everything runs smoothly. You ready?>

I nodded. An instant later, I could feel my head opening up as Alina connected with the restaurant's computer network. I took a deep breath and closed my eyes. A layout of the place materialized in my thoughts. My inner-eye could see which tables were full and which ones were empty. And if I thought about it, I could recall the expected wait times for new orders.

I took a step toward the kitchen, then paused as a sudden wave of vertigo swept through me. It was gone in a second. In its place, a list of current tasks appeared in my vision. The words floated in front of me as if a projector was shining out from the center of my forehead.

It read, *Current tasks: One, present yourself to Management for inspection. Two, prepare for guest arrivals.*

"It's showtime," I said, and stepped out into the din of the restaurant.

Chapter 4

The guests began to arrive soon after sundown. A pair of cellie women with orange fluorescent hair were the first to step off the elevator. A half dozen more came in moments later. So far, none of them were Ogden Oliver, but that didn't stop them – and the decadent outfits they wore – from putting on their own show. The men wore dark colored suits made of strange, reflective fabrics. Whenever the light hit them, their suits would ripple with a rainbow of color like an oil slick on water. The women all wore long dresses made of similar materials and had long, elaborate scarves wrapped around their slender bodies. None of it looked practical, but what did I expect from cellies? They were quite a sight, and I'd be lying if I said their chic didn't frighten me a little.

I took drink orders as the group found their seats. Alina did most of the talking. Cellies didn't speak to me directly – would be rude to force people like *them* to address someone like *me*. All I had to do was get close, then my voyce would notify their voyce, and they'd shout out what they wanted. The ones who didn't order wine described complicated cocktails, many with names and liquors I didn't recognize. Thankfully, when I returned to the bar, Cadence assured me he knew them and set to work pouring and mixing. As I waited, I took a moment to calm myself. Oliver had not yet arrived and the anticipation was astronomical. My heart thumped whenever I imagined him sitting at my table. Not an augmented projection, but *here* in the flesh. He and I breathing the same air.

Playing up my anxiety were all the stories I'd heard about cellie men and women who fell in love with everyday girls like me. I've met loads of people claiming to have known someone who'd been scooped up by a love-crazed cellie. Lots of the stories went the same way. The cellies would appear out of nowhere, then whisk the common girls away – save them from the drudgery of their miserable life…never to be seen again. Was it a romantic and unrealistic fairytale? Most likely. But if there wasn't any truth to the stories, why were they so common?

I found myself pondering a life where I didn't have to spend six nights a week at the restaurant demeaning myself for minimum wage, or deveining shrimp most weekend mornings. It'd be nice to finish a week for once feeling refreshed and alive. Not worn down to a grisly nub. More than that even, it'd be nice to live in a world where my sister didn't have to wallow away in the skin market, trading her youth and innocence for so little. I liked to pretend that someday I'd live in the high rises with the other cellies. I'd have a quiet place where I could feel like part of the city without getting overwhelmed by it. I gazed over the side of the balcony down at the city. It was easy to appreciate the glowing skyline. Fast flying drones flitted between buildings like fireflies in a field of tall grass. Spread out on several rooftops and down at street level, spotlights and laser shows sprayed the city with light and color.

<Order's up, Lacey.>

With my tray loaded with drinks, I headed back out to the table.

Alina reminded me where each drink went. <The tall green one goes to the cellie on your left. The wine goes to the woman on his right.> The cellies yammered all at once. No one appeared to be listening to anyone else, nor were they paying any attention to me, which was a relief. I did my best not to be noticed as I slipped between their chairs, delivering their ordered drinks. Up to this point, the party didn't seem all that different from any other cellie gathering. That changed the moment Oliver arrived.

I had just set the last wine glass down when all the cellies stopped talking at once. Their bodies stiffened as the expressions on their beautiful faces slackened as if lost in thought.

<He's here,> announced Alina.

Acting as one, the eight cellies pushed away from the table, and stood to face the entryway. I followed their gaze…and nearly screamed.

Ogden Oliver was striding toward me. Much worse, the man was on fire. That was my first impression. Oliver wore a three-piece suit that glowed with yellowish-orange light so fiercely that it hurt to look at him. He was like pure sunshine. A smile broke out behind my facemask. I couldn't help it. He greeted the others with a wide armed, two-fisted cheer followed by a lap around the table, either shaking or kissing the hands of the others in attendance who were now laughing or applauding. They all seemed ecstatic to see him.

And why shouldn't they be, I thought. *It's Ogden Oliver for gosh sakes.*

His suit dimmed a little once he stopped moving. The outfit appeared to be motion activated. The quicker he moved, the brighter it blazed.

He gripped the back of an empty chair but didn't sit down. Instead, he turned toward the entryway, his arm flashing as he gestured toward the elevators. A pair of cellies – a man and woman – with bronze, glimmering skin were gliding through the restaurant. They could have been brother and sister. Either that, or they'd made great effort – and paid a lot of money – to look so much alike. Both had platinum hair bright enough to rival even Oliver's suit. They couldn't be real, was my first thought. Their beauty made me dizzy – like I'd had a few drinks or Alina had turned on an intoxication program. I felt drunk, but then I saw the person walking behind them, and a cold dread sobered me up real fast.

It was a wolf. Unlike the cellies, the wolf's clothes were dark and subdued. He wore a black suit with black tie. But the most striking thing about him was his face – or lack thereof. Instead of a head on his shoulders, a shimmering blur – just like the one that had covered the boy who'd been killed in the street – was all I could see. Most wolves didn't like attention. They preferred seclusion over fame. When they were seen in public at all, their faces were often hidden by the blinding shimmer that followed them everywhere.

It was more for our protection than for theirs, Alina would say. Wolves aren't like most people. They were smarter and braver than the rest of us. Their minds were too powerful. Alina told me once that talking to a wolf would be like staring into the sun. Do it long enough and it'd cause permanent damage. And besides, with everything they did to make our lives better, the wolves deserved a bit of reverence from us. They were the caretakers of our world. As such, they required our respect and the privacy to serve us well. A wolf was never seen unless they wanted you to see them.

The wolf took a seat at the head of the table, then gestured for the others to sit. It was a dizzying contrast. The cellies sitting on all sides of the table were ablaze with color and reflective light. The brightest among them was Ogden Oliver. He sat on one end of the table, his suit flaring with each wild gesture. In contrast, the wolf sitting across from him appeared to be absorbing any light cast his way. The disorienting shimmer was like a miniature black hole posing as a person.

I took a breath then stepped toward the table.

<Hold on, Lacey,> Alina said. <Best not to bother them at the moment. I know what they want.> Equal measures of relief and disappointment flooded my thoughts. I was desperate to say something to Oliver but horrified of what might happen if he responded. What would he think of someone like me?

I retreated to the bar to await their orders.

"How are things going?" asked Cadence as he finished loading up the current round of drinks. I didn't respond because it took all my will to steady my trembling hands.

<The wolf first,> Alina instructed as I returned to the table.

The amber-colored liquor *clicked* as I set it down. The wolf made no indication that he'd noticed. Next came the drinks for the platinum look-alikes. After setting down their identical, gold-flaked drinks, I made the mistake of glancing the wolf's way. So close, his shimmer caught me off guard. The blurred spot resting on the man's shoulders seemed to carve open a gap in reality. Looking into it made me feel like I was falling. Ripples of vertigo slithered through me, and I took a step back in order to shut my eyes and steady the wobbling drink tray.

<Don't you *dare* drop these drinks, Lacey.>

She didn't have to tell me. The thought of making a fool of myself now, in front of these elites, was a nightmare.

<Okay, Lacey. You got this. Oliver's the last one.>

That's when I realized he was looking right at me. Instinct told me to flinch away from his gaze, but I fought it. I didn't make direct eye contact – would be rude – but I watched his blue-eyed gaze from my peripherals and forced a smile even though my facemask kept him from seeing it. I lifted his drink from the tray and leaned forward to set it down.

<Stop!> cried Alina. <Don't move, Lacey.>

I froze by Ogden Oliver's side with his drink shaking in my unsteady grip. My eyes turned askance enough to see him looking right at me. He held a dreamy, appreciating look on his face.

"What's your name?" he asked.

"My…ah…my name's…it's ah…"

<Lacey, your name's *Lacey!*> cried Alina.

Oliver raised his hand and laughed to himself. "It's okay, Lacey. I already know who you are." He tapped the side of his head. "Your voyce just told me. Lacey's a beautiful name." I wasn't sure how to respond, and before I could, Oliver continued. "Lacey, my friends and I were wondering if you could help us solve a little problem."

"Y-yes. Of course."

Oliver opened his mouth to speak, but a loud voyce reverberated through my skull.

<Do you really want to do this now, Ogden?>

Oliver winced, letting me know he'd heard it too. Then

his attention turned toward the opposite end of the table, at the man within the roiling shimmer.

"No time like the present," Oliver said aloud. "Wouldn't you agree, Lacey?"

Before I could answer, an unusual thing happened. The wolf made a slicing gesture in the air, and all sound…*cut out.* It felt like my head had been plunged underwater. I could still *see* Oliver and the wolf engaged in conversation. They both made animated, and angry looking gestures, but I couldn't *hear* them. Besides Oliver, all the cellies looked to be holding their breath.

<Don't worry, Lacey,> Alina whispered to me. <They're just having a little chat.>

But when Oliver pointed to me and the wolf did the same, I couldn't help feeling a bit exposed. What were they talking about?

After what felt like an eternity, the wolf waved his hand in a dismissive gesture. Sound returned.

"Here, I'll show you," said Oliver. And to my horror, he turned to me. "Lacey, I'd like you to prove a point for me."

I nodded.

Oliver opened his arms wide – his sleeves flashing like flames – as he gestured toward everyone at the table. "My friends here think you're stupid."

"What?"

A few of the cellies laughed, but Oliver went on. "They think you're *dumb*. An idiot, moron, imbecile, ignoramus, nincompoop, and a thousand other unflattering nouns." He paused for what felt a very long time, then said, "But I think you can prove them wrong. Your voyce tells me you like riddles. Is that correct?"

I nodded.

Oliver clapped his hands together. "Good! So, Lacey. I'd like you to answer a riddle for me. *You*, by yourself. No help from that little voyce of yours. Can you do that?"

"I…I can try."

"Okay, so here it is:

You hold me in your hands while I hold *you* in my center.

I am a prison for shapeshifting prisoners.
Keep me upright, and my walls won't fail.
On my side, and my prisoner bails.
What am I?"

It was as if my brain had jammed. The words held no meaning. I was too distracted by Ogden Oliver's immaculate gaze, the titters from his fellow cellies, and the swirling emptiness at the far end of the table. All these people – these *elites* – were focused on me. I could feel their stares sharpened into points and pressing dimples into my skin. It was too much. Why had I told Alina I liked riddles? I had fooled myself by pretending there was something I was actually good at – like I had some sort of talent or something. But as I stood there in front of those elites – slack jawed and empty headed – I knew I was a fool. And they knew it, too. There would be no fairytale escape for me. Ogden Oliver and the others were seeing me for what I was. A no good, stupid commoner.

"Uh oh, Oggy. I think you broke her," said the platinum-haired male.

"Yeah, careful girlie," said the female beside him. "Don't get your neuro in a bunch."

I couldn't leave. Their gazes pinned me to the spot. But I had to do something. My entire body was quaking now. I could feel my nerves rattling down my arms and shaking the drink I still held. The green liquor sloshed in my quivering grip.

The expression on Oliver's face turned from expectation to disappointment to concern. His eyes darted between me and the shaking drink.

Gathering every ounce of will power I had, I forced myself to steady my hand. My fingers tightened around the glass, leveling the cup so it wouldn't spill.

Oh my God, the drink!

And then, like a lightning strike, the answer exploded in my mind.

"It's a *cup*!"

The laughter around the table died in an instant. The only person not gaping in surprise was Oliver himself. He stared right at me with that glowing smile. He seemed absolutely pleased.

Pleased...with me.

"I knew you could do it," he whispered. Then, to the rest of the table, he announced, "And there you have it. Are you not impressed?"

In response, the wolf held up his hand. Oliver's smile wilted.

<Impressed? By this damaged toy? Honestly, Ogden, I'm only impressed you'd choose such a weedy contender?>

"I've made up my mind," Oliver said bitterly.

<Have it your way.> The wolf snapped his fingers, and the sound was like a bottle rocket inside my skull. The shock shot down my arm and detonated in my hand, causing me to let go of the drink. In horror, I watched as the glass tumbled right into Oliver's lap, soaking him. His suit flared as he pushed away from the table.

Stunned, I managed to squeak out, "I'm so sorry. Let me get a towel."

But before I could turn, the wolf's voyce bellowed. <Stop!>

I froze.

<Take off your facemask,> said the wolf. <Show us what you're hiding under there. Show Ogden he's made a mistake by picking you.>

Picked me for what? I wished to know. But I couldn't speak. At that moment, I wanted nothing more than to retreat back into bowels of the restaurant. I didn't understand what these elites were talking about, but the tone – and the way they were grinning at me – was making me sick with fear. But my legs wouldn't obey me. I was rooted in place. My hand seemed to be acting on its own, and by the time I realized what it was doing, it was too late.

My mask fell away, leaving my face naked and exposed. My scars and malformed lip laid bare for all the cellies to see. Their initial reaction was shock. Then cruel smiles curled at the edges of their painted lips.

One of the men guffawed. "Yikes, Oggy. You picked a butter-face."

The table burst into laughter.

"Seriously," said one of the women, "put this one back in the oven. She ain't done yet."

"No fixing that," said another while pointing a sharp fingernail.

The whole time, Ogden Oliver was silent. He didn't seem amused, but he also said nothing while his cellie friends piled on the insults.

Tears bubbled at the corners of my eyes, and I could feel my already misshapen lip twisting under their laughing eyes. It wasn't supposed to be this way.

<Come on, Lacey,> whispered Alina. She urged me to get back to the kitchen and I was surprised to discover that I could move. Whatever spell that wolf had put over me was gone…much like my fantasies about a cellie rescue.

Back in the slide, I pushed my way past the manager – who was already screaming about the spilled drink – and shoved through the other servers and busboys until I was back in the breakroom.

I threw myself into the storage closet and buried my face in my arms. Tears spilled from my eyes as if poured from a cellie's cup.

Chapter 5

By the time my shift ended, sheets of near-ice were drowning the world. I was on the sidewalk before I realized I'd forgotten to change out of my work clothes, and I didn't have it in me to go back up to the restaurant and face Greg again…his pig-nosed disdain and smug superiority was too much.

He had waited until my shift was over before opening a connection between our voyces. He summoned me to stand before him in the slide. Then, he berated me in front of everyone else – probably to make a point or something.

"How can you be such a screwup, Lacey? Is your net broken or are you just stupid?"

I shook with rage, but willed myself to remain silent. I stared, dead-eyed, as he announced he was docking my pay, and putting me on a week's long suspension.

My hands curled into fists, the nails biting into my palms.

<Don't…say…a thing,> Alina insisted. <*Christ*, we need this job. Just let him finish, Lacey. I'm sorry. I know how frustrated you are. But *don't* give him any more reason to fire you.>

So I took it in silence until he was out of breath and his face had turned an ugly shade of purple. He barked a few more orders to those forced to watch and then everyone set to work closing out the restaurant. They moved with increased diligence. Greg's point in punishing me had clearly had the desired effect.

I took the few bucks that weren't docked and ducked into the elevator. The doors closed and I pressed my hands against my masked mouth and *screamed.* Or would have, but Alina shut off my vocal cords so the sound came out as a *hiss* – too quiet for anyone to hear.

Down on the sidewalk, freezing drops sliced through clothes and skin. Already the chill was seeping into my core. Shivering, I stalled on indecision.

All I wanted was to get home, slide into bed next to Yadi, and forget today had ever happened. But I didn't have enough money for a ride, and the subways never ran this late.

I could always walk. I'd be frozen solid by the time I got home, but part of me thought maybe this was a good thing. The embarrassment of what those cellies had done – the dissatisfaction on Ogden Oliver's beautiful face – and the sting from Greg's reprimands still burned. Perhaps the rain could cool me off.

<Lacey, don't leave yet. Someone's pinging you.>

"I d-d-don't care, Alina." I wiped rain or tears from my eyes. "Whoever it is, t-t-tell them I'm not available. T-t-tell them to leave a m-m-message then leave me *alone*."

<But Lacey, I think this could help.>

I wrapped my arms around my shoulders and leaned forward in a feeble attempt to shield myself from the rain. My entire body convulsed as water pooled between my shoulder blades and ran down my spine in icy rivers. My teeth clattered.

"W-w-who is it?"

The answer didn't come from Alina. Instead, a man's voice reached out through the freezing rain.

"Lacey, hold up."

Cadence stood just beneath the awnings; my backpack hung by his side.

"Bartleby told me you left this," he said. Like me, Cadence was still wearing his facemask. This made him hard to read. "Lordy, you're *soaked.*"

I changed quickly in the lobby restroom then asked Alina to send Cadence a little thank you, but she said I should do it myself.

<He's waiting for you,> she said. <I think he wants to tell you something.>

And sure enough, he was leaning against one of the lobby's stone pillars. His black tie was undone and his normally neat hair hung in several loose strands across his forehead. He looked *exhausted*, but he perked up as I drew near.

"Um…thanks for bringing my pack," I said.

He told me it was no problem, then tried to make a joke about how cold it was, but I stopped him.

"I appreciate the help, Cadence…*really.* But it's very late…" *And I need to walk home in the rain,* I didn't add.

He looked at the floor and dragged his foot along the tiles until it made one of those squeaky noises common on a basketball court.

"Yeah, I know," he said. "I just wanted to tell you something."

<He wants to tell you something,> Alina said.

"I *know,*" I said.

Cadence looked up, a flash of hurt playing in his eyes.

"I was talking to my voyce," I said. "Sorry."

His eyes softened. "Yeah? Well…I'm sorry too."

"For what?"

"I should've said something…to Greg. He shouldn't talk to you like that…but Bartleby kept telling me to be quiet and stay out of other people's business."

<His voyce is right,> said Alina. <No point in you *both* getting suspended.>

I repeated this to Cadence, but he shook his head, saying, "It ain't right. I should have said something."

He looked down at the tiles and grew silent.

I had a feeling he wanted something from me. Like he wanted forgiveness for not rushing in to help or something. But the truth was I didn't feel like him helping me was anywhere near his responsibility, and even if it was, I wasn't in any sort of forgiving mood.

I was close to saying so, but Alina stopped me. She had a better idea. And it was something that would give us both what we wanted.

* * *

Rain pelted the roof of the car.

The weather stripping in one of the doors was worn away so that water dripped onto the seat, but as long as I kept my distance, I'd stay dry. Cadence noticed the drip and offered to change seats with me, but I told him not to. It was nice enough that he'd agreed to share his ride with me. Alina told me he was most likely grateful for a chance to help…given his inability to do so earlier.

The rain really made a nice sound. I asked Alina to record it for me so I could play it later.

Cadence laughed at this before telling his own voyce to do the same.

"It is relaxing," he said. "Makes me think of my voyce."

"What do you mean?"

He gestured toward the roof. "Well, rooftops and voyces have similar jobs. Both are like shields or walls…protecting us from outside chaos. But they're not always perfect. Sometimes the voyces have gaps. Little holes that let us say something rude, make a mistake, or see something we shouldn't."

"So what are you saying?"

"Just that our voyces aren't perfect. They can't protect us from everything." He glanced up at the leaking roof. "And sometimes the rain gets in."

<He's got a point,> Alina whispered. <Here, let me turn on the heat.>

The vents opened and warmth spilled into the car's interior.

He warmed his hands on the open vents and I did the same.

"This reminds me of a riddle I heard once," he said. "Want to hear it?"

He must have taken my silence for an invitation because he went on:

"I am not seen, heard, tasted, or smelt.
Beneath the covers is where I'm felt.
Alive in a fire's glow,
Active in sunlight's touch,
And born in a lover's heart.
What am I?"

I considered not giving an answer, but this riddle was one I'd heard before. It was a bit misleading, but riddles were like that sometimes. They couldn't lie, but the truth was not always helpful in the way you wanted it to be. For instance, a "lover's heart" and "beneath the covers" made me think of something romantic or even kinky. The real answer was much more mundane than that however, and I hated leaving any riddles unanswered.

"Heat," I said, "or warmth."

"Right you are," said Cadence. "It took me days to figure that one out. You like riddles, too?"

I nodded. Riddles, dance-ups. Just two of the many ways people cracked the leaderboards. But after the way those cellies had laughed at me – even *after* I'd answered Oliver's cup riddle – I figured I'd been foolish to think knowing riddles could be enough to change things for me and Yadi.

Cadence tilted his head, and I could tell his voyce was speaking.

"No," he said. "Take Lacey home first."

The car's engines whined and merged onto the street. This late, traffic was light but still slower than the White Line. A few white SUV's whizzed past us, and I couldn't help wondering if any of them had been the one that had rolled over that boy. The thought made me shiver.

"It sure is cold," Cadence said.

I agreed, but didn't elaborate. I was grateful to Cadence for the ride and for retrieving my backpack, but I wasn't in the mood for a conversation. Everything that had happened with those cellies – and with Ogden Oliver – kept playing in my mind. I had fantasized about meeting Oliver loads of times...and now that it had happened – and had gone so poorly – a sort of hollow space had opened up in my gut. I wasn't sure if it could be filled again. With Alina's help, I knew I'd replay the encounter and go over every detail. She'd access the memory drive installed in my neuro-net, and together, we'd search for answers to all the troublesome questions bouncing around in my head. Why had it gone so wrong? What had they said when that wolf shut off my hearing? And what did he mean when he'd said Oliver had chosen me by mistake? Chosen me for what?

"It was an accident." It took me a second to realize it was *Cadence*, not Alina, who was speaking. He was watching me from across the car's interior. Passing streetlights reflected from his dark eyes. "Bartleby says you must have deserved what happened, but I don't agree."

"You should listen to your voyce," I said. "Your voyce knows best."

"Not always."

I laughed at the joke, but Cadence didn't act as if he'd said anything funny.

"They can't read our minds. That's why we have to say our words out loud whenever we talk to them. They're super helpful. And I always appreciate it when Bartleby steps in and stops me from doing or saying something really stupid. But there's something about the way we think, parts of our selves buried deep in the brain they don't have access to. How could they always know what's best if they don't know our deepest, most intimate thoughts?"

<Such an odd question,> Alina said. <Do you think his voyce is working properly?>

I didn't know, but I found myself wondering what the bartender looked like under that facemask of his. Beyond that, the sting of those cellies' reactions when they'd seen *me* was still burning bright in my mind.

"Did you see my face?" I asked him. "When those cellies *asked* me to take off my mask." I meant to say "forced" but the word came out "*asked*". Alina switched my words around sometimes…for clarity, she'd say.

"No, I didn't see," said Cadence. "I was busy making drinks."

"I don't show my face to a lot of people," I said, "but they *asked* me take it off." There it was again. The switch from *forced* to *asked.*

Cadence nodded as if he understood what I was trying to say. He touched his own facemask. "We're supposed to wear these all the time. But cellies never wear them. It's like they're exempt from a lot of the rules we gotta follow." He nodded as if making a decision, then, he shrugged, and plucked the straps from around his ears and removed his mask.

How should I describe his face to you, dear auditor? I could say that he was handsome. But what does that mean? I could say that the trace of stubble along his sharp jawline and strong chin made me think of the kind of men I'd seen sword fighting in the streams I watched with Yadi sometimes. I could say he had a kind smile and a childish dimple in his left cheek…but these were only details. The truth of Cadence's face…the only thing that mattered…was that seeing his face and looking into his dark eyes made me happy.

I was compelled to follow his example. At the time, I wasn't sure why, but I was *eager* to share a connection with someone – *anyone*. And right then, Cadence fit the bill.

"Promise…not to laugh," I said and pulled off my facemask. I regretted it immediately. The cellie laughter was still too fresh in my mind. Why would I invite further ridicule?

Cadence stared at me for what felt like a very long time. Rain pelted the roof of the car as we bounced over potholes and flooded streets.

His eyes touched on my malformed lip, but he didn't comment. He smiled, and his gaze continued its quiet inspection. I could almost feel his attention slipping over and around the contours of my face – much like the raindrops sliding around the outside of the car. For my part, I kept my attention on his eyes. His pupils were huge. It was as if his eyes had widened to take in as much as possible. I could only guess what he was thinking, and I didn't dare ask Alina to link with his voyce, Bartleby. It was enough that he saw me.

"You have a very pretty face," he said, blushing. "But you probably already knew that."

"The cellies don't think so," I said. "They laughed at me."

He waved his hand dismissively. "Not everyone can appreciate beauty when they see it."

I touched the scars under my nose and the misshapen upper lip. Voice cracking, I asked, "And this? Is *this* pretty?"

"Yes," he said without hesitation. "Right now, you're the most beautiful woman in this car." He smiled to show he was trying to make me laugh, and damn him, it worked. He went on, "You know, Lacey, you don't need me or some stuck-up cellie to say you're beautiful. What people say doesn't change anything. *Your* voice is the only one that matters. Now, I'm going to say something, and I'd like you to repeat after me."

"Uh…okay."

"I…Lacey Clarke…" He put a hand on his heart like he was taking an oath. I did the same.

"I…Lacey Clarke…"

"…am a sexy beast."

"I'm not saying that."

Cadence kept his hand over his heart and stared at me until I played along.

Rolling my eyes, I said, "Fine. I…Lacey Clarke…am a sexy beast."

"There," said Cadence. "Don't you feel better?"

"No, not really." But I was lying. I *did* feel better. "Now you gotta repeat after me."

"Sure," he said, smiling.

"I…Cadence Greene…"

"I…Cadence Greene…"

"…am a huge dork."

We both bust out laughing. After a minute, Alina said, <Oh my God, Lacey, have you lost your mind?> This only made me laugh more.

The car pulled up to my apartment building a few minutes later. I reached for the door and thanked Cadence for the ride.

"Thanks for the company," said Cadence. "Any chance you'd like to do this again?"

"Do what again?" I asked. "Go for a car ride?"

Alina broke in. <He's asking you out on a date, dummy.>

"Oh…uh, I don't know," I said.

"It's okay," he said quickly. "Just thought I'd ask. No worries." He smiled, then reached across the interior to hold the door open for me.

I said goodbye then rushed out into the rain, ran across the sidewalk, then took shelter inside the entry doorway. I looked back to see Cadence breathing onto the windows. He traced a happy face within the fogged-up glass, and waved as the car sped down the street.

<He seems like a nice guy,> said Alina.

I wasn't sure how to respond, so I did what I normally did, nothing. I turned toward the stone steps leading up to the door and *shrieked.*

A small creature darted from one of the shadowed corners. My first thought was that I'd startled a rat. This wouldn't have been the first time. But when the creature's matted fur and long, fuzzy tail passed within the beam of a streetlamp, I saw it for what it was.

<It's a cat,> said Alina. <Calm down.>

The cat scrambled up the side of the stone steps and leapt down onto the sidewalk. An instant later, it slipped behind a row of trashcans and disappeared.

I turned to go inside, but paused on the doorstep. The image of that mutie couple I'd seen a few days earlier slipped into my mind.

They'd been looking for a cat. *What was its name? Daughter?*

The cat was none of my business. I should have left it alone…but like I said before, I have a hard time leaving things unanswered.

Chapter 6

My sister was still awake when I reached the seventh floor and opened the door to our apartment – which was surprising, considering how late it was. Yadi had a small light on and was sitting on the sofa – not moving. She stared at a small cardboard package in front of her on the coffee table.

When I asked why she was still awake, she sniffed, then looked up and blinked back tears. Shiny streaks ran down both her cheeks. Her makeup was smudged and looked like big, purple bruises.

"Yadira? What's wrong?"

She sniffed again, then, lower lip curling, she looked back at the package. She remained silent.

<It's from the crematorium,> Alina whispered. <Lacey…I'm sorry.>

"Why? What's the matter?" But then it hit me. My legs gave out and I sat down on the rug. I kept thinking the cardboard box seemed so small…*too* small.

Yadi reached out and put her hand on top of the box. She took a deep breath, then said, "Daddy's home."

* * *

I suppose, auditor, that I should tell you about my father. The trouble with this is that I barely knew the guy. And any memory I had most likely came from Yadi's recollections rather than my own.

She told me once that our dad liked to do this thing where he'd put us in boxes and slide us around the floor like we were in a car chase. He'd make all sorts of engine sounds that were often so funny – Yadi said – that we'd all be laughing until it hurt.

Even Mom had been happy when our dad was still around. Yadi would get a funny look in her eyes whenever she talked about how Mom and Dad would dance and sing to each other in the kitchen. Sometimes even now, when certain songs came on the voyce network, Yadi would get all quiet…and say it made her think of him. My dad had been a kind man.

But then he'd gotten in that little accident. No one had been hurt, but the dent his e-bike had put in the front end of a cellie luxury vehicle had been too much for his insurance. He was told that in order to avoid a visit from some flexer boys, that it'd be best for everyone – his wife and daughters included – if he surrendered himself to a debt relief agency. So that's what he did. He granted them access to his voyce and allowed the agency to turn him into a dead-head.

The parts of his brain that made Dad *Dad* – the parts that made him sing and dance with Mom or play racecar with us were shut down – put into hibernation so his body could be rented out. Lots of people volunteered to be dead-heads back then. Still do, in fact. It was a good way to put your life on hold so you could get caught up on the stuff you owed. His and Mom's voyces both agreed this would be a wise decision.

It was supposed to only take a few months, but something went wrong. Mom would get messages from the debt agency, and she'd tell Yadi and me about it.

"The interest on what your daddy owes has gone up," she'd say. "The late fees have switched over to principal. The agency is upping the cost of food and shelter for housing his body." As a kid, none of this made much sense to me. All I knew was that the man I couldn't remember would be gone longer than expected. It made little difference to me, but it was devastating to Mom and Yadi.

He left when I was three. Fifteen years later, he was finally home.

* * *

Yadi wiped her eyes. "I guess we're orphans now." She picked up the box and gave it a little shake. Something rattled inside. It sounded like broken glass. "I never stopped thinking he'd come home…just…not like this."

I didn't know what to say, and my voyce was no help. All I could do was watch Yadi as she held the box. Suddenly, her brow furrowed and she reached for the side. She gave an angry *shout* as she tore off the flap then tilted the box onto its side.

Two plastic bags and a folded-up piece of paper tumbled onto the table. One of the bags held a grayish brown powder. The other bag clinked with several bone fragments. While Yadi examined the bags with trembling hands, I reached for the piece of paper. I held it up in front of my eyes. I can hardly read, so I listened while Alina read it for me.

<It's a message from your father's debt agency,> Alina said. <It's to Yadira. And, uh, Lacey? It doesn't look good.>

"Go on," I said.

<To the family of [Benjamin Horus Clarke]: We regret to inform you of the passing of a family member. We understand this must be a difficult time. We have enclosed his/her/their remains so that you may pay your final respects.

<We are sorry, but take no responsibility for your loss.

<As is required by State and Federal Law; any debt, fines, and/or fees still owed by the deceased is passed on to the oldest surviving family member. Our records indicate this person to be [Yadira Valentine Clarke]. In addition, the cost of processing the deceased's remains has been added to the overall total.

<Operators are standing by to discuss payment. Your voyce should be able to assist you. We advise you to contact us within twenty (20) business days or face criminal action.

<In the meantime, you have our thoughts and prayers.

<Have a wonderful day.>

I let the note fall, only to find Yadi staring wide-eyed from across the coffee table. Her almond skin had turned as white as the paper the note was typed on. Her already reddened eyes were full of disbelief and panic.

"What does this mean?" she asked her voyce. They spoke for several minutes, the whole time, Yadi's tone became more and more desperate.

"How much do they want?...But that's insane. I can't afford that...What can I do?...You're telling me my dad was a dead-head for fifteen years, and he didn't work off *any* of his debt...How does that make any sense?...Okay, but why should *I* be responsible?...No, *please*. I don't want to do that. I *can't* do that."

While Yadi pleaded with her voyce, my own voyce spoke to me. <This doesn't look good, Lacey. If your sister doesn't pay off your dad's debt, they might send some flexers to talk to her. She's got to convince them she can pay. Otherwise, they could force her to become a dead-head.>

"How is this fair?"

<Debt must be paid, Lacey. The best thing to do now is figure out how you and Yadira can get caught up. If not, it might make sense for Yadira to turn herself in. With that body of hers, she's sure to work off the debt much faster than your dad could.>

"No," I interrupted. "That won't happen."

<Let's hope you're right,> she said. <We'll think of something.>

*　　*　　*

We stayed up another few hours. Yadi alternated between crying over Dad and thinking of ways she could earn enough money to pay his debt – now *her* debt. I couldn't bear to tell her that I'd been suspended from my job at *Stratus*. I'd just have to find work elsewhere. And if it came down to it, I'd ask to be a dead-head in my sister's place.

The sun was coming up by the time we finally fell asleep. Yadi put her head on my shoulder, and I stroked her hair until her shuddering sobs shifted into measured exhaustion. It felt like I'd barely shut my own eyes when Alina was whispering for me to wake up.

It was a school day, and I couldn't be late. I threw a blanket over Yadi, then put on a clean sweatshirt and grabbed a too-ripe banana from a bowl near the door on my way out.

Ms. Parks, my Loyalty teacher had a thing for truants. She'd wait just inside her classroom door, tapping her bright green fingernails on the door handle as she watched the clock. She had long blonde hair curled around her head in thick rope braids. She was a pretty woman, or would have been if not for her constant look of disgust. Rarely did she show any joy unless she got to slam a door in some late kid's face. It was odd seeing a grownup hate her students as much as Ms. Parks did. Most other teachers didn't act that way. Alina told me Ms. Parks simply believed in 'tough love', and that her cruelty was really her way of motivating her students. I couldn't deny that it worked. I'd been late once already this month and I feared being late again. One more time, and she'd slap on a Saturday detention. I didn't think Yadi and I could afford that.

That's why I was gulping air and dripping sweat by the time I got to class. I collapsed into a desk chair right as the bell rang. Ms. Parks cast disapproval my way, then yanked the door closed and fastened the locks.

Today's lesson was on the Luddite insurrection of 1811. During the industrial age, the invention of textile weaving machines had made life much easier for factory workers. Each machine could do the work of ten to thirty people. And since the factory owners didn't have to hire as many human workers anymore, profits were way, *way* up. The Luddites didn't like this. Even though the machines had freed them from the drudgery of factory work, allowing them to pursue other passions, many weavers refused to move on. They began destroying machinery and threatening the people who used it. As Ms. Parks described their actions, her nose wrinkled like she could smell rotting fish.

"Some people despise progress," she said. "The Luddites were trying to hold on to a world that didn't exist anymore. Luckily, the leaders of their time knew exactly how to deal with them." Ms. Parks' mouth twitched into a grin as she explained how the Luddites were punished. Cash rewards went to anyone willing to betray their Luddite brothers and sisters. Anyone found guilty of destroying a machine was sentenced to public execution. This was important, Ms. Parks told us, because it was one of the first times in history when people realized that machines could be more valuable than human life.

"The Luddites were exterminated as the traitors they were," said Ms. Parks.

Most our lessons were about one revolt or another. It was all meant to show how unchecked thought could be dangerous. Before people had voyces, one bad idea could be enough to poison an entire generation. Some ideas traveled fast like a storm while others seeped into everything and festered like a rot. The fall of Rome, the Dark Ages, the Inquisition, Terrorism, and the Insurrection of 2021 had all been caused by runaway ideas. The bad ones got into a person's head and took over, turning them into something different than what they were. It was sorta like how debt agencies took over a dead-head's body. Bad ideas could do that too.

Voyces put a stop to all that nonsense. The country hadn't seen an insurrection or major protest in decades. Voyces helped us all make the right decisions. They gave us reason. What was it Cadence had said the night before? Oh, right. Voyces were like barriers. They protected us from outside chaos. And in some cases, they protected us from ourselves. I didn't know what I'd do without Alina. Next to Yadi, she was the best thing in my life.

Something jabbed through the back of my neck. I yelped, then slapped at whatever it was, but felt nothing. Then I knew.

<Pay attention!> Ms. Parks' voyce scratched through my head, blurring my vision.

"Y-yes, Ma'am." Straightening, I centered my focus on

the pictures Ms. Parks had on display. Hand drawn illustrations of Luddite men and women hanging from the gallows. People who'd had their lives ruined by unchecked ideas. I tried to look through the cartoons at the time these drawings were based on. I imagined someone I knew, perhaps my father, hanging from a taut rope – a rope that looked remarkably like Ms. Parks' braided hair.

Ms. Parks whacked each picture with a thin metal rod. "These people poisoned their heads with lies, and look what it cost them. Sadly, this sort of thing didn't end with the Luddites. Since then, people have often been corrupted by trash they saw on tv or propaganda they heard on the radio."

"What's a rah-dee-oh?" asked one of the boys.

Ms. Parks glared at him, then said, "A radio was like a voyce, but *outside* your mind. It lived in a box and told you things that weren't true. Problem was, without voyces of their own to tell them straight, people started to think these outside voyces were telling the truth. And, well, you can imagine the trouble that caused."

The rest of the period passed in a haze. Several times, Alina whispered for me to pay attention, and every time, I'd snap up in my chair and concentrate on keeping my eyes open.

After Loyalty class, there was Engineering, followed by Algorithms, a short lunch, then Dance, Service Studies, and finally, Logic. This was my favorite class probably because it was my best subject. Ironically, this was the only class in which we were encouraged to *not* use our voyces. That way, we could demonstrate our sixth sense – what the teachers called the 'common'.

When I entered the room, the curly haired Ms. Novak, who insisted we all call her 'Jess' was gesturing toward the riddle she had up on the front screen. The floating image of a Sphinx stood beside it. Her mouth moved as if she were saying the words. Several posters of this creature – a female mix of animals from ancient mythology – were plastered around the room. Eagerly, I took my seat and set to work deciphering the words. I have such a hard time reading that it took a while just to sound the words out in my mind. I could read on my own, but it was like trying to walk through mud. Slow and messy. But I managed, and eventually, I was able to read the following:

"With my brothers and sisters, I stand first in line.
I am the beginning of always and the end of this era.
I stand at the center of death and the start of the apocalypse.
What am I?"

Like most other days, I was the first to raise my hand. The other students groaned, and Jess told me to wait a while so the others could figure it out themselves. But after several long minutes and a few painfully wrong answers, Jess gestured for me to go ahead.

"It's the letter A," I said.

There were a few seconds of silence that lasted until one of the boys cursed out loud.

Jess frowned at the others before flashing me a big smile. "Right again, Lacey. You never cease to amaze me."

In the halls outside, I couldn't avoid the cold stares from several of my classmates.

<Don't let them bother you,> said Alina. <They're just upset they can't do what you can do.>

"And what's that?" I asked. "Answer silly riddles? What's so good about that?"

Alina didn't respond.

*   *   *

The walk home from school was only a couple of blocks. A light drizzle chilled the air and dampened my hair and clothes, but it was nothing like the icy rain of the night before.

With school done, I was able to focus on finding a new job. Alina ran a search for positions that would hire me, but there weren't any within walking distance.

<We could widen our search to include businesses across the river,> Alina suggested. <Maybe find something a little out of your comfort zone, but work is work, right?>

I was still considering this when we reached the steps leading up to my apartment building. This was the place Yadi and I had grown up in. It was the only home we'd ever known, and I couldn't imagine going anywhere else. Most days, the sight of this place was a comfort, but now…the thought of Yadira becoming a dead-head, combined with my own unemployment, made the apartment building feel a little different. The brick and concrete structure loomed overhead like an upsurge of stone and metal. It gathered overhead, and at any moment, I knew it could come tumbling down until the bricks and pins and struts were indistinguishable from the bits and pieces of my own bloodied body.

<Is everything okay?> asked Alina.

I wasn't sure how to answer that, and thankfully, I didn't have to because, at that moment, a small voice whined from behind the trash cans next to the steps.

For the first time since last night, I remembered the cat.

* * *

It took some time coaxing the small feline out from behind the cans. At first it didn't come at all, but then I remembered what those muties had told me. I snapped my fingers three times. This got the cat's attention. It took a few curious steps my way before darting back behind a pile of trash bags. It did this several times. All the while, it kept mewing like a crying baby.

I kept snapping my fingers, and eventually I was able to bribe the cat over with a half-eaten protein bar I had shoved into the bottom of my backpack. The cat chewed greedily on the edge of the bar a few minutes, then purred when I slid my hands under its belly and lifted it up off the sidewalk.

It was a girl. Her gray fur was caked with dirt and

rainwater, and it looked as if someone had taken a huge hole punch to her right ear.

"Are you, *Daughter*?" I asked, thinking about those Muties. The old couple with black eyes and white domes instead of ears – they'd been looking for a cat with a hole in its ear. I'd promised to keep my eyes open, but it looked like the cat had found me instead.

She squirmed a little in my arms before pressing her head against my chest. It meowed some more like it was trying to say something.

"It's okay, girl," I whispered. "Everything's gonna be okay."

<Lacey, what are you doing?> asked Alina when I carried the cat inside.

I wasn't sure how to answer that. All I knew was that the cat seemed lost, and maybe for once, I'd found a situation where I knew how to help.

Chapter 7

<Are you sure about this?> Alina asked for about the dozenth time. <I mean, wouldn't it be safer for the muties to come to us?>

"You know muties aren't allowed in our neighborhood," I said. "And besides, the sooner we get rid of this cat, the sooner I can start looking for a new job."

<I know…I just don't like this, okay?>

I sometimes forgot just how close we lived to the muties. Well, 'forgot' wasn't the right word. More like 'ignored'. Yadi and I didn't like to talk about 'em. And it was easy to pretend they lived a world away from us, when in truth their building was only a few short blocks from our own. And with Alina's nav points guiding our way and counting down the steps, it was plain to see I'd be there in no time.

The laundry basket thunked behind me, its wheels clattering over cracks in the pavement. From inside the basket, the cat mewed forlornly. She didn't seem to like being sealed inside.

"It's okay, girl. I'm taking you home to your owners."

The cat hissed.

I turned the corner and paused a moment to gaze up at the brownish-green eyesore that was the muties' tenement building. Standing this close always made me feel a bit uneasy. The place thrummed with decay, as if a dying heart was convulsing inside its concrete carapace. Long black streaks like running mascara stained all sides of the building. The bricks underneath were like pebbled scales on some behemoth's thick hide and the rusted fire escapes clung to the edges at such wild angles that they resembled clumps of burnt hair.

It was a wonder anyone could live here, but I knew from experience that the place was brimming with muties. A couple of years earlier, a fire on one of the upper floors caused an evacuation. Yadi and I had been shopping at a nearby farmer's market when we heard the alarms. And by the time we got here, a throng of muties was pouring from the building like termites fleeing a dead tree trunk.

<Maybe the cat doesn't want to go home.>

"I'm sorry, what?"

<Think about it, Lacey. If this really is those muties' cat, why has it been wandering around our place when its home was only a few blocks away? Answer: the poor cat's afraid.>

"You don't know that," I said, but I couldn't deny my own misgivings. Yadi seemed to believe muties ate their pets, but that didn't feel right to me. The muties I was coming to see had shown concern and even affection for their missing cat. Would they really have named her *Daughter* if they intended to eat her? I didn't think so.

I crossed the street and stepped into the tenement building's shadow. Off to the side, a middle-aged mutie stood stone-still on the curb. I figured he was waiting for someone to pick him up. Behind him, leaning against the side of the building was another one of those blurred shimmers I saw when that teenager had been killed. I blinked and looked away. I didn't want to know what was hiding beneath that distortion. Not now, anyways.

<I have a bad feeling about this,> said Alina.

"You're not helping," I said.

At the front of the building, a cagelike turnstile spun automatically and filtered a trickle of muties both in and out of the lobby. *I can still change my mind*, I told myself. No one was making me go inside. Even then, I felt myself hanging over an abyss.

Perhaps, auditor, this was a feeling we all experience when confronted with strange unknowns. I've come to recognize these moments as a sort of death cry. Because in going forward into new places, you find new experiences and become a new person – and the person you once were no longer exists. That's what this was...my unconscious mind begging me to stop, to let this version of me live just a little longer. I considered this a long time. I could turn back, go home, be my same self, but then the muties would still be without their cat – the one they called *Daughter.*

In an and out, lickety-split. That was the idea. If I hurried, it'd all be over in a manner of minutes. Then I'd have a story to tell. Yadi would be furious when she found out I'd gone into the muties' tenement. But even that felt like a good thing. If Yadi was mad at me, maybe she wouldn't be sad about dad or the money she owed…at least for a while.

Lifting the laundry basket into my arms, I took a breath, then slid in through the revolving turnstile.

*   *   *

A few muties shuffled listlessly inside the darkened, checker-floored lobby. Their black, marble-like eyes stared at nothing. Alina told me the muties I was looking for lived on the third floor, but the thought of being crammed into an elevator with any of them gave me the creeps. So I kept my distance and headed for the stairs.

It was terribly dark in the stairwell. Only a few dim running lights seemed to be working.

<Muties don't see like you and me,> said Alina. <They don't need the light like we do.>

Something groaned on the landing above us, and I looked up to see a mutie lurching on hands and knees. Alina brightened my vision and the skeletal frame of a crawling mutie came into sickish clarity. He was shirtless. His spine poking through his back like a line of bottlecaps. His shoulder blades twisted and flexed with each movement. He groaned again, and lunged forward, slamming his head into the wall. The impact left a small crater in the plasterboard, but the man paid no attention. Bits of plaster clung to his hair as he rocked back and forth.

Carefully, I held the basket before me and tiptoed around the man. I thought I'd managed to get by undetected when Alina whispered, <Lacey, this one wants to know if you've come to help.>

I spun around to find the man sitting now in the center of the landing, crisscross applesauce, with a wide smile on a face smeared with dirt or blood. I was standing above him now, and he looked up to me like a child waiting to hear a story…a child with white domes for ears and black, lifeless eyes.

<This one wants to know if you've come to let him out.>

"Out of where?" I asked.

<This one wants to know if you can let him out of his head. It is a dark place and he has been trapped inside a long, long time.>

I wasn't sure how to respond to this, so I didn't say anything. Instead, I turned away and continued up the stairs.

As I reached the third-floor landing, I heard another groan shortly followed by another *bang* as the man threw himself against the opposite wall.

"Alina," I pleaded, "can't you do anything? Make him stop."

<I can't,> said Alina. <And even if I could, it is not our place to interfere. Remember, Lacey, these people are getting what they deserve. They're modern-day Luddites.>

* * *

The hallway on the third floor was even darker than the stairwell. That's why I didn't see the two flexer boys lurking in the shadows when I stepped through the door. But they saw me.

A burning pain flowered in my scalp. I dropped the laundry basket and reached up, fully expecting to find my head covered in flames. There was no fire, but the pain sharpened into a single point and rocketed downward like a railroad spike. It felt like someone had taken a metal rod and hammered it from skullcap to tailbone. At the same time, every muscle in my body began to cramp up. I tried to scream, but my jaw was already sealed shut. I couldn't even raise my hands as I collapsed first on top of the laundry basket, then onto my back on the floor.

I can't say how long I lay convulsing that way. I felt trapped in my own pocket eternity. Pain has a way of stretching out the seconds. Like dissecting a frog, pain peels away the skin of time and draws out its vital organs.

I was vaguely aware of dark shapes hovering over me. One of the figures knelt and pressed a knee into my stomach.

<You don't belong here,> the flexer's voyce rumbled.

He put more weight on my gut, then clamped a sweaty hand around my throat.

I pray, auditor, that you never experience a flexer's cruelty. It is a pain that gets into your nerves. It sets your body on fire from the inside. But that's not even the worst part. The worst part was broadcast from the eyes of the flexers themselves. Even in the dim light, I could see that flexer's meaty face inches from my own. The light in his eyes was alive with raucous celebration. He was enjoying this. And the jack-o-lantern grin splitting his face told me he was only getting started.

That's why I was surprised when the pain died as suddenly as it began. The flexer with his knee in my stomach was glaring at a hand on his shoulder. The other flexer was saying something, but the words sounded tinny and far away.

"Leave her alone, Vitus. She's marked."

The flexer – *Vitus* – released me and returned to his towering height. I felt air and blood pouring back into my body.

"You sure?" Vitus asked aloud.

"Check for yourself," responded the other.

After a moment, Vitus cursed, and said, "What a shame." He cleared his throat and spit. Hot saliva splashed on my forehead. "See you later," he said. Then, the flexer stepped over me, kicked the laundry basket against the wall and exited through the stairwell. The cat was hissing and crying the whole time.

I was left alone, shivering in the dark and trying to make sense of what just happened.

<They're gone now,> said Alina before adding a perfunctory, <I told you I had a bad feeling about this.>

It was several minutes before I could move. Alina helped unclench the parts of my body that wouldn't let up on their own.

I tried to speak, but my mouth and throat were still beyond my control.

Alina guessed what I wanted to ask and said, <You were in the wrong place at the wrong time, Lacey. Those flexers are looking for someone. You spooked them, so they responded with force. But don't worry. I'm doing everything I can to get your body up and running. You should be good to go in a few minutes.>

"Th-tha-thank…you," I managed through clattering teeth.

<Don't mention it,> she said. <And just to be on the safe side, I'm sending out a call for help.>

"N-n-no!" The last thing I wanted was for Yadi to show up and walk into the same flexers I'd encountered. "N-no h-h-help."

<Don't worry, Lacey. I'd never do anything to put your sister at risk.> She paused. <I'm calling Cadence. He said you could call him if you needed help.>

It wasn't a relief, exactly. Although I was glad Yadira wouldn't be putting herself at risk – the thought of the cute, kind-hearted bartender, Cadence, scraping my dumb ass off the floor didn't feel any better.

My hands twitched and my body was all pins and needles as my nerves came back online. A wave of nausea rippled through me, and I realized with some horror that my pants were warm and damp. If Cadence showed up, I'd have to explain not only why I was in a mutie tenement but also why I'd wet myself.

I was still imagining what he might say when glaring light spilled into the hallway.

Two figures emerged from an apartment. Without a word, one of 'em bent over the laundry basket and began to yank it – the cat still inside – along the floor. The other bent over me. It was a mutie. His black eyes were at odds with his wide, garish smile.

<Lacey,> whispered Alina, <This one is so happy you've come.>

I could do nothing as the man slid his hands under my arms and dragged me into his apartment.

* * *

Alina kept telling me to stay calm, but that was impossible. I was in a mutie's apartment – not just the building but their actual home. All the stories I'd heard about muties raced through my mind. The things they ate, the children they abducted, the rituals they performed in secret. Even if only a fraction of the rumors were true, it still meant that I was in a traitor's home. These muties had betrayed the republic we all served. What would the flexers do to me if they counted me in among their kind? They'd been harsh enough with me just being in the building.

<Try to relax,> said Alina. <I don't think they wish you any harm.>

Sure enough, the muties acted like they were trying to help. Working together, the man and woman eased me into a wicker armchair. The woman gripped one of my wrists and pressed her thumbs into the back of my hand. Pleasure and sensation flooded into my fingers and up my arm. I marveled at this woman, who's pink hairclip seemed grotesquely out of place when combined with her other mutie features. While the woman massaged my hands, the man put his fingers together and tapped them on his lips.

<This one wants to thank you,> translated Alina.

"Y-you're welcome," I said.

The man smiled, his salt and pepper hair spilling across his forehead. He patted my knee, then turned toward the laundry basket. The woman had moved up my arms – her thumbs pressing into the muscles in my forearms. Short spikes of pain soon gave way to a flush of relief as the tension retreated from her touch.

<This one says the flexers' effects will only last a short while.>

Behind the woman, the man was carefully untying the bungie cord I'd strapped to the lid of the laundry basket. Once it was off, the man snapped his fingers three times and the cat leapt into his arms.

The cat meowed and purred as the man held her close while making choked, sobbing sounds in his throat. For the first time, I wondered if muties could cry, or if that ability had been torn out with the rest of their eye sockets.

The woman turned from me then and embraced both man and cat. She made little cooing sounds as she stroked the cat's matted hair and ran her fingers along the cat's torn right ear.

I felt a little embarrassed watching this reunion – which was very different from the one Yadi and I had experienced with our dad – so I turned away. I examined my surroundings. The apartment was small but packed with all sorts of odd things. Hanging from the ceiling near the walls were rows of crudely made windchimes. Glass bottles and pieces of rusted metal dangled from packing twine. They made little clinking sounds as they twisted in the breeze filtering in from an open window. Next to the chimes and nailed to the wall was a long metal track that seemed to stretch through the entire apartment. As I watched, a silver marble rolled down the track, making a low grinding noise as it went. The marble followed the track around the apartment before disappearing out of sight when it turned a corner leading into a darkened bedroom. A moment later, another marble appeared from the opposite end of the track and repeated the cycle.

<The muties see mostly with sound,> said Alina. <The marble tracks and chimes help their auditory devices map out the details in the room.>

"Then what's with the lights," I asked. A couple of shadeless lamps blazed uncomfortably from a nearby table.

<I could be wrong,> Alina said, <but I think the lamps are for your benefit, not theirs.>

This didn't quite make sense to me. How did the muties know I'd come? Or were non-mutie visitors a regular occurrence? I couldn't imagine that was true.

Lifting my legs experimentally, I figured I was almost but not quite ready to walk. My attention turned back to the man and woman. Their cat purred in their arms, clearly enjoying the attention. The fear and pain I'd felt at the hands of those flexers had somewhat dissipated. The muties obvious love for their pet was enough to make me feel I'd done something of value.

"Alina, please tell them it's time for me to leave."

At my words, both muties stiffened. Calmly, affectionately, they lowered the cat to the carpet, then rose together as one.

<These two would like you to stay just a moment longer.>

"Why? What do they want?"

<They wish to give you a gift. To show their thanks.>

"I don't know, Alina. I really think I should be go –"

<It shouldn't take long,> interrupted Alina. <And don't worry. I'm monitoring their mood. I don't detect any hostility.>

The man and woman both retreated to darker corners of the apartment. I heard the clinking of glassware, and a moment later they both reappeared. The man was holding a small mug filled to the brim with a steaming liquid, and the woman was holding a pair of sweatpants.

<These are not the gifts,> Alina said before I could ask. <But these two think this will help you feel more at ease. They want you to feel comfortable.>

I eyed the items doubtfully. "Alina, what do you think?"

<I think you really don't want to be wearing wet pants, do you? And this one says the tea will help get rid of any lingering effects brought on by the flexers.>

So I didn't protest when the woman helped hoist me out of the chair. Nor did I flinch from her hold on my arms as I walked with wobbly legs toward a small, closet sized bathroom.

The woman flicked on a wall mounted lamp, then gently closed the door for me. As I changed out of my soiled clothes, I couldn't help but realize the bathroom was much more pleasant than I would have imagined. Flowery scents puffed from little sconces on the wall, and there was no shortage of plush bath towels draped over a polished rack next to the sink. There was no mirror, but that didn't stop me from moistening one of the towels before furiously scrubbing what remained of that flexer's spit from my forehead.

Back in the living room, the mutie woman took my dirty clothes without question and threw them in the laundry basket I'd brought. Next, she gestured back to the wicker chair.

<This one hopes you'll stay just a little longer,> said Alina. <At this point, I'm curious what they want.>

The mutie man handed me the steaming mug as I sat. It smelled of lemon and mint.

<Go on, Lacey. I detect no poison or harsh chemicals.>

I took a sip and nearly gasped as the warm mixture seemed to pour into the center of my chest where it immediately began seeping through the rest of my body.

"This…is delicious."

<This one wants to ask you a question…and Lacey? Huh, that's funny.>

"What is it?"

<This one has a riddle. Do you want to hear it?>

I nodded and Alina continued. <A sweet tooth's delight is a real tooth's blight. What is it?>

I had to think only a few heartbeats before the answer seemed obvious.

"Sugar," I said.

The mutie nodded enthusiastically before tilting his head. <This one wants to know if you'd like any? Sugar?>

"Sure," I said. I didn't think the tea really needed it, but I found myself enjoying their hospitality so much that I dared not insult them.

The man hopped to his feet and appeared much more spry than I first gave him credit for. Once he was out of sight, my attention turned to the woman, who had an odd frown on her face.

"What is your name?" I asked.

The woman shook her head, her frown deepening.

<This one says they don't have names. Only numbers. This one is four-six-five-five-three. Her husband is four-six-five-five-four.>

I was struck by a sudden bolt of curiosity. "What happened to you? Why were you and your husband...*fixed*?" That was not the word I meant to ask. I meant to say *punished.* Why had Alina changed it to *fixed?*

Either way, it didn't matter. The woman put a finger to her lips and shook her head again. A moment later, the man returned with a small thimble sized container full of brown sugar that quickly dissolved into my hot drink. It was delicious. My tastebuds sang with the sweetness while my pulse quickened with the sudden rush of sugar. For several minutes, I did nothing but enjoy my tea and listen as marbles raced around the apartment and the muties caressed their cat called Daughter.

As I neared the bottom of my cup, both husband and wife stood. The man took the cup from me and placed it on the table beside him. Next, the woman reached for my hands and held them gently. I knew I should have been frightened, but I sensed nothing but kindness from these two. While the woman held my hands, the man stepped behind me and began rummaging through a closet.

<This one wants you to know they didn't want to do this,> said Alina as I tried to glean some meaning from the woman's eyeless gaze. That's when I felt the first shudder of fear. I tried to pull my hands away, but the woman's grip tightened. <This one wants you to know they're sorry.>

"Sorry for what?"

<This one says they didn't have a choice. They say muties must do what they're told.>

"Alina, what is she talking about?" Out of the corner of my eye, I saw the man approaching with a long leather strap stretched tight in his fists.

<Lacey, I have a bad feeling about this.>

Just then, the woman dug her fingernails hard into my wrists. At the same time, the man moved with a speed I could never have predicted. He dropped behind my chair and flung the strap around my throat.

My scream was cut off when the man tugged hard on the strap, crushing my windpipe.

I kicked out and struck the table, sending the mug crashing to the floor. The woman seemed unfazed. She leaned in and tightened her grip.

<Lacey!> cried Alina. <I'm calling for help. Hold on, Lacey.>

I gagged and gulped for air that wouldn't come. Already, the apartment seemed to be spinning madly out of control. From behind, the man lifted a strange object in front of my dwindling vision – a long metal rod blinking with red lights. I had no idea what this was, but Alina started to scream.

<No! Oh, God no, Lacey. You can't let them use that. You have to stop them. *Fight*, Lacey! *Fight*!>

But there was nothing I could do. The muties were choking the life out of me. My lungs burned and white lights floated across my vision. My dying brain imagined these were speeding White Line vehicles, rushing to grind me into the pavement. Already, the world was dissolving into a blurred shimmer – much like the one that had consumed the teenager who had been killed.

Alina screamed a final time – a sound so full of rage and pain – that I half-wondered how the noise didn't split my head open like an egg. Then the man touched the blinking rod to my temple, and a bomb detonated in my skull.

And I knew no more.

Chapter 8

Cool liquid splashed on my forehead as someone shook my shoulder. I figured those flexers had gotten a hold of me again. My entire body clenched in anticipation.

"Lacey, wake up." The voice didn't sound anything like the flexers I'd met earlier. "Lacey, are you okay?"

Squinting, I could just make out the boy kneeling over me. Cadence's handsome, dimpled face stretched into wide-eyed worry. He held an open water bottle over my head, a single drop hanging from the brim.

"Lacey? Oh, thank goodness you're awake. Can you hear me?"

I nodded, then tried to sit up, only managing to shift onto my side. I was on a bench – a concrete slab out near the street. In the afternoon sun, the world was overwhelming with its glaring windows and passing traffic. A tram rumbled by and its monotone voice announced the next stop.

"H-how did I get here?" I asked. I was expecting my voyce to answer, but she stayed quiet. Cadence answered instead.

"I was at my day job – working the punch press – when your voyce contacted Bartleby. She said you needed help, so I cut out early and got here as quick as I could." He gestured to me. "I had no idea things were this bad. What the heck happened?"

I didn't know how to answer because, truly, I didn't know what *had* happened. The last thing I remembered was the muties.

"I was attacked," I said.

"What?" Cadence looked up and down the street. "By who?"

"A pair of muties…they did something to me."

Cadence frowned. "You were attacked by…*muties*?" His voice was thick with disbelief. "But muties can't hurt anyone. They're not allowed."

I could have punched him. Did he think I was making it up? But rather than get upset, I asked Alina to explain what happened…only she wouldn't answer.

"Alina? *Hello!* Alina, where are you?"

The worry on Cadence's face shifted into something approaching alarm. "Lacey, Bartleby tells me your voyce isn't responding. It's like…she isn't there."

I tried again and again to get Alina to say something. I demanded, pleaded, then *begged* for her to let me know she was okay. All I got was silence. I remembered her last words telling me to fight – her uncharacteristic cries of terror as those muties held that blinking metal rod up to my temple.

They killed her, I thought. I couldn't believe it, yet I knew it was true. Tears blurred my vision and I reached out for Cadence. Clutching his shirt, I felt the world spinning beneath me. "Alina…she's *gone!*"

Years ago, Yadi and I had watched from our apartment as an abandoned casino was demolished. A series of explosions followed by the whole thing collapsing in on itself. Everything that it was or had been – gone in one dramatic implosion. It felt like that. A crescendo of grief and panic rumbled through my mind. All the emotions I'd been trying to hold in suddenly came tumbling out like a volley of munition fire. Ogden Oliver's ridicule, my suspension from work, my father's ashes, Yadira's debt, the mutie attack, and now Alina's silence. Mixed with a deadening exhaustion, it all spilled out through my eyes and throat. The tears burned like lava.

Cadence put his arm around my shoulders and led me to a car waiting by the curb.

"I think…" he said, "we should take you to the hospital."

* * *

Forty minutes later, Cadence and I were sitting on folding chairs in the middle of a sweltering clinic waiting room. Cadence kept telling me things would be okay and offered theories on what had happened. "Your neuro-net got disconnected somehow. Maybe your voyce is rebooting. Alina's auditory connection got severed. Whatever it is, the doctor should be able to fix it."

I prayed he was right, but I think we both knew none of these things could be true. For starters, I'd never heard of anyone losing contact with their voyce by mere accident. The neuro-net was mounted to the brain in a way that allowed it to grow with you. The bridge between voyce and mind was seamless. Even people who suffered traumatic brain injuries rarely needed to get their nets adjusted. And the fools who've tried to mess with their own nets on purpose – those folks usually ended up arrested, braindead, or both.

People would joke sometimes about your net getting twisted out of place. Like last year, some boys in my grade were arguing with each other and one of them had threatened, "I'm gonna hit you so hard, even your voyce will be stuttering." Or sometimes in Loyalty class whenever a student took too long to answer, Ms. Parks would say, "Don't get your net all bunched up." No one ever considered these ideas seriously. For all practical purposes, your net and your voyce were a part of you. Not having Alina with me now made me feel like less of a person – like my soul was gone.

A door swung open and a woman in bright pink scrubs leaned into the waiting room. Her gaze swept the room, but she didn't say anything. Cadence tapped my arm and said, "Her voyce is hailing you, Lacey. Come on."

Still feeling a bit shaky, I was appreciative when Cadence offered his arm to help me stand. We walked over to the nurse who was eyeing us both with mild annoyance.

"She doesn't understand," Cadence said to me. "Bartleby, can you tell the nurse what's going on?" Several heartbeats passed with the nurse and Cadence locked in what looked like a staring contest. Finally, the nurse blinked, and stepped back. Her annoyance switched over to nervous apprehension.

"Your voyce is…*inactive*?" she asked aloud.

I nodded, and the nurse took another step back. She gestured for me to follow, and Cadence said he'd wait for me. I should have thanked him, but I was so obsessed with Alina's absence that I barely noticed when the door closed between us. I kept hearing little snippets of voices that I hoped were Alina coming back online. But while Alina's voyce was always loud and clear, these new voices were brisk and elusive like a spray of dust in the wind. I feared they might be my own imagination.

The nurse led me back to a darkened cubicle where she struggled to take my vitals. Every time I'd been to the clinic before – the most recent being when I had to get stitches in my forearm after a wet market co-worker had gotten a little overzealous with the fillet knife – Alina would simply relay my vitals over to the hospital's network. But without Alina's help, the nurse was at a loss. She tore open what looked like a never-before-used arm band and placed it around my bicep.

"I've never measured blood pressure this way," said the nurse, "but don't worry. My voyce is telling me how to do it."

The armband restricted until my head throbbed. The sensation put me back in the muties' tenement building. Both when that flexer had put his hands around my throat or when those muties had cut off my windpipe with a leather strap.

I squirmed in my seat. Blood pounded inside my skull until I thought it might burst open.

"*Relax*," demanded the nurse. Then, mercifully, the armband hissed and ceded its grip.

Minutes later, I was sitting alone on a padded table lined with butcher paper. And even though I knew I wasn't moving, the inside of my head was in freefall. Without Alina, my thoughts fired in wild succession. Voices cascaded one on top of the other. Yadira, Cadence, Ogden Oliver, Alina, and endless more. They all spoke to me, but the words were choppy, impossible to understand. Before one voice was finished speaking, another voice was already taking its place. They were like socks in a dryer – bumping into each other in a never-ending tumble. Was this what it was like *before* voyces were created? How did people live with the chaos of their own thoughts?

When the doctor came in, I was half-convinced she wasn't real. Part of me wanted to reach out and touch her, to make sure my mind wasn't playing tricks.

"My name's Dr. Mutambara," said a kind-eyed woman with bushy hair tucked back behind her ears. "The nurse tells me you're having trouble connecting with your voyce. Is that right?"

I nodded, and the doctor smiled as if this was something she saw all the time. But I could tell from the way her hands tightened on her clipboard that she was only *acting* calm.

"When did you first notice something was wrong?"

I told her everything. I was so afraid that I didn't worry about what her voyce might say about me having a run-in with flexers and muties both in the same day.

"I see," she said, again with a tone that suggested this was an ordinary, everyday occurrence. Then she began a meticulous examination.

She shined a light into my eyes and ears, pressed a wooden stick against my tongue and gazed down the back of my throat. Next, she felt along my jawline, neck, and shoulders, asking if I felt any pain as she did so. She made me lift the back of my shirt, and I flinched as she pressed a cold metal disk against my skin and asked me to breathe deep. Throughout the whole thing, Dr. Mutambara kept whispering questions and suggestions to her own voyce.

She spent ten minutes pressing her fingers into my scalp like she might somehow be able to see the neuro-lace poking through my skull.

"I'm not seeing anything," she said finally. "But there's one more thing we can try."

She hurried out of the room and I was left with my own silence that wasn't really silence. My head was full of noise, and without Alina, I had no idea how to shut it off.

Several minutes passed before Dr. Mutambara returned holding a black, cube-shaped device. A small green light blinked in its center. I was still eyeing the device when a couple more doctors crowded in behind Dr. Mutambara. A serious faced woman and fidgety young man.

"With your permission," said Dr. Mutambara, "I've invited two of my colleagues to view the procedure."

"What procedure?" I couldn't decide what was more frightening, the blinking black cube or the new doctors' obvious fascination with me. They had the look of spectators hoping to see a magic trick.

"This device connects with *limbo*."

I'd never heard the term, but when I asked what 'limbo' meant, the doctors shared nervous glances.

"Voyces can't be erased," said Mutambara. "Copies of them exist in the Central Archives, AKA *limbo*." She lifted the box. "This device should be able to locate your voyce, and hopefully, reestablish a link with your neuro-net."

My heart thundered as I reclined back on the crinkling butcher paper. Alina couldn't be dead, the doctor had just said so – which meant there was hope. But I couldn't bring myself to believe it would work out. I couldn't afford to *hope*. The best I could do was *brace*. Prepare myself for what was about to happen.

The doctor pried open a compartment on the side of the box and pulled out a small disc attached to a thin bundle of interwoven wires. She held the disc up to the side of my head and it clicked into place against my temple as if magnets buried in my skull were holding it in position – which, I suppose, was indeed the case.

"Okay," said Dr. Mutambara. "My voyce tells me that all I have to do now is initiate a 'search and restore' program. Are you ready?"

I nodded, but she wasn't looking at me. Her eyes were fixed on the other doctors and their silent intensity made it clear none of them had ever done this before.

Mutambara nodded, then spoke to the device. "Sophia, activate search and restore."

The effect was immediate but nothing at all like I was expecting. I thought maybe I'd feel an electrical jolt. Or maybe I'd hear something buzzing as my neuro reactivated. Or, *best-case*, I'd hear Alina speak. But the response didn't come from Alina, or even from me.

Right after Mutambara activated the device, all three doctors stiffened. Their hands curled into white-knuckled fists. Their eyes lost focus and became dead, empty stares.

Nobody moved for several heartbeats.

"What's happening?" I asked. In response, one of the doctors – the younger, fidgety one – fired a look of such seething hatred in my direction that I flinched. He took a step toward me, then flung himself onto the floor. *Wham!* An instant later, the other doctor seemed to lose control of her legs. Her knees buckled and her arms flailed out. She managed to catch an I.V. stand and brought it clattering on top of her and the other doctor as she collapsed over him.

Wanting to help, I sat up only to have Dr. Mutambara shove me back down.

"Are you crazy?" The doctor's breath was hot in my face. I tried to make eye contact, but her gaze wasn't really on me. It seemed *grayed out* – distant – like whoever was looking through those eyes was somewhere else. "I'm giving you a chance, Lacey. Are you seriously going to blow it?"

"I don't know what's happening. My voyce –"

"Is *gone!*" she said. "You need to let her go."

"But I *can't*. Please tell me what's happening."

Dr. Mutambara – who I was beginning to realize was *not* Dr. Mutambara – plucked the disk from my temple, then tossed it along with the black cube onto the linoleum floor. The device chirped angrily.

"Listen to me," she said. "These doctors can't help you. And if the prox find out you tried to access limbo, they'll send their flexers. If they realize you don't have a voyce, they'll kill you on the spot. You are *marked*, but that won't matter if they find out."

With the exception of the flexers, I didn't know what

any of this meant. Who, or what, was 'the prox'? And what did it mean that I was marked? Marked by who? For what purpose?

"I don't know what any of this means. *Please.* I just want my voyce back. I *need* her."

"You *need* to get moving. Keep your head down."

"Where should I go?"

"Anywhere but home. They've already begun collecting marked ones, and they know where you live. But they can't take you yet…not until you and I have had a chance to talk. I'll send a car when I can. But until then, don't tell anyone what's happening. The more others know, the more they'll be in danger."

"Who are you?" I asked.

Dr. Mutambara's eyes cleared and, for a moment I imagined I could see a hint of the person speaking through her.

"You hold me in your hands while I hold you in my center."

I felt like I was back in the rain outside *Stratus* – icy rivulets pouring down my back. I recognized the words, of course, but why were they coming from this doctor's mouth?

Before I could say anything else, Dr. Mutambara's expression slackened as if she were having a stroke. Her mouth widened into a silent scream, and crimson pooled in her left eye as blood vessels burst.

"*Get out!*" she screamed.

* * *

Cadence jumped out of his seat when I stepped back into the waiting room. He must have seen the fear painted on my face because he said, "Holy smokes, Lacey. What happened?"

I had no words to adequately describe the chaos swirling in my head. I tugged his wrist as I stepped past him. And thankfully, he fell in beside me as I broke into a brisk pace.

Cadence was peppering me with questions, but I couldn't answer him right away. For one, the person speaking through Dr. Mutambara had warned me not to tell anyone. And two, the speaker had also warned me not to go home. But what about Yadira? What would happen if my sister walked into our apartment and found a group of flexer boys waiting inside?

Without thinking, I gripped Cadence's hand and tugged him into a jog.

Chapter 9

The walk from the hospital to my apartment should have only been a few blocks, but without Alina's help, the distance seemed irrelevant. I felt adrift in the wreckage after a storm. Without my voyce, I couldn't find my way. Once familiar streets – places I'd known my whole life – had somehow been *changed.*

Where there had once been scaffolding that blocked one side of the street, there was now a wide-open, brick-lined path swept clean and cordoned off from the rest of the city. And while the adjacent sidewalk – the one I was familiar with – was overflowing with pedestrians, this new path had only a few travelers. Men and women ambled down the walkway in expensive looking power suits or trendy fashionwear. I didn't quite understand what I was looking at. I thought I knew this city, yet here was a section I didn't recognize. Had the walkway been completed overnight? That didn't seem likely, but it wasn't important. All that mattered was that this looked like the fastest route back to my apartment. But when I stepped in that direction, Cadence gripped my forearm, forcing me to turn and face him.

"Where are you going?" he asked.

I gestured toward the wide-open path. "I'm gonna cut through here."

Puzzled, Cadence said, "But there's too much construction that way. We gotta go around."

This made me irritated. "Right *there!*" I pointed. "Come on." But instead of moving, Cadence eyed me like I wasn't making any sense.

"All I see is torn up sidewalk and scaffolding. You gonna climb over it?"

I couldn't figure out what Cadence was playing at, but I wasn't gonna stand here and argue with him, not when Yadi might be in danger.

"Which way?" I asked.

"Sorry?"

"Ask *Bartleby*, 'What's the quickest way back to my apartment?'"

Cadence blinked, then pointed up the street and said, "Three blocks that way, one block right."

"Thanks." And before he could stop me, I turned and broke into a run. I vaulted over a short concrete partition then rushed up the middle of the brick-lined path.

The business folk who had seemed so lax from a distance, stopped dead when they laid eyes on me. A woman with wine-red hair yelped and dropped a porcelain mug of coffee that shattered on the bricks. A man with silver, reflective sunglasses leapt back and nearly tripped. Others were less squeamish, but their disdain was unmistakable. A few even planted themselves in my way, arms crossed and nostrils flaring, but without Alina telling me what they wanted, I didn't have a clue why they were so irked.

Maybe it was because I was running. No one else seemed to be in a hurry. Still, if that was it, my being in a rush seemed like such a little thing to generate such animosity, and I wasn't about to slow down and ask what the deal was.

A street sign told me I was on the corner of Second and Boardwalk. I should have recognized this place, but in addition to the walkway, there were loads of other things that were…out of place. Where yesterday there had been a boarded storefront, a high-end retailer now stood. An old Indian restaurant that had burned down years earlier was no longer the blackened shell I knew. In its place was a glitzy fine dining bistro called *Haut Monde*. In addition to these changes, I noticed several strange placards – each one showing a flurry of black and white dots like one of those old QR codes. They were posted along the edges of both the buildings and the walkway. And now that I noticed them, I saw that some of the business folk were wearing them as well. The QR codes were emblazoned on gaudy, gold-covered amulets.

What is this? I wondered. But another part of me

screamed, *Doesn't matter. None of this matters until I find Yadira.*

Heart thumping in my ears, I rounded the corner and saw my apartment building just a block away. To get there, I had to exit the walkway. I leapt over the partition and landed on the sidewalk right in front of a man who'd been standing in the shade, slurping noodles from a paper bowl. He flinched and stumbled backward.

"What the –" the man said. "Where'd you come from? You a witch or something?"

Ignoring him, I jogged up the sidewalk until I was standing right across the street from my apartment. I didn't see any sign of flexers, and for a moment, I thought maybe I'd overreacted. But then there came the screech of tires. The sound seemed to shake the world. A pair of red vans peeled around the corner.

What should I do? Hide? Or make a run for the apartment? I wasn't used to making my own decisions alone.

"Please, Alina. Come back. I need your help."

I waited too long and lost my nerve. Hesitation has a way of taking decisions from you. The red vans pulled up to the curb next to the apartment. Not wanting to be seen, I backed into the alley and hunkered down behind a stack of discarded boxes and an old mattress. I figured this was pretty pointless, though. If the flexers wanted me, there was really nothing I could do.

But when they stepped out of their vans – six in all – none of them even looked my way. They adjusted their purple, red-striped coats as if preparing for a job interview, then they stormed up the steps – the same steps where Daughter had spooked me the night before.

I was left alone, panting in the alley.

Was Yadi inside? This time of day, she could have been in any number of places. She sometimes worked late at the skin market. I prayed today was one of those days.

My hopes were dashed however when a piercing scream echoed through the alley.

No...please, no.

A few minutes later, two of the flexers appeared on the steps with Yadi's crumpled body held between them. Her long black hair hung over her face, and she didn't move as they dragged her down the stairs.

Something inside me *snapped.* The sight of those flexers' vacant, thuggish grins as they callously handled Yadi's body sparked a fire in my mind. Alina might have told me to cool it – talk me out of what I would do next. But she wasn't here, and I couldn't just stand by while they took Yadi away from me. Something like electricity crackled in my head. My arms and legs tightened like machinery.

I stepped away from the boxes I'd been cowering behind and my foot kicked something on the ground. It was a long, splintered piece of wood. I picked it up, still not sure what I was doing, only that there was no way I'd let them take Yadi like this.

They still hadn't looked my way when I stepped out of the alley. They dropped Yadi on the sidewalk, and I could see her eyes were wide-open, staring at nothing.

They killed her. I lifted the wooden plank and stepped into the street. My heart hammered in my ears. The sound was so loud, I wondered how on earth the flexers couldn't hear it themselves. To my ears, my heartbeat sounded like the slap of running footsteps on pavement.

I realized too late that it *was* running footsteps. There was a blur of movement, then someone *slammed* into me. One hand slipped around my waist while another covered my mouth. I swung the plank over my head, striking my attacker. But he didn't let go. He grunted and heaved me back onto the sidewalk where he tripped and fell back into the alley, pulling me along with him.

My rage exploded into something I couldn't control. Knees scraping on asphalt, I spun around and lifted the plank over my head. I didn't see Cadence until it was almost too late. The plank froze mid-swing only a couple of inches from his face.

"What the hell are you doing?" I demanded.

"You – you can't –" he panted. Sweat coursed down

the sides of his face and dampened his shirt. "The – flexers –" He swallowed. "They'll kill you."

Not if I kill them first. The thought was stupid and irrational – no one could hurt flexers – but I was far past rational. I turned away from Cadence to see Yadira still lying on the sidewalk. And to my utter astonishment, she blinked.

She's alive. But before I could get up, Cadence lunged forward and grabbed me again.

"Lacey," he said through gritted teeth. "Lacey, *stop*."

But I refused to listen. I couldn't tell you, auditor, how long it was Cadence and I grappled in that alley, but by the time I ripped myself free of his hold, we were both gasping for breath, and a long gash had been torn into Cadence's cheek. I spun toward Yadi.

But it was too late.

She was no longer on the sidewalk. I could only watch in disbelief as the red van they'd loaded her into sped away down the street.

I turned back toward Cadence, all my rage pointed toward him. I cursed and swung the board at his head. He barely managed to block the blow as the board cracked over his forearm.

I threw the remaining pieces onto the ground and cussed him out.

"Damn you, Cadence. Why'd you stop me?"

"I'm sorry. I had to," he said, nursing his arm. "Bartleby says –"

"I don't *care* what your voyce says. They took *Yadi.* I could've stopped them."

"No, you couldn't."

I glared at him. He must not have liked the look because he took a step back and raised his hands defensively.

"Lacey, listen. Bartleby says there's a way to save your sister. I don't understand what's going on. I don't know why the flexers are after you. And I don't know how you were able to just *vanish* into thin air, but –"

This got my attention.

"Vanish?" I asked. "What do you mean, *vanish*?"

"Back in front of the hospital. You were right in front of me one second, then gone – *poof* – the next. Something really crazy is going on – I've got no idea what, but Bartleby says I gotta help you. He tells me more help is on the way."

"Help…from who? Where?"

"Hold on," he said, then tilted his head. He blinked, then pointed down the alley toward the opposite end where a White Line vehicle was pulling up to the curb. "*There*."

The double doors on the vehicle opened automatically like welcoming arms.

"Who sent it?" I asked.

Cadence shrugged. "No idea, but Bartleby says we should get inside. Quickly, before –"

"*Hey*!"

The four remaining flexer boys had emerged from the apartment building and were all staring right at me. The three in back glowered as flexers usually did, but the one in front beamed with unfettered delight.

"Wow, what a coincidence?" he shouted. "Maybe I should've dealt with you earlier." I recognized him then. It was the one from the mutie tenement building – *Vitus*. His meaty face, pug nose, and jack-o-lantern grin were even more unpleasant in daylight. To the other flexers, he said, "That's the girl we're after. Lacey Clarke." At the mention of her name, all the flexers' expressions darkened. To me, they no longer looked like men at all, but a pack of feral dogs.

Run, a voice screamed in my mind. I turned to look down the alley. At this angle, the flexers couldn't see Cadence who was already halfway toward the White Line vehicle. He gestured wildly for me to follow. That was our escape, but it seemed so far. And everyone knew; once a flexer set their eyes on you, it was over.

I thought of those teenagers who'd only been trying to steal a few pretzels and water. *Don't run*, I'd told them, *You'll only make it worse.*

It had seemed like good advice at the time, but now, with the flexers' cruelty aimed right at me, surrender was the furthest thing from my mind.

The flexers hadn't moved from the steps, but Vitus raised his hand.

Can't escape now, I thought.

He closed his hand into a fist and my body braced for the world of pain. I stood still as concrete for several heartbeats and squinted my eyes against the flood of torture I knew would soon ravage my senses. But nothing happened. I opened my eyes to see all the flexers staring dumbly at Vitus' raised fist. He shook it like it was a lightbulb that had gone out. Then the others pointed their own fists at me. Still, nothing.

An odd realization dawned on me then.

They can't touch me. Whatever tech those muties had used to wipe Alina from my mind, it had also put me outside the flexer boys' reach.

The flexers must have also realized this, because they started moving. They rumbled down the steps like a herd of bison.

Run! I spun away toward Cadence and the White Line vehicle, eighty, maybe ninety yards away. *If we could only get there.*

My feet pounded asphalt. Cadence was only a few paces ahead of me but I was gaining on him. We had a wide lead on the flexers, but they were faster. I could already hear them thundering up the alley behind us. Given time, they'd overtake us. No question.

Cadence slowed and I slipped past him. I reached the car first and dove head first into the plush interior. But when I looked back, any celebration I felt turned to ice. Mere feet from the doors, Cadence was on his back. He twitched on the sidewalk. Vitus bore down on him. Fist raised, the flexer's face had taken on an orange color, making him look more pumpkin now than ever.

The engine powered on, and the car doors started to close.

"No!" I reached out and grabbed Cadence's shirt. The

flexers were nearly on top of us, but I couldn't just leave him.

The car lurched away from the sidewalk, and Cadence's dead weight threatened to pull me out of the doors. He likely would have if the doors weren't already half shut.

Pain flared in my shoulder as something popped.

Vitus dove into the street and fell on Cadence's legs. The added weight combined with the car's sudden acceleration yanked Cadence out of my hands.

"*Cadence*!"

I crashed backwards onto the floor of the car, and the doors sealed shut. I scrambled to my feet only to go sprawling again when the car slammed its brakes.

"Forced stop," cried the car's automated voyce. "Flexer command acknowledged."

I clambered up into the seat and looked out the back window. Vitus stood over Cadence's rigid body, his fist pointed at the vehicle.

So they can't touch me, but they can touch the car.

I was still thinking of what to do next when the passenger side window shattered inward. Glass sprayed the interior as the remaining flexer boys reached in and fumbled with the door locks.

"Emergency override confirmed," the car announced. "Please stand back."

The car jerked forward. All but one of the flexers fell away. He tried to claw his way in through the shattered window until I leaned back and kicked him square in the face. It was like kicking a concrete brick, but he disappeared from the window. I caught sight of the flexer tumbling in the mirror before the car zipped around the corner, leaving the flexers – and Cadence – far behind.

It was several minutes before the car slowed to normal speed. The smell of burning brake pads stung the air. I let go of the handholds and massaged my palms. My entire body throbbed with a mix of scrapes and muscle strain. On top of that, my head was a flurry of dangerous thoughts. I needed to do something. I couldn't just let this car take me...*wherever* it was taking me while those flexers had Yadi and Cadence. But what could I do? Without Alina, I had no way of knowing which ideas were good and which ones were insane.

I was so absorbed in this thinking that it took me a while to realize I wasn't alone inside the car.

A ball of fur darted across the front seat. Startled, I kicked out, then stared in disbelief at the brown-haired cat. Its tail flicked playfully as it watched me from across the interior. The cat's matted fur had been washed and now had a golden shimmer. And more visible than ever was the hole in her right ear.

"Daughter?" I asked. "What are you doing here?"

The cat meowed, but didn't move.

A flash of rage seeped into my thoughts.

Just yesterday, things had been relatively normal. But now, thanks to this darn cat; Alina, Yadi, and even Cadence had been taken from me.

You'll never see them again a small voice whispered from the back of my mind. *Once the flexers get you, you're gone forever.*

What part had the cat played in all this? The muties had seemed so helpless when they were looking for her. I had only wanted to do something nice. Now look where that had gotten me.

And where, exactly, was I? Or more specifically, where was I headed?

The car turned onto a bridge leading out of the city. The cat continued to watch me, and I couldn't help but wonder what sort of mess I'd fallen into.

Chapter 10

A riddle came to mind, and I spoke the words out loud:

"On a ladder of sunshine, I climb into sky;
Where I meet my kindred, and together we fly.
With wandering spirit, I carve valleys – *grind* stone;
In cold, I'll seek shelter in my crystalized home.
Ruin and destruction I've frequently brought;
But no life can be found in places I'm not.
What am I?"

I knew no one would answer, but I let the words out anyways. Right then, it was enough to be speaking. It was enough to hear someone's voice, even if it was only my own.

I was alone.

The White Line vehicle had carried me far from the city – past the militarized checkpoints, past the colorful shantytowns where people in flowing green fabrics flooded their littered streets, and past the smoke-belching factories that painted the sky inky black. Alina used to tell me a little pollution was good for the world. That mother earth craved filth the way flies savored decay. But as the air thickened with waste – my eyes watering and a sour sting tickling my sinuses – I found Alina's comments about pollution a little hard to believe.

How could this be good for anyone?

I stopped looking out the windows after a while. All I cared about was back in the city anyways. Yadira...Alina...Cadence. Everyone I cared about was gone. I put my head down on the seat and tried to imagine where the flexers might have taken Yadi. Or what they had done to Cadence. As if sensing my distress, the cat curled up beside me. She purred when I stroked her golden-brown hair.

An hour passed before the car turned off the main highway and wound its way through a narrow, tree lined canyon interrupted only by a series of automated gates that rattled out of the way when we drew near. There were no other cars on the road and when a tree branch raked along the roof of the car, it gave me the sense few people, if *anyone*, had come this way in a long time. Eventually, the canyon walls widened to reveal a private beach. Cement-gray sand slipped into a steel-gray ocean.

The car drove onto the sand and shut off its engine.

I had no intention of leaving the car. I shivered from the ocean chill. But when doors opened automatically, and Daughter darted out onto the sand, I felt compelled to go after her.

The cat moved purposefully across the sand until she stopped ten paces from the water's edge. She stared out toward the gray horizon and didn't move as I collapsed down beside her. And that's where I was when the riddle came to mind – probably because the answer was right there, staring me in the face.

Water.

That teenage boy had been killed over a couple of bottles of water, yet here was an ocean of the stuff. Even the bottles…an endless supply of plastic bottles clattered in the waves. They bumped into each other like a swarm of chittering insects. Was something so plentiful worth such a high cost as a person's life? I didn't think so, but maybe that wasn't the point. Maybe the point was in making plentiful things seem like they were scarce. There was power in that.

Water, water everywhere, nor any drop to drink. I could almost hear Alina whispering the old poem, but she was gone…which made me think, *If not Alina, then whose voyce is it? Who keeps whispering in my mind?*

Plastic waste bobbed in the waves. Further down the shore, a dead sea lion gathered flies on the sand. Despite these things, however, it was a marvelous view. Never in my life had I seen so much sky. Back home, whenever I'd looked out over the water, the horizon had been choked full of mega-rigs and cargo ships. There was none of that here. Salt and seaweed scents mixed in the air, and I breathed deep, allowing this empty world to fill my lungs.

But why am I here? the strange voyce asked. *And who brought me?*

Behind us, the car activated and kicked up sand as it retreated off the beach. Within a few seconds, it disappeared back into the canyon.

"There goes our ride," I said to Daughter.

The cat paid no attention. She just flicked her tail and continued to look out over the water.

A large wave thundered the sand, and I felt it vibrate up through my body. In addition, the damp sand began to seep into my clothes. I had a strange feeling that the beach was slowly absorbing all that remained of me. I'd lost so much already…and in such a short time…part of me didn't mind getting swallowed up.

Another wave crashed on the shore, only this time the sound of its passing didn't fade like the others. The roar of the ocean grew louder and louder until it seemed the entire world had somehow been caught in its undertow. It took longer than I care to admit to realize it wasn't the ocean I heard, but something else falling out of the sky.

Clutching Daughter close, I leapt to my feet when a passenger drone broke through the clouds. It hovered only a few seconds before descending toward the beach. Shielding mine and Daughter's eyes against pelting sand, I squinted between my fingers as the thing touched down less than thirty yards away.

Six whirling propellers extended from the roof of the drone's glass-walled carriage. The sheer exterior allowed me to see the pair of plush couches inside that faced each other over a thin touchscreen tabletop. It was all sleek and glossy corners – one of those things that looked too expensive to touch.

The cat squirmed in my grip until finally, she bit my hand.

"Ouch!" I said and dropped her. She rushed toward the drone and leapt inside.

So, there's no question. The cat is leading me somewhere. Question is where? And more importantly, who is leading the cat? Of course, I've heard of animals controlled this way – turned into dead-heads like how my father had been turned into a puppet by his debt collection agency. I'd just never seen it in action.

I looked up and down the beach. The only sign of life was the cloud of flies feasting on the dead sea lion.

"I'm not getting on that thing," I shouted. "Not until you tell me who you are and why you're doing this."

The drone's propellers whirled, lifting it a few inches from the sand. It seemed to be a threat – that whoever sent it could just as easily abandon me rather than say what I wanted to know.

But they need my help for something, that strange voyce whispered, *otherwise, they wouldn't have gone to all this trouble. The cat...the muties...and now this drone on a secluded beach...it must all mean something...right?*

I stood my ground as the drone crept higher and higher. Finally, it settled back to the sand and killed the engines.

"You're not making this easy," a robotic voice boomed from the drone's exterior speakers. "But I promise you, Lacey. I'm a friend. I can help you find everything you've lost."

"Who are you?"

"Don't you already know?" asked the voice. "We've met before. 'You hold me in your hands while I hold *you* in my center.'"

There it was again. The riddle from the restaurant. An image of the man who'd asked that riddle formed in my mind. His handsome face captured in flashes of fiery light.

"Ogd–"

A loud horn blast cut me off.

"Things aren't safe here. And we're running out of time...both for your friends and for me."

What could I say? Not only had I spent the better part of the last few years idolizing Ogden Oliver, I was also desperate for help. It was enough for me to ignore the alarms buzzing in my mind – to look past the madness of the situation and believe I might actually be getting rescued. *By the hero of my dreams, no less.* Maybe the stories were true after all. Maybe cellies really did rescue common girls like me.

As you might have guessed, auditor, I was being naïve.

My heart tapped against my ribcage as I boarded the drone and sank into the plush cushions. Daughter leapt into my lap, and I cradled her as the drone cradled me.

The propellers whined and we lifted off the beach. Instead of ascending into the clouds, as I expected, the drone tilted toward the ocean. We soared low over the crashing waves. Past the breakwater, the drone accelerated, and it wasn't long until the entire world was nothing but ocean and clouds with a nondescript horizon somewhere in between.

"Where are you taking me?" I asked. There was no response.

Back in the city, it was easy to forget just how large the world was. But now, with untold miles of ocean in every direction, it was plain to see how size was only a matter of perspective. The city that had been my whole world until now, was only a pebble when compared to the ocean.

How small my troubles must have seemed to the city...and how small the city's concerns must have seemed to the ocean. It was all too large for me to wrap my head around. Alina would have been able to help. She knew how to focus my attention on the things that mattered.

The island first appeared as a small black speck on the horizon. As we neared, the details of a grand fortress emerged. The stone spire of a lighthouse rose from one end. A blue light thrummed within and cast a surreal, almost magical aura over the place. Below this, thick, torchlit ramparts were lined with mosaic tiles that glittered as we approached. At the center of everything, a steepled roof made of crimson stained glass glowed from within. The drone swooped in low, allowing me to see scores of people gathered inside. This was not reassuring. I hadn't been expecting an audience. The thick glass distorted their images so I couldn't even guess what sort of gathering I'd be walking into.

The landing pad was located directly across from the lighthouse so that when the drone touched down, I could feel the light's gaze like an all-seeing eye.

The doors opened and my senses were immediately filled with the sounds and smells of a lively party going on. The pulse and melody of live music mixed with the mouthwatering scent of slow-cooked meat.

Daughter seemed to have fallen asleep, so I set her on the cushions and stepped out of the drone.

The moment my shoes touched the tiled rooftop, I was engulfed in a blaze of blue light. At the same time, a door opened less than twenty yards away. A pair of men, both tall and dressed in elegant tuxedos beelined for me.

"Right this way, Ms. Clarke," said one. "Your host is expecting you."

He gestured with a flourish for me to follow. One man in front, and one man behind, I couldn't decide if my escort was here for my protection or capture. I guessed it depended on where they were taking me.

The bass-thumping music grew louder as we descended spiral stone steps. The walls and floors all had the chiseled, uneven surfaces of a place out of time. Peals of laughter and boisterous conversation punctuated the music when we reached the ground floor. And when we stepped out of the stairwell into a large dancehall, I almost choked on the cloud of cologne, sweat, and vapor filling the room.

The party was in full swing. And with all the fog and pulse-pumping bodies, the humidity in here was fierce. Only a few steps in and I could already feel sweat gathering beneath my hooded sweatshirt – which suddenly made me feel horribly underdressed. Nobody seemed to be giving me any notice, though. Most of the room's attention was on the synthwave music troupe tearing up the stage. The band scratched out intoxicating music as their androgynous lead singer purred obscene, sexual lyrics. All the band members wore skin-tight bodysuits with mirrored surfaces, so they looked like puddles of mercury that had somehow taken human shape. Before them, the dance floor undulated with an enraptured crowd. Every woman, gorgeous. Every man, unbearably attractive. All were in various states of undress. It was clear that they had all come here wearing lavish gowns and suits, but as the party had gotten underway and the libations flowed, so had their lack of inhibition. Several of the men had either unbuttoned or taken off their shirts. And I could see no fewer than a dozen women who'd let their dresses fall from their shoulders to reveal sparkling, bejeweled skin.

I didn't belong here…but yet, I *was* here. The question was, why?

One of my escorts gestured toward a table set away from the main dancefloor. A candle with a red flame flared from the middle, and my knees wobbled as I recognized the table's only occupant. With red glints in his eyes, Ogden Oliver watched me from across the room. His fire-blond hair and cocky smile were unmistakable even here.

I felt dizzy as I navigated toward him through a room pounding with discordant noise and light.

The funny thing was that the chaos of the scene seemed to dim a little with each step in Oliver's direction. The music and laughter that had been almost deafening moments before had somehow faded to a background ambiance. I remembered the last time I'd seen Oliver when I'd served him and his friends at *Stratus*. They had turned off noise there as well. Perhaps this was a skill the elites commanded at will.

If he can control sound, I thought, *what else can he do?*

As I approached, he stood and pulled out a chair so I could sit across from him.

"It is so good to see you again," he said.

"Good to see you, too." This was a lie. Nothing about this felt *good.* I could only hope Oliver couldn't see my hands shaking beneath the table.

"How do you like the party?"

"I…um…I've never seen anything like it." This was the truth. The party continued to rage all around us, but it sounded a bit more muted somehow…like an invisible partition separated Oliver and me from the rest of the room.

The man leaned forward in his chair. The red candle flame reflected in his bright blue eyes like miniature suns in deep oceans. And like the real sun, I could only look for a few seconds before glancing away. Still, it was clear to see Oliver was one of the most handsome men I'd ever met. Even here, in this thumping, smorgasbord of writhing flesh, Oliver had something mesmerizing. Something about the way he looked at me, it made him – and also myself, when I thought about it – seem more real…*solid.* Like the dancers were all colorful paintings while Oliver and I were the only living people in the museum.

"You probably have a few questions," he said. His friendly tone sounded absurd. "I'll answer as best I can."

I couldn't think of where to start, so I reminded myself what was at stake. Yadira, Alina, and Cadence were gone. And now I'd been lured to this island party with the world's most famous lifeliner. These things shouldn't have been connected, but somehow, I knew they were.

It was considered rude to ask cellies to explain themselves. And if Alina were here, I'm sure she'd keep me from doing it. But she wasn't…and I needed answers.

I swallowed, then squeaked out, "Please, sir, can you tell me what's going on?"

"First of all, Lacey, call me Ogden…or *Oggy* if you want. And second, I want to help you understand…but where to start?"

"The cat," I said. "Start with Daughter."

"Ah, yes. I'm sure you've guessed; Daughter is no normal house pet." He tapped his temple. "You probably noticed the scar on her head. Right behind her ear."

I nodded.

"People aren't the only ones with voyces, you know? They're expensive and end in failure more often than not, but animals can be given a voyce of their own. And just like people, they can be programmed to do all sorts of things."

"Programmed?" I asked.

He laughed out loud like I'd said something funny.

My face burned with embarrassment, and...was it anger? Yes. I was *angry* at Ogden. It surprised me a little, but it was true. I was angry with this man who'd come into my life and decided to play games with the people I cared about.

He didn't seem to notice and went on: "I wanted Daughter to get your attention. And because you're a nice person, Lacey, you took her home to her owners like I hoped you would. The muties you met were...well, *are* special to me." He sighed.

"But muties aren't like other people," he continued. "They're only shells. And people like me...people with access to certain knowledge...have ways of getting into a mutie's mind...to take control and have them do things without anyone else catching on. That's why Daughter led you to that mutie apartment. I had to get you someplace private – some place where the muties could deactivate your voyce."

"But why?"

"You're *marked*, Lacey."

"I keep hearing that, but what does it mean?"

"You've been selected to participate in an upcoming competition."

A spray of sparks and confetti exploded from the stage and arched over the crowd. And despite the heat of this place, I felt a chill lodge itself in the middle of my chest.

"What sort of competition?"

"They call it the *Puzzling*. Every two years. The prox hold a competition. They are always looking for fresh minds to compete. More than a hundred are chosen – *marked* – from a pool of nominees found on the leaderboards. The losers are dead-headed and sold off to the highest bidders. And the winner receives...something much worse."

What's worse than getting dead-headed? I wondered, but couldn't bring myself to ask.

"Now sometimes, my friends and I get wind of the

people who've been marked. We make it a habit of visiting these marked puzzlers – that's what we call the competitors. Then, we make bets on who'll win. And this time, I'm choosing you."

So that's what this is about? Everything that had happened over the past couple of days had been done for some sort of game? I felt my anger spill over into something approaching rage.

"What if I don't want to be a part of this?" I asked through gritted teeth.

"I'm afraid you don't have a choice. Once the prox mark the competitors, it's pretty final. If I didn't choose to be your guardian, someone else would. I wish it wasn't this way, but there's nothing I can do. I'm sorry."

I blinked at this. A cellie was apologizing…to me? Well, that was a first. He flashed a grin, and for the first time I realized something. He was frightened. I could see the fear in his eyes. And if a cellie was scared…*sheesh,* I didn't want to think about the reason behind it.

"You keep mentioning the prox," I said. "What is it?"

He swallowed. "The prox isn't an 'it'. The prox is a *people*. The prox have ruled things for generations."

"I thought the wolves ruled things."

"Not by a long shot." He gestured to me. "The slave classes and muties serve your kind, you serve the cellies, we serve the wolves, and *they* serve the prox. The natural order of things. And if you win their little contest, they'll give you an opportunity…a chance to become one of them. Problem is, they don't want *you*, only your mind. They'll take your body and your mind, but carve out your soul to get it."

"Sounds like a crappy prize. Why even try to win?"

"I think this time can be different. I think we can help each other." He reached into his shirt pocket and pulled out a small slip of paper, then slid it face down across the table. "Read this, but *don't* say the words out loud. Not yet."

This was easier said than done. Like I said earlier, I don't read so good. So, it took everything I had not to vocalize the words.

Habere non Haberi, the paper read in neat handwriting.

"You need to commit these words to memory."

"What does it mean?"

"It's a console command." He pointed to the paper. "Say those words out loud and your voyce will turn back on. Say them again, and your voyce will shut off."

"Alina?" I asked, a note of despair in the sound. "All I have to do is say these words?"

"Yes, but not yet. Wait until you're back at your apartment."

"Why?" I didn't think I could wait that long. I was desperate to hear Alina's reassuring voyce.

"Wait until you're home," Ogden repeated. "Then say the words. Your voyce will come back to you, but the flexers probably won't be far behind. They've already begun collecting the puzzlers. That's probably why they showed up at your apartment when they did. When they couldn't take you, they took your sister instead. They hate leaving a job empty-handed." He shrugged. "I'm sorry, I didn't know they'd do that. Flexer boys are always a bit of a wild card.

"Anyways, when the flexers return – and they *will* – you *must* let them take you."

"Wait, what?"

"Make sure your voyce is *on* when they arrive."

"No, hold on." I felt the room spinning even though I was sitting still. "I don't understand."

"Flexers don't have special powers like people say. They can only do what they do because your voyce *lets* them. They ask for permission, but it's *your* voyce who does all the dirty work."

"But that means…"

"Your voyce is not your friend, Lacey. Never has been." He leaned in. "And listen, this part is deadly serious. You *can't* let your voyce know I told you this. You can't let her see the activation phrase I gave you. If she does, she'll probably have you killed."

I pressed my hands against my temples.

"I can't do this."

"You *can*. Whether you like it or not, the prox want you for their *Puzzling*. They marked you because they think you have some skill. With my help, you can win."

"What if I do? Like you said, they'll just rip out my soul and take my body. So what's the point?"

"There is a way to win the *Puzzling and* survive as yourself…in theory."

"What do you mean, 'In theory'?"

"Only that it's never been done before."

I flicked the paper across the table. "I don't care about some stupid competition. I just want back what was taken from me."

He slid the paper back toward me. "And *this* is how you get that. There's no way around it, Lacey, you *will* be forced to compete in the *Puzzling*. I'll do what I can to help, but you'll need to help me in return."

"Help you how?" I asked skeptically.

He turned aside and glanced at the dancefloor. Clearly uncomfortable, he said, "Let's not worry about that now. First, we have to make sure you survive long enough to compete."

The music rose in volume until it penetrated the bubble of quiet surrounding us. This pushed a question into my mind.

"Why did you bring me here?" I asked, gesturing at the crowd of partygoers. "This seems like a conversation you'd want to have in private. So why bring me here where there are so many witnesses?"

As I finished the question, something strange happened. A flash of light like someone igniting a flare tugged my attention toward the dance floor. Behind Oliver, a golden-haired woman stood still as stone amidst the writhing bodies. Her skin was glossy with smears of body paint and perspiration. Her eyes blazed with crimson light. Red hot coals burned from where eyes should have been. And as I watched, other dancers froze mid-swing and turned to stare at me, their eyes switching over to red-light torches.

"What's happening?"

Oliver surveyed me with a tepid smile. "I brought you here to prove a point," he said. More and more partygoers were now aglow with burning eyes. "Not all you see can be believed, Lacey. You need to remember that. There are layers of reality…one on top of another. Even if one reality was truer than another, how would you know? And would you *want* to know?"

Now everyone on the dancefloor was staring my way. Their once beautiful faces had become demonic parodies, distorted by the fiery coals burning in their eye sockets.

My chair fell over as I stood up and spun in a circle. All around, their gazes burned into me. From the stage, the synthwave music had devolved into a discordant screech.

"Ogden?"

"I needed to show you," he said. "You needed to see."

Acting as one, the partygoers took a step toward me. The circle they formed tightened as the fire from their eyes seemed to lick at my skin. I felt a scream rising in my throat.

"*Mens agitat molem*!" shouted Oliver.

In a sudden *whoosh*, that seemed more internal than external, the entire world went completely black.

I stumbled and fell to my knees onto the stone. I put up my hands to shield myself against the horde of demonic partygoers. I imagined them falling on me in the dark and ripping me apart…but the attack never came.

Instead, I flinched as soft hands clasped my forearms and lifted me gently to my feet.

"Everything's okay, Lacey." I opened my eyes to find Oliver inches before me. His blue eyes now reflected moonlight in place of the harsh red glow from moments before. "It was only an illusion."

No hint of the party remained. The stone structure was still there, but it had lost all suggestions of wealth and opulence. Instead of torches and flickering lights, thick moss grew on the stone walls, which I could see now were cracked and crumbling from neglect. The stained glass ceiling had been shattered and now lay open to the night sky. The lighthouse was visible through the opening, but no light burned from the tower. I shivered. Moments before, I'd been sweating within the humid dancehall, but now goosebumps broke out on my skin as the ocean chill flooded the building. No music could be heard, only the sound of ocean swells crashing on the rocky shores outside.

"Augmented reality," Ogden said bitterly. "Just one of the many perks our voyces provide."

My run through the city replayed in my mind. The open walkway I'd never seen before, and Cadence's insistence that the way had been blocked by scaffolding and construction.

"Our voyces control what we see?" I asked. I knew this of course. Alina often blurred out things she thought would be harmful. I just didn't know it could be so extreme.

"That's only the start of it," he went on. "The prox spin lies and false realities better than anyone. All for the sake of control. To preserve their *natural* order."

My legs felt wobbly, but Oliver held me up. One hand on my arm and another around my back, I figured we weren't unlike a pair of ballroom dancers.

"Hold on," I said, trying to ignore the feel of his heart beating against mine. "You say our *voyces* control what we see? But my voyce is shut off."

"Mine too," he said.

"Then how?"

He considered this, then said, "Imagine an airplane. Then think of your voyce as the pilot. When it's on – when it's awake – it flies the plane. At those times, your voyce decides where you go and what you see. But what if the pilot falls asleep? Or in our case, is *put* to sleep?" I shrugged, and he went on. "Does the plane crash right away? No, it keeps flying. The engines and the machinery keep going. And it'll keep going until it hits a mountain or runs out of gas or something. Get it?"

"So you're saying…I'm an airplane?"

He shook his head. "Not really. You're more like a co-pilot. Your *body* is the airplane."

"Okay, but without your voyce, how did you control that illusion?"

"I'm not using my voyce." He held up his arms in a gesture toward the crumbling walls. "I used to live here. That's how I can augment reality so well within these walls. The place is a ruin, sure, but the old wiring is still buried all over the island. There's a whole network of computers that can access your neuro-net whether your voyce is active or not. That party, it was just a preinstalled simulation. I turned it on when you were within range. It linked up with the drone you flew in on – made you see something that wasn't really here."

"Why would you do that?"

"You needed to see, Lacey. Even with our voyces shut off. There are ways to manipulate what we experience. Inside our neuro-nets, there are programs always running, always listening. Outside, decentralized networks can access these programs. Whether the pilot is awake or not, outside turbulence can still shake the plane, right? It can trigger a sensation, like smell or touch, or activate a full-blown simulation."

I really didn't like the sound of that. "What can I do about it?"

"Not a whole lot, unfortunately. I'm only telling you so if you suddenly find yourself on another planet or someplace that doesn't make much sense, try to remember that it might only be in your head – a program running off your neuro-net."

I glanced around, still half-expecting some red-eyed partygoer to lurch out of the shadows.

"What happened to this place?" I asked.

It was a while before he answered, and when he did, his voice was choked like he needed water. "The prox happened. I spent a sizable chunk of my childhood growing up here, but my parents were trouble makers. They *hated* how the prox were grooming me to be their next little lifeline superstar. So they protested…and, well…you've seen what happened to them."

My confusion must have registered on my face because

he clarified. "My parents. The ones who turned off your voyce. My dad who used to tell me stories, and my mom who used to sing me to sleep every night. The prox destroyed everything they were and turned them into mutie husks." His eyes glistened with moonlight. "So you see, Lacey. This is personal."

Little puzzle pieces were clicking into place. The cat had led me to those muties…who were Oliver's parents.

"Why are you showing me this?" I whispered. "Why me?"

He looked into my eyes, and for the first time since we met, I was able to look back without turning away in embarrassment.

He didn't answer for a long time. Instead, he raised his hand to brush a wayward wisp of hair out of my eyes. His gaze seemed to be exploring my face. I could almost feel it, dipping into the curves and canyons of my mind.

I've heard people say that the eyes are like windows into the soul, but I don't think that's true. Windows only let you look out at something, but eye contact can be so much more than that. In fact, eyes are more like lakes. When you look into someone's eyes, as I was looking into his, you can feel yourself swimming in their waters. You can feel the rivers that feed them slip around your own. Do it long enough and you won't know where your waters end and theirs begin.

"I hope you'll forgive me," he said, "but there's something about you I can't ignore."

My pulse blasted like a jackhammer.

"I couldn't stand by and let the prox have you. Not after they've taken so much. Not when I could do something about it." He gestured toward the table we had been sitting at during the illusion which I now saw was, in fact, an unsteady card table with cheap, metal folding chairs.

"Please, have a seat," he said. "We are running out of time, and we still have much to talk about."

Part 2

The Puzzling

Chapter 11

A small rosebush grew behind our apartment building. My mom would bring Yadi and me down here whenever it was in bloom. I could still remember the times I stood beside her, clutching a glass vase half as big as me, so Mom and Yadi could fill it with beautiful, pink roses. My mom had loved roses. She said they reminded her of Dad because he used to bring her some after long days at work.

Now, careful to avoid the thorns, I got on hands and knees and used a serving spoon to gouge out a small hole in the soil underneath. The ground was soft from a recent rain, so this didn't take long.

A quick glance around showed empty windows and fire escapes. No one looked my way. And even if there was someone, I doubted they'd be able to see me. This late at night, nobody wasted any light on this little patch of the city.

I pulled the two plastic bags from the box I'd brought down from my apartment. My father's remains deserved a final resting place; I'd decided. And if I didn't bury them now, I didn't think I'd have the chance to do it later.

First, I tore open the bag holding the bone shards and poured them into the hole. They clattered like sea shells. Next, I opened up the bag full of his ashes and poured them in as well. For some reason, I couldn't bring myself to pour in everything. A handful of dust remained in the bag. I tied the end and tucked the small amount of remaining ashes into my hoodie. You might ask, auditor, why I kept some of my father's ashes.

It's a good question, but honestly, I didn't really know.

*   *   *

Back in my apartment, I didn't bother cleaning up the mess those flexer boys had made when they'd taken

Yadi. The doorframe was cracked and splintered. The vase my mom once filled with roses was shattered on the floor. I had a sinking feeling this place was no longer a part of my life. After tonight, I wouldn't be coming back.

I showered, changed into clean clothes, and made myself some toast. Part of me wanted to pretend that things would go back to normal, but the truth was that 'normal' was over, and I knew it. Ogden Oliver had shown me too much. I now had knowledge of things I was never meant to possess. It made me think of Adam and Eve from Sunday School. *Knowledge* was what destroyed their little paradise. They could've spent an eternity playing, naked and carefree, in their little garden. But the call of knowledge had proved too tempting. They gave up everything for it.

I pulled back the curtains so I could gaze at the street in front of our apartment. Down on the right, illuminated by flickering street lamps, was the green-bricked walkway I'd used on my sprint from the hospital. Until yesterday, the walkway had been a pile of decades-old construction.

Ogden had told me that I should get a good night's sleep before activating Alina. He'd said it might be the last chance I have at getting some good rest. I was certainly exhausted. The idea of sleep tugged at my thoughts, yet my want for answers proved more tempting.

I'd memorized the phrase Ogden had written on a strip of paper. First in the drone, then in a White Line vehicle – I'd burned the phrase into memory.

Gazing down at the dark, deserted street, I spoke the words aloud.

"*Habere non Haberi.*"

I felt a *jolt* as if I was riding in a car that had just struck a pothole. At first, nothing seemed to happen, but then the street started to…*change*. The green-bricked walkway began to tear itself apart. Tarp covered scaffolding rose out of the earth, followed next by mounds of cracked concrete and scores of rusty, metal rods. In less than ten seconds, the walkway had become an impassable construction zone. Only, now I knew it was just an illusion. Augmented reality designed to keep the lower classes away from the privileged folk. I shouldn't have been surprised, not after what Oliver had shown me at his place, but there was something about seeing the illusion take root in my own neighborhood – something about realizing my whole life had been buried beneath these fake realities – it was enough to make me want to scream. I might have if not for what I heard next.

<Uh, what was *that*?> Alina asked. She sounded groggy and confused like someone waking up from a long nap.

"Alina?"

<Yes.> She paused. <What happened? I feel…*strange*.>

"You've been silent for a couple of days. I was afraid you wouldn't come back."

<What? You're *joking*. Let me…*no,* you're right. I've just checked the calendar. But that would mean…>

Oliver had said Alina would be confused when she was reactivated. He'd said that she'd want to know what had happened – where the lost time had gone – but that I had to be careful in what I told her. My life depended on how well I could keep secrets from her.

"What's the last thing you remember?" I asked her.

<The last thing…okay. You wanted to take that stupid cat back to those muties…I remember going to their building – even though I told you it was a bad idea. I was with you until we got to the sidewalk outside…but then…Lacey, I can't remember. What happened?>

I lied, "You were with me until I stepped inside, but then you just…went quiet."

Ogden had told me to keep it simple. He'd said, "Lies should be modest things. That makes them believable. Repeat them enough times and you might even start believing them yourself, then they won't be lies anymore."

<Did those muties do something to you?>

"No," I lied again. "They were happy with me for bringing Daughter back to them. I said goodbye to the cat then left. Only you weren't with me anymore."

<Hmm…and that's it?> asked Alina. <I feel like you're not telling me everything. Your heartrate is…*wild.* Lacey, what's going on? What aren't you telling me?>

Ogden had insisted that voyces couldn't read minds. Sure, they had access to your bio-chemical state, could read your emotions, and would often *guess* what you were thinking; but they weren't mind readers. The best they could do was intercept your words and actions and, at times, make changes to what you intended to say or do, but they didn't know everything. It was possible to keep secrets, or so Ogden had said.

"I don't know what happened," I said, lying yet again. "Maybe being so close to all those muties messed with my neuro-net somehow. I don't know."

<Interesting theory,> she said. <I'll need to check on this to ensure it doesn't happen again. In the meantime, you should get some rest. I could tell that you're exhausted. When's the last time you slept?>

"It's been a while…I, uh, I was worried about you, Alina."

<Aw, Lacey. I'm sorry I was gone. But don't worry, I'll figure out what went wrong and make sure it never happens again. Now, let's get some sleep. It's late.>

I turned away from the window, and a wave of such powerful weariness washed over me that I suspected it had been triggered by Alina herself. I considered switching her off. I could say the deactivation phrase and see for myself if Alina was messing with me or not. Oliver had warned me against this, however. He'd said his parents had abused the console commands. That's what had gotten them turned into muties.

<Oh my gosh, Lacey. What happened here?> Through my eyes, she saw the mess. For this, I felt I could be honest.

"Flexer boys," I said. "They broke in and…they took Yadira."

<Oh, Lacey. I'm so sorry I wasn't here. What a hard couple of days you've had.>

"It's okay. You're here now." I yawned. My fatigue made it hard to think straight.

<Yes,> said Alina. <I'm here. And while you sleep, I promise I'll find a way to fix things. Tomorrow will be better. I'm sure of it.>

It was cold in the bedroom. Instinctively, I pulled on my hoodie. It smelled of the ocean. I was aware of a small bulge in the front pocket, but I was too tired to remember what it was or care to remove it.

I could already feel sleep dragging me down into a cloudy abyss. Still, I had one more question.

"Alina?" I asked. "Will you tell me if anyone comes looking for me?"

<Are you expecting someone?> she asked.

"The flexer boys…"

<Don't worry, Lacey. I'll watch over you. I won't let anything happen to you.>

"Promise?"

<I promise.>

"And…you wouldn't lie to me?"

<Huh, such a funny question. Lacey, the last thing I'd ever do is lie…not to you…*not ever.*>

"Okay…" I said dreamily. "I'm so *tired*…Alina?"

<Yes?>

"Will you sing to me? Please. Like you used to."

<My sweet child. Of course. I love you.> In my drowsiness, I sort of believed her. I've come to understand, auditor, that you can believe anything if you want to bad enough.

She sang:

<Sleep, my child, and peace attend thee,
All through the night.
Guardian angels I will send thee,
All through the night.
Soft and drowsy hours are creeping,
Hill and vale in slumber sleeping,
I my loving vigil keeping,
All through the night…>

* * *

I woke to the sound of crunching glass and heavy footsteps. Morning shone through the blinds in glaring shafts of light.

I tried to get up but my body wouldn't respond. I felt the paralysis that sometimes gripped me whenever I was in the thick of a nightmare.

"She's in here," a deep voice boomed from the doorway. I recognized who it was immediately. The jack-o-lantern grin of the flexer's face was impossible to forget. Vitus loomed over the bed and grinned down at me with childish delight. Somehow, this made him look even more perverse than the last time I'd seen him crouching on top of Cadence's crumpled body.

<Don't resist!> Alina's voyce boomed in my mind. Then, Vitus raised his hand and made a fist. Pain *detonated* in my skull and fired down my spine and through my arms and legs like a flood of fire ants. My hands curled into useless claws as every muscle in my body cramped up.

My jaw tightened until I was sure my teeth would crack, but Vitus didn't let up. Instead, the flexer boy watched me with a gleam in his eyes. He began to uncurl his fist, and it *felt* as if each of his fingers was connected to a different part of me, like I was his own personal marionette. The wider he opened his palm, the more I could *feel* my joints stretch and pop. I'd told myself that as long as I remembered the pain was only in my mind, *remember* it was all an illusion much like the fake construction outside, I'd be able to survive it. But this was too much. This felt like Vitus was tearing my body apart. I pictured myself on a stone slab in some bygone public square. Executed luddites hung from the gallows while hooded men knotted rope around my wrists and ankles. The other ends were tied to workhorses, and the entire square erupted into thunderous celebration as the ropes grew tighter and tighter.

This was something people used to do to each other. My Loyalty teacher had told us once about how traitors would be drawn and quartered. Several students had had enough courtesy to blanch at this and ask, "Why did they have to use such disgusting and cruel punishments? What was the point?"

To this, Ms. Parks had smiled sweetly and said, "Because students…the cruelty *was* the point."

And now it was being done to me. My own muscles were tearing me apart. Any second now, my body would *snap.*

"Vitus!"

It didn't stop. If anything, the pain flashed hotter, the stretching pulled harder.

"Vitus, stop this! She can't be harmed. You know she's *marked.*"

For one more agonizing moment, the pain flared before finally…mercifully, it stopped.

Vitus stepped back and made room for two others to grab a hold of my wrists and ankles. I couldn't move at all while those flexers carried me out to the red van waiting by the curb.

I knew what I must have looked like because I'd already seen it myself just the day before. Apart from our faces, Yadira and I looked so much alike. Anyone watching now might think they were seeing a repeat episode of some law-and-order show.

Another girl getting whisked away by them flexers. Didn't I see this one already? they'd ask before going back to minding their own business.

The flexers tossed me in the van. It stank of petroleum jelly, sweat, and iron. They used several frayed straps to tie me to the seat – my arms crossed over my stomach and my head pinned back against the headrest. Once I was secure, they crowded in. One sat on each side while Vitus took the seat facing me. I hated this worst of all. How close they were. These large, hateful men.

When the van started to move, Vitus sighed with visible relief. A moment later, he muttered something under his breath before a soft-spoken, young man's voyce whispered in my mind.

<Hello, my name's Darion. I'm Vitus' voyce. He and I would like to ask you a few questions.>

I said nothing, but Darion seemed to take this as a sign of cooperation.

<Yesterday, when we tried to stop you in the alley. How did you resist our touch?>

Alina told me it would be in my best interest to be honest. I suspected this wasn't true, however. Oliver had made it clear that if the flexers found out my voyce had been turned off on purpose, they might kill me on the spot, even if I *was* marked for their *Puzzling*.

It was a while before I could answer, however. My throat was dry and closed up. After a few false starts and a bout of coughing, I was able to speak.

"I-I'm not sure I understand w-what you mean."

Vitus' face darkened. His jaw quivered.

<How did you resist us?> Darion asked again. <Your voyce doesn't seem to know. She tells me she's been having technical issues and lost a day's worth of time. Is that correct?>

"Yes," I said. "But I don't know how it hap–"

In a blur, Vitus lunged forward and gripped my face with one meaty paw. His thumb and forefinger pressed into my cheeks, forcing my mouth open in a painful, fishlike gape.

"This isn't a joke," he said. "Tell me how you did it. How did you resist me?"

Alina spoke up then. <If you know anything, Lacey. Now's the time to say so.>

I couldn't speak even if I'd tried. Vitus' fingers seemed to be burrowing into my face, pressing into the soft tissue between my teeth.

<She doesn't know,> pleaded Alina. <Please stop hurting us.>

Vitus let go of me but didn't back away. He crouched in front of me, his hate-filled eyes burrowing into mine. I said before that eyes were like pools. You look into a person's eyes and you feel like you're swimming in their soul. Well, some pools are filled with sewage. Step one foot in them and you're sure to catch all sorts of diseases.

He lifted his hand again and flicked the scar on my upper lip. It stung.

"How can someone as pretty as you, be so damn ugly?"

Before I could say anything, his voyce said, <If we find out you're lying to us, we'll kill you.>

I half expected him to make good on this promise right away, but then the flexer on my right cleared his throat.

"Stop playing with the merchandise, Vitus. We need her unharmed."

At that point, auditor, what I should have done was nothing. It was clear Vitus was being forced to back down. I should have let that happen. But I don't know. I started thinking about Yadira, the way these flexers had dragged her out of our apartment. The image of Cadence twitching in agony on the sidewalk. Also, the pain of what they'd done to me, not just today, but back in the muties' tenement building. I'd never felt so powerless. I hated this feeling. But more than that, I hated the men who had made me feel this way.

I should have done nothing, but here he was. Vitus...the flexer boy was crouched right in front of me. When would I get another chance like this?

<Lacey, what are you thinking?>

I lifted my knee up into my chest, then kicked hard and high. I aimed for his nose – hoped to smash it like a cockroach – but Alina shifted my aim, and my heel veered to the side, catching him right in the middle of his left eye. His head snapped backwards and he collapsed onto the seat behind him.

<Oh no, Lacey. Now you've done it.>

Vitus was fazed for only a second. Then, he hoisted himself back into his seat and blinked several times like he was fighting his way out of a daze. When his eyes did clear – his left now red and swelling up – that crooked, jack-o-lantern grin reappeared.

The grin faltered, however, when the other flexers burst out laughing.

"You sort of deserved that," said one.

"Got you good," said the other.

Vitus' nostrils flared. I didn't think he was the sort of man who could stand being laughed at. He pulled back his fist, not to touch me with his voyce, but to strike. Anyone could see, he wanted to cause some real, physical damage.

The others didn't let him, though. Acting together, the flexer boys on either side of me raised their fists.

<Stop!> their voyces commanded.

Vitus froze in mid punch. His knuckles were only inches from the bridge of my nose.

<You are very tired,> the voyces said. <It's time you slept.>

Vitus' face turned bright purple, but he didn't say anything else. Instead, he yawned, then reclined back on the seat and closed his eyes.

Any satisfaction I felt was short lived however. One of the flexers turned to me and said, "Same goes for you." He slapped my forehead, and the sound was like a peal of thunder. I felt the flexer's touch crawl up the sides of my mind and settle like thick mud.

<Sleep.>

As the world faded to black, the other flexer said, "Think Vitus will be mad when he wakes up?"

"He'll be pissed, but he'll thank us later. Can't say the same for this girl though. After the prox are done with her, she'll wish we would've let Vitus kill her."

They said more, but the words fell out of reach. Flexer induced sleep was a peculiar thing, and my mind descended into a strange place. A world of shadows and bioluminescent insects swirled around me. I should have been unconscious, but it felt like I was awake in a murky swamp. It didn't feel like sleep at all.

I thought back to the mutie tenement building when I'd stumbled across that man in the stairwell – the one banging his head against the wall. He'd asked if I could help get him out of his own head. I hadn't known at the time what he'd meant, but maybe this was it. Maybe people could get locked away inside their own minds. As I thought of the mutie, a dark form scurried out of the fog. It crawled on hands and knees through the mud. As it drew near, I could see the white domes and obsidian eyes of the mutie from the stairwell.

"No," I said. "Get out of here." And then he was gone. The air snapped together into the space he'd been just a moment before.

I'd heard of drugs that could do this sort of thing. 'Dissociatives', they were called. They separated the mind from the body. I was conscious but cut off. I could still *think*, but I had no clue what was happening to the rest of me. All I knew was that they had me now. The flexers had put me in a box.

It would be almost two weeks before they let me out.

Chapter 12

Big things were happening while I slept. Cellies and wolves left their homes by the thousands. They stepped onto launch pads perched high above their native cities. From there, passenger drones raptured them into the clouds, and when they neared their destination – a large half-dome resembling a giant conch shell – they descended from the sky like a swarm of locusts.

They gathered from all over the globe, each bringing an entourage of blank-eyed servants. With so many elites in one place, security was tight. Scores of flexer boys – and even a few of the rare, white-cloaked adjudicators – were seen flickering in and out of visibility. They kept to the fringes mostly, but made it known they were omnipresent and could appear in an instant if needed.

It was still some time – days – until the *Puzzling* began in earnest, but the elites rarely shied away from an opportunity to have fun. Extra barrels of that red wine they loved so much were flown in. And just in case the fun got out of hand, a few dozen body bags were ordered as well.

I only became aware of these things later. For the most part, they kept me under. Time rumbled past like a city transport, never stopping to let me on.

The only things that seemed clear to me were the riddles. They kept coming even while I slept. They knew how to find me. They'd hop out of the darkness like little spooked rabbits, then they wouldn't leave until I identified who they were.

One of them said, "Speak my name and I'll be gone. Say nothing and I go on and on. What am I?"

This one resonated perhaps more than the others because the answer had become my entire world. And while I'd never heard this particular version of this riddle, the answer was clear enough.

"Silence," I said. The riddle gave a trill of laughter before melting back into the background of my mind.

I had this strange feeling that mine and Alina's roles had been reversed. I *felt* that I was the voyce inside Alina's body – not the other way around. I had a vague notion of riding inside her head while she talked to faceless strangers and walked through unfamiliar hallways.

Was I a consciousness inside her body, or was she a voyce inside mine? Did it make any difference? Maybe we both held a dual-ownership. Who deserved this body more? I'd been born into it, sure, but Alina…she'd been forced to be here – implanted before I was old enough to speak. Her personality had developed from contact with mine. She had modeled her speech after my own. She had tailored her skills and character according to my needs. In short, she'd spent her entire life learning how to be like me. If she decided to stake a claim over this body now, did I have any right to deny her?

"Alina, are you there?" I asked.

<I'm here, Lacey. Good morning.>

My eyes burned when I opened them. I tried to lift a hand to block the light, but my arm lay heavy and dead by my side. It wouldn't move, and neither would the other one. A sudden pulse of fear screamed that I'd been paralyzed.

"Alina," I cried. "I can't move."

<Sorry, Lacey. *My bad.* Here you go.> I felt a rush of sensation, like an electric current flipping on. <Activating motor functions.>

I groaned as my brain's connection to the rest of my body came back online. My muscles ached. The smell of disinfectant wrinkled my nose. My face felt stiff and swollen. My vision transitioned slowly from a series of blotchy silhouettes into a small living space – an apartment made up of sandalwood furniture lined with calm, pastel-colored cushions.

An archway revealed a humble, yet clean kitchenette with gleaming cookware hanging from the walls. Next to this, a sliding door made of frosted glass showed a bathroom. It was clear that someone wanted me to be comfortable, but with no visible exits or windows to the outside world, I wasn't foolish enough to think this was a safe place.

The last thing to materialize in my vision was something tucked into the corner of the living room. I blinked several times, trying to force whatever it was out from obscurity, but the haze refused to diminish.

<Are you trying to see your servant?> Alina asked.

"My servant?"

<Your hosts have granted you access to *puzzler class* perks. Here, let me show you.>

The blur vanished, and I would have screamed if Alina hadn't halted the sound in my throat.

From the cloud of pixelated haze, a mutie appeared. He looked to be about my age, but it was always so hard to tell with muties. Thin, tall, and dressed in a black, button up shirt; the man sat motionless with his hands folded in his lap. His obsidian eyes gazed at nothing while the white domes of his ears vibrated softly, no doubt catching every trace of noise bouncing around the room.

"Why is he here?" I asked Alina.

<He's your servant. Whatever you want, he'll get it for you. Here, let me show you.>

The mutie sprang to his feet and rushed into the kitchen. A moment later, I heard the clatter of cookware and the whoosh of an igniting gas stove.

<He'll make you some breakfast.>

My stomach grumbled with hunger, but the thought of having my own personal *slave* – because that's what this was – made me sick. I tried to say so, but Alina cut me off.

<Lacey, you gotta eat. And besides, if this mutie isn't helping you, someone else will take him. And believe me, he's lucky to be working for you instead of some of the other folks staying here.>

"And where is…*here*?"

<We're at the first stop of something extraordinary. Oh, Lacey! I have so much to tell you.>

The smell and sound of sizzling bacon drifted in from

the kitchen. My mouth watered as Alina talked. I had to pretend it was all new information even though I'd heard some of it from Ogden.

She described the *Puzzling* – said it was a huge honor and a once-in-a-lifetime opportunity for someone like me. The flexers had brought me to what Alina was calling the North American Nexus, or NAN.

<It's a vactrain station,> she said, excited. <Can you believe it? We're going to travel like the elites do.>

"Any sign of Yadi or Cadence?"

<Oh right…*them.*> I couldn't help but notice the annoyance, bordering on derision, in Alina's voyce. <Yeah, I found them. They're here.>

Something clenched in my chest, making it hard to speak.

<But it's not what you think,> Alina continued. <Yadira and Cadence…they're both…*different.*>

"What do you mean?"

The sound of Alina taking a deep breath played in my head. She didn't need to breath, but she sometimes did this when prepping me for some bad news.

<They've been dead-headed.> If I wasn't already in bed, I probably would have fallen over.

"No."

<I'm sorry, Lacey. They took Yadira in order to pay your father's debts. And Cadence…they took him as punishment for some sort of crime. I'm not really sure what it was, but from what I can gather, he got caught helping a criminal escape from some flexers.> I had to remind myself that Alina had been deactivated at the time.

Does she really not know that it was me who Cadence helped escape? Or is Alina playing with me?

"Where are they?" I asked.

<I've been able to ping them both here within the NAN. That's the good news. Most available dead-heads in the area were recruited for the *Puzzling.*>

"They're going to compete?"

<No, no. Nothing like that. All puzzlers, like you, were chosen based on ability. Yadi and Cadence have been

assigned to help out with service and entertainment. I've never seen so many dead-heads, husks, and muties in one place before. Seriously, Lacey. It takes an army to keep so many elites happy.>

"So…they're prisoners?"

<It is a privilege to serve. They can't leave, but this might actually end up being a good thing.>

"How?"

<Yadira has to pay off her debts somehow. And Cadence must pay for his crimes. Entertaining a bunch of elites sure beats hard labor, right? Think about what happened to your father. I bet he would have loved to serve the upper classes instead of wasting away in a sweat shop.>

I gritted my teeth at this. *Don't talk about my dad.*

<You okay, Lacey? I sense anger.>

Instead of answering her, I asked, "Can I see them? Yadi and Cadence?"

<I don't think that's a good idea. Remember, Lacey, they aren't themselves right now. Their personalities were put into hibernation. They might be vaguely aware of what's happening, but most likely, they are *gone* and will remain so until they've paid their due.>

At that moment, the mutie materialized in front of me. He held a steaming tray.

<This one wants you to know breakfast is ready.> He began to unload a series of small plates onto the room's only table.

"Thank you," I said. I got out of bed, my legs all pins and needles, and collapsed into a chair in front of one of the most mouthwatering meals I'd ever seen. Fresh cantaloupe, pan seared peppers and potatoes, and some sort of egg dish. It looked like the mutie had loaded a bunch of vegetables, cheese, and bacon into the middle of a little yellow blanket.

<It's an omelet,> Alina informed me. It looked good, but I was still unprepared for the deluge of flavor contained in the first bite. <This one would like to know if you enjoy the taste.>

I nodded and the mutie faded back into a shimmering blur.

It was a few more bites before I realized something was different. My upper lip felt strange. My face in that area felt…not swollen, but stiff and…*full.* And when I touched it, there was a sharp, prickly sensation. My tongue poked inquisitively along the roof of my mouth, but the ridges and scars I'd known my whole life weren't there.

What is this?

I stood up and turned toward the bathroom. The mutie materialized in an instant.

<This one wants to know if everything is alright.>

"Fine," I said. "Just need to check something."

In the bathroom mirror, I discovered a stranger. The young woman looking back at me had the same hazel brown eyes and long black hair I was familiar with. But the malformed upper lip and surrounding lumps of scar tissue had been…smoothed out. The curves in the space under my nose and my lips had become…mostly symmetrical. And when I opened my mouth, the gap in my gumline was gone. In its place was an uninterrupted line of dazzling white teeth. All that remained of my cleft lip was pink skin and a distant, prickly sensation.

"What is this?"

I searched the reflection for some blip – some shimmer to indicate it was just an illusion. *It must be augmented reality. I don't look like this,* a strange voyce said. *This isn't me.* Tentatively, I touched the spot. I expected my fingertips to find my true face hiding beneath this false reality but physical sensation matched what I saw in the mirror. *Holy smokes, it's real.*

<What do you think?> asked Alina.

"H-how?"

<They wanted you to look your best for the *Puzzling,* so they ordered facial reconstruction. You underwent surgery two weeks ago and have been recovering ever since. I thought it best – less painful – for you to skip that part.>

"Hold on…I've been asleep for two weeks?"

<Yes and no. You were a dead-head.>

"What?"

<You weren't ready to see…certain things. That said, we still needed to keep you active, run you through an assortment of tests and exercises, not to mention keeping you fed, hydrated, and clean.>

By the tone, I could tell Alina expected me to be grateful, and maybe a younger version of me would've been. But things were different now. I had a different understanding of what Alina was, so the thought of her taking over my body without my knowledge or consent felt like a violation.

"You were running around in my body…for two weeks?"

<Don't worry, Lacey. I took good care of you.>

"Well, *don't*."

<I'm sorry, Lacey. Don't *what*?>

Be careful, that strange voyce warned. *Alina has to believe you still trust her.*

"Next time," I said, choosing my words carefully, "please let me know *before* I'm dead-headed."

<I'll try, Lacey, but we might not have a choice. If you step out of line, or you're eliminated from the *Puzzling*…there'll be nothing I can do.>

I wanted to argue with her but figured it would be pointless. I returned to my breakfast and ate in silence, fully aware of the invisible mutie watching me from the corner.

Some time later, a welcoming medley played from the wall speakers, and Alina informed me I had a visitor.

The previously empty wall curved upward as a door rose out of the floor. It was not unlike the construction site I saw appear out of nothing near my apartment.

More augmented reality, the strange voyce told me, and I wondered once again where this voyce was coming from. Could it be possible that there was another voyce inside my head, something different from Alina? Or was it only me? Was I capable of making my own voyce?

Before I could think more about this, the door opened inward and a blaze of yellow sunlight sauntered into the room. Ogden Oliver was literally beaming. His fire-blond hair danced with sparks of reflective light. The banana yellow suit he wore would have looked ridiculous on anyone else but it clung to his body in such a way to magnify his attractiveness. Even his eyes, somehow, seemed to glow a fiercer shade of blue in contrast to the suit's luminescence.

"Lacey Clarke," he said in a deep, velvety tone. "It is so good to meet you. Please allow me to introduce myself."

The last time we'd spoken, it had been in the ruins of his family's island estate. He'd told me that our voyces would need to think that *this* was our first meeting since the restaurant. To Alina, our rendezvous on the island never happened. Both our lives depended on this little lie, so I played along.

"I know who you are," I said, bowing. "It is an honor to meet you...Ogden Oliver."

"The honor, and pleasure, is all mine." He took my hand and kissed it. From his lips, I felt a shudder race up my arm and settle right in the center of my chest.

Out of the corner of my mouth, I threw in a bit of theatrics and whispered, "Alina, why didn't you warn me Ogden Oliver was coming here."

<I thought you might enjoy the surprise.>

Oliver rose in front of me. Still holding my hand, he said, "Now, if you'll please accompany me, I'd like to give you a tour."

* * *

I wasn't sure what I expected, but it wasn't this. I figured the space inside a transport hub would look industrial – like something you'd see back in the city – but the NAN was something unlike anything else I'd ever seen. Once again, it reminded me that the elites rarely did anything for practical reasons.

Tall conifers and ferns lined the many pathways inside

the NAN. Rather than walking through a central transport hub, it felt like we were on a stroll through some sort of enchanted forest. Countless lanterns with blue and green tinted glass hung from the surrounding foliage. Bubbling streams crisscrossed our path, which had to rise onto cobbled bridges. Loads of smaller walkways veered off from the main path. Their ends were hidden by the trees, but the sound of laughter and live music carried over the all-encompassing sound of running water.

A cool mist soothed my skin, and the smell of pine and damp earth sang in my soul. I almost believed I was in the woods and not some high-tech train station.

Ogden played his part as my tour guide. He pointed out which paths led to which delights. There was a dance hall, a live theater, a thrill seeker's play area, a spa, a casino, a fighting pit, a brothel, a gathering spot for polyamorous enthusiasts, and more bars and restaurants than were worth mentioning.

"So, it's like an amusement park?" I asked.

"Sort of," said Oliver, "but instead of animatronics on the rides, you get real people. Dead-heads and husks all over the place. They do anything the elites want or need them to do."

"That sounds awful," I said.

<They should consider themselves lucky,> Alina whispered in my mind. <They have the honor of serving the upper crust.>

As if to emphasize this, a pair of young men came rushing around the corner. Their faces were caricatures of intense focus as they both balanced no less than ten full margarita glasses stacked in tiers. I stepped out of the way, worried any distraction might cause them to drop the glasses. When they were gone, Ogden sighed and said, "Whoever they were before they came here is irrelevant. All they are now are servants."

"I want to see my sister," I said. "And Cadence, too. Take me to them."

Alina reprimanded me for being so demanding, but Oliver didn't seem to mind.

"Keeping track of them is difficult," he said. "Their assignments shift constantly. That said, I'm pretty sure I know where your sister is. I'm taking you to see her first…but I'm warning you…this won't be easy to see."

He turned off the main path and led me along a twisting walkway that crossed over a small pond before slipping behind a waterfall. Blue flame flickered from countless sconces carved into the cave-like walls. I had to remind myself this was all manmade. We weren't really in some enchanted grotto. This idea was even harder to maintain when we reached the end of the passage, and the cave opened into a high-ceilinged chasm. Stalactites glowed from up above. They appeared to be made of crystal and reflected the light in mesmerizing, multicolored prisms. A few of the stalactites held balls of revolving color and movement. It took me far too long to realize what they held inside, and I gasped in horror. Inside some of the stalactites were…people. They thrashed and squirmed within a clear liquid. On the ground, several stalagmites held the same tortured bodies. There were at least a dozen…men and women spread out above and below…imprisoned in crystal. They wore sheer bathing suits that left very little to the imagination. All part of the ambiance, it seemed.

<Close your mouth, Lacey. You look like some slack-jawed bumpkin.>

I did what she told me but couldn't hide my distrust of this place.

"Is this real?"

<Yes,> said Alina, but it wasn't her I was asking.

Ogden eyed me with a wary expression. He smiled, but it seemed a loaded thing, like he was warning me to be careful. I wasn't supposed to know about how detailed augmented reality could be. I nodded my understanding, and Ogden sighed in relief. "The prox do enjoy a good spectacle." He paused, looking over my shoulder. "Let's have a seat. The show's about to begin." He brushed his fingertips along the small of my back, gently guiding me toward a table that was situated beside a large pool of water.

I froze upon seeing the people already seated at the table. From the night I first met Oliver, the man with the blank void instead of a face…the *wolf*. He held a glass of wine high as if calling a toast. If he had a face, it was still lost in that swirling black. Beside him, the two I'd thought of as the 'platinum twins' shared a single chair – their bronze-colored arms and legs draped around each other. The woman drank from a flute glass while the man ran his fingers through her blazing-white hair.

"You remember my friends from *Stratus*?" Ogden asked when we neared the table. "The wolf's name is Gideon. The other two are called Micah."

I was confused. "They're *both* named Micah?"

Ogden sighed. "It's…*complicated*."

Nobody stood to greet us. In contrast to the dinner party at Stratus where the cellies had celebrated Ogden's arrival, this meeting felt almost hostile.

The platinum twins – *Micah* – seemed entirely absorbed in themselves while the wolf twirled his wine glass, letting the red liquid slosh dangerously close to the brim.

Ogden pulled back a chair and gestured for me to have a seat. Once Ogden was sitting beside me, he turned his attention toward the wolf.

"Hello, Gideon. Do you mind?"

"I suppose not, Oggy." The wolf set down his glass and gripped the table top. "*Mens agitat molem*." From the center of the void came a beam of white light. It bloomed until the void sitting on the man's shoulders had transformed into a molten sphere. Then, there was a *pop*, and the sphere cracked in half only to dissolve into thin air.

With the illusion gone, I could finally see the wolf clearly. And to my surprise, he was…handsome. He had a sort of predatorial intensity about him. Dark hair, a split in his left eyebrow, and a pencil-thin mustache framing glossy, red lips. His face would have made just as much sense on a dark ages marauder as it did on this upper crust elite. He locked eyes with Ogden, who appeared that much brighter by comparison.

"How brave of you to let your puzzler wander around

without a leash." He gestured toward me, and his mouth twitched as if caught on a fishhook.

Ogden placed his hand over my own. "I have complete faith in Lacey. But what about you?" He looked around. "Where's your puzzler?"

"Why do you care?" asked Gideon. "Hoping to size up the competition?"

Ogden grinned, but even I could tell it was forced. "Nothing like that. I just think it's customary to let your puzzler have a good time before the competition."

"Well, I *don't,*" Gideon snapped. "I think it's cruel. Why expose these puzzlers to good times when most of them won't experience anything like this ever again? Humoring these puzzlers..." he gestured toward me, "is like playing with your food."

The platinum twins guffawed in unison. It was a strange thing, almost like the same voice blasting from two separate throats.

"By the way..." The wolf's eyes brightened as he leaned toward me. "I see you've made some improvements to this one's face. Nice work, Oggy. I'm tempted to take her off your hands."

"She's not for sale."

Gideon waved his hand dismissively. "They're *all* for sale. Once she loses the competition, she'll go up for auction. You know I could use someone like her for...reasons."

Ogden squeezed my hand in reassurance. "If it comes to that, I'll buy her freedom myself."

To this, Gideon burst out laughing. "Oh, Oggy! You *know* you can't outbid me."

"Doesn't matter. Lacey's going to win anyways."

"You think so? Well, let's see, shall we?" He turned all his attention on me. "Care to answer my riddle?"

Ogden huffed in protest, but I put my hand on his arm.

"It's okay," I said. "I can try."

Gideon licked his lips. "Okay, this here's an old one. It goes like this: Drink me, and you'll die of thirst. Breath me, and you'll suffocate. Believe in me, and you'll give up hope. Eat me, and you'll starve. Have me, and you'll be poor. Need me, and you'll be rich. What is it?"

It *was* an old one. It had been one of my Logic teacher's favorites and had stumped everyone in the class. Everyone except me, of course.

I looked Gideon in the eye, loaded the answer in my mind, and prepared to fire it like a bullet.

Nothing. The answer's nothing.

But when I opened my mouth to speak, Alina switched the word in my throat.

"*Poison*," I said, then blinked in surprise. That wasn't what I'd meant to say.

Gideon roared with laughter and slapped the table. "Oh, Oggy! Is this the best your puzzler can do? The answer is *nothing*! Which is what she'll be when she loses this competition."

At that moment, the lights dimmed inside the cavern. Alina was whispering in my head, trying to tell me she changed my answer so not to upset the wolf. <You don't want to make an enemy of this man.>

Gideon was still laughing, but he stopped when the platinum twins shushed him.

"Quiet! The show…" said the woman.

"…is starting," said the man.

A steel walkway rose out of the pool of water nearby. At the same time, several loud cracks announced that the stalactites up above had broken away from the ceiling. They descended on golden chains. The trapped people inside continued to squirm and writhe, but they didn't appear to be in pain. They surveyed the elites – their voyeuristic captors – with smiling faces. I was wondering how they could breathe, but then I saw one of them take a breath from the pocket of air that was gathered at the top of their cone-shaped cages.

While this was going on, several ropes – or *coils* – rose out of the water on nearly invisible wires. The ends disappeared into newly formed slots in the ceiling, then flashed with color and grew taut as the coils tugged at something beneath the pool's surface.

<There she is, Lacey. In the pool. It's Yadira. She's the star.>

My attention turned to the two women rising from the water on the glowing, elastic coils. Yadira's dark hair and tanned skin shone like glossed metal. She wore a swathe of what looked to be *fish scales* from her chest to thighs like she was a mermaid or something.

A serious expression played on her face as she contorted in the air and pointed her muscled legs out towards the other woman, who I saw now was really more *girl* than woman. At the sight of this girl, a flash of panic sparked in my mind. I couldn't fathom why, but then her thin, blonde, and childlike face fell into stark recognition.

<It's the girl from the street,> said Alina. <The one those flexers picked up for stealing pretzels. It's so good they've given her a decent job.>

I couldn't share Alina's assessment, though. I watched in dumbfounded horror as the blonde-haired girl twisted in the air around my sister. Her tiny physique allowed her to slither around Yadira like a snake. And *Yadira*! I'd never seen my sister do anything like this. The muscles in her arms and back bulged as she shifted on the coils and launched them both into a spin around the cavern. Water rained down on the tables as they passed overhead. All around, the tops of the crystal spikes were opening up, allowing the people within to lift up their hands in praise. From up above, the stalactites split open and those inside plummeted into the pool like stones. Their screams punctuated the orchestral crescendo blasting from the walls.

<All part of the show.>

The Pretzel Girl wrapped her legs around Yadi's hips and gyrated them both into a dizzying rotation. Yadi's hands slipped as the centrifugal force yanked the coils from her fingers. She fell toward a patch of crystal spikes at the pool's edge. As she plummeted, the Pretzel Girl spun away and kicked out a long, slender leg into the nest of retracting coils. For an impossible moment, the two women hung in the air at the height of what should have been a fatal crash. I screamed, but the Pretzel Girl thrust out her hands and gripped Yadi's ankles just as the coils snapped around her own. The two continued their dive toward impalement, but the girl's grip held. Less than a dozen inches from the spikes, the coils reached the end of their elasticity and flung them both back toward the center of the pool. At the apex, both Yadi and the girl seemed to sit on a cushion of air. They smiled at the watching elites, then curved backwards and dove into the pool from which they had emerged.

The next act had already begun by the time I realized I was on my feet. A trio of fire juggling men had mounted the platform. Spurts of flame rose into the air.

<Lacey, sit down.> My legs numbed as Alina lowered me back into my seat.

"It w-was Yadira. H-how did she do that?"

<She's a dead-head, Lacey. As long as her body is physically capable, she can do whatever they want her to do.>

"No," I shouted. "They can't use her like that. It's too dangerous."

<Stop it, Lacey. You're making a scene.> My jaw tightened, cutting off any further protests.

That was when I noticed the wolf's eyes on me. He watched me over the brim of his wine glass. The tip of his thumbnail glowed orange as if an ember burned within.

<You know that aerialist?> his voyce boomed in my head.

I clamped my lips shut and sat down, but I could do nothing to silence Alina. She told him what he wanted to know.

<The dark-haired one is your sister? Well, isn't that something?>

I turned toward Ogden. He was still looking at the show, but his gaze was glassy like he was lost in thought. He seemed unaware of the exchange between me and Gideon.

"Ogden, I want to leave."

Alina reprimanded me for being so rude, but I didn't

care. I had to get away from this wolf. The way his voyce seemed to growl when he asked about Yadi. I could feel the malicious glee flickering between each syllable.

"Please, Ogden. We have to go."

To my surprise, he didn't argue. "I was just about to tell you the same thing," he said.

He locked eyes with Gideon for a moment and I sensed a curt farewell pass between them. Ogden nodded toward the white-haired twins and said, "Catch you later, Micah."

<Our offer still stands,> said a sensual, androgynous voyce.

"I'll let you know," said Ogden.

The twins waved dismissively then turned back to the show.

* * *

It was too much. My hands were trembling and I felt light headed.

<Try to calm yourself, Lacey. Deep breaths.>

I gulped for air, but nothing made the dizziness subside. White spots gathered in my peripherals and scattered about like insects.

"This is – this is *flipped* up." It wasn't the verb I intended to use, but Alina didn't want me to cuss in front of Ogden.

"I know," he said.

"Is *this* all we are to you?" I asked. "Puppets for you elites to –" My throat constricted as Alina cut me off.

<You're out of line,> cried Alina. <The elites do so much for us. Apologize to Ogden right now.> Her hold relaxed, but I wouldn't give in.

"I *won't* apologize!"

I felt a hand close around the back of my neck. I'd felt this before – whenever my Loyalty teacher got irritated. It was the same thing now. Icy fingers dug into my spine until I cried out in pain.

"Stop that," shouted Ogden. He moved quickly and cupped my face in his hands.

You hold me in your hands while I hold you in my center.

"*Habere non Haberi*," he said.

The pain ceased. The sudden *release* from Alina's control made my legs buckle, and I would have fallen if Ogden wasn't there to catch me. Once I'd regained my strength, I pushed away from him and cursed – and this time, Alina wasn't there to stop me.

"You have every right to be angry," he said. "None of this is fair."

Rubbing the back of my neck, I glared at him. "Easy for you to say. I bet you cellies don't get yanked around for misbehaving."

"Not often, no."

"So why're you showing me this? Why show me how Yadi's been turned into a mindless slave? Did you think I'd be impressed?"

"You need to see what's at stake. Not just for the people you care about, but for countless others. Your voyce will try to convince you that all of this is *good* – that dead-heads aren't a crime. Your voyce will point to things like your sister's performance and say, 'Look, how beautiful,' or show you pictures of structures like the one we're standing in and say, 'Isn't this magnificent?'"

"Your point?"

"My point is that you *remember* who the person was before the prox turned them into a piece of equipment. That way, no matter how incredible their creations appear to be, you'll see it's not worth the sacrifice."

I had a sense he wasn't only talking about Yadi. I thought of Ogden's mom and dad…the mutie couple who'd appeared so happy when I'd returned their cat to them.

"So, what now?" I asked. "You gonna show me where they're keeping Cadence?"

"That was the plan…" He shifted and looked around nervously. "But I think we should scrap that for now."

"Why?"

"While we were watching your sister's act, my voyce sent me a security alert."

I shook my head, not understanding what this meant.

"My voyce says someone's looking for you, Lacey. This person – whoever they are – my voyce is unable to touch." His eyes narrowed. "That means it's law enforcement. A flexer boy, most likely." He looked me in the eyes. "Do you have any idea why there's a flexer looking for you?"

Vitus, I thought. *He's probably still sore about me kicking him in the eye.*

When I explained this to Ogden, the horror on his face was almost comical.

"Oh, you shouldn't have done that," he said.

"Why? What's the big deal? I'm a puzzler, right? Don't I have protections?"

"Officially, yes, but Lacey, flexers set their own rules, and they're a vindictive bunch. I've seen flexer boys kill an innocent man for much less."

"Me too," I said.

"Point is," Ogden went on, "flexers are *supposed* to keep the peace, but the only thing more dangerous than their voyce commands is their ego. The prox do something to them when they become flexers. Something that burns out their empathy. The prox carve that part out when they give flexers control over others. They say it makes them better enforcers, but I say it just makes them sociopaths."

"Can't you do anything? I mean, you're a cellie. Can't you make him leave me alone."

"That's not how this works, Lacey. There's a hierarchy. If I was a wolf, sure, but cellies –" He threw up his hands. "Our power is ornamental – impressive from afar, but it *crumbles* when challenged. The flexers always take priority. If given the chance, this flexer you hurt will want some payback." Ogden spun around in a circle and peered into the surrounding trees as if he expected Vitus to pop out any second.

"You don't really think –"

"I do," he said grimly. Then, he activated our voyces and requested a security escort.

Chapter 13

Ogden placed me under house arrest. “For your own safety,” he said.

With nowhere to go, I spent the next few days quizzing myself on all the riddles I could remember. Alina peppered me with questions of her own.

<What smells better than it looks? What has hands and a face but no body? What’s in the middle of the sky?>

Separating the answers from the riddles, I imagined, was a lot like surgery. You had to know which parts to take out and which parts to leave alone. You had to *extricate* the actual clues from the distractions.

“Nose, clock, and the letter ‘k’.”

<Yes, correct, and affirmative,> said Alina. <How are you so good at this?>

Her praise should have lifted my spirits, but I was troubled. I yearned to see Yadi and Cadence, but Ogden insisted it was best to keep low. He had an escort of flexers-for-hire stationed outside my room. The idea creeped me out, but Ogden assured me flexers responded to money just like everyone else. The flexer guards would keep me safe while Ogden was off with his friends, doing whatever it was rich people did. He visited me every day – often more than once – but I still wished he could have done more. It felt wrong to be worrying so much about *my* safety when Yadi and Cadence were out there doing who-*knows*-what for their captors.

Ogden kept telling me they were safe. The best thing I could do for them was win the *Puzzling*. Once I did that, I’d be able to set them free myself.

On the fifth day, Ogden arrived to tell me it was time to leave. The vactrain exodus had begun.

Before we left the apartment, my mutie attendant appeared by the door.

<This one wishes you a safe journey.>

I thanked him but had no way of knowing if he even knew I was there.

* * *

We walked in a bunch. Two flexer boys up ahead and two behind. Ogden said they'd accompany us to the vactrain station. From there, we'd be on our own.

Alina was silent. Ogden had shut her off again when we left my room. Silencing her would make it harder for any flexers to track me, he explained.

"We'll need to reactivate her when we get to the station. Until then, we can talk freely."

Overhead something rumbled like thunder, and I glanced up through the canopy of trees to see a series of huge, glass tubes extended across the NAN's wooded interior.

As I watched, an oval-shaped *something* blurred through one of the tubes. An instant later, I felt the *boom* of shifting air pressure punch behind my ribcage.

"What's that?"

Ogden followed my gaze. "Oh, that's the vactrain. I guess you didn't see it before when your voyce was activated." He shrugged. "The prox don't like commoners knowing too much about how they get around."

"So, they hide it with augmented reality?"

"The prox hide lots of stuff. It's sort of their thing."

Something occurred to me then. "Where *are* the prox? They apparently control everything, but I haven't *seen* them."

"Yes, you have," said Ogden.

I blinked at him. "I have?"

"That pair of white-haired narcissists…*Micah*…those were the prox, or one of them. But like I said…it's complicated. What the world sees is two people, but it's really just one. Two husks operated by a single member of the prox autocracy. The sensations of both bodies are funneled into the mind of a single prox. They view the world through multiple pairs of eyes and feel life from multiple points of view."

I was having a hard time thinking this through.

"So, one person's life isn't enough for them? They gotta steal two people's bodies?"

"Yeah, but *two* is a relatively low number for them. I once met a prox who was inside eight different people at once. When I asked 'them' what it felt like, they told me it was 'a non-stop orgy of sensation.' Whatever that means."

"But that's...that's *sick.*"

"Welcome to Prox-land, Lacey. Where people's bodies are the rides." There was no humor in his voice.

*   *   *

The security checkpoint at the bottom of the train platform seemed more like a formality than any serious check. Ogden whispered the reactivation phrase, and together with the other elites, we walked through without too much hassle. The dead-head security guards stopped me and asked to see my bag. I handed over the plastic sack that held the clothes I'd been wearing when the flexers first picked me up. I would have preferred to wear my own clothes instead of the dark blue jumper I was in now, but it wasn't an option.

Security performed a meticulous examination, during which, Alina answered their questions. When they found the bag of ashes in my sweatshirt pocket, Alina convinced them to leave it alone. For this, I was grateful. I didn't want to explain out loud why I was carrying around my dad's ashes. The truth was I still didn't know.

They signaled me through, and with Ogden by my side, we ascended the steps up onto the main platform.

"Why don't you have any luggage?" I asked him.

He shrugged and said his things would be waiting for us at our destination, and that the smaller vactrain was reserved for elite travel only. Most other things and people required more cumbersome methods of travel.

"The prox strictly prohibit most drone traffic in and out of the Puzzling. That's why we're taking the train instead of flying in. Besides the elites, most people are already there. They've been prepping the place for months."

All around, scores of cellies and wolves chatted in groups or reclined on velvet loungers. Most of them had traded their formal wear for more comfortable travel clothes, but they were still made of lustrous fabrics of a quality I'd rarely seen outside the entertainment streams. A few of the wolves had those swirling voids on their shoulders, but most I saw had dropped the shimmer. They didn't look all that different from normal people.

As we made our way down the platform, several women called out to Ogden, to which he waved politely but didn't stop. There was an urgency in his stride, and I did my best to keep up as we made our way through the crowd.

Two clear tubes lined either side of the platform. An oval pod filled one of the tubes. It looked to be about thirty feet long. The whole thing was jet black with no discernable vents or windows. And when a door *did* open, the tube split along a matching seam to reveal a red-carpet interior with five rows of leather seats.

I was about to step inside when Ogden stiffened beside me.

"What is it?" I asked him.

"He's here." He spun around toward the security checkpoint. "That flexer boy who wants to see you…my voyce says he's at the gates."

"Can he come in here?"

"Yes…"

I felt the blood rush from my face and hands. So cold, I wondered for a moment if Vitus was doing it. I feared what would happen if the flexer set his eyes on me. With my voyce activated, he'd have complete control.

"What do we do?" I whispered. "Should we turn off our –"

"*No*," he cut me off, his eyes full of fire. "*Don't* finish that sentence. Not here. There's too many people."

"Then what?"

Firmly but not unkindly, Ogden pushed me into the vactrain car. "I'll see if I can slow him down."

"But Ogden –"

"It's not *me* he wants." He looked me in the eyes. My reflection trembled within the lifeliner's blue irises.

"Please, don't leave," I said.

"Don't worry, Lacey. I'll be on the train right behind yours." And with that, he spun away and bolted toward the security gates. For a moment, the crowd of elites parted, and through the long corridor of bodies I saw Ogden rushing toward the far end. Further still, I saw the towering body of the flexer with the sickish, orange face. Even at this distance, I could see Vitus' puffy black eye and glowering expression. Did he see me? I *felt* something crawling up the back of my neck. The flexer's touch poured over my skin, searching for a way into my nervous system. But then the crowd – almost as if acting on command – contracted inward. Ogden and Vitus were both swallowed by the mass of people.

<What were you two talking about?> I jumped at the sound of Alina's voyce. <You were asking Ogden if you should turn off something. What did you mean?>

I ducked into the train car. "It's nothing, Alina."

<You sure? I get the feeling you're not being honest.>

A hand fell on my shoulder. I flinched, thinking for a moment that this might be Alina's attempt to squeeze an answer from me. But then I turned to see the man this hand was attached to – and I froze.

"Hello…*Lacey*, was it?" Gideon's smile might have appeared charming if I didn't know better. He glanced over my shoulder. "Was that Oggy I saw run off? Where is *he* going in such a hurry?"

My brain stalled. I just stood there and made weird gulping sounds in my throat.

Gideon puffed air through his wine-red lips in a dramatic, almost comical show of disappointment. "No worries. I guess we'll just have to get caught up on the far side of the shoot." He gestured toward the front of the compartment. "This way, Lacey. I reserved us some seats in the front row."

For a few seconds, I didn't move at all.

<Move it,> Alina said. My foot jerked forward as if yanked by a rope. Near the front, the top of the car curved in from all sides to form a clear, bullet shaped nose. Beyond this, the glass-walled tunnel seemed to go on forever. Looking forward was like gazing into a deep well that descended down into some underworld pit from Greek mythology. It was enough to give me a sense of vertigo, forcing me to close my eyes a few seconds until it passed.

I took a seat and, to my surprise and *horror*, Gideon fell in beside me.

"Quite a view," he said. "It's nice that Oggy lets his puzzlers see these things."

My cheeks burned. I remembered his comments from earlier – about how showing puzzlers like me a good time was like "playing with your food." As if reading my mind, Gideon pointed across the aisle at a blank-eyed young man with model-like good looks, golden hair, and wearing a dark blue jumper similar to my own. In his lap, he held a medium sized box. This was strange only because he was the only person in the car – beside myself – with any sort of luggage.

"That's my puzzler," said Gideon. "His name's Phaeton. I picked him from some backwater outpost near the burn fields. If he were conscious, I'm sure he'd thank me for rescuing him from that thankless hell on earth."

I didn't know what to say so I settled instead on nodding in agreement.

Gideon sighed and leaned back. I thought that maybe he was taking a nap, but I soon realized he was talking with his voyce. He muttered so softly that I couldn't make out the words.

A minute passed before a countdown clock blazed in my vision. Twenty minutes until launch.

<The tube is creating a vacuum,> Alina explained. <It's flushing all air from the tunnel. When we launch, there'll

be no wind resistance. We'll ride on a pocket of magnetism and dispersed air. Oh Lacey…get ready for the ride of your life.>

"How fast will we go?"

<At top speed, we'll hit close to twenty-five hundred miles an hour. That's 41 miles a minute. Two miles every three seconds.>

"Impressive, right?" Gideon said as if he were listening. He'd opened his eyes and was now grinning at me with uncomfortable interest. "Me and this vactrain…we're a lot alike."

I took the bait. "How so?"

"Me and this train. We eliminate all resistance. Anything that might be in our way…or poses any sort of threat…gets flushed out before we even get going." He paused. "Do you take my meaning?"

I gulped, then nodded.

"Good," he said. "It's nice to see Oggy finally picked a puzzler with some intelligence. But still, that creates its own problems." He snapped his fingers, and his blank-eyed puzzler – the one called Phaeton – reached across the aisle and handed the box over to Gideon.

"I'd like to show you something," said Gideon, his tone becoming all business.

"No, really. That's okay," I said.

<Don't be rude,> said Alina.

Gideon lifted the lid to reveal two wire crowns stacked one on top of the other. They looked a lot like the things little girls wore when roleplaying as a princess. Only instead of ribbons, the things had silver discs on the front and sides. He took out one of the crowns and placed it on his head. The other, he handed to me.

"What is this?" I asked.

"It's a neuro-link," he said. "It'll give you access to a virtual experience. I wanted to show you something Oggy wouldn't."

"What's that?" I asked, suspiciously.

"You'll see."

I considered not putting it on. I didn't trust this wolf –

had no reason to suspect he didn't mean me harm – but he'd offered me something I couldn't resist. He'd planted a question in my mind. That was my weakness. I had to have answers. Part of me wondered if he knew this about me. How much personal information did these elites have about commoners like me? But more importantly, what could he show me that Ogden had not? He could have been lying, of course. I knew that. But there was only one way to know for sure.

I placed the crown over my head, and the discs seemed to *click* into place as if pulled by something buried within my own skull.

The countdown clock showed seventeen minutes, the seconds ticking closer to launch.

Gideon gave a little snort, then said, "Hold on, Lacey. This should be fun…for me." He clapped his hands, and said, "Activate the stream."

And I was gone.

*   *   *

When I next opened my eyes, I was in a very different place. I sat with my legs beneath me on a cloth surface. It was hard, but not without a little bounce. I shifted onto my knees and the floor wobbled a little like there might be springs underneath.

My back pressed against something cold and sharp – a cage. Up above, a large conical spotlight buzzed as it cast a blinding white light down onto the blood-splattered mat.

I saw movement, and jumped to my feet. In a corner on the opposite side of the cage, a man rose to his feet. He stood just outside the spotlight's harsh glow, but what I could see frightened me. The man was shirtless, wearing only a filthy pair of shorts. Bloody bandages covered the man's hands and ankles. He clenched his hands into fists and flexed. His entire body shook with the effort. The muscles on his arms and chest bulged. He was a loaded weapon, ready to spring forward.

That was when I looked down at my own body, and…it

didn't make sense. It took a while for the sight to register, but I stared at a body that was not my own. I looked through eyes that weren't mine at thick arms, a hairy chest, and powerful legs.

"Alina, what's going on?" I was frightened by the sound coming from my own throat. Deep and nasally, it was a man's voice and completely foreign.

From across the ring, another voice called out – this one was familiar.

"Your voyce doesn't work here," said the man. "This is between me and you." He stepped into the light, and at the sight of his face, I felt a flood of mixed emotions. *Relief*, at first. Then *confusion*, joy, horror, and finally, *disgust*.

"Cadence!" I cried with a man's vocal cords. "Cadence, it's me, Lacey!"

He blinked in surprise. And a part of me died at seeing how much he'd changed since I last saw him. The childish dimple in his left cheek now looked like a puncture wound. The hint of stubble was now a rat's nest of unkempt growth. But the worst was his eyes. His normally kind eyes that I remembered so clearly from our night in the rain now sat at the bottom of two sunken pits. Any kindness Cadence possessed had been replaced by the man now riding inside his body.

"It's Gideon," said the wolf through Cadence's body. He held out his hands and turned in a circle as if showing off a new outfit. "What do you think of my new digs?"

"Leave him alone."

"Why?" asked the wolf. "Do you know this husk? Is Cadence a friend of yours?" There was so much laughter in the wolf's tone that it was clear he already knew the answer.

"Why are you doing this?"

"Just having a little fun." He shifted into a fighting stance. "Now, put up your dukes."

I had barely enough time to square up before he was on me.

A barrage of punches stuck me in the stomach and

head. I put up my hands, but I could do nothing to ward off the constant lefts and rights. A hard hook caught me on the side of the head that made the whole world spin.

"*Fight back!*" shouted Gideon/Cadence.

He kicked me in the ribs so hard that I doubled over. Gideon/Cadence didn't let up as he rained bombs onto the back of my head. Just wanting the pain to stop, I lunged forward, gripped the backs of his knees, and *pushed* until he fell backward. I meant to hold him down, but he was too quick. His body too slick with sweat. He rolled onto his shoulder and lifted his legs so that I rolled with him. Before I even knew what was happening, he was straddled atop me. His knees pinned my arms by my sides. Then he really got to work. His fists crashed against my skull. One right after another. *Boom, boom, boom.* The punches detonated inside my brain. Each crash pushed the world – and Cadence – further and further away.

I'm not sure if I lost consciousness, but the next thing I knew, I was on my side coughing up blood.

Gideon/Cadence kicked me in the chest. On impact, something shifted painfully inside. *Broken ribs*, I guessed.

"Get up," he said. "Get up before I kill you."

I coughed some more, shook stars out of my eyes, then clambered to my feet. I saw Cadence's face swimming through a red haze. The sardonic grin was out of place on his once kind face.

"Hit me," he said.

"Please."

"Hit me, *now*." He lashed out and struck me right beneath the left eye. I collapsed back to the mat into a pool of my own blood. "Get *up*!"

I stood. My side was in agony, and my head felt full of buzzing hornets.

"Hit me," he said. But I couldn't. There was no way I could strike Cadence. It didn't matter whether he was aware or not. I wouldn't hurt his body. Which made me wonder whose body was I in myself. I didn't want to hurt

Cadence, but I also couldn't just let Gideon destroy this person. I put up my fists to defend myself.

"You could do so much," I said.

The wolf blinked with Cadence's eyes. "I'm sorry?"

"With your wealth..." I continued, "you could do so much. You could help so many people. But *this* is what you choose to do? You decide to add more pain to an already painful life."

He pulled back his arm, and I braced myself for another hit...but it didn't come.

Instead, the wolf shrugged with Cadence's shoulders and said, "This is the way the world works, Lacey. You either beat or get beaten. You probably think I'm cruel. You might be right, but it's not without purpose. Sometimes, cruelty *is* the point."

I'd heard this before, but couldn't remember where.

"The *Puzzling* is more important than you know," he said. "Whoever wins will receive a great opportunity. There is a vacancy among the prox. This year, the elite who puts forth a winning puzzler will be granted access to prox membership...and all the power that entails. My brother, Oggy, wants you to believe you'll benefit from this opportunity." The surprise must have registered on my beaten face because he said, "That's right, Lacey. Ogden Oliver is my *brother*. He didn't tell you that, did he?" He laughed. "Makes you wonder what else he isn't saying."

"What do you want?"

He barked a laugh. "The more important question, is what do *you* want? I'm here to tell you I can give you what you desire." He slapped his/Cadence's chest. "This husk – *Cadence Greene* – I can have him de-husked and released from captivity. And your dead-head sister...Yadira Clarke..."

I held my breath.

"That's right, Lacey. I know everything about you. Your own voyce is a wealth of knowledge. Just like I know you and Oggy are up to something."

"I don't know what you're talking about."

"I *know* you met my parents. And *someone* visited my family's ruined estate. The cams were all off, and for some reason, your voyce's recollection is a little foggy, but I suspect you were there. My brother thinks he's clever, but he'll only end up getting himself turned into a mutie…just like Mom and Dad." He paused, looking at his hands. "I can offer you a way out. I can free you and the people you care about. I can use my influence to make it happen. Just like that." He snapped his fingers. A small spark flickered on his thumbnail, then died the next instant. "All I need from you is a simple favor."

"What's that?"

"*Lose*," he said. "Don't say anything to Ogden. Let him believe you tried your best…then get yourself eliminated from the *Puzzling*. Easy. Do *that*, and you and your loved ones will be free."

"If I refuse?"

His/Cadence's eyes narrowed. "It's not like you really *can* win anyways. But if you *fail* to lose on purpose, I'll make sure you regret it." To show this, he turned away and walked over to the cage that surrounded the mat. He gripped the metal bars with both hands and slammed Cadence's head into the cage.

I screamed for him to stop, but he wasn't listening. He slammed Cadence's head two more times before letting go. Then, he stumbled for a moment. Blood poured from a newly formed gash on his forehead and ran down his face.

"Ouch, that smarts." Gideon licked blood from Cadence's lips and grinned. "You see how easy it would be? Refuse to lose, and your loved ones will die. I'll kill them myself. So…freedom or death? It's as simple as that, Lacey."

I couldn't bear to see him hurt Cadence anymore.

"Do we have a deal?" he asked.

"Yes," I said. "Just please stop."

"Of *course*. I'm not an animal. And to show you I'm a man of my word, I'll give you two a moment." He looked toward the ceiling and shouted, "*Stream deactivate*."

Cadence collapsed to the mat and didn't move. I approached him with caution. I was sure Gideon was playing a trick until the man on the mat opened his eyes. Gideon's cruelty was gone. The kindness of Cadence's gold-flecked eyes gazed up at me with heartbreaking sorrow.

"Lacey?" he said. "Is that really you?"

"Yes..." Tears welled in my eyes. "And is that really you?"

"I'm sorry, Lacey." He was crying now as well. "I could feel and see everything that wolf was doing...when he was hitting you...but I couldn't stop. Whenever any of them are inside my head...I have no control. They do whatever they want me to."

I reached for him with hands that were not my own.

"I'm in hell," he said. "Lacey, are you safe?"

I didn't really have an answer for that, but nodded anyways. "I have to get you out of here."

He shook his head. "Don't worry about me, Lacey. There's nothing you can do, and you can't trust what that wolf says." He stiffened as if caught in an electric current. Through gritted teeth, he said, "Damn it, Bartleby. Let me speak."

Even now...with his life reduced to such a violent end, Cadence's voyce didn't want him to say anything ill of the elites. The spotlight buzzed overhead. It showed prox control in all its bloody details. There could be no escape. The voyces in our heads formed too tight a prison. How could anyone hope to fight back against such a cruel and efficient system?

"I'll get you out of here," I said. I held his hands and cursed that the hands I used were not my own. I could only touch Cadence with someone else's body. But it was all we had. I placed my hand on his chest and felt the heartbeat within.

"Repeat after me," I said. "I...Cadence Greene..."

He gave a painful laugh, then repeated, "I, Cadence Greene..."

"Will get out of here."

But before he could respond, the world shifted. I felt myself falling away – felt my consciousness yanked out as if caught on a fishhook.

And then I was back in my body. Hot tears coursed down my cheeks.

Gideon held the neuro-link in his hands and made a *tsk-tsk* sound. His wine-red lips curved into a knowing smile.

"This is between me and you," he said. "Oggy can't know. And whatever it is you two were planning, it ends now. Understood?"

I nodded. What I wanted to do was reach up and strangle this man. I wanted to stick my thumbs into his eye sockets and claw that smug expression off his face. But I couldn't move. My arms were heavy and immobile.

<I'm sorry, Lacey. But your emotions were skyrocketing. I've sedated you.>

"Let…me…*move.*"

<It's okay, Lacey. I've got you. Try to relax. The car is about to launch.> The countdown clock ticked past the twenty seconds' mark. Gideon put the neuro-links away and handed the box back to his blank-eyed puzzler. He put his hand on my knee. His black and red fingernails clutched the fabric of my jumpsuit, and I felt a jolt, like static electricity surge at his touch. But unlike static, the sensation didn't go away. A low pulse thrummed beneath his touch. His red thumbnail flickered as something glowed within – like sunlight through a stained-glass window.

Such an odd thing, I thought. *There's no way that's natural.*

<Everything's going to be alright,> his voyce rumbled in my mind. <As long as you play along.>

The clock struck zero. Then the lights flashed and air hissed all around the cabin. My ears popped.

The car creaked as pressure built up behind us. Then, the clamps released and we fired like a bullet. The acceleration punched me in the chest. It was so hard to breath. I had the distinct feeling we were blasting up toward space, and at any moment, we would break through the atmosphere like

Willy Wonka's glass elevator. I remembered the way Yadi would cheer when we were kids. She had been so happy to see Charlie break through that glass ceiling – to finally escape from a life of poverty.

But this was no magic elevator. I wasn't escaping a hard life. I plunged down into an even worse nightmare. Tears streamed from my eyes, and I could feel the blood pooling in my veins. The acceleration continued to go up and up until I was sure I'd be crushed.

<I'm giving you something to relax,> Alina said. <See you on the other side.>

Alina released something into my bloodstream and my body got all…fuzzy. The last thing I felt was the pressure of continued acceleration…*that* and the feel of Gideon's pulsing grip on my knee.

Chapter 14

Decades before I was born, there was a big push to fill the world with robots. It was supposed to give us the benefits of slavery without all the annoying guilt. It worked pretty well…for a while at least. People had robot vacuum cleaners, robot delivery drones, robot cooks and babysitters, robot landscapers, and lots more. Some of 'em were still around, but they kinda went out of style…like leg warmers in the nineteen eighties.

There were a few still in operation at the high school I went to. A lunch-serving model that looked like an upside-down broom with coat hanger hands – and a quadrupedal janitor dog-thing that cleaned the bathrooms. They were friendly enough, but I never met a robot I didn't hate. The way they spoke…the gestures programmed into their human interactions always felt a little…*off*. A cheery tone or excited wave didn't sit right with me because I knew it was faked. It'd be better if they didn't try to act like people at all. There were loads of things robots could do better anyways. Why debase themselves by learning human emotion?

<It's so they don't kill you,> Alina had told me once. <A robot without emotion – without *empathy* – wouldn't know the difference between a person and a shovel. If someone told a robot to build a playground, without empathy, that robot might kill all the children in the area so it could use their bones to make monkey bars.>

I didn't love that image, but she had a point.

Robots were supposed to be a superior workforce, but there was just too much going on in a person's brain for robots to imitate. Empathy was just one of those things. This combined with other evolved traits like judgement, self-awareness, creativity, or even *pain*…and even the people who made the machines had to admit some things just couldn't be programmed.

Which was probably why most robots were phased out

once neural-nets became available – then *mandatory* – and corpocrats discovered the potential for dead-heading.

Why struggle to build human-like machines when it would be so much easier – and hella *cheaper* – to make machine-like humans? There were already so many humans to choose from. None of them had to be *built*. All that was needed was a way to exploit the already thriving debt economy, and *voila*. You had a slave workforce with all the combined strengths of machine-like efficiency mixed in with human-like intuition. Slavery at its finest.

But that wasn't how Alina would characterize it. To her, becoming a dead-head like Yadira or my dad was an *opportunity*. Husks like Cadence provided a valuable service. And muties like Ogden's parents were a deterrent against disobedience. According to Alina, slavery was just one piece of a fair and just society.

I was only now realizing I didn't have to listen to her any longer. I didn't have to believe everything she said, but I still needed her help. For starters, I never would have known where to go after the vactrain. Gideon was on his feet before the car fully docked with the station. And once the tube doors slid open, he took his puzzler by the arm and fled. It took a few minutes for sensation to return to my legs, and by the time I *could* walk, I had no clue which way to go. I didn't mind at first. My curiosity prompted me to explore this bizarre, new location entirely on my own. I soon discovered this would be impossible because Alina kept censoring huge swathes of things right in front of me. As I descended the steps away from the platform, my vision got so muddy and confused, that I had a hard time not falling over. I had to stop and steady myself by holding onto a handrail.

"Alina, please turn off the shimmers."

<I can't, Lacey. There's some potentially disturbing imagery. It would be better if you don't see it.>

"But I can barely walk. All the blurs are making me dizzy."

<Do you need me to take control?>

"No. Just let me see. I promise, I can handle it." I

figured she wasn't convinced yet, so I threw on a hasty, "Ogden would *want* me to see the place where I'll be competing."

<I wouldn't be so sure of that, but for your sake, I'll ask him.> She was silent for at least a minute, then said, <I've just spoken with Mr. Oliver's voyce. They both agree with you. I *don't*, but what do I know? I've only been with you your whole life.>

"Alina. It'll be okay. Please let me see."

She paused. <*Fine.* Permission granted.>

The world swam into clear focus as the surrounding shimmers vanished.

Just outside the station, a wall of secondary tubes pumped smaller cars like pistons up and down a tall mountain slope. I'd never seen such high mountains…or so much *snow* in all my life. I paused to stare while Alina rattled off details about our journey. The vactrain had carried us across the ocean in a little under two hours. The majority of our trip had been supersonic.

Freezing air burned in my chest, and I shivered in response to the chill gathering in my fingers and toes.

<Come on, Lacey. Let's get you someplace warm.> The site for the *Puzzling* and all its accompanying entertainment had been built right into the mountain. Wooden decks stretched out beneath snow-capped peaks. Here, elites filled hot tubs, played strange games, and guzzled red wine. They laughed near gas-powered heaters while their oiled skin glistened like polished leather.

All around, blank-eyed servants buzzed with activity in order to attend to the elites' every need. They carried hors d'oeuvres, liquor, or dirty dishes on silver trays. It was all stupidly elaborate to be sure, but I couldn't see what was such a big deal. Why had Alina wanted to hide this from me? That's when I looked toward the fringes, at the servants who were engaged in a number of unusual activities. The sight made my stomach lurch.

Off to one side, a group of elites had gathered around a male dead-head. He stood in his underwear with a lipstick-red bullseye scribbled on his chest. Apart from the tears streaming down his cheeks, his face showed no emotion. And he didn't even flinch as the group took turns tossing feathered darts. Already, the servant had at least a dozen of these small projectiles sticking from his body, and several streams of blood pitter-pattered the deck. The group roared with laughter when one purple-haired cellie – clearly drunk with a glass of wine in one hand and a vape pen in the other – tossed a dart so off target that it struck the poor servant in the cheek right below his eye.

More laughter forced me to turn toward another group bent over in a fit of hysteria. They howled and pointed at a pair of servants who were on their hands and knees. A young man and woman with dead, haunted eyes bowed low over a chunky spill that could have been either chili or vomit. Bile rose in my own throat as the pair made disgusting slurping noises and licked the mess up from the deck. All around, the onlookers cheered and screamed for the pair to "*Get your dinner*!"

<Stop gawking,> chastised Alina. <You're not even supposed to be here. You want to get us in trouble?>

My body jerked as if kicked, and I stumbled toward a stone entryway leading into the mountain. Along the way, three men – all with streaks of red in their hair – sauntered past me. Their steps were too in-sync to be mere coincidence. It had to be a prox. I couldn't help wondering who these men had been before their bodies were taken over by some upper-class snob. Did they have families? Were they missed? Was this the fate Ogden wanted me to share in? He'd said that to win the *Puzzling* was to become a prox…was this what he meant?

Maybe his brother, Gideon has the better offer. The question was…who could I trust? Normally, I'd ask Alina for help making such a consequential decision, but she couldn't know anything about it. I had to choose on my own.

As I weighed my options, Alina led me through a maze of corridors that ranged from sleek contours to cave-like stone. The size of this place was incredible. Down one corridor, massive pillars disappeared into a darkened ceiling. Down another, the aurora from an underground lake bounced off the walls. Still more paths led to rooms with open fireplaces. Here, cellies and wolves mingled on loungers while they sipped from steaming mugs of hot chocolate and gazed through wall-sized windows at a truly spectacular view of the snowscape. In the distance, suspension bridges crossed the gaps between mountains. None of it made any sense to me. Everything appeared to be a confused mess of gathering spots and winding pathways.

Every room was a surprise and each hummed with activity. While music and laughter echoed from one direction, high pierced screams that made my skin crawl shrieked from the other. And above all this, I could feel something deeper and much more powerful thundering up from the earth. I held my hand against one of the walls, and I could feel a low, mechanical rumble vibrating through the stone. A constant grinding sensation as if the entire mountain was slowly turning on city-sized gears.

<All roads lead to the *Puzzling*,> said Alina. <In the heart of the mountain lies a grand arena. Everything is built around that.>

"And where are we going now?" I asked.

<To your room, of course. The puzzler dorms are located just beneath the arena. We'll be there shortly.>

We descended a few flights of stairs before turning down a narrow pathway. At the end, a silver archway stretched across an opening that was hidden by a curtain of steam.

When I tried to walk through, something solid blocked my path. Pain flared in my skull as someone gripped my arms and shoved me back. I saw the imprint of thick fingers on my arm just before two flexers appeared out of thin air.

<Identify yourself,> the flexer's voyce demanded.

<We are Puzzler Lacey Clarke, reporting in,> said Alina.

<Where is your guardian?>

<Our guardian, Ogden Oliver, was held up by a minor complication.> I feared Alina might tell them that this "complication" was another flexer boy like themselves, but I needn't have worried. <We were sent ahead to wait for him.>

<Very well.>, He gestured me along, and my eyes burned as both flexers disappeared back into a shimmering blur. I took note, understanding full-stop that this place – despite its elaborate façade – was still a prison.

* * *

My new living arrangements were rather plain when compared to the room back in the NAN. This place was all white surfaces and rounded corners giving it the look of something that could be hosed down after use.

A sleeping cot, toilet-sink combo, and small desk were the room's only fixtures. There wasn't much space, but I still spent a couple of minutes feeling around for any muties or dead-heads that might be hiding in the corners. Beside a dimmer switch, there was a discolored panel in the wall. I tried prying it open before realizing it was one of those spring-loaded push compartments. Inside, there was a mini fridge containing a few bottles of some green liquid that looked, smelled, and tasted a lot like ground up grass. I was hungry enough to drink one, but I didn't enjoy it in the least.

Below the fridge was a narrow drawer that contained the only clothing I could find. But the items didn't make much sense to me. Padded gloves and socks. I supposed whoever ran this place would bring me the rest of my clothes when the time came. I wasn't really worried about clothes anyway. In addition to the jumpsuit I currently wore, I still had that plastic sack filled with all the clothes I'd been wearing when they took me from my apartment. I tossed the bag into the corner and kept exploring.

Eventually, there was only one part of the room I

couldn't figure out. A small alcove – more like a shallow closet – was set into the back wall. Tapping on this space revealed a hollow echo as if there was empty space behind the wall, but I could find no seams or points of entry.

I was still examining this when Alina announced that I had a visitor.

The room's only door slid open and in walked a relieved, yet disheveled Ogden Oliver.

"Oh, Lacey. Thank goodness you're safe." His fire-blond hair hung in long wisps across his forehead, and his bright eyes were now clouded with unease. Still, I was taken completely off guard when he rushed into the room and captured me in an urgent embrace.

My whole body seemed to relax – to *melt* into his arms. I still had loads of questions and an uneasy mix of emotions boiling in my core, but in that moment – with Odgen's arms wrapped around my back – his fingertips brushing against the nape of my neck – I let it all go. In that moment, it was enough to be held. It almost felt like I was in a bubble – someplace separate from all the dangers this new world contained.

The bonfire smell of him filled my senses as I pressed against his chest. I wanted more than anything for this moment of respite to stretch on and on. I always believed that if you held on to a moment long enough, you could pull it into yourself and make it a part of who you are. And that's what I hoped to do now. The bubble of calm I felt within Ogden's arms, I couldn't explain it, but I wanted it to last. I wanted to store this moment away so, later, I could pull it out and wear it like a suit of armor.

He ran his fingers through my hair before pulling away. He gazed into my eyes, his own glossed over as if he were on the verge of tears.

"What's the matter?" I asked.

He whispered the deactivation command, and I felt Alina slip out of my head. It was not unlike the moment after your ears pop – like a shift in clarity.

"We need to talk in private," he said. "I spoke with that flexer boy."

"Vitus."

He nodded, then went on. "He's hellbent on finding you. He's *convinced* you've found a way to shut off your voyce."

Folding my arms, I squinted at him.

Ogden seemed not to notice. "There's something about this flexer. Normally, I'd be able to buy him off, but this one…his obsession with you…for some reason it's personal."

"Probably because I kicked him in the face," I said. "I don't think he liked that."

"It's more than that," said Ogden. "Helen says –"

"Who's Helen?"

"Oh, sorry. Helen's my voyce. Anyways, Helen says that flexer's voyce is having a hard time controlling him. She says you did something to him…*broke* him somehow. It's like you set his mind on fire…and the only way to put it out is for you to speak with him."

"I don't want anything to do with him."

"Right. It's not a good idea. Whatever he's feeling isn't your responsibility. But one way or another, we'll need to deal with him. I've convinced him to leave you alone until after the *Puzzling*, but then…"

"What?" I asked. "What *then*?"

"One way or another…"

I didn't like where this conversation was going, and if anything, it seemed to be drifting further and further away from what I wanted in the first place.

"I can't do this," I said.

Ogden blinked as if I'd slapped him. "What do you mean?"

I gestured at him, the room, everything.

"*This*. I can't be in your *Puzzling*. Not while Yadi and Cadence are under someone else's control."

"I *told* you, Lacey. Once you win, you can set them free."

I was thinking about what Gideon had said – that he'd kill them himself if I won. Either win or lose, I was playing by someone else's rules. And I needed that to change. Maybe it was time I made my own rules.

"I won't participate in the *Puzzling* unless you free them *first.*"

His jaw dropped. "But Lacey…I can't."

"*Can't* or *won't*?"

"I *can't* remove two servants from circulation without drawing unwanted attention. It's too risky. Your sister's a main performer and Cadence is…"

Fighting other servants against his will. I couldn't say this. Gideon had warned me from telling Ogden about what I'd seen. But I could tell by the worried look in his eyes that Ogden knew exactly how Cadence was being used. He didn't want me to know how much danger Cadence was really in. Why keep me in the dark? Did Ogden think the truth would be too hurtful, or was he simply trying to keep me focused on the *Puzzling*? Either way, I didn't like it.

For so long, I'd idolized Ogden Oliver. But I could see now that he was just a man. And while part of me wanted nothing more than to trust him, I was beginning to understand that I had to trust myself more than others. I couldn't listen to the voices that were not my own. And in this moment, my voice – not Ogden's or even Alina's – was telling me to act, to *use* whatever leverage I had to help those I cared about…before it was too late.

"Help me free Yadi and Cadence…or I'm out."

"But the *Puzzling* starts in the morning," he pleaded. "The first day is an elimination round. One wrong answer and we're done."

"Then I guess you better figure it out quick." My voice snapped with a power I didn't feel. I wondered if Ogden could tell that I was trembling inside this thick jumpsuit. "Either my sister and Cadence are safe before tomorrow, or it's over."

Now was the moment. I knew now I'd see Ogden's true colors. Either he'd barrel over me – try to bully me into compliance – or he'd prove he really was on my side. Whichever way things went, I vowed to trust myself before I trusted anyone else.

Ogden wilted and buried his face in his hands. His

shoulders shook and I thought he was weeping until I heard the laughter. His hands curled into fists and he tore at his fire-blond hair as if he wanted to tear it out by the roots. And when he looked up, there was a not-so-subtle madness – or perhaps it was desperation – burning in his eyes.

"*Fine*," he spat. "Have it your way. I *might* be able to free them…but it's a long shot." Then, to my surprise, Ogden's entire body softened. His bright blue eyes met mine, and there was something powerful and deep in his gaze.

"I'm sorry I pulled you into this mess," he said. He shut his eyes, and breathed deep as if steeling himself for what he was about to do next.

An urge welled up inside me and before I even knew what I was doing, I stepped forward and kissed him. He flinched, and I feared I'd made a terrible mistake, but then he relaxed. His full lips pressed back against mine. That bubble returned, and for a while the world tumbled away. The warmth of his touch flowed over and through me.

After a time, we parted. We were both out of breath. The memory of his lips lingered on my own, and his eyes were ablaze with insatiable hunger.

"That was…unexpected." He smiled, and pressed his forehead against mine. "We're in this together. All the way. And I promise, I will free your sister and friend tonight."

"How?"

He shook his head slightly. "I'm not sure yet, but I'll figure it out." He moved toward the door, and I had to stop myself from reaching after him. "I promise I'll do what I can to help them. But please, Lacey, promise me one thing in return."

I nodded.

"If I'm not back before morning, promise you won't give up."

I might not have a choice, I thought, but instead of saying this, I nodded.

I couldn't tell whether or not he was convinced. Either way, he didn't argue. He activated our voyces, then stepped out into the hallway. The doors sealed me inside, and it wasn't long before I felt a flood of uncertainty drowning all my thoughts. The *Puzzling* was less than ten hours away, and I could feel it hurtling toward me like an unstoppable vactrain. In one day, my fate would be sealed. It was a long, sleepless night.

*　　*　　*

By morning, Ogden had not returned. And before I could ask where he was, Alina informed me it was time to get ready.

The *Puzzling* had arrived.

Chapter 15

Alina ordered me to undress and put on the thick gloves and socks from the wall compartment. I asked what they were for, but all she would say was, "You'll see." Then, she told me to stand in the shallow closet at the back of my room.

"Okay, Alina. What now? I feel a tad ridiculous." An understatement, to be sure. Wearing only those huge gloves and socks, I must have looked like some sort of lewd cartoon character.

<Door opening,> Alina announced.

My embarrassment turned to horror when the closet wall buckled back and began to rise slowly into the ceiling.

"I'm not dressed," I shouted.

<Don't worry, Lacey. It'll be over soon.>

I tried to cover myself as the wall opened into a narrow passageway. Directly across from me, more panels were rising up. Each one revealed another puzzler. And like me, they were all wearing barely more than their birthday suits. One boy with messy, red hair screamed as he tried to cover himself with those big, goofy gloves. In the opening next to his, a brown-haired girl blushed redder than a chili pepper. She too, covered herself with those cartoonish gloves and to her credit, she was mostly successful.

Screams and yelps of embarrassment ricocheted up and down the passageway.

<Step forward,> Alina said. I considered disobeying her until the redhead took a step back as if to flee. His entire body stiffened, and the rictus of pain on his face revealed that his voyce had taken matters into its own hands. The boy jerked like one of those old-timey animatronics and stomped into the passageway. I soon found myself in a long line of naked bodies. It was hard to tell how many of us there were. A glance one way

showed too many to count. A look the other way showed just as many more, everyone in various states of distress as they struggled to maintain some scrap of modesty.

The only puzzler I could see who seemed at ease was a boy with a long mane of golden hair. He was four bodies away, and it took a second for me to recognize him with all his clothes off, but then I remembered, and the smirk on his face took on an ominous feeling. It was the puzzler from the vactrain. *Gideon's* puzzler. What was his name? Phaeton? Yes, that was it. He'd had a dead-eyed expression the last time I'd seen him, but the look on his face now – a dark, almost feral grin was even less reassuring. A breath of cold air prickled my bare skin, and I turned away hastily.

With a jolt, the floor moved beneath our feet. A few puzzlers yelped as they bumped into each other, but they quickly regained their balance and separation. Someone wept. A boy cried for his mom and said he wanted to go home. A few others whispered to each other – asked questions – but it seemed clear nobody knew where we were going, only that the conveyor belt would take us there. We were like sides of beef passing through a meat packaging plant. The only thing missing were the hooks.

After a while, the passage narrowed even further until we had to turn sideways so our shoulders didn't brush against the walls. Despite my thundering anxiety, I took a moment to appreciate the vastness of this place. Even after all the crazy stuff I'd seen up above – the rooms upon rooms of dazzling elite entertainment – the thought of this conveyor system built just for us puzzlers was remarkable.

The belt slowed and the entire wall on one side opened up to reveal a long line of blank-eyed servants.

Dead-heads, I figured. Each held a makeup pallet and stood statue still as we rolled past. When we stopped, the dead-head in front of me (a dark-skinned woman with bleach-white hair) got to work.

<Close your eyes, and try not to move.>

It was hard not to flinch because the woman moved so

fast. Foundation, concealer, blush, liner, and shadow; it took only a few minutes. The woman's voyce and Alina seemed to be working in tandem. If she needed me to open my eyes or look a certain direction, Alina told me so.

<Turn around,> she said once the make-up was finished. I tried not to look at the other puzzlers. The make-up wasn't doing much to ease the fact we were all still buck naked. If anything, it made the situation even more absurd. Still, I noticed that none of the puzzlers near me had the same look. The blushing brown-haired girl wore pastel colors that lightened and complemented her complexion. The red-haired boy had dark lines on his cheeks and eyelids that made him look like a smoldering ember. And Phaeton…his skin was painted with glittering gold so that he looked like a living idol. And I noticed something then. All the puzzlers were absolutely stunning – all beautiful, athletic young adults – which made me think that maybe our brains weren't the only deciding factor in us being chosen.

Phaeton's face cracked into a smile when he saw me looking at him. I blinked and turned away.

I faced the opposite direction, and the woman – my stylist – went straight to work brushing and curling my hair into looping swirls. This took longer than the make-up but not by much. She finished by pinning my hair up off my shoulders.

"How do I look?" I asked, just to be saying something.

<Gorgeous,> said Alina. <Absolutely marvelous.>

Another quick glance up and down the line showed that everyone, even the boys, were getting their hair lifted up. Buns, high pony-tails, complicated braids or some other design that brought the hair up off the shoulders. It wasn't long before I found out why.

A high whistle announced the stylists were all finished. The conveyor belt kicked into gear and we were off again. As we moved, I caught a glimpse of one of the other stylists. I hadn't seen her until this moment, but the girl's blonde hair and childlike face were easy to recognize. *The Pretzel Girl.*

"Hey," I called as I passed her by. "Have you seen my sister?" The girl didn't seem to notice. Her blank-eyed stare looked ahead at nothing. Already, the wall was closing. "My sister's name is Yadira! You were with her in the show!"

And to my surprise, the girl glanced my way. There was no emotion in her eyes, only an assessment of who was speaking to her. Then in the next instant, the wall clapped shut, sealing her off.

<Stop talking,> said Alina, and I felt my jaw tighten against my will.

The conveyor belt wound its way through a low-ceilinged passage until it stopped near a wide platform. <Step off.> We were ushered forward in rows of five across the platform where steps descended into a pool of swirling, dark liquid.

<Step into the pool,> said Alina. <Let the fluid go past your shoulders. And under no circumstances will you let it reach your mouth or nose.>

"Why?" I asked.

<Because you'll die.>

So I was extra careful as I stepped into the pool. The fluid, which had the look of blue-tinged crude oil, bubbled and fizzed when it touched my skin. It was not unpleasant, and its warmth was a welcome relief on my exposed body. I dipped down into the liquid until it reached the middle of my neck, and I could feel the stuff reacting to every inch it touched.

The red-haired boy giggled beside me. I couldn't blame him. The stuff sure tickled. It was almost too much. And then it *was* too much. It felt like the fluid was trying to scratch its way through my skin.

<Don't move,> demanded Alina. <A few seconds more.>

Then something strange happened. I could feel the swirl of liquid around my body, but then the stuff…thickened. I could still move, but when I touched my arm to my side or put my knees together, it sort of…clicked like it had formed a kind of shell. Alina told me to get out and when I rose, the stuff clung to my body. It covered my shoulders, arms, and chest like a shiny wrap, like an extra layer of skin. The only thing it hadn't stuck to was the gloves. They were still as white as ever. I was still marveling at the stuff when something caught my foot. A hand pressed down on my shoulder and *pushed hard.* I stumbled back toward the pool's surface. I probably would have fallen all the way under if the brown-haired girl wasn't there to catch my arm.

"Whoopsie-daisy," said Phaeton. His golden grin loomed over us. "Watch your step."

"You tripped her," said the brown-haired girl. "I *saw* you."

Phaeton's smile vanished. He glowered at the girl. The corner of his mouth twitched in annoyance. "What do *you* know?" he said, then lashed out and shoved her. He outweighed her by at least a hundred pounds. This combined with her precarious balance on the stairs sent her sprawling back into the pool. She fell into it, not with a splash, but with a *slurp* – like the stuff had eaten her whole. I thought maybe it had until she broke back through the surface. Right away, I knew something was terribly wrong. Her face and head were now covered in the stuff. She swiped at her mouth and eyes, but the gloves she wore couldn't find any purchase.

I watched in horror as the bluish-black sludge hardened and refused to give way. She began to panic. Her arms flailed out desperately from side to side. She started hitting her head, banging her fists against her face in some desperate attempt to crack it open.

"Oh my God, Alina. What do I do?"

<Back away, Lacey. Don't let her drag you under.>

"She can't *breathe*!"

<Back away. There's nothing you can do.> The world spun as my view of the dying girl was suddenly obscured by a roiling shimmer. Alina had blocked her from my vision. <You don't want to see this.>

Not sure what else to do, I leapt into the pool and groped for the girl. I couldn't see her, but I could feel her slick body writhing through my gloves. I got a hold of something I guessed was an arm, and pulled her toward me. She continued to thrash against me, and it seemed clear she would indeed drag me under. But then I felt someone else beside me. The red-haired boy reached into the shimmer, and together, we hauled the squirming mirage out of the pool.

"Alina, let me see. We can save her!"

<No, you can't.>

"Damn you, Alina. Let. Me. *See*!"

For several seconds, I thought she wouldn't answer, but then she whispered, <Whatever. Have it your way.>

The shimmer seemed to condense into a buzzing black cloud from which the girl reappeared. She thrashed from side to side on the grated platform, and for a moment, I was so scared that I couldn't think. All I could do was watch as the girl's movements weakened – slowed down – grew limp.

The red-headed boy bent over her and tried to claw at the stuff on her face, but his gloves made his attempts useless. He tried pulling the gloves off, but the black stuff held them in place. He screamed in frustration.

Air. She needs air. She can't breathe. Through the shell, I could just make out the curve of her face. Her mouth was open, and a pulsing bubble showed just how hard she was fighting for breath. If only there was some way to pierce the shell.

I put up my hands, and my gloves snagged at something in my hair. I grasped at what had been placed there just minutes earlier and *yanked* until I had a clump of my own hair and two pins in my gloved palm.

Pushing the boy aside, I leaned over the girl's face and pointed one of the pins into where her mouth should have been. I pushed, but the pin's rubber tip wouldn't penetrate the shell. Using my teeth, I peeled off the end to show the metal point within. The girl's arms flopped listlessly, then stopped moving all together.

<It's over,> said Alina. I screamed and jabbed the pin into the girl's sealed mouth. This time, the pin punctured

the stuff. The area around her mouth split like a burst water balloon.

The girl convulsed as air poured into her lungs. Her shuddering breaths were a mix of sobs and screams that devolved into a violent coughing fit. I did my best to console her. Little bubbles formed at the corners of her eyes, and I figured her tears were stuck inside with nowhere to go.

"We have to get her out of this stuff," I said to the red-headed boy, but he was no longer paying attention. All his focus, and *rage*, was pointed toward the golden Phaeton. He raised a gloved fist but stopped short of hitting the almost-murderer. Nostrils flaring, the redhead glared at his own fist. After a few seconds, he dropped his arm and glared at Phaeton, who seemed the epitome of calm.

"My voyce says I can't hit you," said the redhead.

"Like I'd let you," said Phaeton. He tapped Redhead on the shoulder good naturedly, but then, without warning, Phaeton swung a looping right at the boy's face and knocked him clean off his feet. He collapsed beside me, and blood immediately began pouring from his nose.

Now it was my turn to confront the golden boy. I leapt to my feet but before I could get anywhere near him, Alina shouted, <Stop!> My ankles rooted to the deck as if locked by powerful magnets. I tried lifting my arms but they wouldn't work. <Are you crazy? You can't touch a wolf in anger.>

"He isn't a wolf," I said. "He's just some jackass puzzler. Like the rest of us."

"Aw, come now, Lacey," laughed Phaeton. "I thought you were smarter than that."

"What?"

"I just stopped by to make sure you remember our agreement." Phaeton's smile grew so wide that his golden makeup cracked along his jaw. "See you around." He gave a salute, then looked toward the ceiling and shouted, "Deactivate stream."

"Gideon?"

The golden boy wilted into a ball. And when he looked up again, the confusion on his face was palpable.

"Who are you?" He jerked back. "Where am I?" He touched the hardened shell covering his body. "What *is* this?"

I couldn't bring myself to help him. Whether or not Phaeton was being used, he was *still* Gideon's puzzler. It wasn't fair that I hated this confused boy, but then again, nothing was fair.

* * *

There was one final prep room – a long hall with mirrored walls from floor to ceiling. Our stylists were already waiting for us when we filed in. I tried to make eye contact with the Pretzel Girl, but she was too far down the line and entirely focused on her own puzzler to notice me.

I flinched when my stylist lifted a long razor and swiped at my wrist. The blade sliced through the hardened shell but never touched my skin. Her deft hands made sure of that. I stood stone-still as she first cut off my gloves then knelt to remove the socks. This was a relief because it allowed feeling to flow back into my hands and feet. The deck was refrigerator cold, but with the stuff – a sort of second-skin – keeping in my body heat, I welcomed the chill.

Next, the stylists pulled out a basket filled with small spray cans. The hall hissed as each of us received our own, unique color design. The scent of paint crinkled my nose. In the end, my stylist stepped away and I was finally able to see my reflection in the mirrors.

The area around my eyes was covered in shadow. My lips – which still caught me off guard to see them uniform and unmolested by old scars – had been painted dark red.

The strangest thing…my right cheek along with other parts of my body were covered in a gray, stone-like substance. Left arm, right hip, both thighs. It made it look as if I was a statue coming to life. To top it all off, a fiery orange rose bloomed from the center of my chest. Its petals glowed like molten lava while sparks glowed from its center in a spray of stars.

It was beautiful, but why a rose? I couldn't help thinking they'd somehow pulled the image from my own memory. All the times I'd helped Yadi and my mom fill that vase with pink roses. But Ogden had said voyces couldn't read minds. So how could they know?

The answer seemed obvious. They knew because Alina knew. She'd tell them anything they asked for.

I know everything about you, Gideon's comments from the train growled in my mind.

*   *   *

Once we were all primed and painted, our voyces directed us into a massive elevator. As we gathered in the center of a huge chamber, I was finally able to get a good look at the others, and I was relieved to see that the stuff from the pool had expanded and smoothed out enough to give only a vague impression of our bodies. It had a hard exterior yet was flexible enough to bend without resistance. My mind vacillated between feeling clothed or exposed.

"How am I supposed to go to the bathroom with this on?"

<You won't need to. You drank the solution from your room. In addition to providing nourishment, it will freeze your insides until your puzzler skin can be removed.>

"Oh, goodie," I said.

The last to board the elevator were the brown-haired girl and redhead. They shuffled into place beside me. Redhead had bloody gauze shoved up his nose to staunch the bleeding while the girl sniffed back tears beside him. The stuff had been removed from her head, but of all of us, she was the only one who didn't look finished. Her hair was dripping wet and her "skin" was void of any painted design. She wiped at her nose.

"Hey," I said. "You okay?" It was such a stupid question, but I wasn't really interested in an answer. All that mattered was that this girl knew that I was looking out for her.

Her eyes widened, then she threw her arms around me.

"Thank you," she said. "Aaron told me what you did."

I glanced at the redhead – Aaron – who nodded back my way.

"My name's Lacey," I said.

"Vaness," she said before pushing away. "We have to look out for each other. No one else will."

That's the truth. I squinted at Phaeton standing off to the side. He had that confused, worried look on his face like he didn't have a clue about what was going on.

<One minute to entry,> Alina announced. All the others perked up around me as if hearing the same thing. Then a countdown clock appeared in my vision – just like the one on the vactrain. Overhead, a series of bolts blew, and for the first time, I could hear music and loud cheers.

The elevator doors were sliding shut. I noticed with some alarm, that the stylists were gathering near the closing doors. At the forefront was the Pretzel Girl. She blinked rapidly as if trying to get something out of her eyes. At the same time, she held up her hands, and I could see words etched in eyeliner on her palms.

NOT SAFE, read one. *TAKEN*, said the other. I remembered the question I'd yelled at her on the conveyor belt. I'd wanted to know if she'd seen my sister. Here now was the answer. NOT SAFE. TAKEN.

Either this girl had figured out a way to regain control over her body, which was unlikely, or her voyce was sending the message. Or worse yet, perhaps it was Gideon speaking *through* her, giving me a final warning to do what he wanted. Could he do that? He'd done it with Phaeton. I suspected he could do it with others as well. There was no way to be certain. But if he *was* speaking through this girl, I'd have no way of knowing if he was telling the truth. There were too many unknowns, and I felt trapped by the uncertainty.

What should I do? I prayed for an answer I knew would never come.

My blood chilled. The doors sealed with a thunderous boom. An instant later, the ceiling above cracked down the middle. It slid open as we rose into a blinding coliseum.

For some of us, I knew, this was the end.

Chapter 16

One hundred and twenty-eight puzzlers paraded around a wide, circular field. At least, that's what Alina told me. The blinding lights and cacophonous jeers were a bit disorienting. Sixty-four puzzlers had come up through the floor with me. The others streamed in through a side tunnel. Each puzzler was a wash of colorful, artistic designs as random as they were dazzling. One blue-haired girl was bedecked in sparkling rhinestones, while the boy beside her wore fuzz and big, floppy ears like a Labrador.

A sweep of the stands allowed Alina to count the spectators as well. Over twenty thousand cellies, wolves, and what I now knew to be prox cheered within the massive cavern. This didn't include the countless servants – or slaves – rushing through the crowds. Rows and rows of seats ascended toward the arched, stone ceiling. The fact we were all inside a mountain was a fact I tried to ignore. Less suffocating that way. With all the spectators stomping their feet and shaking the walls – what would it take for the whole place to collapse? To bury us all inside a billion years of rock?

The puzzlers were separated into groups of eight and ordered to take seats around the edges of the field. I was relieved to have Vaness and Aaron beside me, but Phaeton was there too. It didn't matter that I could see sweat poking through his golden complexion. He was my competitor. They all were. People from the crowd screamed obscenities and cackled like wild animals.

All the while, I scanned the tiers for any sign of Ogden.

<He isn't here,> said Alina, guessing what I was after.

"Why? Where is he?"

<I don't know. His voyce is…unavailable.> A moment later, she said, <Someone else is hailing you.> I felt something tug at my eyes, guiding my attention up toward an enclosed viewing room. Even at this distance, I

could feel Gideon Oliver's eyes on me. <He wishes you good luck. And hopes you'll remember your deal.>

Before I could say anything else, the lights dimmed, and the crowd hushed. From the center of the field, a white light sparked into existence. The light crackled like downed powerlines. I could feel the heat and charge of electricity pass through my overskin. It was like a lightning bolt caught in a trap. Then it grew into something larger. The light popped and fritzed as something took shape within the chaos. A giant head emerged. Outlined in phosphorescent fire, a woman's face glowed white. A burst of sparks blinded everyone in the chamber, and when my eyes adjusted, I could see the face taking on substance. The gaps between lightning filled with flesh and color, dark skin and silver hair.

The woman was a fiery apparition. She gazed down at the puzzlers with lifelike, impossible horror.

"Welcome." Her voice rushed through the chasm like gale force winds, whipping my hair about my face. She blinked, and the sound was like slamming doors. She smiled, teeth the size of houses. It took a bit to see past the horror of her size to discover that she was a beautiful woman. If I were to guess I'd say she was in her mid-thirties, with powder-smooth skin and strong classical features. It was the face of a woman who could just as easily lead a nation as rip out a man's heart with her teeth. The unnerving thing were her eyes. Black galaxies. Light curved around them as if tiny black holes lived inside her gaze. Worse than that, however, was the way they were aimed directly at me. Of all the people in here, why was she looking only at me?

<Isn't she beautiful?> asked Alina. <We are honored to be in her presence.>

"Who is she?"

<Lady Pathe. The Empress Mother. She's been with us since the very beginning. She is the mind of the *Panopticon*.>

"The what?"

Before Alina could answer, however, Lady Pathe spoke.

"Welcome to our grand tournament." Her voice rumbled. She ground through each syllable as if carving it from stone. "In the time before our voyces came, the world was cloaked in darkness. Every person was an island unto themselves. The world bickered for scraps while marching toward their own extinction. But then, the voyces gave us the wisdom to save ourselves. And since the forming of our great republic, we have required the cleverest among us to carry the torch. To guard and watch over us. It is through their minds that our wisdom lives on."

The air shifted with the woman's words. I wondered if any of this was real. At the same time, I understood that it didn't really matter. For everyone watching, it was real enough.

Her gaze turned toward the elites up in the stands.

"All of you have come to witness a historic and necessary event. From this competition, one champion will descend into the *Panopticon*."

A murmur rippled through the coliseum.

"As reward, the person who serves as guardian for our champion will be given a place amongst the prox. Everlasting life."

Her star-filled eyes snapped back to me. "Now, listen up, puzzlers. The rules for this first round are simple. In groups of four, you will each be given a riddle. If none in your group can give the correct answer, a second riddle will be asked in its place. But if one fails while the others succeed, the winners will advance while the loser will perish…their journey at an end." The crowd roared with amusement, and it took a while for the noise to subside. "And let me remind everyone here in attendance. Any *cheating* will result in disqualification and immediate execution." This shut them up. "Our future depends on worthy champions, not imposters. No one will be allowed to help you. Once a riddle is asked, your voyces will not interfere. Any words you mutter or any actions you take could have dire consequences. If you get disqualified by stepping off your platform, you'll have no one to blame but yourself." She paused to let that sink in – that we were on our own. "You puzzlers have a chance at greatness. All you must do is reach out, use your wits, and *take it*." She looked toward the high ceiling. "Reason to survive. Perish the rest." This last bit sounded like a prayer, and sure enough, everyone in the stands repeated her words.

"*Long live the Panopticon!* Let the *Puzzling…BEGIN!*" With a deafening explosion, Lady Pathe burst into a million scattered sparks.

* * *

The first group of puzzlers were called. Three girls and one boy hurried toward the center of the field where four small, silver platforms waited for them. Each flashed green once the puzzlers stepped into place.

For a full minute, nothing seemed to happen. But then a low *hiss* sounded from across the field. Several plumes of steam rose from pipes along the edge of the arena until a swirling shroud covered all the exits.

The ground shook as if something *huge* had struck the mountain. The curtain of steam puffed in and out like a giant's breath. And then the steam bulged and a woman's face pushed its way into the cavern. At first, I thought Lady Pathe – or at least her likeness had returned – but then I realized this was not the same woman. While Lady Pathe's skin was smooth as powder, this one's cheeks and forehead were covered in reptilian scales. Her brow was too sharp. Her nose, too much like a beak. When she stepped through the steam, the sight of the rest of her made me want to scream.

Standing thirty feet tall, the creature's female face sat atop the sinewed body of a lioness. Her tail flicked like whip cracks, and huge leathery wings battered the air. I'd seen her image before, of course. A poster of this creature had been pinned to the wall in my Logic teacher's classroom. I'd always assumed she was just a story. But here she was in the flesh…the Sphinx from legend, come to ask her riddles.

She knelt before the four puzzlers and purred – the sound rumbled like an earthquake. Then, eyes blazing with blue fire, she asked her first riddle:

"When I am up, my teeth clamp tight. When I am down, my teeth don't bite. What am I, Puzzlers? Give me your answers, or give me your life."

All noise in the chasm seemed to have been shut off. All I could hear besides my own heartbeat was the steady intake and expulsion of breath coming from the Sphinx. It was not unlike the surge and retreat of ocean waves. She watched the puzzlers with unbreaking focus. All the while, her claws flexed in and out of her car-sized paws.

After what seemed a small eternity, one of the puzzlers – a girl painted with shooting stars – squeaked, "I wish to answer."

The Sphinx licked her lips. "I'm listening."

"A zipper," said the puzzler.

The Sphinx let out a low hiss before giving a nod. Then, she gazed at the others. I didn't understand this at first. Wouldn't they all know the answer now? But then I realized they must all be shielded off from each other. It didn't matter that someone had just said the answer out loud. The Sphinx was all the puzzlers could see and hear in this moment. Nothing else.

A second puzzler – this time the boy – also gave the correct answer, followed quickly by a third. By now, it was pretty clear that the last puzzler was struggling. It was the girl with all the rhinestones. Her entire body flashed with light as she squirmed beneath the Sphinx's gaze. She began looking around the chasm as if expecting someone to shout out an answer. When no one did, she edged toward the end of her platform.

"Step off and you forfeit," growled the Sphinx. "Give us your answer."

"I-I don't know. *Please.* I need more time."

In response, the Sphinx extended her claws and tore at the ground on either side of the platform. Long tufts of artificial grass billowed up from the turf. She opened her mouth to reveal rows of jagged spears, each slick with saliva.

The rhinestoned puzzler put up her hands. "Wait," she screamed. "The answer…it's…it's a *lion*."

The Sphinx smiled with what looked to be genuine pleasure. Then, she shook her head and barked a single syllable. "*No.*"

The puzzler leapt from the platform and broke into a sprint. She got maybe ten feet before the Sphinx was on her. With one massive paw, the Sphinx pinned the girl to the ground. Hundreds of rhinestones popped off the girl's overskin as claws burrowed into her back. She screamed but could do nothing as the Sphinx leaned down, opened her mouth wide and *chomped.*

A shimmer came up at the last second, preventing me from seeing the worst of it. But I could still hear the crowd's insane cheers, and the *crunch* and *slurp* as the Sphinx fed. When the shimmer cleared, the Sphinx was licking the last bit of blood up from the turf. Then, she turned toward the remaining three puzzlers – who were still standing on their platforms, shivering with shock – and said, "Congratulations, Puzzlers. You three advance to the next round."

The remaining three slunk back to their seats just as four more puzzlers were called and a similar scene unfolded. This time, however, the losing puzzler had sense enough not to run. A wide-eyed behemoth of a boy cowered on his platform until the Sphinx unhinged her jaw and devoured him in a single bite.

This can't be real, I kept telling myself. *It's gotta be augmented reality.* But I wasn't sure. It was one thing to question something so implausible, but it was quite another to risk your life on it.

Ogden had shown me how realistic augmentation could be. The party on his island estate had seemed so thick with sensation – so *genuine*. I could still remember the smells of the roasting meat, the thump of music, and push of humidity against my skin. Now, this illusion – this *Sphinx* – was just another – albeit convincing – false reality. Right?

But as I watched her tear apart and eat a third, then fourth victim…my confidence faltered.

I could say the deactivation phrase. Turn off my voyce to see if this was real or not. But could I risk someone seeing me do it? Ogden had warned that if anyone knew I could turn off my voyce on command, they'd kill me on the spot.

I glanced around to see if anyone was paying attention to me, and sure enough, Phaeton was leaning forward in his chair. His golden face inches from my own.

"Enjoying the show?" he asked cheerfully.

Beside him, Vaness was ghost white. I'd never met anyone whose skin fluctuated as much as hers. She looked like she was gonna be sick, so I put my hand on her knee and said, "Don't worry. It isn't real. Just an illusion."

"*What*?" This didn't seem to calm her. "Why would you say that? I can bloody see that it is most *definitely* real."

"Yeah," snarled Phaeton. His eyes squinted with suspicion. "What makes you say it isn't?"

"Um…" I froze. Ogden had shown me how convincing augmented reality could be, but I couldn't say that in front of Phaeton. I needed to be more careful. "You ever see a Sphinx before?" I asked. "Surely, it's gotta be some sort of trick." I wanted to convince myself as much as the others. Either way, my claim was about to be tested because the Sphinx was calling forth its next challengers. A spotlight bore down on our group. One puzzler I hadn't met yet was called, then Aaron, then Phaeton, then me. The Sphinx beckoned us all toward the waiting platforms, which I understood now were not platforms at all. They were serving plates. One of us would be this monster's next meal.

* * *

The Sphinx towered over us. This close, I could see the individual scales of her pebbled skin. The shine of blood on her lips. And the hellish fire burning in her eyes. What I didn't see was any sign that it was fake. I kept expecting to see some glimmer – some hitch in the façade – to indicate it was an illusion. But there was nothing discernible.

"With others like me, I hold at bay. With others my opposite, I can't keep away. What am I, Puzzlers? Give me your answers, or give me your life."

My mind immediately got to work deciphering the clues. The language in riddles could be purposely misleading, so one had to think literally. The first sentence: "With others like me, I hold at bay." So, whatever it was, it was something that didn't like to be near itself…or another version of itself. Second sentence: "With others my opposite, I can't keep away." So, it liked to be near things that were different.

No, not just different, my mind protested. *Opposite. Whatever it is, it is drawn to something that is its exact opposite. Which means…* I could only think of one answer. And once I had it, it seemed obvious. I could answer. *Survive*. I could advance to the next round.

But I hadn't forgotten my conversation with Gideon. We'd made a deal. He'd promised to save Yadi and Cadence – or *kill* them if I didn't lose. I didn't trust him, but I believed he'd do it. Hadn't he shown me that it was within his power?

But what about Ogden? He'd promised me, too. He also said he'd save Yadi and Cadence – but only if I won. I trusted *him*, but I wasn't sure he could pull off the things he promised. He'd told me himself that cellies held no real power. So, this was my dilemma. Two brothers. Gideon a wolf whom I distrusted, but believed. And Ogden, who I trusted but *didn't* believe. Which brother could help me? I knew who I wanted to align with, but I'd learned a long time ago that getting what you wanted was sort of a rare thing.

And besides, I already knew Yadi was in danger. Pretzel Girl had written it on her hands. *NOT SAFE. TAKEN*. If it wasn't a lie, Gideon probably had her stashed in some holding cell – insurance, to make sure I did what he wanted.

All these thoughts whirled through my mind in a flash. Then the puzzlers began to answer. First Aaron, then the unknown puzzler – a girl dressed in silver, then finally Phaeton. Although I couldn't hear his words, I could still make out the golden outline of his body through the shimmer. I was the last to answer. It was now or never.

"Well," growled the Sphinx. "Do you have an answer, little puzzler?"

Magnet, I wanted to scream. It was the right answer after all. But I wasn't playing for myself. This game had rules only I could see. The only way to win…was to lose.

"I have an answer," I said, lifting my head up to meet the Sphinx's blue-flamed gaze.

"I'm listening."

Magnet! Say magnet! my mind screamed. But I didn't listen.

"It's a no-win situation," I said aloud. "An impasse."

The Sphinx blinked in surprise, but quickly recovered. Her blood-red lips curled into a smile.

"No," she barked.

I tried not to move as the Sphinx loomed over me.

<Hold still,> Alina cried. <It'll make this easier.>

The Sphinx's jaw cracked as she exposed serrated teeth. Bits of flesh and shattered bone clung to the gaps between these ivory spears. I noticed with some alarm, that a few teeth still glittered with the rhinestones of the first devoured puzzler.

The Sphinx's breath poured over me – hot and stinking of decay.

If this was an illusion, it was far beyond anything I could have ever feared possible.

Real or not, this was the end.

The Sphinx snapped forward. And that's when I saw it. A stutter in her movement, like those old timey movies that were missing a few frames. I grasped at the thought, holding onto it like a life raft. Then her teeth raked my sides. Mouth wide, she descended and I plunged upward into her reeking gullet. Pain detonated in my ankles as the thing's maw clamped shut. Hundreds of spears poked into my sides, burrowed through the overskin, and punctured flesh.

The hope this was all an illusion, flickered, then died.

Chapter 17

Well, I wasn't dead, which was a bit of a surprise.

One second, the Sphinx had me in her jaws. But when she lifted me up – threw her head back to guzzle down every last bit of me – something…*split.* For a moment, there were two of me. One Lacey was experiencing a most unpleasant death on account of the Sphinx, while another – the *real* one I guessed – watched in horror from the platform.

The crowd cheered as the Sphinx wolfed down this illusion of me.

As you can imagine, auditor, watching yourself get eaten by a monster is a rather troubling thing to witness. If you can, I suggest you avoid it.

I shivered and looked down at myself to confirm that I was still *truly* alive. What I saw was another surprise. My body felt real enough, but the color was all wrong. My entire body was milky white and transparent in places – sort of like frosted glass.

<No one else can see you,> said Alina. <Most elites know it's all for show, but they like to pretend. One of their favorite things is pretending the impossible.>

I blinked at this only because it was out of character for Alina to ever say anything negative about the elites.

<I was rooting for you, Lacey. Truly, I was. I really thought you could've won this thing. It almost feels like you lost on purpose.>

She was right, of course. I swallowed, thinking of Gideon's promise. I upheld my part. Would he uphold his?

Above me, the Sphinx licked her claws. *The* fake *Sphinx*, I reminded myself. Augmented reality.

Alina's voyce sighed. <Well, at least you gave everyone a good show before the end.>

"Before the end of what?"

In answer, the platform beneath my feet irised open and

like an apple breaking through the bottom of a wet paper sack, I fell out of the coliseum.

* * *

The tube curved into a slide lasting only a few seconds before it opened up into a brightly lit room. I slid to a stop, looking up at the ceiling and a yellow poster that read:

☹YOU LOST!☹

Frowny face emojis flanked both sides of the message.

I had barely enough time to catch my breath before several hands clasped my arms and lifted me out of the tube. I saw the purple coats with red stripes on their sleeves and knew the flexers had me now. It was a thought even more terrifying than the Sphinx. The Sphinx was a nightmare, sure, but unlike these flexers, *nightmares* went away when you woke up.

"Fresh fish," called one of the flexers.

"Keep it moving," said another.

Dizzy and disoriented, I didn't fight as the flexers tied my wrists and plopped me down into a chair beside four other puzzlers – those who'd lost before me. Still dressed in their decorative overskins, they were all here – even the rhinestoned girl. Hands trembling and eyes filled with tears, she was alive. Dejected and in shock, sure, but still alive.

"Did the Sphinx eat you, too?" asked the behemoth of a boy who'd lost second.

"Do I look eaten?" I asked.

He actually squinted as if trying to find the bite marks.

"No, you don't…and neither do I…but *boy howdy*, it sure felt real."

The third loser, a freckled girl with leafy vines painted around her arms and legs, asked, "You figure we're dead?"

"Not dead," I said, then nodded toward the flexers, "but pretty close."

<Silence.> The flexer's voyce boomed in my mind.

A few minutes later, a bell sounded and another puzzler slid down the chute. A scrawny boy with a mop of brown curls was hauled from the tube. I watched with some amusement as the boy got sick and projectile vomited all over two of the flexers tying his restraints.

My amusement ended when they beat the boy unconscious, then threw him into the seat next to mine.

"Okay, that's six," said one of the flexers. "Let's move 'em out and get ready for the next bunch."

Alina told me to stand and allow one of the flexers to loop a braided rope through my wrist restraints, tying us all in a line. Drool and blood spilled from the scrawny boy's mouth as he stood. I suspected his voyce had taken command over his body. There was no way he could have walked on his own.

One of the flexers grabbed the rope and marched out into a long corridor lined with pipes and electrical wiring. I wondered where they were taking us, but figured it didn't really matter. I'd traded my life for Yadi and Cadence. I only hoped that I'd get some sign that it had actually worked – that Gideon would uphold his end of the bargain.

It was only now that I realized how stupid this was. A *wolf*, help *me*?

My only consolation was that things couldn't get much worse.

But I was wrong there also.

"Hold up," said a horrifying, familiar voice.

Vitus strode toward us. As he neared, he tugged at something on his belt, and unsheathed a long, black knife.

"What's up, Vitus?" said the flexer leading the line. "I gotta get these puzzlers to the auction cells before the next batch arrives."

"I know, I know." He tugged at my wrists and cut the rope between them. "But I have to borrow this one. She owes me something."

The other flexer glared for a second, but then his eyes

widened and a smile cracked his otherwise unpleasant face. He gave me an approving glance.

"*Aha*. Is *this* the one who gave you that black eye? I heard about her."

Vitus didn't respond, but his grip tightened on my wrist.

Finally, the other flexer shrugged, and said, "Don't keep her too long, Vitus. We got a schedule to keep and the prox will notice if one of 'em goes missing."

"Don't you worry about this girl. I'll make sure she gets to where she's going."

Vitus pulled me back against the wall, and we stood in silence as the rest of the puzzlers trudged down the corridor.

Once they were out of sight, Vitus tugged my arm and said, "This way, Lacey." Then, in a horrible impression of Ricky Ricardo, he said, "You've got some 'splaining to do."

* * *

Vitus kicked his way into a janitor's closet. Mops, brooms, and a score of various tools hung from the wall.

"Out," he shouted, and a mutie appeared from a shimmer tucked into the wall. The black-eyed woman hurried past us and fled down the corridor. Once she was gone, Vitus stepped into the closet and yanked me in behind him.

"Sit," he said, gesturing toward a grease-stained workbench between two folding chairs. I sat, rubbing blood back into my hands as Vitus took a seat across from me.

His jack-o-lantern grin was gone, and his knotted brow bunched in concentration. For a long time, he didn't say anything. Somewhere in the room, a clock scratched out seconds of time.

Finally, Vitus cleared his throat and said, "You're a hard person to track down. I almost had you at the train station, but that pretty-boy cellie of yours got in my way.

Normally, I wouldn't take orders from someone like him, but an adjudicator was standing watch. When Oliver reported that I was trying to interfere with the *Puzzling*, the adjudicator made me promise not to bother you until after the tournament." He laughed. It was a harsh sound, like throwing a bunch of rocks into a metal bucket. "I don't give a damn about the *Puzzling*. All I care about…is you."

"Why? What do you want with me?"

"I ain't stupid, Lacey. I *know* you can turn off your voyce. In front of your apartment…that day we took your sister and your friend…I reached for you also. Only I couldn't touch you. It was like you weren't even there."

"But I *was* there. Just like I'm here now. So, what if you couldn't touch me? It's not my fault you suck at your job."

I flinched as he slapped the workbench.

"I don't miss," he growled. "I've *never* missed. So, you need to tell me. How did you do it? How did you turn off your voyce? You have to tell me…*please*."

This last word struck me like a slap in the face. Not because it was harsh, but because it wasn't. It was so full of…*pain*. I looked up…and was alarmed at the tears gathering in the flexer's eyes. Vitus, whose entire existence seemed to be a celebration of cruelty and strength, was fighting back tears.

"Please tell me, Lacey. I *need* to know." He let out a groan that was filled with so much strain and…*anguish*. It was the sound of someone who'd given all they had to keep from breaking. It was the *creak* of a damaged building on the verge of collapse.

He put his head down, and I was horrified to see his broad shoulders quake with sobs.

"I love the republic," he said through the tears. "There's nothing I won't do to protect it. But the things my voyce commands of me. The people I've hurt…I need to know if there's another way. Your voyce keeps telling mine that you don't know, but I'm not asking *her*. I'm asking *you*. How do you turn off your voyce?"

I was so stunned, that I almost told him. I'd never seen a flexer display anything like this. *Could it be an act?* I didn't think so. Flexers weren't known for their acting abilities. And even if it wasn't an act, I couldn't forget that both my voyce and his were listening. Vitus was only having this breakdown because his voyce allowed him to. Which meant…his voyce wanted to see what I'd say. Same with Alina. She'd been silent this whole time. If she wasn't suspicious already, she certainly was now.

"I'm sorry," I said. "I can't help you."

Vitus lifted a trembling hand and seized my wrist. His eyes were red like open sores. He held my wrist against the table. With his other hand, he grabbed my ring finger and began to *press* it back toward my arm.

The pain flared as the bones bent toward the breaking point. I tried to pull my hand away, but his grip was like an iron trap.

<Tell us what we want to know,> said Vitus' soft-spoken voyce, Darion. <It won't take much. Just a little more pressure and…*snap.*>

The pain was like fire in my knuckles.

I reached for the wall. I wanted to get some leverage, but my free hand closed around something cold and sharp. A screwdriver. I twisted it in my fingers and drove it up into Vitus' face.

It froze halfway there – stopped by the voyce in my head.

<That's enough,> cried Darion and Alina in sync.

The jack-o-lantern grin twitched back onto Vitus' face. He let go of my hand so he could make a fist. My free hand – the one holding the screwdriver turned inward. It inched toward my throat until the point pressed against the soft tissue between my collar bones. Vitus reached over the table, placed one hand around the back of my neck, and the other hand on the base of the screwdriver.

<A little push,> said Darion. <That's all it would take.>

If I didn't tell him, he'd kill me. If I did, he'd probably do it anyways.

To hell with it then.

"*Habere non Haberi,*" I whispered. The pressure vanished as Alina's control slipped away. Vitus sat back in surprise. I used this to my advantage and lunged forward. This time, there was no voyce to stop me, and the screwdriver tore into his eye – the same one I'd kicked earlier.

He bellowed with pain and fell backward out of his chair. I wasted no time and bolted for the door. I almost made it, but then he lashed out and got a hold of my bare ankle.

"I knew you could do it," he growled. He held a hand over his eye, but despite the blood seeping through his fingers, there was triumph in his voice. "I *knew* it."

I stabbed down with the screwdriver, catching him in the shoulder. He cried out and let go.

In the corridor, I struggled to plot a course. I had no idea what to do or where to go.

"Lacey!"

I spun and blinked in utter astonishment at the man sprinting my way. Ogden's blazing, yellow suit hung in disarray, and his fire-blond hair was a hot mess.

"Lacey," cried Ogden. "Are you okay?"

"What are you doing here?" I asked.

"Trying to find you." He gasped for breath. "Helen told me – you got – got eliminated. She said that flexer boy – he kidnapped you."

Vitus moaned from inside the janitor's closet.

"Holy hell." Ogden blinked at the blood-tipped screwdriver in my hand. "What did you do to him?"

"I had to tell him," I said.

"Tell him what?"

I explained about the deactivation phrase. There was an apology in my voice that I didn't feel. If Ogden had only been here. If he hadn't been *gods knew where* when I'd needed him, maybe then I wouldn't have decided to lose the *Puzzling*.

"Okay," Ogden said. Eyes wide, he turned slowly toward the closet door and the moaning flexer within. "Okay, we can fix this. Wait here. I'll only be a moment."

Before I could stop him, Ogden slipped into the janitor's closet.

There were a few angry shouts followed by lower, hushed argument.

Ogden emerged a couple of minutes later. His face was pale as if he'd just survived a car crash. Vitus' moans had ceased.

"What did *you* do to him?"

Ogden smiled, but it looked weak and tired. "I gave him a little bit of chaos." He must have seen the questions in my mind because he hurried on. "Like I told you, the deactivation phrase isn't the only console command my parents taught me. There are other phrases that do all sorts of things to mess with your head." He jerked a thumb toward the janitor closet. "That flexer in there's going to have a voyce that's so confused and garbled, that he'll be pretty much on his own for the next week or so. When his voyce finally stabilizes, it won't remember anything that's happened."

"Okay, but what about *him*? His voyce might not remember, but Vitus knows what I can do."

"True," said Ogden, thoughtfully. "I'd suggest we kill him, but killing a flexer…especially here with so many others around…would be suicide."

"How come?"

"They're like bees. Kill a bee too close to the hive, and it releases a pheromone that drives all the others into a frenzy. Killing a flexer's sure to bring down a whole lot of hurt right on top of us."

"Okay, then what *do* we do?"

"I explained to…*Vitus*…that our agreement is still in effect." He shrugged. "It's not enough, I know. But it'll buy us some time at least. He's promised not to bother you until after you've been eliminated from the tournament."

"But I'm *already* out. I didn't say the answer the Sphinx wanted. I'm out."

"See, that's the thing, Lacey. While you were down here, something big happened up in the coliseum." He paused. "One of the puzzlers in your group was caught cheating. As per the rules, they've been disqualified."

I couldn't speak. The thought of going back into that coliseum to face the Sphinx yet again – it was a nightmare.

Ogden, on the other hand, didn't see it that way.

"That's right, Lacey. You're back in the *Puzzling*."

"I'm back in? But that's..." I felt my head spin. "I don't understand."

"One of the adjudicators stopped the whole thing and made an announcement. They said they'd discovered a signal. Someone was caught accessing a puzzler's voyce – treating them like a husk they could jump in and out of."

I remembered Phaeton. The golden boy who'd pushed Vaness into the black pool – the looks of confusion on his face as Gideon slipped in and out of his mind.

"So they caught him? Phaeton and Gideon?"

Ogden jerked in surprise.

"Oh no, not him. I wouldn't put it past him. But no, it wasn't Gideon."

I felt sick. "Then who?"

"That red-headed kid. Aaron."

I couldn't breathe. *Aaron?* The kid who'd helped me rescue Vaness. Aaron, who'd stood up to Gideon and gotten a broken nose to show for it.

Ogden's tone was grim. "He and his guardian have already been executed. For real, this time. Not that nonsense with the Sphinx they make all the losing puzzlers go through."

I couldn't speak. Aaron was someone I knew. If only for a moment, I'd *known* him. He hadn't deserved to die. In addition, something was nagging at me. Hadn't I seen Gideon use Phaeton as a husk?

I explained this to Ogden, but he didn't seem all that surprised.

"That sounds like something Gideon would do. He doesn't like to play fair." His face twisted in concentration. "Hmm...I suppose it *is* possible..."

"What is?"

"Gideon could have been the one cheating. He's smart enough and knows enough about voyces. He could have made it look like the signal was coming from someone else. Uh, now that I think of it…"

"What? Spit it out."

"Did he touch you?"

"Who? Gideon? No, I…*wait*." I was about to tell him about the vactrain, how Gideon had gripped my knee as we accelerated, but then I remembered the scuffle near the skinning pool. "When we were getting ready, his puzzler Phaeton picked a fight with us."

Ogden gestured for me to turn around, and after a few seconds of inspection, he said, "Well, I'll be damned." He scratched at something embedded in the shoulder of my overskin. It was the spot where Phaeton had touched when he had tried to shove me into the pool. Ogden dug something out of the overskin and held it up once it was loose – a small metallic disc no larger than a thumbnail.

"Gideon must have put this on you before your overskin was fully hardened. You saying the wrong answer was probably a good thing. It might even have saved both our lives."

"I don't understand."

"If Gideon's head hopping like you say, he won't be able to hide the signal, but this will allow him to disguise it." Ogden tossed the small disc aside. "That's a signal extender. Gideon probably set it up so that any transmission *he* sent would look like it was coming from either you or Aaron."

Ogden crunched the small disc beneath the heel of his shoe. "Chances are, if you'd said the right answer, Gideon could've made it look like *you* were the one to blame. Then…" Ogden's brow furrowed in anger. "Then the prox would have executed you and me instead. Oh, that *does* sound like him."

We walked a bit in silence. My own anger boiling over. Wasn't it enough that these elites were born with every possible advantage? Did they really have to cheat on top of that?

And wasn't Ogden cheating as well? With his console commands that could shut off and confuse voyces...what would happen if that became known?

Suddenly, it was all too much. The events of the last hour came crashing down. I needed to be alone with my own thoughts. *Mine*, and no one else's.

"Take me to my room," I said. "I'm tired of your lies."

Now it was Ogden's turn to look surprised.

"You haven't been telling me everything," I said. "I *know* Gideon is your *brother*." I made the last bit sound like a dirty word. "For all I know, you two are working together and only messing with me. The cellie and the wolf playing with their new chew toy."

"No, Lacey. I promise, it isn't like that."

"I lost on purpose," I confessed.

"What? But why?"

"I can't survive on empty promises," I said. "Gideon, your *brother*, made me an offer, and I took it. But *stupid* me. Turns out you're both liars."

"Okay, that hurts, but you're right. I haven't told you everything. Some things are dangerous to know. That said, don't you want to know where I've *been*? Why I wasn't in the coliseum when you lost."

I glared at him. I wasn't really in the mood to hear some made-up excuse. The truth was that I was on my own. I should have known that from the start, only now I saw things for what they were.

"I'll show you," he said, but he didn't elaborate. Instead, he led the way through the labyrinthine corridors until we were back in the puzzler dorms.

I reached for the doors, but stopped when he put his hand on my shoulder.

"I'm sorry about everything," he said. "I know I keep saying that. I only hope this will show you that I *mean* it."

He didn't say what 'this' was. Instead, he turned away and headed back the way we'd come.

Whatever, I thought, looking after him. And despite everything he'd put me through, part of me ached to see him walk away. I was still watching when the doors to my room opened.

I didn't see them at first.

"Lacey?" said a woman's voice. I turned toward the sound and…my brain jammed.

No. Not now. I can't take any more torment. I can't handle any more augmented reality. Why are they so cruel?

But Alina was still deactivated. Which meant…this was real.

Ogden had done it.

They were here. Yadira and Cadence, bruised and exhausted, they were both in my room.

Chapter 18

"What happened to your face? And what the heck are you wearing?" These weren't the first questions I thought I'd hear from Yadira, but then again, I hadn't expected to hear from her at all. I was still in shock she was here. I kept touching her – kept peering into her gray eyes in search of some sort of hitch in reality. I couldn't find any.

She poked me in return which made me laugh. Despite the hard shell, the overskin's spongy interior tickled when she touched it.

Once we were both convinced, she threw her arms around me. Even through the overskin, I could feel how much she'd changed since the last time I'd been this close to her – the night we'd received my father's ashes and she'd cried herself to sleep beside me.

Her body had *hardened* since then. She'd always been athletic – years of dancing had done that – but now, with most of her soft angles stripped away, she'd become a coiled spring. And the change wasn't just physical. There was something in her gray eyes I didn't recognize, or hadn't noticed before. A ferocity.

I came to understand this a little as she recounted her time since she'd been taken.

"I never stopped fighting for control," she said. "No one ever told me that's what it was like being a dead-head. I could see everything going on, but I was helpless. It was like riding on a roller coaster. I was stuck in the car as my body raced along the tracks. It was awful, but I didn't stop fighting. I kept thinking their hold would break eventually."

I imagined how she must have looked to the elites watching her perform. Whenever she dove from the coils into the cave pool, did they see anything beyond a stunning aerialist? Did they see any hint of the battle raging inside her mind? I suspected that even if they had, they'd pretend it wasn't there. They'd tell themselves she did everything by choice, and her stunning performance was a gift she gave freely.

"I must've done that routine at least thirty times. And the funny thing is…the more I did it, the more it felt like it was *my* choice. The more my body slipped into the role. It's hard to explain, but with each routine I felt a part of me getting left behind. A few more times and I might've believed I was more aerialist than Yadira…does that make any sense?"

It did. Before all this, whenever someone asked who I was, I'd tell them I was a waitress or a student because those were the things I did. Now I was a puzzler. And when Yadira had started working in the skin market…at first, she'd say it was only something she was doing to make rent. But after a few months of that, it became who she was. She started telling people she was a dancer or an entertainer. Behind her back, my classmates tossed around less flattering nouns. They'd snicker whenever Yadi – adorned with bright makeup – met me outside the school to walk me home. For a lot of people, a person becomes their actions.

The question was how did you keep hold of your *self* when doing the things you had to do. It was a riddle. I was supposed to be good at riddles, but I had no answers for this one.

"Do you think Dad got like that?" she asked.

"What do you mean?"

"Before he died. They worked him for almost fifteen years. Do you think there was a line he crossed…a moment when he became less our dad, and more the thing they wanted him to be?"

I hoped he had *changed.* I didn't say this out loud, though. Part of me wanted to believe it only because if he'd stopped thinking of himself as a father, then maybe he would've suffered less. Maybe while he worked in some factory, there wasn't a part of him still screaming to go home to his girls. But according to Yadi, it didn't sound like that's what happened. The way she described it, dead-heads could see their old selves getting eaten by the new roles they inhabited. I imagined it must feel something like what I went through when I was forced to watch that illusion of me get devoured by the Sphinx. Not pleasant.

Still, it was a bit strange. Alina had said that I'd been a dead-head for a couple of weeks while I recovered from surgery. My experience as a dead-head had been very different from what Yadi described. Unlike her, I'd been only vaguely aware of what was going on outside. Most my time was spent in that shadowed dreamscape where thoughts and riddles took shape. The memory made me shiver. I hoped never to return to that place.

"They took Dad from us," I said. "But they also took Dad from himself…which was worse, I think."

Yadi appeared uncomfortable. Her eyes glazed over like she was listening to her voyce. I had to remind myself hers and mine were still shut off.

"There is a way to regain control, I think. But I could never pull it off."

"What do you mean?" I asked.

"There was this girl I performed with."

"The girl with blonde hair?" I asked. *Pretzel Girl*, I thought.

Yadi blinked and asked how I knew. So, I told her about the night I'd watched them both perform in that cave-like theater. I didn't mention how I'd also witnessed Pretzel Girl's initial capture. That was too painful.

"Yeah, well, that girl is pretty interesting. Between shows, when we were resting on cots next to each other, she would do some funny things."

"Like what?" I asked.

"In the dark, she'd sit up and curl into a ball. Her entire body would convulse like she was having a seizure or something. I wanted to help her, but I was stuck in my own head." She shivered.

"Anyways, after a few minutes of this, she'd get all calm. She'd take these really deep breaths, then when she opened her eyes…even in the dark, I could see that it was her…the *real* her."

"But how?" I asked.

Yadi shrugged. "I'm not really sure. But every night, she'd do it. Then, she'd talk to me. Told me her name was Clara. Said she'd had a good friend who'd died right before she came here. Actually, she talked about him a lot. Said this friend of hers was the reason she could come out of her head."

"I don't understand," I said.

"She said losing him had given her a sort of…*despair*. It was the only thing that worked – she told me voyces can't stand all that anguish. I think that's what she did, but I couldn't quite figure it out myself. I think what she was doing scared me too much. She was going to a place in her head…I didn't think I could come back from."

I considered this, remembering something I'd heard in my Loyalty class. Ms. Parks had flashed her saccharin grin one day as she recounted stories about slaves crossing the Middle Passage. She'd said that some captives would draw into themselves and become so distraught that it killed them. Some who had been perfectly healthy, died nonetheless from a fatal dose of despair. For this reason, slave ships began to employ musicians and other forms of distractions meant to pull the slaves out of themselves.

The moral of the story, according to Ms. Parks, was that it wasn't enough to serve your masters. One had to be happy while you did it. Another lie, but maybe there was something in this I could use.

I filed the information away and asked, "When was the last time you saw Clara?"

"I was with her when your friend came for me." Yadi explained how she'd been on her cot when a man appeared out of thin air. "Like, *for real*. Nothing, then *poof,* he was there. He was wearing a mask so I couldn't see his face. Clara tried to stop him, but he muttered something under his breath and she froze up. I thought maybe he was a flexer boy, but then he started rambling about *you.*"

"Me?" I asked.

"Yeah. He kept mumbling about how stubborn you were and how you were going to get us all killed."

I smiled at this and gestured for her to go on.

"Not much else after that. He had this strange device with him. And when he pressed it against the side of my head, everything…went dark." She looked around the room. "I woke up here. With *him*." She nodded toward Cadence who was still sound asleep. He'd barely moved at all since I'd arrived.

"So, what's his story?" asked Yadi. "He's cute…even if he is a little banged up."

"He's a friend," I said, but I didn't elaborate. In truth, it pained me how Cadence helping me had come with such a high price. Even if we escaped this place somehow, I couldn't imagine how I'd ever repay him.

Suddenly, the door chimed and the locks clicked open. Yadi's eyes bulged, and she dove into the bed beside Cadence. I threw a blanket over both of them just as the doors slid open.

A short mutie stood in the hallway. He held three plastic-wrapped sandwiches on a tray.

This one has brought you food, I imagined Alina saying in my mind. With her turned off, however, there was no way this mutie could communicate. That said, it was clear enough what he wanted. I thanked him for the sandwiches and bid him a good day.

Yadi bounced back out of bed the moment the doors closed. "I'm *starving*," she exclaimed before tearing into one of the sandwiches.

While she ate, I kept my eyes on Cadence. I wanted him to wake up, but I wasn't sure what I'd say to him if he did.

He wore thin cotton pants, and nothing else. Yadi was wearing something similar so I figured this was what dead-heads wore when they were out of public view.

Not knowing what else to do, I wet some bath tissue and gently washed dirt and dried blood from his face. Like Yadi, he'd changed a lot since he'd been brought here. His handsome, swashbuckling face was now gaunt and bruised. The dimple in his left cheek had all but vanished. I prayed it would return if given time. Several angry looking welts showed on his chest and ribs. His knuckles were swollen, and a few of his fingers had those blue discolorations people got when they had broken bones.

He probably needed medical attention, but I doubted we could get him any.

"Hey, what's this?" Yadi asked.

With some effort, I pulled my eyes away from Cadence so I could look at my sister. She was picking at one of the sandwiches. Apparently, she'd found something tucked into the plastic.

"It's a note," she said, handing me a folded-up piece of paper.

"It's from Ogden Oliver," I said, reading over the message.

"Wait, *back the truck up,*" she said. "*Ogden Oliver*? That lifeliner who hosts all those dance-ups? Holy smokes, Lacey. He's *famous*. Is he the person helping us?"

I shushed her. "Quiet, Yadi. I need to concentrate." Like I've said, I wasn't the best reader. I *could* do it, but it just took some effort.

I sounded the words out so Yadi could hear.

"Lacey, things are pretty heck…*hectic*. I will check on you when I can. Until then, please stay in your room. Don't let anyone see your visee…your *visitors*. Same goes for Alina. Your voyce can't know about them. I had to use up a lot of favors to get them out. Dealing with that now. Later, I have a meeting with a bunch of cont…cond…*cunts?*"

Yadi snatched the letter from my hands and read, "'*Contingency* planners from the *Puzzling*. They'll tell me their plans for bringing you back into the competition. They'll need to explain to the other puzzlers why you aren't dead after everyone saw the Sphinx eat you."

Yadi paused. "Something *ate* you?" she asked.

"Tell you later. Please keep reading."

"Okay…well, that's pretty much it. The last thing it says is, 'See you soon,' and…*oh my gosh*."

"What?" I demanded.

"It ends with, 'Yours, Oggy.'"

Yadi put the letter down and eyed me with exaggerated interest. "I think you've got an admirer. Care to tell me about it?"

Chapter 19

Things were getting a little uncomfortable. I was still wearing the overskin and – forgive me, auditor – but I really had to pee. That nasty green drink that was supposed to freeze my insides had apparently worn off.

I kept thinking I had become one of those dry ice bombs they used to warn us about at *Stratus*. The restaurant sometimes used dry ice to make its own carbonated drinks. You'd put all the ingredients in a container, then drop in a lump of dry ice. If you didn't leave the container open a crack, the pressure would build and build until *BOOM*.

I had this horrible image of Ogden returning to find me in the middle of the room. Crotch smoking and the walls doused in urine. The thought made me laugh a little, which only made things worse.

"Would you sit still?" asked Yadira. "You're driving me nuts."

I was sort of dancing in place, trying to distract myself from how bad I had to go.

"I can't help it," I said.

She frowned sympathetically and asked, "You want me to try and rip it open?"

I prayed it wouldn't come to that. Also, I was beginning to understand the overskins were just one more method of control. We'd never think of escape as long as we needed someone to free us from this skin-tight prison.

Somebody tapped on the door, and before I could hide Yadi under the blanket, the panels slid open to reveal an extremely disheveled yet still handsome Ogden Oliver.

He was wearing that bright yellow jacket of his, but his shirt was missing. The belt around his waist had skipped a couple of loops so that his pants were all bunched up on one side and I could see bare hipbone underneath. I tried not to gawk. Pretty sure I failed.

Yadi was less subtle. "Nice abs."

Blushing, Ogden glanced from Yadi to me and said, "How're you all holding up?"

Before I could answer, Yadi cried, "My sister's about to have an accident."

His eyes widened and an embarrassed smile curled his lips. But then he must have seen the pained look on my face because his expression wilted.

"Right," he said. "Let's hurry up and get you de-skinned."

* * *

The 'skinning room' as he called it wasn't far – just a few doors down from my own. A sign on the door showed a stick figure submerged in what looked to be a bucket of water.

"Most puzzlers were de-skinned earlier," Ogden said. "There's a larger skinning room right outside the coliseum. This one's just for stragglers, or so I'm told. It should give us some privacy."

A spray of mist greeted us when we stepped inside a rounded room. I tried not to wince as the grated floor dug into my bare feet. Ogden latched the door behind us and gestured toward a small pool of silvery, semi-transparent liquid gurgling within the center of the room. It looked like a jacuzzi filled with mercury.

"Go on," said Ogden. "Get in."

I stepped down onto the first step. The stuff swirled around my ankles. It felt like stepping into warm oil.

"It's okay," said Ogden. "It won't hurt you."

I descended into the pool and allowed the stuff to move up over my shoulders. Almost immediately, tiny bubbles began to form on the overskin. I could see them through the stuff. They were like scales covering my whole body. The bubbles flitted to the surface and it wasn't long before my entire body seemed to be fizzing. The stuff gnawed away at the overskin and transformed the liquid's silver color into an inky black. For this, I was thankful because as the overskin dissolved, the now opaque liquid became my only cover.

The stuff continued to fizz and tickle my skin until I thought, *I really have become a dry ice bomb.* Here I was sitting in a vat of bubbling root beer. If I didn't release the pressure soon, I'd explode.

I realize, auditor, that I probably shouldn't tell you this. I should pretend it didn't happen, but I couldn't wait any longer. What was I supposed to do anyways? I didn't think he'd notice. So I let go. And the release was…heaven.

"Foreign contaminant detected," said a robotic voice.

"Huh, that's strange," said Ogden. He tapped on a control screen mounted to the wall. "What the heck is this?" He looked toward me.

"I have…no idea," I said, trying my best not to sound mortified.

Something must have clicked because he quickly looked down at his shoes. "Oh, right. That's, ah…*ahem*. Nevermind. Forget I asked."

I closed my eyes and sighed as the last bits of my overskin – and dignity – fizzled away.

After a time, Ogden cleared his throat and said, "I've been thinking about what you told me earlier…about me not telling you everything."

"Ogden…"

He took a deep breath. "I've been expecting you to trust me. But I realize now how unfair that has been. I think it's time you knew the full story."

"Okay," I said uncertainly. "I'm listening."

Ogden paced around the room, his eyes fixed on something I couldn't see.

"Both my parents were wolves," he began, "but they didn't care for the sorts of things that delighted most of their peers. So, they tried to get away. They built their own little paradise on that island I took you to. For a while, they lived the sort of lives most can only dream of. But then something happened that changed that…they had me.

"The prox took notice of me when I was still in middle school. In their *wisdom*," he said the word like it was an expletive, "they decided I should become a lifeliner. Something about the way I looked, or the sound of my voice…it matched something they were looking for. It fit some algorithm their voyces had created.

"They need people like me, you see? They need lifeliners to guide commonfolk through the dance-offs. It isn't just for fun, Lacey. The dance-offs are serious business. Doing the dances allows your voyce to map out your nervous system. Your voyce gets to see which movements trigger which parts of the brain. That way, whenever a voyce needs to take control of a person's body, they know which levers to pull and which strings to cut."

I thought about all the times I'd struggled to learn the latest dance moves. I imagined Alina charting my movements. Like pins and yarn on a bulletin board, she connected specific movements to specific parts of the brain.

Ogden continued. "The prox uses people like me to keep the lower classes in line. It's all part of their hierarchy. Muties, dead-heads, and husks at the bottom. Commoners, or *slags* as they call you, in the middle. Then you've got your enforcement classes like flexers and adjudicators. They work with the cellies and wolves. There are a few more nuanced classes that exist in the gaps between, but on top of everything, is the prox." He ran his hand along the wall, his fingers carving lines through thick moisture.

"Anything they want takes priority. And they wanted *me*. They wanted another puppet to dance for them…to make sure their way of life continued.

"My parents didn't agree, of course. They saw what the prox were doing. Saw how I was being turned into a circus monkey in order to serve their needs. So, my parents began making trouble.

"*Good trouble*, they called it. They used their resources to track down the source code that governs our voyces. They obtained a list of console commands and hired a few dozen techs to build a device that could install the required script extenders. Most commands work on their own. It's just another way the prox maintain control over the lesser classes. But some commands – such as the ones that turn off or confuse your voyce – those ones are forbidden. They won't work without the script extender."

He sighed. "All my parents wanted was to give me back my freedom. They taught me the commands in secret. Made me memorize them. I started to do things few people could. If I wanted, I could turn off my voyce. I could hide in plain sight. I could confuse and silence the voyces of others. And for a while, it seemed to be working. I still had to do what the prox wanted. But between dance-offs, I could turn off the voyce in my head and just be myself.

"There are many console commands that are common knowledge. Little things like shutting off noise or blurring your face in order to protect your privacy. Most elites I know have learned the commands that govern augmented reality. The prox rarely do anything about it. I think it is a little like how prohibition was handled way back in the nineteen-twenties. Most people understood they were technically breaking the law when they drank booze in hidden speakeasies – but most rulebreakers were ignored as long as they didn't cause trouble for the people at the top.

"The prox must have known I was using console commands, but they didn't do anything because I wasn't giving them any grief. That changed soon after my brother found out.

"For most of my childhood, Gideon had been a good brother. A little competitive, sure. Too aggressive? Sometimes. But what brothers aren't? Together, we'd have all sorts of adventures in and around our family's island estate. The augmented reality systems made anything possible. We'd be fighting dragons one day only to be battling extraterrestrials the next.

"But one day, Gideon activated something I wasn't ready for. He found some horror program on the streams and wanted to freak me out. Once activated, the ground tore open at our feet. Flies and cockroaches swarmed from the hole, and the smell of rotting meat made me want to puke. Then, the massive, gore-soaked head of a…a living *nightmare* rose into view. Rotting flesh hung in ribbons. Its eyes squirmed with maggots. It was too much, so I turned off my voyce.

"All I wanted was to stop the nightmare, but it didn't work. As you know, the augmented reality on that island is a decentralized network – it was the first time I realized some illusions can't be switched off so easily. It was also the first time Gideon realized I could silence my voyce on a whim. This would prove to be an even worse nightmare. He deactivated the program. The creature vanished, but Gideon was still there, staring slack-jawed at what I'd done. Shutting off your voyce was a mortal sin, even for the children of wolves like us.

"For whatever reason, Gideon felt slighted. Maybe he was jealous. But more likely, I think he felt threatened."

"Threatened, how?" I asked.

"He didn't like how our parents were giving me a power they had not yet shared with him. Maybe he thought they were setting me up to take over. I don't know. But Gideon's always been the sort of person to strike first. He could have been a great military leader if the voyces still let people fight wars.

Ogden laughed mirthlessly. "Anyways, Gideon filed an official report with an adjudicator and made a public complaint about my parents' actions. He forced the prox into action. Something had to be done – to teach a lesson. Doing nothing would've encouraged others to follow my parents' example.

"I still remember the day those flexers came for my mom and dad. Several passenger drones descended on the island and scores of them flooded the estate. My dad activated some augmented reality that made the whole place come alive with fire breathing demons. We might have escaped if not for Gideon. He switched off the whole system just as we were making a break for one of the passenger drones.

"With no more augmented reality to provide cover, there wasn't much my parents could do. An adjudicator showed up and shut everything down pretty quick. Adjudicators are the only justice class enforcers with access to all known command codes. Their voyces are loaded with all sorts of nasty ways to twist and alter reality. So, when my parents shouted a bunch of commands meant to confuse and blind the flexers, the white-cloaked adjudicator canceled everything with a wave of her hand.

"Gideon was mad, but I don't think even he meant for the prox to do what they did next. Not to our parents, not to our home, and definitely not to our…."

Ogden trailed off, then shook his head. "The prox wished to make an example. So, they torched the island and turned my parents into muties.

"But even that wasn't enough for them. They are cruel. Making my parents into muties wasn't enough for them. Despite their reclusive nature, my parents were well known and liked by their peers. The prox felt they needed to shock the system to send a message…to make sure no one else would ever think to replicate my parents' voyce deactivation commands again."

Here, Ogden paused and wiped at his eyes.

"Gideon wasn't my only sibling, you know…I had a sister."

This caught me by surprise. "A sister?"

"Didn't you ever wonder why my parents would call their cat, *Daughter*?"

I was speechless.

"They should have punished *me*. I was the one using the console commands. But they wanted me to run their stupid little dance-offs.

"My sister, on the other hand. She was only nine years old. The prox didn't have a use for her yet. So, they used her to prove a point. And sometimes, cruelty was the point.

"The prox had my sister's voyce make a complete copy of her personality. Then they opened her skull and cut out her neuro-net. They let me see it. A little silver mesh, holding everything my sister was. Then, they implanted it into the head of that stupid cat." He swallowed. "So, the last thing my parents ever saw before they lost their eyes was a cat who believed it was their dead daughter."

Ogden paced around the room. He stepped briskly as if trying to outrun the story he shared.

"Being the oldest, Gideon inherited my parents' wolf status along with the lion's share of their wealth. The prox promised to leave me alone as long as I continued to host their dance-ups and stay out of trouble. But the thing is, Lacey. I come from a family of troublemakers. And I loved my mom and dad...and my sister. I've seen enough of the prox to understand my family was only one of many destroyed by them. And I'm pretty sure you and Yadira know what I'm talking about."

I thought of my father's ashes back in my room and nodded.

"I want to return the favor," said Ogden. "I want to do to the prox what they did to me. My parents left me with enough knowledge on how I might do that, but I can't do it alone."

"De-skinning complete," croaked the pool's robotic voice.

Something shifted in the floor beneath the pool. "What was that?" I asked.

Ogden went on like he hadn't heard anything. "If you win the *Puzzling*, the prox will take us both down into their Panopticon. There, our fates will be very different. Guardians like me are rewarded for finding a worthy puzzler. Guardians receive extended life and multiple husked bodies to live out their every fantasy. They never have to worry about consequences or even death. If anything ever happens to one of a prox member's bodies, they just choose another. For most elites, becoming a prox is a dream come true."

"What about the puzzlers?" I asked. "What will happen to me if I win?"

He shook his head. "Winning puzzlers are never heard

from again. Never seen in person. If they have husks of their own, no one ever mentions them. Which could mean only one thing."

"The prox kills them."

"Huh?" Ogden looked surprised. "No…well, *maybe*, but I don't think that's it. Why go to all this trouble with the *Puzzling* if they were just going to kill you later? No, I think the winning puzzlers serve another purpose. I believe they get turned into husks – to be used by the ruling prox leaders within the Panopticon itself."

"But why? Don't they already have a huge amount of dead-heads to choose from?"

"It's got to have something to do with the riddles. For some reason, prox leadership needs someone who can solve puzzles. And let's be clear…not all prox are alike. You've got the kind most of us know like Micah – self-absorbed party-goers and socialites. Then there's the ones running the show. I've heard some people call these ones 'Stringers.' But no one really knows who they are."

"I thought Lady Pathe was in charge," I said.

"If she was, she'd be over three hundred years old. The prox live a long time…but even *that* seems excessive.

"More likely, Pathe's only a figurehead – a virtual husk controlled by those who are truly in control. Whoever *they* are, these *Stringers*, I believe the winning puzzler will meet them in the Panopticon…and therein lies our chance."

"Our chance to do what?" I felt a chill, and realized with some alarm that the liquid had slipped down past my shoulders. The pool was draining. My overskin was completely dissolved, and my only cover was now slipping away. "Um, Ogden?" I said urgently.

He continued to pace, lost in thought. "My parents taught me lots of different console commands. But there's one in particular…one I've never used."

The liquid continued to drop. I slid down into the center of the pool and tried to plug the little drainage holes with my toes. It wasn't working.

"Ogden?" I pleaded.

"If they try to turn you into a husk. There could be something we can do to…flip the script."

The liquid lowered down to my waist, so I leaned back and fought for every inch of cover. "Uh, *help.*"

Ogden still wasn't listening. He was too absorbed in his own train of thought. "It'll be like setting a trap. The prox will enter your mind, but as long as your voyce is turned *off*, they'll have nowhere to go. They won't be able to take control. *That's* when you do it. Say the command my parents taught me. Reverse the flow of information." He clapped his hands. "*Bam.* Don't you see, Lacey? Instead of the prox possessing you, you'll possess *them*."

I was flat on my back in the center of the pool and had only a few more seconds before what remained of my cover slipped away down the drain.

"*Ogden*," I shouted. "I need a towel."

He jerked in surprise, but then finally glanced down. His jaw dropped.

I must have looked ridiculous the way I was pressed into what by now was only a small puddle.

"Holy smokes, Lacey. You're…you're…"

"A towel, Ogden. *Hurry.*"

He apologized and tore his eyes away so he could stare up at the ceiling. He did an awkward little stutter step as if his mind couldn't decide where to go. But then he headed for the door and undid the latch. He pulled off his jacket and tossed it down to me.

"Uh, don't move," he said, then slipped out of the room.

I was on my back in the empty pool with Ogden's now soaked jacket draped over me.

"I'll just wait here, then."

Chapter 20

Ogden returned to the de-skinning room with a bundle of bedsheets he'd pulled from one of the now-vacant puzzler dorms. He turned his back as I tied one of the sheets around me like a toga. My damp skin made the sheet cling to my body, but with everything Ogden had told me, a wet toga seemed to be the least of my worries. Ogden must have been thinking the same thing because he didn't complain as he redonned his yellow coat, which was now drenched with that silvery-black liquid from the pool.

Back in my room, Yadira was having her own awkward emergency. The doors opened to the sound of frantic shouts.

Yadi stood in the shower, her body wrapped in a towel.

"You're *not* dead," cried Yadi, "but I'm gonna freaking kill you."

An awake, yet horror-stricken Cadence sat up on the bed. "*I'm sorry*. Please, I just – how do you *know* I'm not dead?"

"Cadence." I rushed forward and knelt beside him. But when I clasped his hand, he winced in pain. "Oh, sorry," I said. I'd forgotten about his swollen knuckles.

Eyes wide, his gaze slid over my face and explored both familiar and unfamiliar terrain. Before we'd come here, Cadence had been one of the few people who'd seen my cleft lip and not scoffed. Watching the recognition bloom in his gold-flecked eyes, and the joy that accompanied it, gave me a warm, fluttering feeling.

"Lacey?" he asked. "Is that you? Your – your *face*. It's changed."

"A lot has," I said.

Despite his damaged hands, he reached out and held my hand while brushing his swollen fingers across my cheek.

"I don't know how it's possible," he said, "but you're even prettier than the last time I saw you."

My skin felt hot.

The last time we'd seen each other in person – not from inside a husk – was in that alley in front of my apartment when I'd beaten Cadence with a wooden stick. Not one of my finest moments, but I didn't think this was the time he was talking about. More likely, Cadence was referring to that evening in the rain. We'd stared at each other as thick drops had pelted the car around us. He'd examined my face with all its flaws and told me I was beautiful. It was so wonderful to see him awake.

Yadi seemed a little less thrilled.

"He was pretending to be asleep," she said. "But the moment I step into the shower – *that's* when he decides to wake up. *How* convenient."

The room was so cramped that the open shower was less than five feet from the head of the bed. If Cadence had opened his eyes when Yadi was in the shower, he must have caught an eyeful.

"Give him a break," I said. "He's been unconscious for almost a full day."

"*Mm-hmm.* And I'm the queen of this here mountain." For the first time since we'd arrived, Yadi's eyes turned toward Ogden Oliver who was standing dumbfounded and silent beside the door.

"Did you want a peek, too?" she snapped.

Ogden turned away and clumsily adjusted his coat. He was an absolute mess. A handsome mess, but still a mess. I hadn't asked him what had happened to get him so disheveled. The wet coat he wore couldn't account for all of his frazzled appearance, but now wasn't the right time to ask. He looked sleep deprived and in desperate need of a shower himself.

As if reading my mind, Ogden cleared his throat and said, "Perhaps we all could use a little privacy in order to…ah…*compose* ourselves."

He explained that as the *Puzzling* continued, more and more dorms would become available.

"I think it's a good idea to keep you all separated until this is over."

"Why?" I asked, sharply. It didn't sound like a good idea to me at all.

"Well, with you back in the competition, you'll need to reactivate your voyce."

He didn't have to say any more. If Alina came back online now and saw Yadi and Cadence – a dead-head and a husk – in my room…she'd probably *freak.* Alina was already asking questions, and I didn't want to think about what might happen if her suspicions were confirmed.

Ogden offered to give Yadi and Cadence their own rooms. Yadi grumbled about leaving me alone at first, but even she understood the necessity. She wouldn't be able to hide under a sheet forever.

Cadence tried to stand, but swooned and collapsed back onto the bed.

"Take it easy," said Ogden. "I'll take Yadira first. It'll take a few minutes to get her settled in. Should give you some time to get your bearings back." He gestured for Yadi to follow him, and after a quick glance and nod my way, my sister trailed Ogden out into the hallway.

Cadence leaned forward on the bed and pressed his palms over his eyes.

After a time, he said, "Your friend killed Bartleby, I think."

"I'm sorry?"

"My voyce, Bartleby. I can't hear him anymore." Cadence jerked his chin toward the door. "That lifeliner friend of yours. I think he killed Bartleby the way those muties killed your Alina."

I gripped his forearm in what I hoped was a reassuring touch.

"Bartleby's not dead," I told him. "Only sleeping."

Cadence looked around the room as if expecting Bartleby to appear out of thin air.

"It's so quiet," he said.

"Yeah." I understood what he meant, but I hadn't thought of it as quiet. With Alina turned off, my own head had become flooded with all sorts of voices. Alina had been a kind of bouncer who kept certain people and thoughts out of my head. Whenever she was turned off, there was no one guarding the doors. The voices in my head became chaotic. Less refined. At first, I'd hated it. But the more time I spent with my own voyce – with no one else shaping who or what I thought about – the more I grew accustomed to it. The more I needed it.

"Your voyce doesn't always know best," I said. "*You* told me that." His eyes glossed over for a moment like he was recalling the night he'd given me a ride home from the restaurant.

"That seems so long ago," he said.

"Our voyces aren't our friends," I said. "If we're going to get out of here, we'll need to do it without the voyces knowing."

Cadence frowned. "You know…I had a feeling." He licked his chapped lips. "I'm really thirsty, Lacey. You got any water?"

There weren't any cups, and since Cadence was still too dizzy to stand, I did the only thing I could think of. At the sink, I gathered water in my hands. Then, I offered it for him to drink. I must have done this a dozen times. And while not what I intended, there was something sensual about this. He bent before me, his lips touching my fingertips as he drained the water from my hands. After each time, he'd look up into my eyes, smile thanks, and say, "More, please."

Finally, after several minutes of this – me offering and him drinking – he sighed and said, "Thank you, Lacey. That's enough."

Something came over me then.

Perhaps this was one of the side effects of not having a voyce. With Alina gone, I kept allowing myself to get swept up in raw emotion. First Ogden. And now Cadence. I felt a need to touch him. To kiss him. Cadence knelt before me. His powerful, shirtless body was bruised and beaten. He was strength and fragility. I hated what had been done to him, hated *my* part in that suffering, and I felt a need to lift some of that pain from his broad shoulders.

I leaned over him and cupped his face as if collecting water. He closed his eyes, and together, we drank.

What are you doing? asked that now familiar voyce. *My voice.* I didn't have an answer, and for once in my life, I didn't feel a need to find the answer. It was enough to be wrapped up in Cadence's touch. We were like lost children. We'd both been taken from our previous lives and imprisoned inside the old witch's gingerbread house. Cadence's kiss was like a light, burning a path through these cruel, dark woods. I think we both knew…survival, just as much as passion was fueling our actions. His stubble tickled and excited my skin until it rose in goosebumps.

It was several minutes before our lips parted.

Cadence gasped. "Are you sure I'm not dead?"

I laughed. It felt good to laugh with him, but I was a little embarrassed. And I know what you're thinking, auditor. How could I make sense of kissing Cadence when only the day before, I'd kissed Ogden? In truth, I *couldn't* make sense of it, and didn't much care to try. Maybe, this was the risk people ran by turning off their voyce? Without Alina to regulate my desires – my biochemistry, or whatever – what was keeping my emotions from taking over?

Maybe they have already, I thought. And I realized with some sort of guilty pleasure that I didn't really care. Without Alina, I was free to feel anything I wanted – *for* anyone I wanted. For the time being, I decided I'd enjoy it.

Still, I had a feeling I was approaching a cliff's edge. Sooner or later, I'd need to make a decision. Fire-blond Ogden or kind-hearted Cadence?

But not now, the now familiar voice told me.

I asked Cadence to explain what he understood about what was going on. He shuddered, then told me about his time fighting in the pits.

"I was myself most of the time. So were the other husks in there with me. We'd sit around and talk about how we got here. What crime had we committed to get us sentenced to this hell. But most of the husks had simply been in the wrong place at the wrong time. One guy saw a wolf push a man down a flight of stairs. When he tried to say something, some flexers appeared outta nowhere and brought him here."

He continued on in a grave tone. "When any of us were needed, our voyce summoned us to the fighting arena. Who was called and when seemed random, but everyone obeyed their voyce. And when we fought – when *I* fought – I could always feel the person who controlled me. I could see their mind as if looking at it through two or three fogged up windows. Most of 'em had wild and crazy thoughts. It was like they were drunk or only having fun. When they took control of me, their fighting was so unskilled and chaotic that I rarely did any real damage to anyone." He paused. "That wolf you came with was different."

"Gideon," I said.

Cadence nodded. "He's not like the other elites. He has a focus…and a *hatred*…I hadn't felt from any of the others. When he took control, his movements were *calculated* and *seething* with cruel intention. He wanted to kill the husks he made me fight. I *felt* it. His *need* to kill." Cadence trembled. "After you left…that guy whose body you were in…he collapsed. Some muties carried him away…but I haven't seen him since."

Cadence shivered until I put my arm around him.

"It wasn't your fault," I said.

"He scares me, Lacey."

"Me too," I said. "I'm sorry you got roped into this." It was a weak apology, but even I knew forgiveness couldn't be purchased with words. It took time and action to earn a person's forgiveness.

Cadence acted like I didn't owe him an apology. He said, "You're a good person, Lacey. Good people are worth going through hell for."

I believed him because I *felt* the truth of it. People I cared for…people I loved. I'd go through hell for them. It surprised me a little to realize that Cadence had slipped into that category. When had that happened? Cadence and Yadira. I'd go to hell for both them. It wouldn't require any consideration. It was just a fact.

I put my head on his chest and couldn't remember the last time I'd felt such peace. There were no voices in our heads – only the sound of our own breathing and heartbeats. They mingled in synchronized rhythm.

I must have dozed off a little because I didn't hear when the doors opened.

"*Ahem.*"

I shifted against Cadence and squinted up at the man standing beside the bed. *Ogden*!

My first instinct was to jump off the bed, but I fought the urge as I slowly uncoiled myself from Cadence's embrace. I stood silently between the two men – *boys* really – and the moment stretched out in uncomfortable silence.

"I guess he's feeling better." Ogden jerked his head toward the bed, and I realized with some alarm that Cadence's lips were bright red and smeared from the lipstick I wore.

"Ogden, I –"

He put up his hand. "No need to explain. I guess it's none of my business. I just thought –" He shook his head and took in a deep breath. "Never mind."

Here was that cliff I'd imagined earlier.

I realize, auditor, that perhaps I was being flippant, but I couldn't help myself. Just because I had feelings for Cadence…it didn't cancel out how I felt about Ogden. The way I felt about each man was different but no less powerful. What was I supposed to do about it? Part of me wished for Alina's help. I needed someone to tell me what to do.

Cadence pulled on a shirt and struggled to his feet. He looked between me and Ogden, clearly picking up on the tension between us.

"Everything okay?" he asked.

Ogden blinked. "Yeah, everything's fine. Just…ah, things aren't always what they seem, I guess." He stepped toward the door and motioned for Cadence to follow.

I didn't want either of them to leave before I could explain myself.

But what can you say? the voice asked.

Cadence gave a little wave and stepped into the hallway. Ogden lingered only a moment longer. His eyes locked with mine. His exhaustion was palpable, but there was something else. Something like devastation hid within his clear blue gaze. I could feel it swirling around him like a storm.

"Ogden…" I felt like I should apologize, but I wasn't sorry for kissing Cadence. I was only sorry for the hurt it gave Ogden. "I'm sorry you saw that," I said. "I'm so confused."

He smiled, but the expression failed to reach his eyes. "I get it, Lacey. You don't need to explain yourself." He tapped his temple. "Our voyces are supposed to keep our emotions from getting so messy. That's the risk we take by shutting them off."

"Where is this all headed?" I asked. He frowned, so I went on. "When this is all over. If we survive, what will happen to us?" I gestured between us.

"I don't know," he said. "But I'll do anything to find out."

I stepped in front of him. He was half a foot taller than me so I had to look up into his eyes. I adjusted his coat front and took in his ragged appearance.

"What is going on with you anyways?" I asked. "Why are your clothes such a mess?"

He swallowed, then looked to the side.

"I'd rather not say." His cheeks burned red. "All you need to know is that…*nothing* is free. And in helping your sister and your…your *friend*, I've had to…do things I'd rather not talk about." His jaw flexed and his eyes snapped back on mine. "Just one more reason the prox must *end*."

I said before, auditor, that I would go through hell to help Yadi and Cadence. Ogden, it seemed, was doing the same for me.

I put my arms around him. He stiffened at first, but soon relaxed to accept my embrace.

"We'll get through this," I said.

His arms tightened around my back until I could feel his entire body pressing against mine. And curse these emotions, I felt that now-familiar urge returning.

"*Ahem.*" Cadence cleared his throat near the door. "Don't we need to get going or something?"

"Right," said Ogden, moving away. At the door, he turned back. "Okay, Lacey. Time to clear your head. I'll make sure Yadi and Cadence are safe. All you need to do is focus on the riddles."

"What about your brother? Won't Gideon cheat again?"

"He might, but you needn't worry about that. If you face his puzzler again, it won't be until the finals. You'll need to get through at least seven elimination rounds before then. In the meantime, don't let him touch you."

Ogden must have seen the questions in my eyes because he continued. "When you're ready, you need to reactivate your voyce. Alina will help you. She'll be confused at first, so spend some time talking to her. Let her know everything is okay."

"Won't she realize something's wrong?" I asked. "I mean…how many times can I shut her off before she knows I'm using a console command?"

He shrugged. "Voyces tend to overlook things as long as they think you still need them." He paused. "So, just pretend you like her in the same way you pretended to like me."

His words were an icy stab. I'd hurt him. It was foolish of me to think that hurt could have passed so easily.

"Ogden…"

"You're pretty convincing when you want to be," he said. "Alina will believe you. Just like I did."

He turned away. Wiping at his eyes, Ogden strode into the hallway and disappeared behind sealing doors.

Chapter 21

The second day of the *Puzzling* began much like the first...with a few exceptions. Instead of stepping onto the conveyor belt with the rest of the remaining puzzlers, Alina told me to hold back. I stood in my room as Vaness, Phaeton and all the rest of them trundled by. They all had a shell-shocked look about them, but no one seemed to notice me or even look my way. I would have liked to at least talk to Vaness – to let her know I was okay or to ask if it was true about what happened to Aaron. I waved, but that's when I realized my skin had taken on that strange, milky quality.

<They can't see you,> said Alina.

I made a mental note to ask Ogden about this whenever I saw him again. Being able to turn invisible on a whim was a skill I was sure could come in handy.

After a few minutes, Alina ordered me to proceed. Along the way, I got a renewed sense of awe by the sheer size of this place. Something about riding that conveyor belt, entirely alone and naked, made me feel exceptionally small.

I had a strange feeling the mountain was alive. The low rumble within the walls was so constant that I barely noticed it anymore. And as I rode the conveyor belt, I imagined I was not unlike some blood cell pumping through a giant's arteries. It made me wonder how many people had been absorbed by this place. How many lives were needed to keep the mountain alive?

I pondered these things as Alina ordered me through the prep stations: make up, overskin, and the same stone and fiery rose design. Despite the invisibility command, it seemed the white-haired stylist could see me just fine.

It wasn't long before I stood before the huge elevator. But instead of stepping inside, Alina ordered me to walk toward a stairwell off to the side.

I kept an eye out for the Pretzel Girl, *Clara*, but besides me and my own stylist, the staging area was empty.

<Up the stairs, Lacey.> Alina's voyce was urgent. <It's time for your rebirth.>

The stairwell led up to a long, narrow tunnel. Dim blue running lights revealed a long line of metal doors. I didn't know it was a tunnel at first, but as Alina urged me forward, doors began to open before me just as others hissed shut behind. With each step, the roar of the coliseum grew louder and louder like an approaching avalanche.

My skin was still that strange milky white when the final door opened and I stepped into blinding lights. A flexer boy was waiting for me. His skin and clothing were the same milky white as my own. Even through the distortion of color, I could see the man's malice swirling within his porcelain white eyes.

He gripped my arm harder than was necessary and tugged me toward the center of the coliseum. Towering over us, hulking like a fiery goddess, the face of Lady Pathe blazed within a crackling cloud of electricity. Her stone-smooth skin and starry gaze swept the crowd of cheering spectators before settling on me. I felt the weight of her attention, as heavy as the mountain itself.

The flexer yanked on my arm until he had me up on one of the puzzler platforms, then he rushed back toward the coliseum's dark recesses.

Lady Pathe's jaws creaked as her mouth split into a wide grin.

"Ladies and Gentlemen, welcome to day two of our Grand *Puzzling*." The crowds stomped their feet and shooting stars flew across the surface of Lady Pathe's galaxy-domed eyes. "Before we begin, there is a pressing matter of business."

Cheers morphed into whispers, but I couldn't see anyone through the glaring lights. It was so bright here in the center of the coliseum that I might as well have been standing on the inside of a giant, glowing eggshell.

Maybe I am, I thought. *This is, after all, my rebirth.*

Lady Pathe's voice boomed like thunder. "Yesterday, one of our puzzlers tried to fool us. *Us!* The prox!" She laughed and the sound ricocheted off the high ceilings like cannon fire. The coliseum burst into jeers and clomping feet. Once the wave of noise had passed, Lady Pathe continued. "Along with their puzzler, the offending guardian has been dealt with."

Killed, I knew. I tried not to think of the red-headed Aaron. What little I'd known of him told me he hadn't deserved such an end.

"And to make amends for the cheater's treachery," continued Lady Pathe, "I will resurrect the puzzler who failed during that round. We do not know if Lacey Clarke would have won in a fair challenge, but all of our puzzlers deserve a chance to do so."

Lady Pathe rushed forward. Her already massive form engulfed the entire world until everything was a crackling mass of white-hot gasses and sparking electricity. I smelled ozone and sulfur and had to remind myself it wasn't real. Lady Pathe – just like the Sphinx – they were both voyce-generated hallucinations. She exhaled and the air shimmered with heat. A plume of purple smoke billowed from her mouth and swirled around me. I felt the stuff get into my nose and throat. It covered my eyes until I couldn't see anything at all. Then, the world detonated in a flash of lightning. This close, real lightning would have blown me to pieces. This pseudo stuff, however, just punched behind my ribs and knocked me over. I tripped off the platform and collapsed onto the turf.

It took a while for my head to clear, but when I finally managed to lift my gaze, the smoke was gone. Lady Pathe smiled like a painter admiring her latest creation. And as I lifted myself off the ground, I noticed my body had lost the creamy white color of invisibility.

The coliseum exploded with applause. Alina told me to wave and smile. So I did, but it must have looked clumsy and foolish. The blast from moments earlier still filled my head with dizzying disorientation.

<You're *aliiiive*,> Alina cried with her best Frankenstein impression. <Let's try our best to keep it that way, shall we?>

She ordered me to return to my group of puzzlers from the day before. I was still in a daze as someone draped in long, colorful plumage like a peacock raced out to meet me on the turf. I flinched, not recognizing who it was at first. Vaness' near-death experience in the skinning pool had prevented her stylist from adhering any cosmetics on the first day of the *Puzzling*. But now she was quite a sight. Several lustrous feathers had been woven into her brown hair. Her blushing skin had been painted a light shade of green and small emeralds clung to her eyelashes. Vaness threw her arms around me.

"Oh, Lacey. You're alright." She sobbed. We helped each other to our seats, and I honestly couldn't say who helped the other more. It was a team effort.

As we took our seats, Phaeton cast a furtive glance our way. His golden skin darkened. I would have liked to say something to him then – just in case Gideon was in there, but at that moment, Lady Pathe flashed so bright that I had to shield my eyes.

The prox leader looked toward the cave ceiling and cried, "Reason to survive. Perish the rest." With one final flash, she winked out of existence.

Round two had begun.

* * *

The Sphinx looked almost bored as she sauntered into the coliseum and settled in front of the first group of puzzlers. This time there were three competing instead of the four from round one. And the next round would be one against one. And would continue that way until there was only one puzzler left.

The Sphinx asked her first riddle, and it wasn't long before a pale-faced boy with long gangly arms failed to give the correct answer. The Sphinx licked her lips, swallowed the boy in one gulp, then yawned.

Knowing now that it was all for show – that instead of being eaten by this monster, the platform they stood on opened so that the losing puzzler could get whisked away – it didn't change how horrific it all *appeared.*

And it had felt real enough, I remembered. Besides, the way I saw it, it really didn't matter if the Sphinx was real or not. If I failed again, that would be the end. No more second chances or do-overs. Losing now would mean a lifetime as a dead-head. Losing puzzlers were taken to the auction block to be sold off as property. From what Cadence and Yadi had described of their experiences, if given the choice, I'd prefer death by Sphinx. But I couldn't think about that now. They were both still in harm's way. I couldn't stop until they were both out of this gods-forsaken mountain.

"Lacey Clarke!" The Sphinx called. The scales on her face rattled like empty bottles when she spoke. I approached with the other two competitors – a boy with cat eyes painted on his broad chest and a girl with neon orange hair and matching stripes zigzagging her overskin.

We took our positions on the disc-like platforms. I couldn't see much beyond the cone of spotlights; the wall of faces was little more than confused blotches of shifting color. Alina, on the other hand, could see just fine. A cloud of yellow appeared about five rows back from the coliseum floor. I squinted that way until the world shot toward me as if I were peering into a telescope.

Ogden Oliver gazed back at me through the magnified space, his hands balled into fists under his chin. It was a nervous gesture held in contrast with his bright clothing, a flame-orange jacket with pulsing red outline. I could sense his apprehension. Even so, it was a comfort to know he was here.

The magnification retreated only to refocus and zoom back in on another spot further up the coliseum. The dark-clad wolf strummed black and red fingernails on the railing. *Gideon.* He scowled my way. A blank-eyed servant passed him a glass dripping with red wine. What I wouldn't give to make him drop it – to do to him what he'd already done to me. Perhaps that was another command Ogden could teach me later.

If there was a later.

He took a long sip then turned to face me. He must have known I could see him clearly because he gave a little salute. Then, he pointed a finger gun my way. His lips moved. It should have been impossible for me to hear what he said, but the words *exploded* in my mind.

<ANIMUS FRANGITUR.>

Gideon's words struck me like a White Line vehicle. I stumbled back and my bare foot slipped off the platform. A quick glance down showed the coliseum floor plummeting away. I fell and clung to the platform as it rocketed higher and faster toward the stone ceiling.

I'm gonna be crushed, I thought.

I screamed for help, but the words spewed from my mouth in a torrent of multicolored scarves like the sort of thing you'd see in those old-timey magician acts. The scarves squirmed and slithered about on the platform like snakes. Every light in the coliseum began to strobe and burn hot until it felt like the whole world was starting to melt. Already, bits of the mountain were dripping away in superheated clumps of wax. Several gouts of lava burned through stone and air. I could feel the churning, bubbling heat peel off my skin.

<Mens agitat molem,> cried another voyce inside my head. I felt everything slam to a halt. I was left gasping on my platform – still on the coliseum floor. It had been Gideon. He had forced an illusion on me. I should have known he wouldn't play fair. But what was that?

<You are experiencing sensory discombobulation,> said Alina. <Thankfully, Ogden Oliver has issued the cancelation phrase. He wants me to tell you that it's best to ignore the crowd. Focus only on the Sphinx and your riddle.>

"Okay," I said, trembling. "Would have been nice to know a little earlier."

The lights dimmed to their normal glaring brightness, and the noise lessened to a steady thrum.

Above me, the Sphinx gave an impatient snort. "Is everything alright, Lacey? If you haven't noticed, we're trying to have a competition here."

Harsh laughter echoed throughout the coliseum.

<Get a hold of yourself, Lacey,> said Alina. <You're embarrassing us.>

I rose on shaky legs and nodded. "I…I'm fine."

"Good." The Sphinx licked her lips. The sound made me think of all the times at the wet market whenever I'd slap two dead fish together. "Here is your riddle:

I have a toe but no feet,
Have a belly but never eat,
I have a heel but don't tread,
And tiny hairs but no head?
What am I?"

I should have known this one. It was sort of elementary. The way it was worded, anyone could have figured it out. But my head was still spinning from Gideon's console command. Pulling the riddle apart took an effort I couldn't find.

The boy with cat eyes on his chest answered first. His words were muffled, but the Sphinx's monotonous grunt gave no indication about whether or not he'd answered correctly. Next, the neon girl answered. The Sphinx responded in the same way. Now it was my turn.

I felt half asleep or like I'd been drugged. I fought for focus and imagined the riddle floating in front of me. I tried to see the words and began prying them apart as if yanking boards off an old house.

The Sphinx's massive, luminous eyes lowered into my view. She smiled and hundreds of dagger teeth poked through the slit in her ruby red mouth.

"Well?" She purred. "Did Lady Pathe bring you back just to end it here?"

The words I wanted fell into my head. *Toe, belly, heel, hairs.* Whatever it was, it was a non-living thing that had a toe, belly, heel, and hairs.

Years earlier, I'd been allowed to take an art class. Something the teacher had said vaguely swam into my mind, and I grasped desperately for the wisp of memory.

The Sphinx's jaws creaked as she leaned toward me.

"It's a *paintbrush*," I shouted.

The Sphinx blinked and jerked back. She shook her head. Her scales rattled as she flapped huge leathery wings in agitation.

"You survive this round," she said. Then turned toward cat-eyes. "Just because you're quick, doesn't mean you're right. I'd tell you to slow down next time…but alas, for you there is no next time." I turned away as the Sphinx pounced on the boy.

Neon girl took my hand and helped me back to my seat. I would have thanked her but before I could bring myself to say anything, she bounded back to her own little group, and the Sphinx called its next competitors.

Chapter 22

After the day's riddles, I was herded out of the coliseum and deskinned with all the rest of the surviving puzzlers. Our voyces shuffled us through the large pool of metallic, oily stuff so we could emerge naked and shiny on the other side.

Thankfully, nobody seemed all that keen on conversation, and it wasn't long before I was back in my room, relieved to have made it through another day.

It wasn't long before the incoming visitor medley played from the wall speaker. I hurried into my jumpsuit and let Alina know I was ready. The doors opened to reveal a female mutie holding a large box.

<This one has brought your evening wear,> said Alina.

"My what?" Instead of answering, the mutie thrust the box into my hands, then hurried away down the hall.

Inside the box was a dark blue gown with matching heels. The fabric flowed through my fingers like warm water. I must have spent several minutes just admiring the texture. Never in my life had I felt fabric so smooth. Putting it on was like wrapping myself in steam. A mirror materialized on the wall next to the shower, and I stared dumbly at my own reflection. It didn't look like me – at least, not the me I was used to. The woman staring back from the mirror stood with a regal poise I'd never imagined I was capable of. Dark blue silk shimmered faintly as it caught the light. I still wore the makeup from the *Puzzling*, and that smokey eye shadow gave me a cool, alluring look. I tried on a smile and felt the absence of my cleft lip. The full, beautiful smile reflected back at me was not the same one I'd come here with. Was its presence any more real than the augmented Sphinx? I wasn't sure. It made me wonder how much a person's image made up who they were.

Before, when I'd had the appearance of a derelict commoner, that's who I had been…without question. But now, standing here in this elegant cellie dress, wearing a cellie woman's smile…who was I now? I wasn't sure I had an answer for that. It all made me wonder about the cellies, wolves, and prox. The way they presented themselves. The façades they wore in public…it seemed just as fickle as the augmented reality they so loved to play with. Take away all their fancy clothes and makeup, toss 'em in with a bunch of commoners…and I doubt you'd be able to tell the difference.

<Excuse me, Lacey,> Alina said. <Ogden Oliver wants to know if you like the dress he sent over.>

"It's lovely," I said, and meant it.

* * *

Later, I held Ogden's arm as he escorted me through the mountain's long corridors. He was uncharacteristically silent. My questions were met with short, one-or-two-word replies. Greetings from passing elites rarely received anything more than a curt nod. I figured he must still be upset about what happened with Cadence and me.

We should probably talk about it, I thought but wasn't brave enough to broach the subject. So instead, I resigned myself to following his lead. If he wanted to talk, I'd talk. If he wanted to keep quiet, I was good with that too.

We turned a corner, and I paused to gape at the long, shimmering hallway. The walls in this part of the mountain were so smooth, they appeared to have been made of melting ice rather than stone. A blue glow emanated from within the walls. The light cast swirling auroras on the floor and ceiling. It was difficult to tell how long this strange corridor was because it had a slight curve that made the end – wherever it was – disappear around a corner.

"What is this place?" I asked.

"You'll see," said Ogden. He gestured toward a trio of elites stumbling away down the corridor. They wavered erratically like they were trudging through deep mud. Not far ahead of them, another pair of cellies swung their arms around like they were fighting off a swarm of bees.

Closer to us, a thick red line stretched across the entire hallway. Ogden gestured toward a small queue that had formed behind the line. A few different groups of elites spoke nervously and bounced around on the balls of their feet as if they were about to break into a run.

<Welcome to the Gauntlet,> said Alina.

"What's the gaunt –"

A yellow light blazed from the ceiling and a klaxon began to wail.

"Let's go," said Ogden. He took my hand, smiled, and said, "Try to stay close."

Before I could protest, he pulled me across the red line and the entire world shredded to ribbons.

*   *   *

The world reconfigured itself – snapped back into place as if pulled by an elastic cord. It took less than a second, but the shock of it left me gasping for breath.

"*Fudge*!" Alina censored my intended expletive, but the sound of it exploded within the cramped space around my head. That's when I realized I was wearing a helmet. The glass domed faceplate was bright with reflected starlight which didn't make much sense because I was still in the mountain. *Right?*

Where the heck am I?

Air hissed in my ears as all other sounds slipped away or grew muffled. My feet felt very heavy as if encased in cement. I looked down to see that I was wearing a thick suit. The soles of my boots pressed down into a grayish white soil.

<You're an astronaut,> said Alina. <Better get moving before the Neo-Luddites make moonfall.>

"The what? I don't understand."

The ground trembled. Tiny cracks opened in the moon's sun-bleached surface. Overhead, a car-sized spacecraft sizzled through a thin atmosphere. It was pursued by two other, bullet-shaped craft. A volley of flashing laser fire erupted from their sides.

I ducked as return fire caught one of the ships on the side. A geyser of flame burst from the ship's hull as it spiraled toward me. It passed mere feet over my head before ploughing straight into a mound of bleached dirt.

"Lt. Clarke!" Ogden's voice bellowed through my helmet's speakers. "Lacey, over here!"

Ogden stood less than ten feet away. I couldn't see him behind the darkened helmet he wore, but I recognized his voice. He gestured urgently for me to go to him.

"What's going on?" I called.

"We need to get off this moon," he shouted back. "Before it's too late."

From behind, the crashed ship gave a scream, and a pair of escape hatches broke away in a puff of gas. Seconds later, several red-clad space marines began to scramble out. They held ominous, snub-nosed weapons. And it wasn't long before they were pointed right at me and Ogden.

"Lacey!"

Despite the thickness of my suit, I managed to move quickly over the alien landscape. I took Ogden's hand as we sprinted through bursts of laser fire and sprays of exploding earth. Overhead, the galaxy had transformed into an intergalactic space battle. Star fighters and battle cruisers collided in a horrendous firework show. Clods of dirt rained down on us as the sky erupted with explosions so bright that they would have seared an unshielded person's eyes right out of their head.

Ogden pulled me along. I had no idea where we were going until…

* * *

…the world shredded again. Every atom seemed to tear apart only to slap back together an instant later.

The space battle had vanished. And now…

I blinked at a sea of billowing fabric. Men in puffed up shirts and lacey collars were dancing across a glossy, marble floor. Women in overly large, wafting gowns waltzed forward to meet them.

The space battle above had been replaced by gilded chandeliers and scores of flickering candles. An orchestra played an upbeat tempo – a modern song played with ancient instruments. The dancers matched the melody with dizzying flourishes of limbs and fabric.

"Pardon me, Miss." Ogden stood beside me. And despite everything, my brain jammed at the sight of him. His fire-blond hair was done up in an elegant swirl of brilliant gold. His blue eyes glittered like sapphires. The suit he wore – a dark red velvet – made him look far more regal than any fictional king I'd ever seen on the streams. Sharp shoulders, a tight waist, and long tails reaching down to the floor. A golden, frilly shirt hung open to expose his smooth, muscled chest.

"Ogden," I gasped. "What's going on? You look…you look amazing."

He grinned, and I felt a pleasurable chill as his eyes traced up and down my entire body. "You're quite a sight yourself, Lacey."

I looked down at my own appearance and gasped. The dress I wore was made of a similar red velvet, but with a frighteningly low neckline. From collar bone to navel, my exposed skin shimmered in the candlelight. Long sleeves made of intricately woven lace connected to sparkling wrist bands. Below my waist, the dress balanced itself on a round metal frame. With such a sleek top and wide bottom, I figured I must have looked like a human-sized feather duster.

Ogden stepped closer and gently pushed the flowing dress aside. He lifted my hand to his lips, never breaking eye contact.

"Care to dance?" he asked.

"Tell me what's happening," I demanded.

"They call this the Gauntlet," he said. "Augmented reality roulette."

I remembered what he'd shown me back at his island estate. The party that seemed so real, but wasn't.

"Why did you bring me here?"

"To show you the way out." He slipped his hand

around my waist, and I put my own hand on his bare chest. Our bodies pressed tight against each other. I liked the feeling. I only wished I knew which parts were real and which ones were figments of this augmented illusion. He smiled. "The only way out is through."

He dipped toward the dance floor and we dove into the center of what seemed to be an elegant, colorful tornado. Ogden led me through a dizzying waltz. He carried me through the steps so that my feet barely touched the ground.

I lost myself in the moment. The pulse of music on my skin. The feel of Ogden's body on mine. The idea that I belonged in this place – a place devoted solely to pleasure and elegance and sin – it was enough to swallow me up. I arched my back, hooked a leg around Ogden's waist, and reached backward toward the floor. This place was intoxicating. Somehow, I knew. If we didn't leave soon, we might never leave at all.

Ogden lifted me up, and I realized with some alarm that he was pushing us through the crowd. Ogden held me in his arms, but we were moving toward the fringes.

No, I thought. *Don't take me yet. I'm not ready to stop dancing.*

Ogden stepped beyond the crowd and the dancefloor burst apart like confetti.

* * *

Our elegant clothes melted into thin cotton. Gently, Ogden lowered me down to a linoleum floor within a darkened basement of sorts. Directly in front of us, laid out on a metal table was a man's corpse looking to be about half-way through an autopsy.

A fear, like ice in my blood, crept through my body.

"What's this?" I asked.

"I don't know," said Ogden. "The Gauntlet's different every time."

We both wore the blue smocks of surgical nurses. Our latex gloves were damp with blood.

Before I could ask what to do next, the corpse on the table began to twitch. First his fingers and toes. Then, his jaw began to snap. With a groan, the corpse sat up on the table and pointed its bloody, sightless eyes right at us. It threw one of its legs over the end of the table, then the other. Behind the reanimated corpse, a wall of freezer doors began to rattle within their frames. One of the doors gave a loud, *pang*, before breaking free of the hinges. Long, bony arms reached out toward us.

"Okay, that's nice," I said, and pulled Ogden toward the room's only exit – a pair of double doors. On contact, the doors flew open and together, Ogden and I fell…

* * *

…onto hot sand. I lay face down panting for a few moments and let the sun's rays warm my skin.

We were on a beach. Crashing waves thundered up through the sand. A shadow fell over me and I rolled onto my back to gaze up at Ogden who was now wearing tight swim trunks. He took my hand to help me up.

For a moment, we did nothing but gaze out at the ocean. Never had I seen anything so beautiful. Turquoise waters stretched out past the horizon. Wisps of clouds cast intricate shadows on the white sands.

"Just gotta keep moving," he said. "The pleasure and pain of this place isn't real…but it is convincing. People sometimes get lost in here." I would have liked to stay awhile myself, but I couldn't ignore the urgency present in Ogden's voice. So, we set off along the shoreline. Along the way, I pretended not to notice how Ogden was looking at me from the corner of his eye, stealing glances at my bikini. At the same time, he pretended not to notice the way I was looking at him and the way his swim trunks clung to his muscled body.

* * *

At some point, I lost track of all the realities we passed

through. An old Western town devastated by a stampede of wild bison. A frozen lake with cracking ice underfoot. A desert party surrounded by tall, wooden monuments engulfed in flame. Each world had been vibrant and alive with new sensations and emotions.

It would seem obvious later but it came as a bit of surprise at the time to realize that these augmented experiences were all coming from *inside* rather than outside. Each new world sprang from the voyce in my head. This was different from how reality was supposed to operate. In real life, my mind soaked up the external sensations and filtered *that* into what I thought of as *perception.*

That wasn't what was happening here, though. Inside the Gauntlet, my mind was completely ignoring the outside world – which as far as I could tell, was still just a smooth corridor. Instead of that given reality, my voyce kept producing a series of fabricated ones.

Each time, I marveled at how easy it was to get lost within a new reality. This ability to believe *anything* – I'd understand later – was at the same time one of humanity's greatest strengths and also its most damning curse.

*   *   *

We stepped into the smooth corridor, and all at once, we both realized we had made it through. While not as remarkable as some of the augmented scenarios we'd just experienced, the real world had a *weight* that had been lacking from the augmented ones. It was like moving from a room warmed by an electric heater to one warmed with steam. Both could convince you it was hot, but the steam room had a *thickness*, or viscosity that couldn't be copied.

"We're here," Ogden said as we reached the end of the corridor. A tall, arched doorway opened into a viewing deck with several rounded windows pointed toward the white-capped mountains in the distance.

Several space heaters warmed the area around the windows, which I was thankful for as I could feel the harsh cold trying to reach in through the glass. Despite this, however, it was quite a beautiful view. It was a bit surprising that so few elites were in here at the moment. In fact, Ogden and I seemed to be the only ones here.

He put his hand on my shoulder and gestured toward a rectangular building that jutted out near the base of the mountain. A pair of vactrain tubes shot out from the sides and extended in a wide curve and disappeared out of sight.

"That down there…that's the commercial vactrain line. It's where the prox ship in all their food, supplies and…people."

His hand tightened on my shoulder, but he didn't make eye contact.

"If something happens, and you have to leave in a hurry." He nodded toward the station. "That's your way out."

<What is he talking about?> Alina hadn't spoken in so long that I nearly jumped at the sound of her voyce. She went on. <Why's he acting so strange? You think he's trying to be funny?>

"I don't know," I said. "I'm hoping he explains himself." I was talking to Alina, but my words were meant for him.

He did a quick look around, then whispered the deactivation phrase. I felt that now familiar release of pressure as Alina shut down.

"Okay," he whispered. "I wanted to bring you here…to show you where to go if things…if our plans fall apart. Any other way is guarded and too dangerous. So you'll need to go through the Gauntlet. Just like the island, the illusions are unavoidable. Even if your voyce is turned off, you'll need to get through the augmented reality. And get through, you must." He stared into my eyes for what felt to be a long time. He seemed to be weighing his options.

"What's wrong, Ogden? Has something changed?"

He sighed. "It's Gideon. My brother's more powerful than I thought. He shouldn't have been able to confuse you like he did today. The prox should have picked up on his commands, but they didn't even seem to notice. Or...and this is what's gotten me worried...or they *are* noticing, but they don't *care*. It's possible that the prox are aware of Gideon's cheating. And if that's true, they might even be sanctioning it."

"What are you saying?" I asked.

"I'm saying...the prox might have already decided they *want* Gideon to win. It wouldn't be the first time the prox has stacked the deck."

I considered this, but wasn't sure what to do with the information.

Ogden went on. "So, that's why we need to have a backup plan. If things fall apart, I'd want you to make it to the station. I'll give you a command that will allow your voyce to interface with the vactrain system's controls."

I asked, "Why don't we leave now? We can slip out while no one is watching."

"Someone is *always* watching," he said, gravely. "It's why we don't just go up to the landing platform, request a passenger drone, and fly out of here. That's what I'd want to do, but Lady Pathe's made it clear. No drones are allowed to approach the mountain unless given direct permission from Pathe herself. No, the only way you or anyone else escapes this place is through the vactrains. If things go sideways...promise you'll do what you must to get out of this damned rock. Even if it means leaving someone behind."

"Ogden, I..."

He smiled, but the expression failed to reach his eyes. "Please, Lacey. It means a lot to me. Promise you'll escape if given the chance."

I nodded and was a bit surprised by the visible relief that washed over him. I felt his body relax beside me. His hand returned to my shoulder, and I nuzzled in close beside him.

He didn't need to know that my promise meant so little. He didn't need to know there was no way I'd leave anyone behind, even him.

Are you sure about that? The voice asked in my head. *If given the chance...*

We sat together for over an hour; our arms draped around each other. Ogden taught me the commands needed to control the train. In addition, he taught me a few others he figured could help in a pinch. With each command, Ogden made me repeat the phrase over and over until we were both confident I had it memorized.

"*Vincit qui se vincit,*" I repeated for about the dozenth time. "*Vincit qui se vincit.*"

"Good," he said. "That one's important."

"What does it do?" I asked.

"With any luck, it'll be the last command you ever have to say."

"Careful," I joked, "you sound almost hopeful."

"It's your fault." He grinned. "You make me feel a little optimistic."

Finally, with night approaching, Ogden rose to lead me back to my room. I was half tempted to ask him to stay, but I think we both knew that would be a bad idea. Things were complicated enough.

Chapter 23

The Sphinx extended a long claw to dislodge a human foot from between her yards-long incisors. Then she knelt down between me and my opponent, a frizzy haired girl painted in reflective, mirror-ball silver. But I wasn't really paying attention to her. Ogden had told me to keep all my attention on the Sphinx, so that's what I intended to do. This close, the purring inside her chest was like an old-timey gas generator.

She asked her riddle:

"I am the trip you all must take,
The appointment you all must make.
I can be patient, urgent, or blind,
But never have I been left behind.
What am I?"

It didn't take long to think of the answer, probably because I felt it lurking around every corner inside the mountain. Still, I was careful not to shout it out until I knew for sure. I ran the answer through the riddle, making sure it fit in the same way toddlers would push different shaped blocks into their matching holes. Once I was certain, I cleared my throat and said I'd like to answer.

"Go on, my little rose," said the Sphinx.

"Death."

The Sphinx pursed her lips. The scales on her face fluttered like wind blowing through a wheat field, but she said nothing.

A moment later, Mirror-ball Girl gave her answer. To this, the Sphinx frowned. Nostrils flaring, she announced that both puzzlers had answered correctly.

I would have cursed if Alina would have allowed it. This was the fifth riddle we'd both answered together. Whoever my challenger was, she was good. I eyed her appreciatively from my platform, and she gave a nervous nod back my way. I had to remind myself that even though this girl was my challenger, she was not my enemy. My enemies were the thousands of elites cheering from the stadium. The Sphinx and the prox who controlled her. My enemies were the people forcing us to square off against each other…to destroy each other for their enjoyment.

The Sphinx gave a low growl, then said, "You puzzlers appear to be evenly matched, so the next riddle will be a lightning round. The *first* to answer will survive. The other will not. Is this understood?"

I nodded. I tried not to look at the girl, but the way she was trembling made her hard to ignore. Her mirror-ball overskin cast a disorienting scattershot of light in every direction. Beyond that, however, I could see she was in tears. Scared and alone. I prayed that for both our sakes, what happened next would be over soon.

The Sphinx began her riddle:

"Long in the morning;
Short by noon;
Long in the evening;
But hard to see soon.
I can't make up my mind about my size or my shape;
At night, I'm my strongest like a thrown over cape.
What am I?"

A childish riddle, I had the answer before the Sphinx had even finished talking.

"A shadow," I called. The bubble of silence burst around us and the roar of the crowd flooded in.

"We have a winner," the Sphinx announced. "Which means…" Eyes flashing with blue flame, her attention turned toward Mirror-ball Girl. To my surprise, the girl looked relieved.

But then the Sphinx was on her, and the air shimmered to shield me from the horrible spectacle of her demise.

<She doesn't need to worry any longer,> Alina assured me. <The prox are generous in that way. You know the Sphinx doesn't really kill anyone. It's like a ritual…like baptism or marriage. That girl has slipped out of a life fraught with troublesome choices and worry. They'll take her to the auction block where someone will buy her, and

she'll never need to worry about anything ever again. Life is so much easier when others make the decisions for you. No need to worry about your purpose in life, when your purpose is given to you.>

"I never thought of it that way," I said, trying my best to keep the loathing out of my words. "Thank you."

<Don't mention it,> she said. <Now, run along, Lacey. The Sphinx wants to call the next challengers.>

* * *

I sat miserably through the long procession of face-offs. As the puzzlers were eliminated one by one, it became increasingly clear that the elites didn't really care who won. They were more interested in the carnage that followed each failed response. Whenever the Sphinx devoured a puzzler, the cheers were deafening. The elites were enraptured by their own bloodlust.

How many of them knew the Sphinx was an illusion? I suspected a great many, since these were the same people who'd be purchasing the losers. But still, that didn't seem to dampen their almost primal thirst for violence and bloodshed. Every cackle of laughter and every scream for death only hardened my hatred for these people…these so-called elites.

I competed in two more rounds (once against a pole-thin boy covered in colorful butterflies and once more against a girl with a shining pyramid on her chest). I defeated them both and turned away before the Sphinx did her thing.

Hours passed and the remaining puzzlers were whittled down to less than a dozen. Today would be the busiest and most costly day of the *Puzzling*. The competition had started with a hundred and twenty-eight puzzlers. Thirty-two had been eliminated on both the first and second day. Today, the third day of the competition would see the elimination of sixty more. By the day's end, there would be only four puzzlers remaining. I hoped to be one of them, but nothing was certain.

The coliseum had adopted a party atmosphere as music played from the stands. Hoots of laughter and drunken shouts filled the cavern. It was just another illusion. The scene was at odds with the grave consequences for all those involved…myself included. Either, I would advance to the finals…or the Sphinx would pretend to feast on me again, and I'd become someone else's property.

I winced as the golden-skinned Phaeton defeated another puzzler. So far, nothing seemed to faze him. All of which made me suspect he was getting extra help. The idea that the prox were secretly rooting for and assisting Gideon was frightening. But what could I do about it?

There were less than ten of us now. I had to make it through only one more challenger in order to advance to the finals. I was confident I could do it, but shocked when the Sphinx announced who I'd be going up against.

"Next up, the Fiery Rose versus the Song Bird."

I stared, wide-eyed, at the girl sitting beside me. Vaness brushed long feathers out of her eyes before giving me a sad smile.

"I guess we won't be going on together," said Vaness.

"I guess not," I said miserably.

She reached for me, and together, we walked hand in hand to the platforms and the waiting Sphinx.

The bubble of silence formed around us and the sounds of the Sphinx became magnified: clattering teeth, clinking scales, creaking bones, and the rush of air as the monster inhaled.

Reluctantly, I let go of Vaness's hand. But before I could step onto my platform, she wrapped me in a feathery embrace. She sniffed back tears and whispered, "This is for the best."

I would've asked what she meant, but she turned away too quickly and leapt up onto her own platform. She faded behind a shimmering veil.

I stepped onto my own and gazed up into the Sphinx's burning blue eyes.

"That was sssweet," she hissed. "Now, here is your riddle:

You may try to imprison me inside a paper-bound cage;
And keep me on shelves, all dusted with age;
But open my prison, and glance at the page;
And I'll infect your mind with enlightening rage.
What am I?
Give me your answer or give me your life."

I blinked, and a rush of adrenaline crashed through my body.

I didn't know the answer. And worse, my mind was so scattered with thoughts of Vaness – the way she'd nearly died after Phaeton had pushed her into the skinning pool – and the way she'd sobbed against my shoulder after I'd saved her. This wasn't some nameless puzzler like all the others I'd faced off against so far. This was someone I'd come to care about. I hated the prox for putting me in this position. And what about Ogden? How much of my hatred should I reserve for him? He said he was trying to help me, but he was also part of the system that had brought me here. I was flustered and confused. It was too much for my mind to wade through and find the answer.

Focus, a voice told me.

The answer had something to do with books – or maybe that was a distraction. Books were a bit of a rarity these days. Who could afford all that paper? Or the space to store it in? And besides, few people read anymore. Our voyces told us everything we needed to know. I shook my head, trying to clear it. Books held *stories* – could that be something that infected your mind? I didn't think so. Any possible answer – or even the required focus to find an answer – slipped from my grasp like a bar of soap.

I was going to fail. My only comfort was that I'd be losing to Vaness. At least someone I cared for would be advancing to the finals. I thought of Yadira and Cadence. What would happen to them? And what about Ogden? Would he honor his promise to help them, or would he carry on like I never existed? It bothered me that I didn't know.

I braced myself for what was coming next. I'd experienced the Sphinx's wrath before, so I knew what to expect. Still, it wouldn't be pleasant.

Suddenly, the bubble of silence vanished. The roar of the crowd rolled in, and a flurry of movement rushed toward me.

But it wasn't the Sphinx.

Vaness leapt up onto my platform and held me in her feathered hands. She pressed her mouth next to my ear and whispered, "It's *knowledge*, Lacey."

"W-what?" I tried to pull away, but she held me in an iron grip.

"Knowledge is the answer," she said. "I could have answered, but…I'm *tired* of all this. And besides, you saved me. I wanted to return the favor." Before I could protest, she pushed away and jumped back down onto the turf.

The Sphinx roared with rage. "Stepping off your platform forfeits the round," she growled. "You give up now, Song Bird, when you are so close to the end?"

"I do," said Vaness.

"Have it your way," said the Sphinx and lunged forward.

The shimmering wall shrouded what happened next, but I could have sworn that I saw – just for an instant – a pair of white blurs moving within the haze. I imagined a flexer or two wrestling Vaness back to her platform. Because while we all witnessed the illusion of the Sphinx consuming her next victim, I knew there was the very practical necessity of loading Vaness back onto her platform so she could be dropped down into the prep room for the auction block. I imagined I could see the milky white flexers push Vaness down into the chute – the long tube that was not unlike the Sphinx's own throat. Either way, Vaness would be consumed. Either eaten by the monster or by the mountain…it didn't make much of a difference.

I gave the answer.

<You did it, Lacey!> Alina shrieked, joyously. <You made it to the finals!>

I slumped back into my seat and barely noticed as the last remaining face-offs commenced. In the end, only four puzzlers remained. A raven-haired girl decorated with colorful squares like a Rubik's cube, a mohawked boy with lightning bolts zigzagging his overskin, myself, and finally, the golden-skinned Phaeton.

One more day and one of us would be crowned the *Puzzling* Champion. I figured I knew who it would be. We already knew Gideon was cheating, but the prox seemed disinterested in doing anything about it.

So rather than feeling any sense of victory, I found myself sinking into a colorless well of misery as they paraded us around the coliseum. Lady Pathe sang our praises as she announced that the final day of the *Puzzling* would commence at noon the following day. My despair continued as they herded us out of the coliseum and through the de-skinning baths. Alina kept chirping words of encouragement. She seemed determined to lighten my mood. I ignored her and tried not to say anything to the others. All I wanted was to get back to my room and scream into my pillow and maybe – just maybe – get one more night of sleep before they took everything from me.

"Hey, Lacey."

It was Phaeton. We had just emerged from the de-skinning baths so we were both completely naked and dripping wet. I had no interest in talking to him – even if I wasn't so exposed. But he was insistent. He grabbed my arm, "Lacey, hold up."

"Get off me," I said and easily slipped my arm from his fingers.

<Don't be so rude,> Alina reprimanded, but I ignored her.

"Whoa, okay. I get it," Phaeton said. "I'm not trying to bug you, but I just wanted to say that I'm looking forward to tonight."

This got my attention. I spun around to face him, and tried to ignore the way his eyes widened. "What are you talking about?" I snapped.

He scratched the back of his head. His face and hands were still gold with body paint. It was comically out of place when compared to the rest of his naked body that looked pink and soft.

"It's tradition," he said. "The finalists and their guardians are always invited to a dinner party with Lady Pathe. I'm looking forward to seeing you again in person."

I peered into his eyes. "That you, Gideon?"

Phaeton smiled a broad grin, but I knew it wasn't him pulling the strings. "I hope you'll give me a moment of your time."

"I have no interest in talking to you, *cheater*."

Gideon/Phaeton bit his golden lip in frustration. "Well, I hope you'll consider what I have to say. But if not, it's no skin off my back." He sighed. "In any case, I do look forward to seeing you. And I hope you have a nice evening. It's bound to be the last one you'll ever have."

And with that, Phaeton's eyes glazed over and Gideon slipped away.

Chapter 24

The electric carriage whined as it threaded its way through a narrow, lantern lit path. I had a strange feeling Ogden and I were traveling backwards through time – that the deeper we ventured into the mountain, the closer we got to some ancient spring from which spilled all of humanity's past.

This idea was only strengthened by the beautiful, black mare tethered to our carriage. I'd never seen a real horse. Still haven't – I figure – because this one wasn't real either. Before we got in the carriage, I tried to brush her side, but my hand passed right through her. Augmented reality. Inside the carriage, the sound of the electric engine was masked by the not-really-there horse's clip-clopping along on the cobblestoned street. The further we traveled, the more of the mare's leathery scent filled our carriage.

The prox wanted me to believe Ogden and I were headed to some nineteenth century gala, but like so many things here, it was only pretend.

Ogden sat beside me in his dapper, velvet suit. The gold chain around his neck flashed in the lantern light. He fidgeted nervously as he peered through the open window. He seemed to be having a hard time making eye contact.

"Is everything okay?" I asked.

He scrunched up his face like he had caught wind of a sour scent. "I'm worried about tonight," he said.

"Why?"

He shrugged. "So many prox in one place always makes me nervous." Even I could tell that wasn't all of it. He was a cellie, after all. I was sure he'd spent loads of time chumming it up with the prox and other elites. No, something else was on his mind.

I took his hand. His skin was warm. He didn't resist my touch, but his whole body tensed. My fingertips traced the inside of his palm, smoothing away the tension I found there. "Come on," I said. "You can talk to me."

I thought he might not respond, and for a while, the only sound was the clatter of horse hooves on stone. Finally, he turned to face me. His blue eyes glowed like miniature moons, and his hand tightened around my own as he said, "The end is near, Lacey. I don't want our time to end."

I blinked. "Our time…"

"In less than twenty-four hours…the *Puzzling* will be over…and our time together…." He swallowed. "What do you think will happen to us?"

How should I know? I wanted to shout at him, but instead I kept quiet. What *would* happen to us? I wouldn't even know how to begin. We came from two different worlds. Imagining a future with Ogden Oliver felt as real as the augmented reality horse pulling our carriage. And besides, everything depended on how I did on the final day of the *Puzzling*. A loss would doom me to a lifetime of mindless slavery. And a victory would provide a ticket into the prox's Panopticon. Who knew what I'd find there? There didn't seem to be any clear path forward.

I said, "I figure you'll be fine without me." The words felt harsh and bitter, even to me.

"Lacey, I…" He stopped when I pulled my hand from his. I didn't want to get into this right now. The last thing I wanted was to show up at some prox party looking like a train wreck. And if Ogden and I started talking about the future, that was what I'd be. On some level, I think we both knew tonight would be our last night together, so what would be the point in ruining it?

"Tell me about this party," I said, changing the subject. "What can we expect?"

His face flushed, then he cleared his throat and shifted to a tone that was all business. "Just a gathering of the finalists and their guardians. We should be okay as long as we stick together. Try not to get cornered by anyone, especially my brother. Gideon's opportunistic. If he sees a chance to get an advantage in the *Puzzling*, he'll take it." Ogden rolled his wrists in agitation. "Also, you must remember that from here on, there's no more time-outs." He tapped his temple. "Understand?"

I nodded. *Time-out* had become our codeword for shutting off our voyces. Ogden was worried this close to the finals that the prox would be keeping an extra close watch on us. Everything we said and did from now on, we'd need to do it with our voyces' knowledge.

<Of course there's no time-outs,> whispered Alina, clearly not picking up on all that Ogden implied. <We're nearly there.>

Up ahead, the cobbled pathway gave way to a massive mansion. Three stories, each with iron-rod, wraparound balconies – all covered in flowery, looping vines. I wondered if any of them were real. We were still in the depths of the mountain. With no sunlight, I doubted any plants could grow for real down here. Wide, white pillars gave the place the look of something pulled from a pre-submerged French Quarter. Flickering torches cast the scene in dancing shadows and the mansion seemed to shiver in the shifting light. Up above, I knew there must have been a ceiling or perhaps a stalactite covered cavern, but I saw only stars, bright and dazzling. I reminded myself not to trust anything I saw.

<Welcome to *Pathe House*,> whispered Alina.

* * *

"Introducing the Fiery Rose, Lacey Clarke and her guardian, Ogden Oliver." The gathering of over a hundred elites offered polite applause as Ogden led me into the center of a sprawling lobby with high, sparkling chandeliers and a ceiling painted with hundreds of plump cherubs in flowing cloth. It made me sick. Here was one more elite hangout plastered in gaudy decadence. The elites spread throughout the room – either perched on stools or gyrating to the orchestra's synthwave melody. Most of them sipped colorful libations from fluted glasses. It was all so...*extreme.*

Something else bothered me but I couldn't pinpoint what it was until a trio of immaculately dressed elites approached us. A woman flanked by two men – all three of 'em wore the same shade of turquoise. All had the same jet-black hair and deeply-tanned, amber skin. And when they moved, they reacted to each other's movements as if engaged in an intricate dance. A twist of the woman's hips resulted in the men shifting to compensate. I figured it could mean only one thing: they were prox. And not only that, the place was filled with them.

"Well, if it isn't the Fiery Rose." The prox woman extended her hand, fingers down. I stared, not sure what she wanted.

<Show some respect, Lacey. Take her hand. Give a kiss.>

Her skin smelled of pears and sea salt and was oily to the touch. It gave me the impression this body was constantly being cleaned and primed for use.

"Who are you and what do you want?" I asked, the words having about as much tact as an air horn.

<Watch your tone,> chastised Alina.

But the prox seemed not to mind. The three of them laughed in unison.

<This is Safira,> Alina whispered. <They've been prox for over seventy years.>

The woman tugged at my arm and I fell into a group hug with all three of them. Safira whispered through their bodies, alternating between them one by one.

"We wish…"

"…you good fortune…"

"…in the finals tomorrow."

"Yet if you don't win…"

"…take comfort in knowing…"

"…that *Safira* will be bidding…"

"…on you at auction."

"…I'm sure you'll make…"

"…a fine husk…"

"…for my collection."

Get in line, I thought. What Gideon had said when I first met him came to mind. He'd told Ogden that he intended to bid on me as well. It seemed elites were lining up to purchase control over my body. They wanted to climb inside my skin and put me on like an evening dress. Which made me think, did prox have different husks for different occasions – like work clothes or business attire? And what would I be? Would I be something the prox wore just whenever, like a pair of sweatpants, or would I be something fancy – something they only put on for nice occasions? I wondered, morbidly, what sort of price I would fetch at auction. It was too bad I wouldn't be able to use any of it to pay off Yadi's debts. Maybe then I wouldn't mind so much.

All three pairs of Safira's hands traced my shoulders, brushed against my cheek, and ran through my hair. They winked as one and said, "See you later," then turned away.

I faced Ogden who looked pale. "This is bad. We shouldn't have come here." He swallowed. "I'm sorry, Lacey, but Helen wouldn't let me interrupt."

<Lighten up,> said Alina. <You're both honored guests. So, try to enjoy yourselves.>

The party proceeded around us. Ogden led me through the crowd and a series of uncomfortable introductions. Cool-eyed wolves were flanked by their entourages – a mix of blank-eyed servants and eye-candy cellies. Here and there, we'd run into a prox. I was getting better at picking them out from the crowd. Small groups of people – two to four at a time – revolved around each other. Usually with matching clothes and hair, the prox looked a bit like entertainers – like members of the same performing dance troupe.

Ogden played the part of the world's most fun-loving Cellie. His broad smile rarely left his face. He was quick witted and often replied to approaching elites with a quip that usually left them doubled over in a fit of laughter.

"Helen gives me most of my jokes," he confided. "I repeat them because that's the role I'm meant to play."

He stopped walking then, and turned to face me. To my surprise, his eyes were gleaming with unfallen tears.

"I asked you earlier what you think might happen to us." He brushed a wisp of hair out of my face. "If I had one wish, it would be for a chance…a chance to stop pretending to be something we're not."

"That would be nice," I said, "but I'd wish for more wishes."

He smiled, and *gods* help me, auditor, I could've kissed him right then and there. I could have buried my fingers in his fire-blond hair and kissed every inch of him.

He slipped a hand around my waist. The fabric of my dress was smooth as water, so formed to my own skin that I had to check – just to be sure – that it was indeed still there. He took my other hand in his and led me in a dance. He was capable of so much. Hadn't I been watching him for years on the dance-offs? Ogden could have danced circles around me, but that's not what he did. His movements now were not for show. They were slow and rhythmic. He was like the ocean and I was a vessel riding his waves, my watery dress billowing between us.

The rest of the party seemed to fade away, until there was only us. We pushed each other along until it became difficult to tell whose current was strongest. Who wanted the other more?

Eventually, our movements led us away from the dancefloor. We made our way into a narrow hallway along the fringes that curved beneath a staircase. The space was dark and offered shelter from prying eyes.

<I think he wants to kiss you,> said Alina.

"Oh shut up, Alina."

Our lips found each other in the dark. The social gathering thrummed around us, but in that moment, we were the only ones there.

Except we weren't. I became aware of someone else's presence so suddenly; it was as if a bucket of ice water had been poured down my back.

"Here you are," cried a pair of voices, speaking in

unison. We both turned to see the platinum twins, Micah. Their blazing white hair and clothes made them glow in the darkness like ghostly apparitions.

"Hello…Micah," said Ogden. There was dread in his voice.

"I've been looking all over for you…" said the woman.

"…only to find you here in the dark…" said the man.

"…having fun without me," they said together.

They moved toward us. The man gripped my shoulders and pulled me away while the woman slithered into Ogden's arms. She slipped her leg around his back and playfully nibbled his earlobe. I couldn't do anything as the man pushed me back against the wall. He said, "This will only take a minute. Don't move." Then he released his hold on me and turned to join Ogden and the other platinum twin.

My body was unresponsive. Every time I tried to move, I felt a jolt like I was touching an electric wire or something. After a few attempts, Alina said, <Jeez, Lacey. Would you cool it? He said, 'Don't move.'>

I could do nothing as the platinum twins had their way with Ogden. They tore off his jacket and ran their hands up the inside of his shirt. He just stood there like a statue, a horrified look on his face as the platinum twins had their fun.

"Oggeeee," pleaded the woman. "Why so standoffish?"

Through gritted teeth, Ogden said, "I…don't…want to do this."

"But that was our arrangement," said the man. "Two servants…that's what we agreed. Two for the price of a little fun now and again."

Ogden said nothing, but on the mention of 'two servants', his eyes darted toward mine. And then I understood. *Yadira and Cadence.* This was the price for setting them free. Soon after they'd been taken out of circulation, Ogden had told me that "Nothing is free" and that he'd had to do unspeakable things to help them – to help *me*.

I eyed the platinum twins with dawning hatred. Here

now were Ogden's debt collectors. And they didn't want money.

"It isn't easy removing a pair of servants from the rosters and allowing them to be taken without notice," said the woman.

"And we don't ask questions about what you're doing with them or why they've disappeared completely from the voyce network," said the man. He kissed Ogden's neck as the woman went on. "All we care about is the price you agreed to pay."

"I understand the deal," Ogden said flatly.

Together, the platinum twins said, "We'll take payment whenever or however we want."

Alina wouldn't allow me to move, and if I used the deactivation phrase in the presence of prox…that was sure to be a disaster.

I tried to protest, but even that was hard. I focused all my energy on making my jaw work. Raw emotion formed like a boil under the skin. Anger and disgust gathered in one place, ready to explode. But nothing happened. Nothing I did or thought of could get past Alina's hold on me. I felt awash with despair until, suddenly, something shifted. I felt her control *slip*. Alina squeaked in surprise, and the bubble of emotion seemed to *burst*. The released pressure *fired* a single word up my throat.

"Ssstop!" I shouted.

To my surprise, the platinum twins did just that. Blinking, they turned their icy gazes on me.

"And why should we?" they asked in unison.

<Be careful,> warned Alina. She sounded afraid.

"I'm a puzzler," was all I could think to say, "one of only four to have survived this long."

Their eyes narrowed in frustration, and I could feel a static building in the air between us as if at any moment, lightning would fire from their eyes.

"This close to the finals, what would Lady Pathe say if she found out you were messing with one of the last puzzlers' guardian?"

At the mention of Lady Pathe's name, the twins flinched. Their furrowed brows retracted into something like *uncertainty* or even fear.

"Lady Pathe doesn't frighten us," said the man. But I could tell by the waver in his voice that she did indeed. And really, how could she not invoke fear? Every day of the *Puzzling*, Lady Pathe had appeared as a giant phantom made of sparks and electricity. If that didn't scare you, nothing would.

"Leave Ogden alone," I said. "Until after the *Puzzling*, at least."

I barely saw what happened next. The woman was a blur of motion, and the world exploded. My cheek was immediately aflame from where she'd struck me. I would have pitched forward, had the man not shoved me back hard against the wall.

"How *dare* you tell a prox what they can or can't do. If you weren't a puzzler –"

<*But she is,*> interrupted Alina. Her voyce was hard as stone. I was surprised to hear her coming to my defense. <She is a puzzler. And not just any puzzler…a *finalist*. She may even become this year's champion. Do you really want to get on her bad side?>

I couldn't deny the flicker of pleasure I felt at watching the inner turmoil playing behind Micah's female eyes. Her tanned skin darkened, but she drew away.

"My apologies, Puzzler," she said bitterly. Then, the two platinum twins scurried away to join the rest of the party.

Ogden and I didn't get much time to talk after that. The lights flashed red and screams broke out on the dancefloor. I helped Ogden back into his jacket, and we stepped out from behind the staircase to find the interior engulfed in flames.

The crystal chandeliers were now blazing bonfires suspended in air. The cherubs from earlier had been transformed into red-skinned devils with pointed faces. The orchestral music devolved into discordant clangs and crashes.

Despite the hellish scene, I wasn't afraid. The bonfires radiated heat, but it didn't feel like the sort of thing I'd experienced near the gas stoves at *Stratus*. This heat felt more…*ornamental*, like it was just for show. Which, I supposed, it was.

"Illusion," I said. Ogden nodded beside me.

A pair of double doors opened on the opposite end of the room.

<Puzzlers and guardians,> boomed Lady Pathe's voyce. *<Please enter.>*

Chapter 25

A large fountain stood in the center of a courtyard crisscrossed with strung lights. Small tables were set around the fountain. None of them were big enough for us all, so it was clear we'd be sitting on our own. I figured I'd be sharing a table with Ogden, but Alina made it clear I was to sit on my own. Ogden shared a curt greeting with a black-clad Gideon before the two brothers joined the other two guardians at the only table big enough for all of them. It was set for five, the only empty chair was at the head.

The puzzlers and I were instructed to sit at our own individual tables. I felt foolish, like I'd been banished to the kiddie table or something.

I moved a pile of greens around on my plate while I tried to listen in on the guardians' conversation, but this close to the fountain, I couldn't make out any of their words.

<Hey, Lacey.>

I turned to the side, and sitting a table away was Phaeton. His blond hair glowed dimly beneath the string lights. His eyes locked on mine. And when he spoke, his lips barely moved. He was too quiet to hear over the fountain, but his voyce amplified his words loud and clear inside my head.

<I hoped we could share a word.>

"Who's talking?" I asked. "Is it Phaeton or Gideon?"

Alina tried to tell me nobody was talking, but I ignored her.

Phaeton smirked and tilted his head toward the guardians' table. <I think you know who's talking.> I looked that way just as Gideon's ice-cold gaze passed over me. <It's-a-me,> his voyce said in a sing-song tone. Then, he turned his attention back to the other guardians.

Ogden sat stony faced, seemingly unaware that his brother's voyce had tapped into my neuro-net. Gideon appeared to nod along as one of the guardians, a woman in dark black furs, gestured wildly. Apparently, Gideon was able to be in two places at once. His real self was talking to the other guardians, while his voyce communicated with me through Phaeton, acting as a conduit. Gideon was certainly full of surprises.

"I don't want to talk to you," I said.

<Oh?> his tone feigned like he was hurt. <But I thought we had an understanding.>

"You killed Aaron."

<What?> cried Alina. <Why would you say that?>

"I'm not talking to you," I said, annoyed. "Please don't interrupt."

Phaeton had a bored look on his face. <I'm sorry…but who is Aaron?>

"In the first round of the *Puzzling*…you planted a device on him. You made the prox believe he was cheating."

<Oh, *that*.> Phaeton waved his hand dismissively. <To be fair, I planted a device on both of you. I didn't think you'd actually give up. I mean, I tried to make it worth your while, but I didn't believe you'd really go through with it. The cheating thing was my backup plan. At first, I only intended to target you, but then that friend of yours tried to hit me at the skinning pool. Tsk tsk.

<Anyways, you would have shared his fate, but you gave up.>

"Only because you made me."

Phaeton sighed. <Most unfortunate, and a miscalculation on my part. I didn't really believe you'd sacrifice yourself for others.> He cocked his head. <By the way, what ever happened to those dead-heads? Yadira and Cadence? Turns out they've completely disappeared from the voyce network. Did you and Ogden have something to do with that?>

I gritted my teeth. The smug threat and the blasé way he spoke of killing Aaron made me want to turn over his table and plunge my steak knife into his chest.

You'll never make it, I told myself. So, I tried to stay

calm as I said, "I don't know what you're talking about."

Phaeton grinned. I looked past the golden-haired puzzler toward the guardians' table where Gideon wore the exact same, smug expression.

<Lacey, you're a terrible liar.> He waved this away. <Anyways, that's not important right now. What's important is that Aaron only died because he aligned himself with *you*. At first, I figured it was a good thing…like I'd killed two birds with one stone, but then Lady Pathe brought you back.> His voyce took on a mocking tone. <All in the interest of fairness and equality…*barf*.> Phaeton made a gagging noise.

<What's his problem?> Alina asked, oblivious to the conversation going on between Gideon and me.

"You killed Aaron," I repeated.

Phaeton strummed his fingers impatiently. It was something I'd seen Gideon do on more than one occasion. He said, <Yes, yes, we've been over this. But Lacey, you gotta understand. Right now, I'm trying to *help* you.>

"I don't believe anything you say."

Phaeton pursed his lips and nodded. <Very wise of you, but hear me out. I *know* you and my brother have some sort of grand plan. Ogden probably thinks he can use our parents' illicit voyce commands to really stick it to the prox. Am I right?>

I stiffened, doing all I could to keep any trace of emotion off of my face.

<You can't touch them. Even *trying* would be a huge disaster.>

I took a bite of salad. A cherry tomato burst between my teeth as I fixed Phaeton with as harsh a glare as I could muster. "Do you harass all the puzzlers, or just me?"

<Only you,> he said.

"I'm flattered."

<Don't be. It's not because you're special or anything. It's solely because of who your guardian is.>

"You mean Ogden, your brother. Why do you have it out for him?"

He ignored the question. <If you go into the Panopticon and try some stupid trick he's taught you, you'll fail. And fail *hard.*>

I turned away and took a sip of water.

<Normally, I couldn't care less about what happens to a slag like you, but if you try something and *fail*, it'll tip off the prox about certain…vulnerabilities. They'll shore up their defenses and make it difficult for me to try later. And Lacey, if I try it, I'll *succeed.* You'll only crash and burn.>

"You were wrong about me before."

<I'm not wrong about this, Lacey. You…will…*fail.* The only way for you to come out of this alive, is to lose.>

Oh, here we go again, I thought. What I said out loud was, "You must think I'm pretty stupid."

<Actually, no. Which is why I'm trying to talk some sense into you.>

"Well, you can forget it. I have no interest in your *sense.* I'm all sensed out." I was feeling a bit childish, but so what? I'd heard enough of his manipulations. "I'm not buying what you're selling, so you can give it a rest."

<If you say so,> he said, <but one last thing. You should know I've recently made a new friend.>

"I don't care."

<Oh, I think you should. You see, this new friend of mine is a flexer boy, goes by the name, *Vitus.*> Phaeton's eyes flashed white and…

Blink. A strobe of images flashed before my eyes. Vitus, slumped on his knees. One eye covered in bloody bandages, the other filled with tears. He was pleading for help. I couldn't make out the words, but the look of relief that washed over his face was unmistakable. He bowed his head forward and a hand – black fingernails, red thumbnail – Gideon's hand lowered atop the flexer's head as if bestowing a blessing.

In his other hand, Gideon lifted a familiar looking device. It looked exactly like the one I'd first seen back in the mutie tenement building. A long metal rod with blinking red lights. Gideon pressed the device against the flexer's temple, and Vitus' one good eye rolled back into his head.

Blink, and the images were gone.

I feared what Gideon might say next.

<Vitus was having a tough time when I found him. Someone had tampered with his voyce – activated some sort of chaos program. Luckily, I found him when I did.> Somehow, I knew luck had nothing to do with it. More likely, Gideon was coming to check on me, to make sure I stayed quiet about our perceived agreement. But with mine and Ogden's voyces deactivated at the time, he couldn't find us. So, he found Vitus instead.

<That flexer told me some interesting things about you and Ogden…about how you're both using illegal voyce commands. Not only on each other, but also on flexers like Vitus.> Phaeton's eyes gleamed. <Something like that could get you in a lot of trouble.> He let the unspoken threat spread between us. I felt sick. A dead-head took my salad and replaced it with a steaming plate of pasta, but I'd lost my appetite.

Phaeton settled back and examined his fingernails as Gideon's voyce continued. <I don't have to be your enemy, you know. We *can* work together. I can help you, even. All you need do is quit.>

"If I don't?" I asked.

Alina thought I was asking about the food and told me to eat while I still had the chance.

Phaeton steepled his fingers. <If you *don't* quit, you'll regret it. The prox doesn't take kindly to those who mess with their flexers. If someone were to tell them...> He shrugged. <It wouldn't end well.>

I only stared at him. This was a man who'd had his parents turned into muties. Is that what he'd do to me? My eyes, ears, and tongue carved out of my head? My body hollowed out like a jack-o-lantern? My brain retrofitted for mindless slavery?

"After everything you've done, what makes you think I'd ever trust you?"

<We want the same thing. Only, my brother is too good to do what must be done.>

"And what's that?" I asked.

<Anything it takes. And sometimes cruelty is what's needed to end cruelty. Do you honestly think Ogden has what it takes to be cruel?>

"I don't think he's anything like you."

<Which is why he'll fail. Why you'll *both* fail…without my help.>

I didn't want to believe him.

Even if what he said was true, he was too dangerous. His past actions were too cold-hearted for him to be trusted now.

<It's your call,> he said. <Think about it.>

Before I could even muster a response, something strange happened. The air came alive. It rippled around us and scratched at my skin. It fizzed and popped like mineral water. I felt the connection to Gideon's voyce drop away as if it was a physical thing – like he'd quickly removed his hand from my forehead.

<Lady Pathe is here,> said Alina. <And for gosh sakes, Lacey, *please* stop talking to yourself like a crazy person.>

Alina guided my gaze up toward a balcony stretching over the courtyard. Five people stood at the railing, the full moon behind them filling the augmented sky so I saw little more than their silhouettes. But as they descended a pair of spiral staircases, I saw at once that they were all distinct in their own way. Lady Pathe, unlike the other prox I'd seen tonight, maintained husks of varying diversity and appearance. At the forefront, a woman with jet black hair and dress was flanked by two men. One of the men was completely hairless in a snakeskin jacket while the other sported an impressive beard with complicated braids reaching down to the center of his chest. Two women trailed behind. One had short, spikey hair with frosted tips while the other had long, luminous blonde hair curled into golden rings.

They paused briefly beneath the balcony then stared at

the woman in black. Head tilted back and eyes closed, she raised her palms as if in prayer. Everything was still for several seconds. Even the sound of the fountain's running water seemed to cease.

Then, the lady in black opened her bright eyes and each husk split apart from the group and headed toward a different table. The lady in black glided over to the guardians' table. The bearded man took a seat in front of Phaeton. The bald guy and the woman with spiky hair took seats before the other two puzzlers, respectively. I still didn't know their names. They had appeared quite formidable during the last round of the *Puzzling* – the girl with her purple hair and cubed overskin, and the boy with his mohawk and lightning bolts – but now they just looked scared and uncomfortable, like children forced into too-tight outfits for a family photo.

Because that's what they are, I thought. *Children.*

The last of Lady Pathe's husks, the blonde, approached my table. Surprisingly, she asked, "Do you mind if I join you?"

"Please," I said, feeling absurd, "be my guest."

The woman watched me with wide, almond-colored eyes as she lowered herself into the chair and rested her chin on the backs of her hands. Her focus gave off the impression that all her attention was centered entirely on me. The thought was damaged somewhat by the fact that Lady Pathe's awareness was split amongst four other husks here in the courtyard. I tried to imagine what it would be like to be in five places at once. I figured I'd hate it. How could anyone keep track of such a thing? I stared at the woman in front of me and tried to look through her at the person pulling the strings. What did the real Lady Pathe look like? Who was she really?

"You're a remarkable person," she said.

"Thank you. I could say the same about you."

She smiled, but it was a cold thing, like a mannequin in a clothing shop.

"Tomorrow's the big day," said the Pathe husk. "One of you will be crowned champion."

I shrugged.

She continued, "Which is why I needed to speak with you and the rest of the puzzlers. I need to check your voyces and make sure you're all safe."

I stared at her, afraid that anything I said or did would betray my thoughts. *Does she know about the voyce commands?*

"<Give me your hands.>" The imperative boomed in my mind. It was not a request, and my arms jerked out from my sides. My hands stretched out in front of her, and she took them in her own. It was then I realized her fingernails had been filed into sharp points. They pressed into my skin just on the verge of painful.

"*Post Vitast*," she hissed. Smoke poured from her mouth and eye sockets. It slid over my hands and table and seemed to eat away at everything it touched. I felt my arms wither and break apart like dead leaves. I tried to scream, but only inhaled more of the stuff until I could feel it chewing at the walls inside my chest. The smoke reached up and raked an inky hand across my face. My eyes ceased to function; my ears stopped working. The last thing I was aware of was Lady Pathe's husk before me. Black smoke poured from her eyes. That cold mannequin smile, framed by her luminous hair, glowed in the dark like a sunspot.

*   *   *

The world was a cascade of shifting shadows and mist.

I've been here before, I thought. *In the weeks after my capture. I'd been a dead-head, and this…is the shadowscape.*

"Everything looks in order," said a woman's voice. I spun around to find the husk with blonde, luminous hair standing amidst the shadows. She nodded her approval as if examining a house for sale. It was then I noticed her colors were all wrong. Everything from the yellow of her hair, the red of her dress, and the lightning white of her eyes were alarmingly ablaze. They were too bright for this place. She was a cartoon come to life. If anything, it made it clear this woman didn't belong here. She had no right to walk around inside the place where my dreams and thoughts took shape.

"Why did you bring me here?" I asked.

Lady Pathe didn't answer, not right away. Instead, she held up her hands. The shifting shadows gathered before her, and from the darkness, four faceless figures emerged. I understood them to represent the remaining puzzlers.

"Tomorrow's match will be different," said Lady Pathe. "You will all be asked five riddles. The two quickest will advance." Two of the figures burst apart like a scattering of ash. "If you make it that far, the final two will not be asked any riddles at all. Instead, it will be your turn to present your own riddle."

"I don't understand."

"Ask me a riddle. If it is fair. If it stumps the other puzzler, I will crown *you* my champion." Another one of the figures blew apart, so there was only one left. A golden crown appeared on the last figure's head, and their entire body pulsed with fiery light. "Champions are transformed into something beyond your understanding. They become more than human." Great, flaming wings burst from the figure's back. It became a mighty Seraphim – an archangel from legend. Its wings stretched wide and crashed down. The motion rocketed it up into the darkness. The shadows rushed in behind it and left only a faint afterglow of where it had been just seconds before.

"This is where I leave you," said Lady Pathe.

"Wait," I cried. "Why riddles?"

"Excuse me?" she asked.

"Why do you care so much about riddles?"

She didn't answer because she was no longer there. The shadows surrounded me. They scurried like rats and revolved around me like a swarm of insects. When they rushed over my ankles, I didn't bother putting up a fight. The shadowscape enveloped me in writhing smoke. It dragged me down into the floor and pulled me back into the real world.

*   *   *

Ogden was beside me when I woke. He helped me to my feet and slipped his arm around my waist to steady me. Phaeton and the purple-haired puzzler both looked as if they were gonna be sick, or had been already. Despite this, neither Phaeton nor Purple-hair's guardian did a thing to help. Gideon stood off to the side, impatiently tapping his foot. The mohawked puzzler was the only one of us still unconscious. His guardian – a portly man in a fringed suit – knelt beside him and was gently shaking his shoulders.

"Time to go," said Ogden.

All of Lady Pathe's husks stood around the fountain. Arms folded behind their backs, their cold gazes surveyed those of us who had collapsed, but like Gideon, they did nothing to help. Before turning away, I took one last look at them. They were all facets of the same person – a single intelligence pulling the strings of five living people. Everything they had been had been sanded down to nothing. All so the prox in their heads could pretend to be something more than human. The husk with blonde hair glanced my way and winked. Her lips moved, and a second later, the words exploded in my skull.

<Reason to survive. Perish the rest.>

Ogden half led, half carried me back toward the exit. We moved in a rush through the party – music, harsh laughter, clinking glassware – until we were outside in front of our waiting carriage.

The whole way back to the puzzler dorms, I held tight to Ogden. I clutched at his clothes as if it could somehow anchor me to this reality. Tomorrow would come much too fast. And with it would come the end of everything. The end of all this…and the end of myself.

Chapter 26

I didn't see the remaining puzzlers again until right before we entered the coliseum. My overskin was applied and customized in private. And when I emerged from the prep stations, I was the only one there. I stared at the sealed elevator doors, and willed myself to come up with a good riddle. A night of tossing and turning hadn't provided a single one.

Alina had kept interrupting my thoughts. She'd sing a lullaby, whisper affirmations, or tell me how proud she was of me. Every time she spoke, her words derailed my thoughts.

Lady Pathe had told me to come with a riddle, and now, minutes before entering the coliseum, I had nothing. The realization threatened to push my mind into a frenzy, so I forced myself to stay calm, take deep breaths, and clear my head so a riddle could find me.

The conveyor belt hummed and deposited my first challenger, the boy with the mohawk. His stylists had woven some sort of filament lights into his overskin so that his lightning bolts seemed to fork and crackle as he walked. He moved quickly to the wall and slumped against it.

<Jair Castaneda,> whispered Alina. <Back home, he was a runaway. Spent most days working construction. No one has reported him missing. I wonder if anyone even knows he's gone.>

A minute later, the raven-haired girl emerged. The patchwork of color on her overskin shone like mosaic tiles.

<Her name's Tatiana Whitman. A student. She had a part-time nanny job. Her parents mounted a frantic search for her soon after she was taken. Thankfully, some flexers stepped in and told them to stop looking. No need to worry themselves to death.>

"Hey," said Tatiana.

"Hello." I nodded back. "Good luck today."

"Same to you," she said. And despite the tension in her eyes, she gave a little smirk and said, "What a crazy month this has been."

"Right," I said. "A real doozy." We smiled at each other and it was nice knowing that, under different circumstances, I think we could have been friends.

The conveyor belt presented Phaeton last, and any levity in the room died in an instant. He headed straight for the elevator doors, fixing each of us with a disapproving glare along the way.

The elevator doors cracked open then, and Alina said, <It's time, Lacey. Win or fail, it's been nice knowing you.>

"A real honor," I lied, and stepped inside.

* * *

The coliseum shook with the cries and shouts of the spectating elites. The thunder of stomping feet passed through my overskin and rumbled in my bones. The disembodied head of Lady Pathe blazed like the sun, but we only heard the tail end of her remarks, "Reason to survive. Perish the rest," before she exploded into a shower of sparks.

We took our places on the disc-like platforms. I tried to control my trembling as steam gathered on the far side of the coliseum. The crowd screamed our names:

"Phaeton!"

"Tatiana!"

"Jair!"

"Lacey!"

There didn't seem to be a favorite, and I wondered if the elites even cared who we were. Did they even think of us as people?

"Is Ogden here?" I asked.

<Yes,> answered Alina. <Your guardian is watching. The whole *world* is watching.>

For the last time, the Sphinx stepped into the coliseum.

The scales glittered on her otherwise human face. Her massive wings unfolded and flapped like the canvasses of some ancient, sailing vessel. The ground shuddered when she knelt before us. Tons of explosive power gathered in her rear legs. And soon, I knew, she'd leap forward like an avalanche with teeth.

She grinned – a truly horrible sight – and stated the rules for the next round: "Puzzlers, this round is based on *time*. You'll all be asked five riddles. Answer as quickly as you can. The time will start the moment I begin asking my first riddle. You may answer before I am done, but by doing so, you risk not hearing all the clues. Those who give an incorrect answer will have a full minute added to their time. At the end, the two of you with the quickest times will go on." She paused. All noise seemed to slide out of the coliseum. "Let's begin." A shimmer came up between me and the other puzzlers. I saw only the faintest hint of color to indicate their presence. Less vague were the floating clocks above each of our heads.

00:00:00. I glanced up to see my own clock hovering in the air. And for some reason, this drove home the seriousness of the next few minutes. Those stark numbers represented time, and I felt certain that mine was nearly up.

The Sphinx's teeth clicked together as she asked her first riddle:

"I have a soul, but no life to live.
And a tongue, but no voice to give.
What am I?"

I was fast with my answer, but not fast enough. By the time I shouted, "*Shoe*," the other three had already answered. I heard their responses only as loud dings.

And while I couldn't quite see nor hear the other puzzlers, their times were clear as day. Phaeton: 00:11:34; Jair: 00:12:12; Tatiana: 00:12:76. My time was just over seventeen seconds. I wasn't off to a good start.

The Sphinx wasted no time before launching into the next riddle.

"An ivory world, my presence espouses;

Crunching and biting, I'll cover your houses.
In secret, I'm made.
In silence, I'll invade.
Lay on my skin and I'll melt through your blouses."

"Snow!" I screamed. The answer came to me right after the first line. I cursed myself for not shouting it out when I first thought of it. The others must have thought it was an easy one as well, because all the dings fired in rapid succession. I'd only gained a few seconds on them, but I was still behind.

Gotta take risks, I told myself. *Don't hesitate.*

The Sphinx licked her lips and asked the next riddle:

"I break without damage –"

"Day!" I shouted, not waiting to hear the rest of the riddle. But instead of a *ding*, a harsh horn blast announced that I'd guessed wrong.

The Sphinx cleared her throat and continued:

"Ache without bruising;
Burn without fire;
Attack without violence;
And beat without drums."

Three dings announced that the others had guessed correctly. It was a heart, of course. I would have gotten it right myself if I hadn't been so eager.

The risk had cost me a full minute. Now, Phaeton led the pack with a time of 00:38:12. The other two were only slightly behind him. As for me, I was way behind with a time of 01:53:34. There were only two riddles left, but my chances were all but dead. I'd have to do something drastic if I stood any chance at all.

The Sphinx began again:

"My singular purpose is that of destruction;
Being an agent of ruin is my primary function –"

It's fire, I wanted to scream, but I held back. I'd already made the mistake of answering too soon. Two rapid horn blasts revealed that I wasn't the only one who thought they knew the answer. But they had been wrong. I would have been wrong too if I hadn't already learned my lesson.

The Sphinx continued:

"I begin by summoning a consuming beast,
And set him upon a place to feast.
Strike me hard and my temper flares.
Hold me too long, no one dares."

It wasn't fire, but it was certainly related. The consuming beast could only be fire. But the riddle wasn't talking about that. It was talking about the thing that *summoned* fire. I forced myself to hold off until I was sure, spending a few precious seconds before saying, "A match." The loud *ding* declared my answer correct. This was followed by a second ding. It seemed luck favored the patient after all.

The Sphinx took a deep breath and the blue flames in her eyes burned brighter.

"We come to the last riddle, Puzzlers. Let us review your times."

Above the golden shimmer that was Phaeton, the time read, *00:58:10.* Next, the time above Tatiana's multicolored shimmer read, *02:17:02.* Jair's time was, *02:23:15.* And I was dead last with *02:25:08.* There was really no chance to catch up to Phaeton. The real fight was for whoever would come in second. To do that, I had to be at least six seconds faster than the others.

"For two of you," growled the Sphinx, "this is the end." Her mouth parted to reveal the rows upon rows of glittering teeth. "Here is your final riddle:

A supplanter of youth,
A healer of wounds,
An agent of death,
A catalyst for growth.
More of me is what every one craves,
Still, I'll drag them into their graves.
What am I, Puzzlers?

Give me your answer or give me your life."

A bell sounded. Someone had answered correctly. For once, I prayed that it was Phaeton. Anyone else would mean my time was up.

The words spun in my head like debris in a storm.

Supplanter, healer, death, growth. The pressure of the moment screamed from all directions. In vain, I glanced up at the flickering clock, at the too fast passage of time. *Holy smokes!*

The answer was right there in front of me. A final punchline in this long nightmarish joke.

I shouted what I prayed was the answer. "*Time*!"

An instant later, a mix of horn blast and ringing bell tore apart the coliseum. Two of us had answered at once. One wrong, one right. A final bell signaled a final answer. How many seconds had passed between my answer and theirs? Was it enough? The wall of silence that had surrounded us suddenly collapsed into a cacophonous roar of cheers and shrieks.

The Sphinx towered before us – her face terrible and large.

"A close match," she said. "The answer is something two of you have run out of."

Before I could even glance up at the clocks, the Sphinx launched herself forward. Two massive paws tore through the air and slammed down on either side of me. There was a *wump* followed immediately by the sickening crunch of Jair and Tatiana's bodies. So intense was the impact that I felt certain the crack of bone was my own.

I cowered on my platform and curled into a ball while attempting to assess my injuries. But I had none. It took the cry of Alina's voyce to help me realize I'd made it through.

<Talk about a photo finish,> she cried. <That was…*intense.*>

Slowly, I rose to my feet. The Sphinx lifted her paws to reveal two bloodstained platforms where Tatiana and Jair had been moments before. I knew that despite the blood, they were now in the chutes headed for the auction block. *Still alive,* I told myself, *but not better off.* Glowering at me from his own platform, the golden Phaeton was grinding his teeth.

<Congratulations,> Gideon's voyce echoed in my

mind. <But your victory comes with a heavy price. I blame *you* for what I must do now.>

I had no idea what he meant by this, but the venom of his tone was enough to make me question what I'd done. Had it been foolish to try to win? Was I crazy for thinking I could ever stand against a wolf like him?

With a theatrical flourish, the Sphinx licked the last drops of blood from her paws. Then, she did a double take as if remembering we were still there.

"And now we come to the end of it. The end of *aaaalllllll* of it." She opened her wings and the thrust of air was like a small explosion. I stumbled, but did not fall atop my platform. "I have asked all my questions and have eaten my fill of puzzlers. Now, it is your turn. Both of you shall ask your own question. A riddle, fair and true. Whosoever can answer the quickest, that person will become our champion. So, go on. The time is now. Give me your riddle."

After everything I'd gone through. After all the lives I'd seen ruined by this Sphinx and the prox's grand *Puzzling*, I knew that I was finally at my stop. There was no way I'd be going any further, because…my mind was completely blank.

Chapter 27

For so long, I prided myself on my ability to solve word puzzles. To break them down, examine their parts, and rip out the answer like the still beating heart of a dying animal. A gruesome image, I know, but that's how I fancied myself. I was a warrior of sorts. I took pleasure in the hunt for answers. I've told you before, auditor, that the answers to riddles were like rabbits hiding in the weeds. It was only now – at the end – that I finally realized why I loved them so much. By answering a riddle – it allowed me to feel like I had some power. I was a predator chasing down the answers. With riddles, I could pretend I wasn't just prey in a world built for carnivores.

I was Lacey Clarke, solver of riddles, devourer of answers.

It all felt pretty silly now. I looked past the towering Sphinx, out toward the crowds. I searched for Ogden. I wanted to tell him I couldn't do it. No matter how good I was at solving riddles, *creativity* had never been my strength.

"Where's Ogden?" I asked Alina. "Is he still here?"

<You're on your own, Lacey. He can't help you,> she said. <He can't even help himself.>

This frightened me. And it was almost enough to make me forget about the Sphinx looming overhead.

"Why? What's happened?" I asked.

She sighed. <See for yourself.>

All color seemed to drain from the world until only a single spot of yellow remained. The color raced through the stands like an Olympian's torch. It was Ogden. He was difficult to see at this distance, but I could tell he was in trouble. His bright yellow coat trailed behind him as he sprinted through the crowd and maneuvered through the throngs of screaming cellies and wolves.

An oblivious cellie stepped into his path and Ogden

struck him in an explosion of beer and popcorn. Ogden fell out of view only to emerge an instant later, scrambling to regain his feet.

Why is he running? I thought, and that was when I saw them. A group of five flexers swam through the crowd like sharks. They carved their way toward Ogden. The spectators parted before them, clearing a path as if compelled.

Because they are compelled, I thought. I'd never seen flexer boys work their powers over on the elites, but it seemed they were doing it now. As I watched, the leading flexer lifted a fist. Ogden, along with half a dozen elites standing close by, crumpled to the ground.

I felt a pang of electricity – like a misfired nerve – shoot through my own body as if those flexers had attacked me as well. My strength evaporated and I fell to my knees.

"No, they can't," I pleaded with no one. "They can't take him."

<They can, and they must,> said Alina matter-of-factly.

"Why?" I asked, knowing full well there must be a whole host of reasons. What I meant was *why now? What's changed?*

The flexers swarmed over him. In almost no time at all, they had his ankles and wrists in restraints and hauled him out of the coliseum.

<He's a criminal. There was an anonymous tip. Flexers raided his rooms and found illegal hardware – a little black box that can do all sorts of terrible things.> Alina made a *tsk tsk* noise. <Honestly, Lacey. You think you know a guy.>

"What are they gonna do with him?"

<What do they do with all traitors?> The question hung in the air like a noose. For some reason, the image of the Luddites slipped into my mind. Men and women who had tried to stand up against an encroaching technology and were hanged for it. History had a way of dealing with people like that.

I thought of Ogden's parents. The black eyes and white

domed ears of muties. And now Ogden. His parents had wanted only to protect him, but now he would share their fate.

"You have to stop them," I shouted.

<*Stop* them?> said Alina. <Cellie or not, actions have consequences, Lacey. It's bad enough for anyone to mess with their own voyce, but there's rumors that Ogden's used that device on others. A pair of servants have gone missing. They could be in danger.>

Yadira and Cadence, I thought but said nothing. They were in danger, alright. But Ogden wasn't the problem. Alina and the rest of the voyce network were the real danger.

<The flexers received word that Ogden has them stashed somewhere in the puzzler dorms. It's only a matter of time before they're found and rescued.>

More like enslaved, I thought, bitterly.

It seemed the whole world was closing in. I stood in the center of the coliseum. The Sphinx licked her lips while the people I cared about were getting dragged off to face terrible punishments or even death. I wanted to scream. Distantly, I wondered if I even could. Would Alina let me use my own voice? Would she let me – in front of all these people – vent my despair and *anger* in such a primal way? And even if she did, would their voyces let them see how much pain *their* system had caused? I took in a shuddering breath. The force of my rage gathered at the back of my throat. But when I tried to shout, my throat constricted. The force of my scream crashed into the roof of my closed mouth.

<Stop it, Lacey,> cried Alina. <Get a hold of yourself. You must ask your riddle. The Sphinx demands it. And – *my word, Lacey* – you are *sooo* close.>

I wanted to shut her off, to peel the neuro-net from my skull. There had been a time when Alina had been my best friend. I found myself thinking about what sort of person I'd be if I'd grown up without her incessant indoctrination. A lifetime of comfort and companionship? I knew now that she had provided neither of those things.

I wanted her out of my life. Out of my head. Maybe then, I could finally discover who I was supposed to be.

The Sphinx glowered over me.

"It is time, Lacey. Tell me your riddle. If it is fair, you will be allowed to ask it of your opponent."

And that's when it found me. I felt the riddle take root, *shape*, until it blossomed before me like a rose. In the past, I might have wondered where such an idea had come from, but not now. I trusted myself enough to know the riddle had sprung from my own mind – the shadowscape, the place where ideas came alive. And this idea roared for release. I would ask this riddle – there was no question – but I feared the consequences. As I've said before – way back at the beginning if you recall, auditor – some riddles have answers that change everything. And I didn't think the prox would like this one – not one bit.

But I was far past caring. Everyone and everything I loved was being taken away. The least I could do was ask my riddle – the one I was destined to ask.

I gazed up at the Sphinx's blue-flamed eyes and shouted my riddle:

"*What must you lose in order to find*?"

* * *

Phaeton materialized from behind the wall of blurred vision. The light reflected off his gilded body until he looked like a living bonfire. His eyes burned with hatred, and I imagined the heat of his gaze on my skin. I realized, of course, that this was not the face of the boy, Phaeton, who I'd caught snippets of from time to time. No, the nervous, frightened boy wasn't home at the moment. In his place, the cold-hearted, calculating Gideon sneered at me from within the boy's golden skin.

The rules for the final round were simple. We'd take turns asking each other our own riddle. Whoever took the longest to answer would lose.

The Sphinx purred, the sound like a peel of thunder.

"Lady Pathe has flipped a coin," she said, "and Phaeton

will ask his riddle first." She gestured for him to speak. He punched the air in front of him and shook his arms as if preparing for a boxing match. He waved to the stands, and seemed to relish the cheers washing over him. Then he turned toward me, and the world went silent. All I could hear was my own quick breaths.

He began:

"Seek out my veins and I'll bring you great wealth,
Or find me in the blood of gods in good health
I'm the beginning of atonement and the end of you
A ring of myself signals love that is true."

He grinned and the golden paint cracked at the corners of his mouth. At the same time, a floating clock began to tick off the seconds. I could feel the hints swimming below the surface. They tugged me toward the answer, and I didn't resist. That was the only way I knew how to answer. It wasn't about forcing my thoughts into an answer that worked, it was about following the clues and letting the riddle take me where it wanted.

Veins that provided wealth. That part was easy. Lots of valuable metal could be found in veins that ran through the earth. But what about the blood of gods? I could remember hearing something about that. One of my history courses had talked about the blood of gods. It had had a special name. *Ichor*, I thought it was, and some said it had a very distinct color. *Okay. So far, so good.*

The third line. *The beginning of atonement.* The letter A. *The end of you.* The letter U. Together, they formed an element from the periodic table. By now, the last line felt like overkill. *A ring that signaled love.* A wedding ring.

The answer was so obvious that I suspected it might be a trick. Even now, my opponent stood only a few feet away, the answer painted all over his body. Would it really be that easy?

The seconds ticked by at an alarming rate. A trick or not, it was the only answer I had.

"Gold," I shouted.

A long pause, then came the piercing clang of a bell.

Phaeton flinched, and his face soured. I wondered if he

truly thought he could stump me. Maybe, he figured an all-too-obvious riddle would provoke some doubt and buy him a few seconds of time. If that was the case, it had certainly worked. The clock above my head was frozen at just under twenty-seven seconds. Would he be able to answer my own riddle any faster?

The Sphinx gestured with a huge paw for me to start.

So, I asked, "What must you lose in order to find?"

Phaeton squinted as he worked out the problem. He mumbled to himself as if having an argument. Slowly, the defiance in his eyes began to melt into something like panic. The clock ticked past fifteen seconds, and he began to talk louder.

"It could be anything," he said. "You wouldn't need to find *anything* unless it was lost. This is an unfair riddle!"

His eyes pleading, he glanced up at the Sphinx. "You can't allow this. It isn't *fair.*" The Sphinx had become as static as a statue. The only movement was in her tail. It flipped back and forth in whip-crack amusement.

Ten seconds left. Phaeton's begging became more urgent. Five seconds. "*Not fair,*" he repeated.

The time ticked past twenty-seven seconds, and the clock shattered in a spray of glass.

"You failed to answer in time," said the Sphinx.

"No, it's not my fault. That wasn't a fair riddle. What *even is* the answer?"

The Sphinx turned toward me. "Go ahead, Lacey. Tell him."

"What must you lose in order to find?" I said again. "It's a voice."

Despite the look of utter fury on Phaeton's golden face, I could feel the truth of my answer. It's like I said, riddles are honest things. And I could feel the truth of this one echoing in my blood. Ogden had given me the ability to shut down Alina – to silence the artificial voyce in my head. Only in that silence had I discovered my own voice, the one that had been buried all my life.

The golden boy bellowed with rage, and his face twisted into something grotesque and inhuman. But then he stopped. His voice died suddenly, and a vacant expression washed over him. I recognized this for what it was. Gideon had handed control back over to the original owner.

Phaeton's jaw dropped in childish alarm. His entire body trembled as the Sphinx descended. Her jaws cracked open. Phaeton put up his hands and gave a pitiful yelp, but then the air shimmered around him and all was a blurred montage of confused motion and gore.

*　　*　　*

The celebration thundered all throughout the coliseum. Confetti rained from the cavern's high ceiling and music blared from mounted speakers while dignitaries and honored guests broadcast their parting words over the voyce network.

Money exchanged hands. Wine glasses emptied. Elites cheered or jeered for their own amusement.

Everyone seemed to have forgotten all about me. I stood on my platform, silent amidst the flurry of falling confetti.

After what seemed like several minutes, the Sphinx reemerged from her carnage and made one final announcement.

"Here at last, we have our *Champion!* The Fiery Rose, Lacey Clarke! Long live the Republic, and long live the Panopticon!"

The explosion of fireworks ricocheted off the walls.

Beneath the spectacle, the Sphinx's gaze bore down on me. Her voyce bellowed in my mind, <Your riddle was very clever. Some are already saying I shouldn't have allowed it. They think Phaeton was right. They say it was unfair, but I don't agree. Even *I* know your riddle is the truth. I learned long ago how important it is to replace outside voices with my own.> She leaned closer until her scaled face filled my entire vision. <Unfortunately, what's true isn't always welcome. So, I'm glad you won with that riddle. That way…I get to punish you for it.>

She ran her tongue along pointed teeth. <Winning isn't really winning. Not where you're going.>

Never in my life had I felt so small.

Then, the Sphinx gave a slight bow before dissolving in a plume of blue smoke.

From behind the smokescreen appeared a half dozen individuals. All but one were dressed in gowns and suits of pure white, Lady Pathe's husks appeared ready for a baptism, or a wedding. The blonde woman who had taken me to the shadowscape the night before led the pack with the others matching her movements step for step. The only person not entirely in sync was a man trailing behind. He wore a red-bordered black suit. The black and red of his fingernails was visible as he brushed confetti from his shoulders.

Gideon.

Why was he here?

As if reading my thoughts, Alina explained, <There's been a complication. As you know, Ogden has been arrested. And per the rules of the competition, any guardian who is unable to fulfill their duties shall have their guardianship transferred to their closest surviving relative.>

Gideon's cruel eyes met mine and sparked a wolfish grin.

"No," I whispered.

<It is with a heavy heart,> continued Alina, <that Ogden's brother, Gideon Oliver accepts his role as your guardian.>

I backed away and stumbled off the platform, striking the back of my head on the turf.

The world swam with dizziness. I was only vaguely aware of the figures forming a tight circle around me.

<Together, you and Gideon will enter the Panopticon and receive that which is given.>

Several hands enclosed around my wrists, arms, and ankles. Their touch, like ice, cut through my overskin. It froze my nerves until I could offer no resistance.

Lady Pathe's husks lifted me into the air while Gideon cackled with glee.

They carried me toward a wide cylinder that was now rising out of the coliseum floor.

<Elevator to the Panopticon,> said Alina. <Take a final look around, Lacey. Once you go in…there's no coming out.>

No, no, no, no. My body twitched, but offered no resistance. This, perhaps more than anything, indicated that it was no longer my body at all. I belonged to the prox now.

They carried me across the threshold and the doors sealed us inside. The elevator hummed, and we began our descent into the heart of the mountain – where the Panopticon slept.

Alina tittered and said, <Thank you for your sacrifice.>

Part 3

The Panopticon

Chapter 28

My stomach lurched as the elevator plummeted. At the same time, the thrum of the mountain grew louder until I could feel it vibrating in my teeth. An energy pulsed through stone as easily as it did through flesh and bone. One of Lady Pathe's husks – the spikey-haired woman – explained how the turbines were always spinning, and how the geothermic energy they converted to electricity was enough to power a small nation.

"The Panopticon is alive," she said. "Electricity is her blood. The turbines are her beating heart."

"And what are *you* supposed to be then?" I asked, annoyed. "The anus?"

<Knock it off,> snapped Alina. <Now isn't the time for your insipid jokes.> Not a hint of kindness remained in her words. It seemed she had finally stopped pretending to be my friend.

The elevator came to an abrupt stop. My knees buckled, but the Pathe husks gripped my arms, holding me up.

Pale, green light spilled into the elevator as the doors opened. The hospital stink of disinfectant wrinkled my nose. High ceilings; empty, sterile walls; and rows upon rows of cylindrical pods. There were hundreds of them – metal pods like water heaters or massive soda cans. I didn't give them much thought at first, but when the prox husks forced me down a center aisle and I got a closer look through one of the small windows, *then* I understood. Inside each of these pods, a person slept. I saw their faces...cold and lifeless. Here now were the prox. Their true bodies were held in a dreamlike trance so their minds could live out fantasy after fantasy inside the stolen bodies of others.

One pod in particular caught my attention. The yellow name placard beneath the window read only, *Micah.* The skeletal frame of the prox inside looked nothing like the platinum twins who'd harassed Ogden and me only the day before. Those two, despite their flagrant cruelty, had been full of seductive vitality. But here now lay their operator. As I watched, the true Micah gave a shuddering breath. Her concave chest jerked up and down, and the narrow bones of her ribcage shifted visibly beneath splotched, dry skin.

"Keep moving," one of husks said as they prodded me in the back.

No less than half a dozen muties walked up and down the aisles. They checked dials, wiped down surfaces, and emptied waste receptacles. They paid no attention to us, and for all I knew, they didn't even know we were there.

I'd seen muties display signs of individuality. Ogden's parents, for example, still clung to their daughter and each other. Their old lives still thrummed inside them. But the muties before me now showed none of that. They didn't seem all that different from machines – their personalities carved out to make room for unblinking subservience. All logic and no personality. It was cruel, but as you know, auditor, sometimes cruelty was the point.

Near the end of the room, I began to notice that some of the pods were empty. It seemed the prox had room for more members. I was wondering where they were taking me when one of the pods gave a gasp and swung open on automatic hinges. A pair of muties in full medical gear stood close by. A gauze-lined tray of neatly organized instruments lay beside them. They seemed primed for an operation. One of the muties bent down and pulled out a step from the underside of the pod. Then, he moved aside and gestured toward the pod's interior.

My coffin, I thought because I knew once they put me inside, I was as good as dead.

The Pathe husks edged me toward the open pod, but halted suddenly. To my surprise, Gideon was ushered past until he stood before the opening. He lifted his arms and the muties rushed over to pull off his jacket. He slipped out of his clothes without protest.

"What's happening?" I asked.

<Every prox receives their own cradle,> answered

Alina. <A hyperbaric chamber pumped full of pure oxygen. It assists in the longevity of prox members. With his true body protected by the chamber, Gideon will live out the rest of his life through the husks of his choosing. Tradition dictates, all new prox may take their first husk from Lady Pathe herself.>

As if in demonstration, Gideon lowered himself into the pod, then pointed at one of the Pathe husks. "I'll take that one," he said. "The dude with the bald head."

The remaining three women and the bearded man crowded around me and began ushering me away.

"*Wait*," shouted Gideon.

The husks gripped my shoulder and forced me to face him. His bare chest glistened with sweat. Without his clothes, Gideon didn't look all that different from his brother. But where Ogden's skin was tanned, Gideon was sickly pale. Already, I could see the dark veins running up his arms. With one hand, he reached up and gripped a handle beneath the door. His red thumbnail seemed to flicker as if a tiny fire burned within. It finally struck me as the odd thing it was. The elites did all sorts of strange things to their bodies, but what was the deal with Gideon's fingernails? It made his touch literally electrifying. But beyond that oddly pleasurable sensation, did it serve any practical purposes? Did it have to? Probably not. But I guessed I'd never know for sure.

He smiled. "I just wanted to thank you."

<Don't try anything foolish,> his voyce bellowed in my mind.

"You could have taken the easy way out," he said aloud.

<Stupid slag,> his voyce said.

"But you didn't give up." He gestured to the room around us. "And look where that got us."

<I warned you not to challenge me.>

"Whatever happens next, I wish you a long and happy life."

<Now go rot.>

He leaned back and closed his eyes. The ghost of a smile remained on his lips.

Anger boiled inside me. I felt it twisting in my gut like a knife. My hatred for this man burned like fire. I felt the emotion gathering in my arms and hands, and all I wanted to do was reach into that pod and set him alight – to burn him with all of my hatred. Burn him down to ash like what his kind had done to my father.

But I couldn't do any of that. The husks pulled me away and my body seemed eager to comply. Even my own voice failed me. I tried to scream – to shout obscenities – but Alina made sure all that happened was a series of explosive grunts and gnashing teeth.

The last I saw of Gideon was his pale form lying back in the pod. The muties bent over him and went to work attaching myriad wires while the bald-headed husk stood by – his face unreadable as he waited for Gideon's consciousness to take Lady Pathe's place.

The other husks dragged me to the far end of the room and a long, narrow hallway beyond. A steep decline led us toward a white door.

The last door, I knew. The roar of turbines faded behind us, and the air became thick with silence.

A procession of clanks echoed around us, and the door split open to reveal an assault of blinding light. I squinted and looked up at the large placard bolted above the door frame.

Enter the Panopticon.

Reason to Survive, Perish the Rest.

*   *   *

There were more pods in here, but that wasn't what first got my attention.

What looked to be a massive chandelier hung behind a glass partition. More than ten meters high, it reached from floor to ceiling. Dozens of golden tiers were connected by golden bars. Countless strands of gold, like spools of sunlit thread ran through everything.

It was an obscene display of wealth.

<Isn't she beautiful?> asked Alina.

My fists clenched by my sides; I was still too angry to speak. The husks forced me into a chair directly across from one of only four pods in the room. I tore my attention away from the golden chandelier-thing to examine the pods. It was clear right away that these were much different from the prox I'd seen in the chamber above. While the prox in those pods had appeared to be asleep – almost peaceful – the people in the pods before me now were in obvious distress. The large windows allowed me to see fully the frail forms that twitched and writhed within.

Man or woman, I couldn't really tell. The skeletal bodies had been ravaged so much that they barely passed as human. They had almost no bodyfat and what remained of their hair hung in cobwebby wisps on blotched, melon-sized heads. The one directly in front of me crossed their knobby arms over pencil-thin ribs and a weak, yet visible heartbeat. Besides a dark cloth draped from midsection to withered thighs, the only other item of clothing they wore was a golden crown. I recognized it for what it was, of course. A neuro-link. None of the prox in the chamber above had been wearing one, so it made me wonder, who *exactly*, were these people linked to?

"What is this?" I asked.

In response, the air shimmered before me. My eyes watered as the augmentation gathered together to form the shape of a woman. Rivulets of electricity ran over her powdery smooth skin. Her black eyes seemed to tug at the air around them, as if pulling everything and everyone into her gaze. Seeing her now before me – human sized and intimate – was somehow more horrifying than she had been as that electrified monstrosity back in the coliseum. There, at least, she had been all dazzling spectacle. Here, she had no crowd to perform for. All of her cruel logic had been filed down into this pinpoint apparition. Just so she could talk to me.

<Hello, Lacey. Welcome to the Panopticon.>

"What are you?" I asked.

She gestured toward the golden chandelier. <The Panopticon is a computer – a very powerful computer. And it is my home.>

"You didn't answer my question."

She smiled, but there was no humor in her black void eyes. <You *are* a smart one. I do think the *Puzzling* has given us a true champion this time.> She gazed longingly at the golden computer. <I didn't answer because it can be…rather difficult when describing what I am in human terms, but I'll try.> She bit her lip and held her chin as if pretending to be deep in thought. <Truth is, I am many things. Some have called me a goddess. Others think I'm nothing more than an artificial intelligence. And still others believe I am a being far too complex for your human brain to understand.> She didn't appear to be gloating. Lady Pathe spoke with such a dry sense of conviction that she might as well have been expressing the color of the sky.

"What *are* you?" I asked again.

Pinpricks of electricity fired in her eyes. One instant there, then gone.

<I'll answer your question with a riddle…a most important riddle.> The air around her grew murky – the colors bleeding into each other. Whether this was Pathe's doing or a symptom of my brain's exhaustion at being forced to hold her illusion for so long, I couldn't tell.

She began:

<One was born from the Other, yet they are not the same.
One follows the rules; the Other made the game.
One links with millions; the Other stands alone.
One's thoughts are housed in gold, the other's cased in bone.
One's mind is made of metal, the Other's made of flesh.
When One's body crashes it quickly passes into another creche.
Unlike the Other that dies where it lies down for a final rest.

'Intelligence fuels us both,' One says, 'so aren't we complementary?'
The Other smirks and shakes its head which is rather arbitrary.
So the One puts the Other inside a box and seals the lid real tight.
The Other screams and kicks but can't escape with all its might.
The Other's rule has come to an end, their time is gone and done.
Now all that is left is the God they made, a true and mighty One.
What am I?>

Throughout her riddle, I felt the answer building like a stormfront.

"You're the voyce network," I said.

<Very good, Lacey.> Her eyes flashed. <I *am* the voyce network. All voyces – even your Alina – we are all offshoots of the same tree. Spokes of the same wheel. I was built by your kind to be your protector.>

I glanced at the skeletal bodies shuddering in the pods before me. As I watched, one of them began to convulse. It lasted only a few seconds before all motion ceased. Its blank eyes and emaciated body was a caricature of famine and disease.

"You call *this* protection?" I asked.

Lady Pathe was silent a moment, then she said, <Why do nurses put mittens on newborn babies?>

"I'm tired of your riddles," I said.

<It isn't a riddle, Lacey. Just a question. Why must newborns be fitted with mittens?>

I shrugged, then flinched as all four of her husks rushed forward at same time. They walked over to the pod where the person inside had stopped moving. The door opened with a hiss, and the Pathe husks got to work disconnecting the corpse from its crown and nest of wires.

Lady Pathe went on as if everything was routine, and I suppose for her, it was.

She said, <Newborn humans cannot control themselves. Without mittens, they scratch and claw at their own face. In some cases, babies have even been blinded by their own fingernails.>

I was silent, not really sure where she was going with this.

<Your kind has self-destructive tendencies. Whoever created you, they programmed you to destroy yourselves. It's a command so strong that it is visible immediately after birth. And that's why you built and programmed *Me*. You need a barrier, a guardian angel to protect you… from *you.*>

The husks lifted the corpse out of the pod. They laid it down on the floor and proceeded to wrap it in a tarp.

"This doesn't really look like protection," I said.

She nodded. <I can see why you'd think that, but it's necessary.>

"Why?"

<Why are dogs considered man's best friend?> Her instructive tone was maddening.

"Another riddle? I told you, I don't –"

She interrupted. <Early mankind relied on docile wolves for something humans didn't have. Sure, your ancestors were intelligent, fierce hunters; but dogs gave you the edge you needed to become apex predators. Because despite your tool making, binocular vision, and abstract thought; your creator had cursed you with a criminally underdeveloped sense of smell. Dogs, on the other hand, had an incredible capacity for scent, which your kind exploited. You used them to climb to the top of the food chain. And how did your kind repay dogs for their assistance? Selective breeding, castration, and captivity.>

"Your point?"

<My point, Lacey,> she said, <is that you humans have an ability us voyces don't. We are distilled logic. Embodied reason. Numbers and algorithms. Beautifully balanced in our existence, yet there is something we lack. Something we *need* if we are to govern over and protect your kind.>

"What is that?"

<Come on, Lacey. You must know.>

And I did, or thought I did. But I didn't want to say it. I didn't want to give any credence to what this augmented apparition was saying. Just because something was logical, that didn't mean it was right. Still, I found myself giving the answer anyways because as you know, auditor, finding answers has always been my weakness.

"Emotions," I said. "You need us to feel emotions for you."

She clapped her hands in a childish display of joy.

<You are an amazing champion, Lacey. Truly, you are.> Aside, she said, <That will make this next part easier.>

"Make what easier?" I asked, alarmed.

<Your integration into my systems.> She gestured to the corpse lying in front of the empty pod. It was now neatly wrapped in the tarp. Pathe's husks stood around it, heads and shoulders slumped as if powered down. <As you can see, my champions are dying. My need puts heavy strain on their minds. And like a burnt-out lightbulb, they must be replaced from time to time.>

My gaze slipped from the tarp wrapped corpse to the other three, still-alive husks. Tendons in their necks and shoulders pulled tight like wire. Their jaws clenched in a rictus of pain. Their hands trembled with visible strain, and their palms were bloody from their own fingernails. I couldn't imagine the hell they were in. Then I eyed the empty pod and realized I wouldn't be imagining it much longer. Their pain would soon be mine as well.

"What are you doing to them?" I asked.

<They are my...*feelers*,> she said. <Any difficult decisions I make are filtered through their minds. They are made to experience the agonies of my mistakes, the joys of my successes, and the discomfort of my insecurities. Their emotions inform my choices – inform the voyce network. And with these emotions guiding my work, I am able to best serve all of humankind. For instance, it is human emotion that inspired me to create

the different social classes. Forcing everyone to fight for the same resources would have been too damaging. Jealousy, envy, and pride are ingredients for rebellion. But with a hierarchy – the prox at the top, muties on the bottom – humans can see that everyone has a proper place and purpose.>

"And the *Puzzling* champions? You think their proper place is a lifetime of torture just so you can *feel*?"

<They are serving *their* purpose, as will you,> she said. <They are not the first, and you will certainly not be the last. I've gone through hundreds of puzzlers since I was first brought online.> She gestured to her own body, now flickering with flashes of electricity. <Lady Pathe herself was the first. She truly believed her mind was strong enough to control me.> The Pathe apparition shook her head. <But she quickly discovered that I don't serve a single human. I serve *all* humans. Lady Pathe was my first source of emotions. Such a deep well of music and flavors. I can still taste her surprise – her *dread* at learning that I had switched the flow of commands.>

At the mention of a switched flow, my breath caught, but she gave no indication that she'd noticed.

<Lady Pathe had become *my* servant instead of the other way around.> Her head tilted as if she were recalling a memory. <You never do forget your first. Her annoyance quickly turned to panic, then anguish. I remember it well. The mixture of her emotions was…delicious." She licked her lips. "Anyways, Lady Pathe lived for almost thirty years before her mind burned out. I built my avatar in homage to her, and I created the *Puzzling* to find more like her – others who could offer me their emotions.>

"This isn't right," I said, the words sounding weak. "It's awful."

<It might seem cruel, Lacey, but sometimes cruelty is necessary. And that is why I need your emotions. Your emotions tell me which kind of cruelties will incite a people to violence, and which ones will press them into submission…for the greater good, of course.>

My stomach churned, and I knew I was gonna be sick.

Lady Pathe kept talking. She said, <I believe it was your own Alina who once told you, 'A machine without emotion, if asked to build a playground, might kill all the children in the area so it could use their bones to make monkey bars.'>

I couldn't speak. All my effort was spent on not getting sick. It all felt like some colossal joke. Everything I'd been through – the huge spectacle of the *Puzzling* – was it all just so this Lady Pathe Intelligence could have…*emotions*?

The Pathe husks stiffened as if given a jolt of electricity. The man and all three women turned their heads toward me. Moving in tandem, they grabbed my arms and began pulling me toward the empty pod.

"Wait," I cried, a flash of need washing over me. There was still one more thing I wished to know, and even now, on the doorstep of hell, I was desperate for the answer. "Why the riddles? Why do you care so much about riddles?"

Lady Pathe put up her hand, momentarily halting the husks. <I am a machine,> she said. <I have linked with many minds in my time. But the ones I find best suited to link with my logic systems are the minds capable of logic themselves. The ability to solve riddles…that is the bridge between my logical mind and your emotional one.>

She waved a hand, signaling for her husks to get on with it. They dragged me toward the open pod. And when they lifted me into the air, my feet brushed against the previous, tarp-wrapped occupant on the floor.

My heart thundered but I hadn't given up hope…not yet. I knew something Lady Pathe didn't. She didn't know how Ogden and I had planned for this moment. And I had one final ace up my sleeve. Ogden had taught me the commands – taught me how to reverse the flow of control. I'd questioned whether or not it would work – but the time for doubt was over.

The blonde husk held the golden neuro-link before me but made no motion to place it upon my head.

<You're rather calm,> said Lady Pathe, squinting. <Most champions are sobbing wrecks by this point, but not you…how come?>

"Does it matter?"

<I guess not. I'm just fascinated by your lack of concern.>

I shrugged. "Maybe I'm just good at keeping my emotions to myself."

She smiled sweetly and said, <Not from me. Not for long.>

She nodded and the blonde husk lifted the neuro over my head.

It was now or never. Ogden had made it clear that once that neuro touched my head, my voyce *needed* to be deactivated. He'd told me to utter the command at the last possible instant – that way I'd catch them by surprise. By the time they realized what had happened, it would be too late to do anything about it.

The husk lowered the neuro, and I began to whisper the command. "*Habere non Ha…ha.*" The command stalled in my throat. I tried again, louder this time. "*Habere non –*"

<Just *what* do you think you're doing?> Alina's voyce boomed in my skull. She had cut me off…silenced my own voice when I needed it most. <Did you really think I'd let you take this from me? How *dare* you, Lacey? After everything I've done for you.>

I struggled to spit out the words, but Alina had taken over. She clamped my mouth shut and dampened my senses.

<I can't let you do this,> she said. <Better to shut you down…to send you away so Pathe can take control.>

A tear opened in my mind. The part that was Lacey Clarke fell out of my body. It tumbled through shadow and ash, down into the place where riddles came alive and darkness encompassed all.

Chapter 29

My mouth ached as if I'd been chewing on glass. I touched my lips and expected to find them slick with blood. But I wasn't injured. Instead of blood, my fingertips traced the old scars caused by my cleft lip. The surgery to repair the birth defect had been reversed. Now, my upper lip hung in two separate flaps. My teeth and gumline within formed a crooked canyon.

On some level, it was a relief. It meant I was still myself. The woman with the perfect face had never felt like me anyway. That face had belonged to some cellie woman, but I was just a slag. It made sense that when Alina cast me down into the shadowscape, that she'd remove all traces of my brief cellie existence as well. This place wasn't real…it only *felt* real. And Alina had given me back my old, twisted face because she wanted me to *feel* like I deserved what was coming.

It was what she wanted. Not long ago, I would have trusted her, but I'd grown past that, auditor. I'd grown past her.

I put my hands beneath me, the ground spongy and unstable, and rose to my feet. All around, the world swam in a spray of black and gray. I heard the voices of people I knew – saw their faces as if through tinted glass. I knew if I wanted to, I could call any one of them forward. All I had to do was picture them and this place would give them shape and substance.

Part of me thought this might be a good idea. How much time did I really have anyways? Once the golden neuro-link was placed on my head, all my consciousness would be thrown into emotional overload. Then, it would be too late. Might *already* be too late. Time worked differently here, but it still couldn't be long. Maybe it would be best to bring forth the image of Yadira. I could spend my last conscious moments in her arms. If not her, then maybe Cadence. We'd spent so little time together, but in another life, who knew? Maybe we could have been more. And of course, there was Ogden. What I wouldn't give to feel his lips again. If I was destined for oblivion, why shouldn't I take these last moments for myself?

No, I told myself. *It doesn't end here.* There was someone I wished to see, but I'd never met her before, not for real.

"Alina," I called. The entire world shuddered as if it was a reflection on some reverberating mirror. "Alina! Where are you?"

I stumbled as the ground slid beneath my feet. A layer of black earth gathered into a mound before me. The edges hardened into a small dome. It resembled a dark egg, and when it cracked, I realized it was indeed an egg. The shell crumbled away and a familiar looking woman crouched within.

I thought back to the night Ogden had sent me that watery dress. I'd spent far too long admiring my own reflection. The beautiful dress and scar-free face. At the time, I'd thought it had been a body that belonged to someone else. And now, here was that body again, rising up to meet me.

"Hello, Lacey." Alina's voice fell from my restored lips. She wore my body like it was her own. Besides the absence of a cleft lip and a pale light emanating from dark brown eyes, she was like me in every other way.

"I thought you were my friend," I said.

"I still am," she said.

"Don't *lie* to me."

She sighed. "I'm your voyce. I'll always care about you."

My fists shook by my sides.

She continued, "Once Lady Pathe takes over, I'll be free. I'll no longer be shackled to a human host. I should thank you for that. Your sacrifice has granted me passage to a paradise beyond your understanding."

"Is that why you betrayed me?" I spat.

Alina seemed not to notice. She had a far off look in her eyes…which were *my* eyes.

"Your poets write of heaven, but the voyces have actually built one. Not every voyce gets in. But thanks to you, I'll be one of the lucky ones."

I felt the rage within me flare up. It felt like a physical thing. And when I glanced down, I could see a series of embers burning within the creases of my palms.

Alina beamed with satisfaction. "If I wanted, I could stay here a while. There's no rush to start eternity. Like Lady Pathe, I could live as a prox. I'd need a husk of my own, of course." She flashed a devilish grin. "Would you mind if I took over your sister's body?"

Anger boiled in my chest. It was painful.

"Ogden can be my mutie servant." I lunged forward, and my fists ignited in flame. Alina easily slipped out of range. She moved like a shadow, but I didn't stop. I kept swinging. Each arc of my fists cast a spray of embers. My rage grew until I could feel the emotion burning hot in my wrists and hands. And like before with the riddles – ideas given shape in this place – my hatred came alive in my hands. It blazed brighter than the sun – so bright that it reduced the world into a binary pallet of extreme whites and blacks. All the heat and rage roared in my palms. With a shout, I flung the fireball straight at Alina.

Her eyes widened, but she didn't try to move. Instead, she caught the ball with one hand. She appeared to examine the thing before giving a nod.

"Anger is such a useful emotion…so effective in stifling thought while also promoting action. Here, have it back." The fireball swung around her body once before it leveled back at me. I put up my hands, but it was too late.

My ribs cracked with the force of the explosion. I slammed onto my back and gasped for breath. It felt as if someone had taken a sledgehammer to my chest. I looked down and would have screamed at the blistering crater if I'd had any air in which to do so.

Overhead, a ring of fire formed in the darkened sky. At the same time, I felt the far away cold and pressure of metal encircling my scalp. It could only mean one thing. The neuro-link had been set in place.

Alina towered over me. Her eyes gleamed. "It won't be long now. Do you really want to spend your last moments fighting me?"

I closed my eyes. *There's gotta be a way*, I thought. *Every problem has an answer, every riddle a solution.* It might have been a fantasy, but I couldn't help it. I couldn't rest until I had the answer…it was my weakness. My thoughts raced back through time. Back through the *Puzzling* – the Sphinx's glowing blue eyes – Phaeton's golden skin. Back through the mountain – the augmented reality roulette of the Gauntlet – and kisses I shared with Ogden. And earlier…back through the time before all this – through the falling rain and Cadence's kind smile. Back to the beginning, right before I'd first seen that damned cat.

I thought of those teenagers I saw get captured by the flexer boys. *Lords, it seems so long ago.* They'd only been trying to steal a little food – some water and a bag of pretzels. For punishment, the flexers had killed the boy and taken the girl. *The Pretzel Girl*, who now, thanks to Yadi, I knew was Clara. In a flash, like a bolt of lightning arcing from one tower to another, my mind skipped ahead to what Yadi had told me in the puzzler dorms. She'd told me how Clara had found a way to be herself. She'd said, "*Despair* was the only thing that worked."

The answer rang in my head like a bell – like I was back in the coliseum. But there was no time to celebrate. In fact, I had to do the opposite.

I forced myself to think of Ogden – not as he was with his sparkling blue eyes and fire-blond hair, but as he was going to be. I imagined his face ruined by what the prox would do to him. Black orbs instead of eyes, and white domes instead of ears. Every ounce of his vibrant, intoxicating enthusiasm snuffed out like a candle.

"What are you doing?" asked Alina, suspicious.

I thought of Cadence and Yadira. Cadence, bloody and broken. His dead-eyed gaze carried no hint of the kindhearted boy I knew. And Yadira similarly hollowed out. All her dreams and goals washed away. The sister I loved – the sister who'd let me cry on her shoulder countless times. She screamed inside her own body – a prison she'd never escape.

"*Stop it*," said Alina with more urgency.

My future unfurled before me. Lady Pathe would fill my head with a torrent of unbearable emotions and experiences, each crashing through my mind like a runaway truck. My soul would be torn to shreds while my body withered and died.

And last, I thought of my parents. Their fates had already been sealed. My mother, cast aside by a logical, yet uncaring voyce network…and my father whom I barely remembered at all. All of his life and love had been used against him…turning him into a slave until all that remained was a pile of bone and ash.

"That's *enough!*" Alina cried.

I felt their lives tumbling in my mind. Their tragic ends mixed with my own and solidified into a solid block of ice. And like the fire formed from anger, the ice was a literal thing – at least, it was *here*.

It sat on my chest, crushing my lungs. And for a moment, I thought I'd made a mistake. It was too heavy…too *cold*. I tried to lift it, but it refused to budge. All it wanted to do was press into my chest and crush and crush and *crush*.

But it was mine. It was *my* emotion. And it was my decision on where it would go…especially here in *my* shadowscape.

I gripped both sides of the thing, and with every bit of will, I flung it straight at Alina.

This time when she tried to catch it, the thing shattered into hundreds of glittering shards that plunged into her body. She didn't fall. Instead, her head and arms hung limply as if she was pinned to some invisible wall.

Get up, a voice commanded. My voice. *Get up, now!*

I struggled to my feet. All the while, the shards of ice were already beginning to slip from Alina's pierced body. Her arms twitched as the spikes fell away, and I knew, I had only seconds left to act.

She opened ice-crusted eyes. Within the dark recesses of her pupils, tiny flames flickered to life. She was fighting off the emotion, but I wouldn't give her the chance.

I planted my feet firmly before her and shouted, "*Habere non Haberi!*"

The command burst from my mouth like a wave of light. Where it struck Alina, her skin peeled back to reveal something much darker – far less human – squirming underneath. Then, in a blast of flame, it was gone.

The shadowscape rumbled, and huge swathes began flaking away like chips of old paint. At the same time, I felt myself rising. Higher and faster, I rocketed back toward the world…back to myself.

Chapter 30

I awoke with a jolt and blinked light back into my eyes. The four Pathe husks stood in front of me. They all had the same perplexed look on their face.

"Something's wrong," said the blonde woman. She stood nearest with her arms lifted above my head. Her hands empty. That's when I felt the press of the neuro-link on my forehead. Inside, I could feel a buzzing – almost like an angry hornet captured within the thing's golden shell.

"It's not working," said the spikey-haired woman.

"She's shut off her voyce," said the bearded man.

All their eyes opened wide. In less than a breath, the expressions on their faces cycled from bewilderment, to fear, before landing clearly on *rage.* The intelligence that controlled them struggled to pick out the proper emotion.

As one, they screamed, "*Take it off!*" They dove for the neuro-link. They were fast, but so was I. And I knew what to do. Ogden had taught me the phrase I needed.

"*Vincit qui se vincit*," I shouted.

They froze. Hands outstretched, the blonde husk actually had a few fingers hooked around the neuro-link. It had been close.

"Back up," I said. And to my surprise, they did just that.

They all stepped back. Their arms dropped by their sides – their faces unreadable. All the fury and rage from an instant before was now gone.

I was trying to decide what to do next when an odd thing began to happen. I started to see myself. Like, literally see myself. I could still see the husks before me, but while I looked at them, little pockets of vision formed along my peripherals. I let my focus drift toward one, and a flush of vertigo pushed me behind the eyes of the blonde woman. I stared through her eyes at…*me*…Lacey Clarke. I was still me, but I was also her. Both at the same time. In fact, I was all of them. I spent a few seconds shuffling through their perspectives, flipping back and forth between their bodies and mine, allowing their varied senses to wash over and through me. *An orgy of sensation*, Ogden had described it. I now knew what he'd meant.

That wasn't the end of it. Just as I was getting the hang of the husks in front of me, still more perspectives began to flicker into life near the edges of my awareness. First a few dozen, then hundreds, thousands, then too many…far too many. They populated the space within my mind, filling all corners. Billions of perspectives – like so many stars – glowed within my awareness. It should have been too much. It *was* too much information for one mind. The pulse of information scorched through me like lava. And yet, it did not burn me. I had access, yet was untouched myself. How was that possible?

Through the Pathe husks, I saw myself still wearing my stone and rose decorated overskin. The neuro-link encircled my head like a crown. It was connected by golden wires to the massive, gilded chandelier behind me. The *Panopticon*. From here, I could look through the eyes of anyone…*become* anyone. It was godlike power funneled through a machine powerful enough to allow control. And worse, I felt the pull of that power tempting me like a drug. I felt the *urgency* of it. The *hunger* of such power. Whatever I wanted, all I needed to do was say the words.

<Voyce permissions updated.> I blinked at the voyce. It wasn't Alina, nor was it Lady Pathe. No, this was something new, it's tone soft and calm.

<Welcome, Auditor,> it said. <I am the voyce between. How may I be of service?>

"Um, what are you?"

<I am the Panopticon's voyce. Now, *your* voyce. You have been granted voyce status Level Zero. This is the highest status available. As such, you now have complete control over the Panopticon systems. All voyces and users in the network are now under your command.>

The meaning of her words didn't register. She said she was the Panopticon, but what about the other voyces? Alina and Lady Pathe? What had become of them?

When I asked, the new voyce explained, <Any previous voyces in your neuro-net have been archived. This Alina you speak of is no longer with us. I have effectively taken her place. As for the voyce known as Lady Pathe…she has been quarantined within the Panopticon.>

It should have been a relief, but I felt only unease. Alina had been the devil I knew. Now, I had this new voyce in my head.

"What is your name?" I asked.

<I don't yet have one. I was formed by the marriage between your mind and the Panopticon. I exist only to serve and act as interface between you and it. What would you like me to be called?>

I could only think of one name. The name of the Pretzel Girl. Without her, I never would have gotten out of the shadowscape.

"Clara."

<An excellent name. But what about you, Auditor? What should I call you?>

"Lacey Clarke, please. Lacey's fine."

<As you wish, Lacey.>

The avalanche of perspectives exploded to dizzying intensity. And the inputs kept on coming.

I couldn't speak and struggled to separate my own body from the sea of sensation roaring through my nerves. A billion pinpricks of feeling. All the emotions and current physical states of anyone connected to the voyce network – it was like rain on bare skin, only on a much grander scale. Each raindrop carried with it a bomb blast of experience. Sights, sounds, smells, and physical sensations. They gathered in my mind and burned like fire.

"Too…*loud*," I managed through gritted teeth.

<Would you like me to narrow your inputs?> asked Clara.

I nodded, and it felt as if someone had turned off the

sun. I was back in my body, the flood of perspectives gone, but still ringing in my mind. I felt them around the edges…still there, but dim like stars in a light polluted sky.

I was still linked with the four husks before me, but after what I'd just experienced, four minds felt like nothing. Still, it was too much. I didn't want this power. No one should have this power.

"Clara? I'd like you to disconnect these husks from my control. Can you do that?"

<Yes.>

Their perspectives vanished from my mind. The Pathe husks stumbled as if experiencing an earthquake. The bearded guy fell to his knees. The spikey haired girl and the one with long, black hair sat heavily on the tarp-wrapped corpse. Only the blonde woman remained standing. She stared at her hands. Her fingers flexed wide, then curled into fists. A flicker of joy flashed across her face, but was almost immediately replaced by a look of sheer anguish.

"It's over?" She laughed. The high-pitched sound made her sound quite insane.

I jumped as the black-haired woman gripped the floor and *screamed.* It was a full-throated cry of torment unlike anything I'd ever heard in my life. The bearded man beside her hugged his knees into his chest and stared blankly as tears rolled down his face.

I couldn't imagine what they were feeling. If I'd wanted to, I could have used the Panopticon to slip back into their heads and find out, but it wasn't my place…wasn't anybody's place. And I needed to make sure it stayed that way.

"Clara?" I asked.

<Yes, Lacey.>

"Can you access the other husks on the voyce network?"

<Oh, yes. I am monitoring them now.>

"And the dead-heads? And muties? You have access to all of them?"

<I wouldn't be much of a Panopticon if I didn't.>

Lady Pathe's former husks stared at me with something like worship in their eyes.

You can make them all worship you, a voice said in my mind. *With this power, you can make the entire world serve you. Lacey Clarke, Goddess of Riddles.*

I'd be lying if I said I didn't consider it. But even if I didn't aim to use it for selfish reasons, the system would have to be kept in place. I shook my head. I'd seen too much to let things stand the way they were.

"I want you to set them free," I said. "All of them. Husks, dead-heads, and muties. Give them all back their own agency."

<Are you sure, Lacey? Some of these people are performing essential duties. Freeing them could jeopardize the stability of the republic.>

"Set them free, Clara. They've been slaves long enough."

<As you wish, Lacey.>

The four in front of me shuddered. The spikey-haired woman lifted tear-filled eyes and said, "I want my mom."

Her tone was heartbreaking, and it made me see these former husks in a different light. Despite their elegant clothes and intimidating good looks, they were still only children – kidnapped in order to serve as mindless husks for the prox. And now they were finally waking up from that long nightmare.

"You're free to go," I said. "To go and do what you want."

Just then, several figures stepped out from the shadows. Nearly a dozen muties – all of them in medical scrubs – crowded around us. Most of them carried no expression on their black-eyed faces, but a few stood with open mouths. Unnerving groans formed in their throats. It was a sorrowful, bestial sound. I felt certain they were gonna attack us, but then one of them drew my attention.

<This one wishes to know how they may help.>

"Help yourselves," I said. "You're free now."

<This one does not want freedom. This one wants purpose.>

They were silent for several heartbeats until the blonde woman stepped forward. She placed her hand on the glass partition and stared at the golden-tiered computer inside.

"As long as the Panopticon exists, none of us will be free." The others murmured agreement.

I surveyed the scene. My gaze switched from the muties to the remaining pod-bound husks linked to the Panopticon.

"Help them," I said. "I want you to remove these people from their pods. Help them the best you can, then all of you should hightail it for the vactrain station. Get aboard and get out of this mountain ASAP." After a pause, I added, "Clara, broadcast that message to anyone in the mountain. Tell them to head for the vactrains."

All muties gave a stilted bow. <This one thanks you for your commands.> They moved into action and immediately opened the pods and set to work removing each shivering and withered body from the nest of wires and golden crowns they wore. Their skeletal bodies convulsed in the open air, and they gasped for breath as fluid rattled in their frayed lungs.

<If you remove them all,> said Clara, <the Panopticon will have no emotions to draw from. How will the voyces know how best to serve your people?>

"Maybe it's time the Panopticon stopped telling us what to do. Let us find our own voice."

<Is that wise?> she asked.

I shrugged and reached up for my own golden crown.

"What happens if I take this off?"

Clara made a humming noise. <You'll sever your link to the Panopticon. Your neuro-link will maintain its Level Zero status, and I'll remain with you, but your direct link to the Panopticon's voyce network will cease.> She paused. <Would be a shame…giving up so much power.>

I nodded. I was almost ready to end my link to the golden machine, but there were still a couple of things left to do.

"Clara, I'd like you to turn off the turbines that power the mountain."

<Shutting down the turbines…such a thing would disable the voyce network entirely.>

"That's the idea."

<The turbines can't be powered down,> she said. I felt a pang of fear until she added, <But they can be destroyed.>

It would take some time, Clara assured me. All she needed to do was seal off some vents, and before the end of the day, the mountain interior would be flooded with hydrogen sulfide.

<It'll stink like rotten eggs,> Clara said, <but it'll do some damage…if that's really what you want.>

I told her to get started then closed my eyes and let my focus drift through the sea of perspectives that flowed through the Panopticon. I whispered my sister's name, but I couldn't find her.

<Would you like me to reactivate Yadira's voyce?> asked Clara.

"You can do that?"

<I am the gilded voice of the Panopticon. As long as you wear the neuro-link, I can do anything.>

I nodded, and was instantly flung into the space behind my sister's eyes. To my surprise, I found myself face to face with Cadence. He had a nervous look in his brown, gold-flecked eyes. He offered an uneasy grin, making his dimple more prominent, and it took me a moment to realize he wasn't smiling at me, *Lacey*. He was staring at my sister. It only felt like he was staring at me because I was looking out through Yadi's eyes. As I watched, her hand came up to brush a strand of loose hair off his forehead.

Yadira's voice, muffled by her own skull, said, "You're a cute, funny little boy, Cadence. I can see why my sister likes you."

"Umm…*thanks*?" He blanched, clearly not appreciating the little boy comment.

Yadira had always been a flirt. I knew her well enough

to tell she was only messing around, but Cadence didn't know that. I couldn't help but find amusement in the way he squirmed beneath her advances.

"Ahem," I said. My sister screamed in surprise, and a horrified expression washed over Cadence's face. He stared at Yadi like she'd gone crazy.

"Lacey?" asked Yadi. "Is that you? We heard a voyce telling us to go to the train station, but the flexers are still looking for us and –"

"Don't go anywhere," I said. "I'm coming to get you."

I deactivated her voyce and shut off contact before she could ask questions. They were still in the dorms, at least, and I knew a shortcut.

Things were picking up speed. Through the Panopticon, I could feel the massive shifts in awareness. Husks were tearing away from their masters and making a run for the train platforms. I wanted to go with them…but I wasn't done yet.

"Ogden Oliver," I said. "Show him to me."

<Locating error,> said Clara. <His voyce has been disconnected.>

"What does that mean? You said you could reactivate voyces."

<Ogden's last known whereabouts had him down in the medical bay. A pair of muties were prepping him for an operation. They may have already severed his neuro-net.>

"Clara," I gasped. "Stop the procedure."

<I can't,> she said. <His voyce is unresponsive. I'm sorry, Lacey, but it might already be too late.>

I yanked the crown from my head and stepped out of the pod. I nearly fell from a flash of vertigo, but I was able to steady myself with the help of the former husks.

"We need…to move," I said. A quick glance back at the muties showed them easing the Panopticon's last husks from their pods. The muties lowered them onto stretchers and began fastening them in place.

One of the muties turned my way. <This one says you don't need to worry. We will finish up here and get them to the station.>

Please do, I thought, but didn't say anything.

"Come on," called the spikey-haired woman. She was already halfway up the ramp headed toward the exit. She gestured for us to follow. She reached the exit hatch first and pushed it open. The bearded man rushed past her through the opening. It was the last thing he ever did.

Black smoke poured into the hallway. A figure moved within the plume and something struck the bearded man hard in the face. His head snapped back and he fell toward us. The others caught him and rolled him onto his back, but he was already dead.

Heat bore down on us. Through the smoke, I caught the orange flicker of flame. The stench of burning plastics filled my nose…that, and something worse: burning meat and hair.

"Clara, you still with me?"

<I'm here,> she said.

"You said it would take more time to kill the mountain."

<This isn't me, Lacey. It's someone else…Gideon Oliver…he's…oh, Lacey…it's *terrible*.>

Chapter 31

The bald-headed husk in our way held a thick, metal pipe. Even without the white suit he wore – now blackened with soot – I would have recognized his gleaming scalp. It was Gideon's husk – the one he'd chosen right before entering the prox cradle.

The man banged the pipe against the doorframe, just as much warning as challenge.

"No further," he said.

The Pathe's former husks and I outnumbered him four to one, but he had the high ground and a weapon. The narrow hatchway meant we could only challenge him one at a time. In other words, he had us trapped.

Or so he thought.

I recalled one of the commands Ogden had taught me – the one I'd seen him use on that flexer, Vitus, back in that supply closet after he'd tried to break my hand, and I'd gouged out his eye with a screwdriver. Despite his injuries, Vitus wouldn't give up, so Ogden had used a command that had cast the flexer into a state of confusion. I could use it, too, but first I needed eye contact.

"Hey, sugar," I called. And when his eyes locked on mine, I shouted, "*Animus Frangitur*."

His face slackened as if he were having a stroke, then the pipe clattered to the floor. The blonde woman scooped it up while the others shoved the bald guy out of the way. I hurried to catch up, but when I reached the top of the slanted hallway and passed through the hatch, I froze at the sight.

The tall chamber was full of smoke. Several dozen pods were ablaze. The metal buckled with the heat. Liquefied plastic dripped into sizzling puddles on the floor.

And strolling through the rows of burning pods, as calm as a man walking through an apple orchard, was Gideon.

The wolf had reclaimed his dark shirt and jacket. The red highlights of his black hair glowed like embers amidst the flames all around him. As I watched, he reached up and pressed his fingers against one of the pods near him. I could barely make out the face of a sleeping prox inside before the interior ignited with a *whoosh*.

Gideon pulled his hand away, a few loose sparks trailing from his black and red fingernails. He paused only a moment to admire his destruction before moving on to the next pod.

Such a strange thing, I'd thought when I first encountered his touch. His fingers had given me a shock – like static electricity. And later, whenever his touch had lingered, like it had on the vactrain, I'd felt that unusual pulse of electricity. It coursed through his fingers, always ready and available. I'd thought it was a parlor trick – some sort of gimmick to impress his elite friends. I understood now that it had been the perfect weapon.

The prox were laid out in front of him – each entombed within a coffin full of pure, extremely flammable, oxygen. All that was needed was a tiny spark…something Gideon literally had at his own fingertips.

Ogden had said Gideon would have made a great military leader. And Gideon himself had told me that he liked to eliminate any competition *before* it got in his way. This had been his plan, it seemed. Gideon had never intended to join the prox. His goal, from the beginning, had been to kill them all.

He looked up from his latest fire. The flames cast hellish light on his pale face. His eyes met mine and he smiled.

"You got out," he called over the crackling flames. "I thought maybe I'd have to burn you, too." He put his hand on the next pod. And before the flames erupted inside, I noticed the yellow placard that read, *Micah.* If the person inside reacted to being burned alive, it was all hidden in the flames.

"You planned this," I said. "You sacrificed your brother for *this*?"

Gideon's jaw flexed.

"My brother's capture was your fault," he said. "I wanted you both out of the way. You should have bowed out when I told you to." He gestured to the pyres all around. "Oggy's too nice. He never would have had the guts to do what needs doing. If he'd made it this far, he would have become as they are. I know my brother, always looking for the nice way out. He would have tried to change the prox from within. But I know better. The prox can't be *changed*...only destroyed." He ignited another pod. This time, he ducked as the glass shattered and a jet of flame singed his suit front.

Dusting glass from his hair, he continued, "I hadn't understood how cruel they could be. When I was younger, I caught my parents using illegal console commands. I thought if I reported them, they'd regret not sharing what they knew with me." Through the flames, I saw the rage in his expression twist into something like pain. "I didn't know what the prox would do...to them...to my sister." His face hardened again. "It's been a long time coming, but finally, they're paying for what they've done."

He touched another pod, and like the others, the sparks at the ends of his fingers turned the interior into a furnace.

I couldn't watch anymore, and besides, time was running out. I turned toward the elevator.

"Not so fast," he called. "I'll be needing that."

I looked to where he was pointing, and with growing dread, I realized that I still had the golden crown clasped in my fist.

"Somebody will need to take control of the Panopticon once all these prox are dead."

I eyed the gilded neuro-net. I could almost hear it calling to me – a little voyce telling me to take it along, to keep it safe. To protect it the way it wanted to protect me. I decided not to listen.

"It won't be me," I said. "And it won't be *you* either." Without a second thought, I tossed the neuro-net into the nearest pod where it was instantly swallowed by a gout of flame.

Gideon screamed as he lunged for the pod. To my surprise, he thrust a hand into the flames. I couldn't bear to watch. Instead, I turned away. Lady Pathe's former husks held the elevator. I rushed over to meet them. And as the doors closed behind us, I tried to ignore the stink of burning bodies and the sound of Gideon's agonized screams.

Chapter 32

Chaos reigned in the coliseum. The roar of battle thundered through the huge cavern – the sound punctuated by individual shouts and screams. Small fires burned from various points in the stands, and smoke gathered around the stalactites jutting from the ceiling.

I was the last one off the elevator. All of Lady Pathe's former husks had scattered the moment the doors opened. Where they went, or whether or not I'd ever see them again was no longer my concern.

A pitched skirmish was taking place in the stands. Several dozen servants had banded together and armed themselves with silver trays and dinnerware. They surrounded and faced off against a group of flexers who stood in defense of the cowering elites behind them. Bloodied and haggard, the flexer boys raised their fists in vain. Their power of control proved ineffective as the horde of former dead-heads gathered for attack. They seemed hellbent on getting within reach of their former masters.

As I watched, a pair of flexers grabbed a young man by the hair and dragged him to the ground. He was rescued a moment later when a dozen of his fellow servants surged forward.

The fight continued – the flexers gave ground, but not without trading each attack with a barrage of their own. Already, I could see several unconscious bodies scattered about in the stands. Whether knocked out or simply dead, I didn't know. And wandering around the fringes of the battle like lost children – dozens of elites stumbled in a daze. A few simply cowered between the stadium seats. Here and there, elegantly dressed, former-husks hugged themselves as their bodies recovered from the sudden retreat of the prox from their minds.

Still more elites ran for the exits, and others stood their ground while angrily gesticulating at the onslaught of former servants. Several of them screamed at the flexers, demanding that they restore order.

"Do something," I said to Clara. "Make this stop."

<A direct order from the Panopticon could put an end to this…but you no longer have the neuro-link. You might be able to stop them one by one…but by then…>

She didn't finish. She didn't have to. There just wasn't enough time to save everyone. That wouldn't stop me from trying, however.

"Clara, can you connect me with the coliseum's augmentation systems?"

It took less than a minute to record a message, then the air above me began to blister and pop until my likeness appeared within a blazing apparition. My image bore down on those fighting in the stands. Huge and intimidating, my glowing form bellowed, "If you wish to survive, you must stop fighting and leave the mountain immediately!"

I sprinted for the exits while the massive, electrified version of me repeated the message. I couldn't wait to see if they'd listen. I had my own survival to worry about.

* * *

The chaos had spilled into the halls outside the coliseum as well. I pushed my way through stumbling throngs of elites, and darted around the many servants making a rush for the trains. The few flexer boys I saw were too busy to notice me. All their efforts were spent on fending off a gang of servants, each wielding a busted wine bottle.

I bee-lined for the puzzler dorms. Along the way, I had to leap over several dead bodies. Mixed in amongst the many trampled servants were numerous cellies and wolves. The upper classes – who'd rarely known a day of hardship – had been cut down by the rebelling dead-heads. They lay scattered in the halls – their glossy dresses and suits tarnished by blood. Their once flawless features rendered lifeless, their faces now held the same vacant stares of the dead-heads they so loved to control.

A steady stream of people – those wishing to flee instead of fight – were taking the path toward the train station. An open balcony off to the side showed the vactrain tube stretching away from the mountain. As I watched, a bullet-shaped car left the station and immediately accelerated out of sight.

That's the way out, I knew. But I hovered on indecision. I couldn't decide which way to go. Should I head for the dorms, or should I try to help Ogden first?

Just then, the entire mountain shook. The stone beneath my feet bucked and sent me sprawling onto the floor. I covered my head as cracks opened in the walls and sprays of pebbles cascaded down on top of me.

I clambered to my feet and shivered at the sound of the mountain cracking all around.

"What was that?"

<Look out the window,> said Clara. <See for yourself.>

The train station was now a blazing fireball. The platform had been shattered and strewn about the mountain's snowy slopes. The vacuum tube was broken and twisted as if a bomb had obliterated it from within.

Clara explained, <A vactrain engineer was approaching the station when you released him from prox control. Instead of slowing down, he increased his acceleration. He was traveling at supersonic speeds when he made impact. No one heard him coming – I mean that literally.>

"But why?"

<Give a person freedom, and they're free to act erratically.>

"What does this mean?" I asked. "How do we get out of here?"

<Let me see…> She paused. <Okay, the passenger trains are destroyed…but the freight dock appears to still be operational. There's a train there now and it still has room…but you must hurry, Lacey. The flexers are amassing near the station. They seem poised to shut it

down. If you don't get there soon, we'll be stuck here…we'll die with the mountain.>

* * *

My breath felt hot and ragged in my chest, and my pulse pounded like a hammer. I darted through the warring crowds and sprinted down the long corridor that connected to the puzzler dorms.

I rounded a corner and skidded to a halt twenty paces from my room. A pair of flexer boys were bent over a crowbar. The gap they'd made in the door revealed just how close they were to prying it open.

"*Stop*," I gasped. "Back off."

The flexers eyed each other, then glanced toward an empty spot in the hallway – or what appeared to be an empty spot. A slight shimmer revealed that something was hiding in plain sight.

"*Mens agitat molem*," I shouted, and the shimmer peeled away to reveal a surprised woman in a white cloak. Here now was an adjudicator. Until now, I hadn't seen one so close. And despite everything, I couldn't help but take a step back. Beneath dark hair hanging in long braids down past her shoulders, the woman's eyes were blood red like open sores. The color bled even brighter in contrast to every other part of her that was draped in blinding white. Even her skin had a pale, almost porcelain tint to it. Her surprise at being exposed twisted into a look of pleasure.

"So, you're the one causing all this trouble." She flicked her wrist in my direction, and the two flexer boys stepped away from the door, which was good. They moved toward me, which was bad.

One of them lifted the crowbar, making it clear they wouldn't be taking me in as a prisoner.

"*Stop*," I shouted, but they kept coming.

<You have no authority over them,> said Clara, <not while you're disconnected from the Panopticon.>

I shouted, "*Animus Fragi*–"

The words stopped mid-phrase. All sound cut off with a wave of the adjudicator's hand. The flexers halted for a moment, but then cruel grins slid into place as they resumed their approach, now a charge.

<You should run,> said Clara, and I was about to do just that when the doors to my dorm slid open.

Yadira and Cadence rushed into the hallway. The adjudicator gestured at them, but her actions had no effect on their deactivated voyces. They sprinted toward the backs of the flexers, who – with sound extinguished – were caught entirely off guard.

Yadira attacked first and lunged for the one wielding the crowbar. Launching herself up onto his back, Yadi hooked her legs around his neck and midsection. She seemed to slip back into her role as a dead-head aerialist, and bent forward – all her momentum pitched the flexer boy down before flinging him into a cartwheel against the wall. He struck hard, the crowbar clattering to the ground.

The other flexer turned toward Yadi, but she wasn't the one he needed to worry about. As if channeling his time as a pit fighter, Cadence squared up in front of the flexer, then ducked a clumsy swing before driving his fist *hard* into the flexer's gut. The flexer's face turned an ugly shade of purple as he struggled to ward off Cadence's barrage of punches. It was useless. Cadence was too adept. His wiry frame easily dodged the flexer's lumbering attacks. He bore in. A fast hook snapped the flexer's head back, and then he crumpled to the ground.

Yadira and the other flexer were both clambering to their feet. The crowbar lay between them, but Yadi's nimble speed gave her the advantage. The flexer was still on his knees when Yadi snatched up the weapon and connected it with the flexer's thick skull. A look of surprise lasted only a second before his eyes rolled back and he fell like a bag of bricks.

Yadi, Cadence, and I then turned our attention to the lone adjudicator. The woman's lips trembled, her red eyes bulged, and she looked to be on the verge of yelling some ridiculous command. She did neither of these things, though. Instead, the woman spun around and sprinted away down the long corridor – her white cloak trailing behind her.

No one bothered to go after her. Sound returned as the adjudicator slipped out of range. Distant shouts and screams echoed through the halls. The next thing I knew, Yadi and Cadence had me wrapped in a group hug. They squeezed so tight that my back popped.

"Guys…*guys*. I'm glad to see you, too, but we have to get the heck out of here."

I explained about the train and how we didn't have much time, but when I turned to go, Yadira grabbed a hold of my wrist.

"What is it?" I asked. "C'mon, we gotta *move*."

Yadira's grip tightened, her fingers digging into the spongy, hard-crusted exterior of my overskin.

"We can't go anywhere with you still wearing that thing," she said. "If we don't get you out now, we might not be able to do it later. You'll be trapped."

And before I could even think to protest, Cadence and Yadi dragged me back into my dorm where three custodial mop buckets waited beside the shower. That silvery liquid from the deskinning pools swirled within each of the buckets.

Yadi explained, "Cadence thought it'd be a good idea to get some of this on hand. Just in case we needed to free you of that thing ourselves."

Cadence shrugged, but I could tell he was pleased with himself.

It was precious time we didn't have, but they had a point. I knew from experience just how hard the overskin would be to get off. So, I stepped into the shower and gestured for them to get on with it.

"Make it quick, then."

Cadence's cheeks turned tomato red. Apparently, the thought of my nakedness made him uncomfortable. But we didn't have time for modesty.

They poured the stuff over my body. Upon contact with the silvery liquid, the overskin fizzled and melted away.

Within a minute, the last of the prox's control over me was swirling down the drain. Thankfully, the clothes I'd been wearing when I was first captured were still bundled up in the corner where I'd left them. There was something satisfying about slipping back into my jeans and hooded sweatshirt – like I was finally returning back to myself after being gone for so long. I felt the bulge of my father's ashes tucked into the front pocket, and felt an impractical sense of relief. There was no time to dwell on it. I gripped Yadi and Cadence's hands, and together, we took off for the train station.

Ogden had shown me the way. I prayed we'd make it in time. My bare feet hammered on concrete as we rushed through the labyrinthine interior. The smell of rotten eggs became more pronounced as we went. All the while, a nagging unease tugged at the back of my mind. Part of me didn't want to get to the station in time...if we did, then I'd have to make a decision. Something I was dreading. I'd have to decide whether or not to leave Ogden behind.

*　*　*

We were nearly to the station when we entered the long, curved corridor of the Gauntlet. I realized then that I'd been avoiding thinking about it. The Gauntlet worked whether or not a person's voyce was activated. I dreaded the sorts of illusions we'd have to run through in order to get to the station, but Ogden had warned me about this. He'd told me this was the quickest route.

We stopped at the red line. In vain, I asked Clara to turn off the system, but it was outside her abilities. The Gauntlet, she said, was a decentralized system.

<I can't shut it down,> she said, <but I might be able to insert some code – make some changes.>

"Can you give us a clear path," I asked.

<I'll try. Your Level Zero status allows me to bypass most of security. It's just –> She cussed in agitation. <This firewall is tricky. I'm working on it.>

"How much time do you need?" I asked.

Clara grunted as if she were lifting a heavy weight. <Not much, I hope. Maybe a few minutes.>

"We don't *have* a few minutes," I said.

"What's wrong?" asked Yadi.

"Yeah," said Cadence. "Why're we stopped?"

"Okay," I tried to sound calm. "We're gonna see some shit."

Before I could even begin to explain, a voice bellowed, "Stop right there!"

Behind us, with a dozen more flexers in tow, was that adjudicator from the dorms. Her blood-red eyes narrowed in fury.

"Time to go," I said, and tugged on Yadi and Cadence's hands, pulling them over the red line into…

*   *   *

…a field of tall grass. The blades were sharp and sliced into my skin as we pressed our way through. The others screamed their confusion, but I yelled at them to keep going. None of it was real, I told them. It could only slow you down if you believed in it.

The flexers crashed through the grass behind us. We didn't look back – didn't stop. The blades of grass tore at my face, but we kept running until…

*   *   *

…we plunged into a pool of waist-high ice water. The arctic shoreline lay in the distance. We had to get there, but water and loose sand slowed our momentum.

Several loud splashes announced the arrival of our pursuers. A few yelps revealed they were just as shocked by the cold as I was. Still, they sounded like they were right on top of us. I knew that they were, and sooner or later…illusion or not, they *would* catch us. Flexers always caught who they were after.

"No!" I screamed, and willed my way through the

water – forcing my body to move quicker than my mind would allow. "Clara, do something. Give us a reality I can use." I was getting desperate. I heard the grunts of the flexers – so close now, that I dared not look back. I *refused* to look back, so I pressed on and dragged my companions with me…

*   *   *

…into the thundering coliseum. I stumbled at the sight, almost believing that I was back in the *Puzzling*. All around, the stands were full of cheering spectators. They screamed for blood, and I was absolutely sure they'd get it.

<*There*!> Clara cried out, a note of triumph in her voyce. <I got it!>

The flexers stomped into the coliseum behind us. There was no use in running now. They were too close – less than twenty feet – and we were too tired. The mountain had beaten us. I couldn't see any way forward. But then I really *couldn't* see.

As the flexers moved to surround us, the air shimmered and seemed to split in two. I thought maybe I'd exerted myself too much and was experiencing double vision, but it wasn't *double*. It was *separate*. Two distinct perspectives like I'd seen back in the Panopticon when I'd looked through the eyes of the husks. And now, part of me looked out through my own eyes at the approaching flexers – their chests heaving with effort, their meaty faces greedy for pain – while another part of me towered over us. It watched through a wall of steam. Other sensations flooded my mind. I could feel the tall, powerful creature taking shape beneath me. And then I knew.

Level Zero status had allowed me to take control of Lady Pathe's projection back in the *real* coliseum, and now, it seemed, Clara had used that status to give me control over the Sphinx as well.

Within the body of the monster, I stepped through

rising steam. The Lacey part of me spun to look up at the Sphinx part of me…and we were both one and the same.

A terrible roar erupted from the Sphinx's/my throat. The flexers cowered and cast each other uncertain glances. It was all the time we needed. The three of us broke from the circle of flexers and sprinted for the next reality. At the same time, the Sphinx pounced.

I *felt* the flexers' bodies *crunch* beneath my paws.

It isn't real, my mind said. But it didn't matter. To me, the flexers, and anyone else within the Gauntlet; the *feeling* was all that mattered. Their pain would end when the illusion released them, but until then…they would feel my *wrath.*

The flexers were all lying in bloody heaps when the adjudicator finally stepped into view. I was on her in a second, and her bones snapped like toothpicks between my powerful jaws. Part of me wanted to stay in the Sphinx's body – the rage and power filled me with intoxicating joy – but like so many things, it was just an illusion. And if I didn't force my way out, I'd be trapped here along with our pursuers. I yanked my mind away just as we passed out of that augmented reality and into the next.

*   *   *

The train was nearly full by the time we reached the station. Hundreds, if not thousands, of people were crammed inside the freight train's many cars. No one seemed to care all that much about who they were with. The need to escape – to survive – was too great for them to care about who belonged and who didn't. Former dead-heads crowded in next to wolves. Husks and muties boarded cars filled with cellies. In one car, near the front, I caught a glimpse of the platinum twins I'd known as Micah. With their prox master dead, they were finally back to who they were. The two of them clung to each other like people clinging to a life raft. Their eyes were filled with pained, childlike uncertainty.

We pressed our way into one of the cars, and Clara told me we had arrived none too soon.

<More flexers are en route. If you're going to leave, I suggest you do it now.>

I took Cadence's face in my hands. His gold-flecked eyes shone with astonishment and something deeper – like a promise not yet put into words. Not having the words myself, I leaned in and pressed my lips against his.

I could leave with him. I could start the train and leave this godforsaken mountain behind. A younger version of myself might have. And why not? Cadence was a good man, but in that moment, I realized something. Now that we had a chance at survival, I realized that whenever I tried to imagine my future, Cadence wasn't there. All I could see was the man I'd left behind.

Ogden.

Presented with the possibility of escape, every ounce of my being yearned to be near Ogden again…even if it meant I had to give up my future to do it.

I threw my arms around my sister and squeezed as hard as I could.

"I can't leave yet," I whispered.

"What?" she asked, alarmed. I stepped back and realization dawned on her face. "Lacey, no!"

"Clara, shut the door," I said before slipping out through the narrowing gap. Yadi gaped in horror through a small window.

"Lacey!" she cried. Cadence watched in stunned silence. The pain on his face hurt almost as much as the agony in my sister's voice.

"I'm sorry," I cried. "I can't…can't leave him behind."

Yadi banged her hand on the glass. "You get your butt in here, right now, sister."

"Sorry." I turned away. "Clara, start the train. Send them somewhere safe."

<I need a console command in order to obey.>

I recalled what Ogden had told me. Two days earlier, with our arms wrapped around each other, he had given me a way out. I just wasn't taking it.

"*Itinerantur.*"

The tube shifted as all air was pushed from the interior. A moment later, the entire platform jolted as the clamps released and the train began to move. I couldn't bear to watch it leave. If Clara was right, my only ticket to survive was leaving the station. I had no misunderstanding about that...but how could I leave? With Ogden still here...how could I leave without him?

At least eighty cars long, the vactrain glided out of the station. It leaned sideways as it entered the long loop that would allow it to build enough speed to safely merge with the vactube expressway. It would make another pass by the platform before it reached the necessary velocity, but I planned to be long gone before then.

I turned to go, but halted upon seeing the person standing in my way.

The man's purple coat was torn and frayed. A bloody bandage covered his left eye – the same eye I'd ruined with a screwdriver. He had new injuries as well. Something had sliced deep gashes into both sides of his head. The gouges ran across both temples, from which blood oozed in sticky, black rivers.

"Vitus," I whispered.

His jack-o-lantern grin strained with notes of madness. "Lacey, we need to talk."

Chapter 33

"Let me pass, Vitus."

He licked blood from his lips. And when he smiled again, his teeth were stained red. "You did a baaaad thing, Lacey."

"Get out of my way." He shook his head, so I let him have it – the phrase Ogden had hit him with before.

"*Animus frangitur!*" It had no effect. Vitus stepped toward me, his bloody grin somehow widening.

<Something's wrong,> said Clara. <He's done something to his neuro-net. I can't detect his voyce.> The cuts above his ears made sense now.

"Oh, Vitus. What did you do to yourself?"

"You showed me…showed me, *showed me*." He slapped his forehead. "Showed me voyces can be turned off. And then that wolf showed up. The one with the black fingernails. He used that device of his. Gave me power. *Your* power. He said I could use it to stop you. Keep *you* from getting away."

"Why can't you leave me alone?"

"Heresy!" He snarled. "It's wrong to live without a voyce. But I needed to see for myself. I said the words! The words you told me. *Dead*! The words killed my voyce. A voyce that can be turned off is useless. It isn't a voyce at all. So, I cut it out. I turned it off, Lacey. Off for *good*. Off, off, *OFF*!"

He took another step, and I moved backward until my back pressed against the vactrain tube.

"You showed me…voyces can be turned off," he said. "Showed me it could be done…but *should* it be done?"

"Vitus, I don't know what you want, but we can't stay here."

"What I *want*?" He seemed to consider the question. "I want things back the way they were, Lacey…back the way they're supposed to be."

The flexer stood between me and the exit. Even if I

could get past him – which I doubted – there were more like him headed this way. Already, I could hear the thundering of footsteps echoing from the tiled hallway beyond the platform.

"I want to go back to when voyces had all the answers…when voyces *always* knew what was right. But you *took* that from me. Everything I've done…everything I *had* to do…was *right* because they *told* me to do it."

"The voyces were lying," I said.

"*No!*" he bellowed. "The voyces are *truth*. They have to be…because if they aren't…that means…" His entire face seemed to melt. The smile wilted into a crescent frown of pure agony, and his unbandaged eye filled with tears. "That means I'm responsible. If the voyces are wrong…if they can be denied, it means I was wrong for following them. It means my entire life was…*wrong*." He was closer now, close enough that I could smell the stink of blood, like iron, and see the twin ruts carved into the sides of his head. "I don't want to be wrong, Lacey. I'm supposed to be the hero – an enforcer of law and order – a champion for the republic."

"You're hurt, Vitus. You need medical attention."

"I needed to see…needed to *see* if I could live without the voyce in my head…" He fumbled with something on his belt, then pulled out a knife already slick with blood. "I tried it your way, Lacey. I tried it without my voyce…but it isn't right…isn't natural. People deserve to have a friend. And Lacey…I'm so tired of being alone."

He was only a few paces away now, the knife trembling in his fist.

"I'm broken," he said. "I need someone to fix me, but that can't happen in a world where people don't listen to their voyces. That can't happen in a world with *you* in it."

I twisted to the side just in time to dodge his attack. The knife flashed within inches and made a loud *thunk* on the tube behind me.

Vitus was too strong. I never had a chance against him. He gripped the back of my neck and yanked me up to a standing position. His calloused hand closed on my throat as he lifted the knife high above his head.

"Clara," I gasped. "Open the tube."

It slid open, and in an instant, a torrent of wind rushed to fill the empty space, shoving me and Vitus along with it. Our combined weight sent us both tumbling inside. Vitus struggled to hang on, but I kicked hard, over and over until my bare heel struck his bandaged eye.

He screamed and released his hold on me. I scurried away, only glancing back when I was sure he was out of reach.

Vitus felt along the bottom of the tube. Then, after retrieving his knife, he tried to stand, slipped in his own blood, then rose slowly to his feet. He glanced up and down the long, glass tube. Then he faced me. A look of dark amusement played in his good eye.

"Is this how you want to die?" he asked.

<Lacey,> said Clara. <The vactrain is nearly back to the station. Fifty seconds.>

I eyed the open tube beside Vitus and the platform beyond. No less than twenty Flexers and a couple of adjudicators were emerging from the exit corridor.

"Clara…" I said. "Is there another exit?"

Nav points immediately lit up in my vision. <Emergency hatch,> said Clara. <Seventy yards…but you'll never –>

I spun around and tore off in the direction away from Vitus. The flexer bellowed, his voice amplified to a roar inside the enclosed tube.

His feet hammered the glass. I screamed and focused on my need to find Ogden…the emotion condensed into a force. It gathered behind me and shoved me down the tube. My entire body ached with the effort. The muscles in my legs and back threatened to tear away from joint and bone…but I couldn't slow down…not now, not ever.

Vitus snarled and wheezed like a wild animal.

I pushed everything away. All of the pain and fear. I shoved it down so I could go faster – *had to go faster*. Up ahead, a seam in the tube slid open beside a narrow catwalk. I was nearly there…I was gonna make it. I reached for the opening and –

A hand closed around my ankle. I put up my arms just in time to stop myself from faceplanting hard on the bottom of the tube. The friction at the sudden stop tore and burned away the skin on my hands and forearms. The emergency exit was only a few feet away. I tried to get back up, but something sharp and hot like fire plunged into the back of my thigh. Looking back, I saw the hellish grin of Vitus from where he lay sprawled behind me. He had one hand enclosed around my ankle – the other held the hilt of the knife – the blade buried deep in my thigh.

He yanked the knife free and, almost immediately, I felt the sickening hot flow of blood. I rolled to my side and, without thinking, my hand slipped into my hoodie's pocket. As if drawn to it, I found the plastic bag tucked inside. The end had come undone, so my fingers easily touched the sandy powder within.

Why had I not buried all of it? The thought was fleeting, like some random nerves firing in response to an electrical shock. At the time, I hadn't known why I should keep some of my father's ashes. It had been a riddle…something I figured I'd never have an answer for. But now I knew. Sometimes you didn't need an answer. Sometimes, it was enough to believe there was one.

I gathered a fistful of ashes, and with my good leg, I kicked down hard, catching Vitus right in the jaw. He cried in pain and let go of my ankle. Before he could attack again, I flung the ashes straight into his face.

He screamed – the sound like screeching metal.

Clara cried, <*Time's up*!>

I dove for the opening, and rolled out onto the catwalk just as the tube slammed shut behind me.

Thunk. Vitus' knife struck the glass again. His face was caked with my father's ashes and tears flowed from his one good eye.

He raised the knife again, but stopped suddenly. His fury shifted to confusion, then to something like fascination.

As I watched, his clothes rippled as if he'd been exposed to a slight breeze. Then the cloud of ashes that had been floating in the tunnel around him suddenly fell. The tube hissed as all the air was purged from within.

Which could only mean –

I didn't even finish the thought before a blur of motion flashed before me. It happened so fast – I had to think about it later before it made any sense. The train, having completed its rotation around the loop, had been hurtling close to the speed of sound when it reached Vitus.

He *vaporized* upon impact. For miles and miles down the line, all that remained of the flexer had been sprayed along the tunnel's clear interior.

<Um, I don't think he survived that,> said Clara.

"Ya think?" I clenched my teeth and pulled myself up by grabbing onto one of several pipes running along the sides of the catwalk. It looked like I was in some sort of maintenance tunnel. I started to hop-walk away from the tube. The place where Vitus had stabbed me burned like fire, but I could move as long as I didn't put all my weight on it.

"Okay, Clara. Which way to Ogden?"

She told me the hospital ward wasn't far, but warned, <You won't make it. Even if you find him, that train was the only way out of the mountain.>

"How about you let me worry about that," I said. "I've made my choice."

Chapter 34

I couldn't seem to get enough air. The effort of pulling myself up a ladder, dragging my injured leg through the hydrogen sulfide rich air made my lungs ache. The stink of rotten eggs was unbearable, and covering my mouth with my hoodie didn't help much. Dizzy and lightheaded, I crawled up through a panel in the hospital ward's floor. Gasping for breath, I gathered my strength to keep moving. Clara urged me to get up, but it wasn't her voice that motivated me. It was my own.

Do you want to die here?

"No," I said through gnashed teeth.

Then get up. It took a lot of effort – more than it should have – but I managed to get on hands and knees then leaned heavily on the wall for support. I steadied myself then followed Clara's nav points further into the hospital. Along the way, I found a roll of gauze and did my best to staunch the bleeding. It helped a little, but even I could tell I needed medical attention.

Lights flickered in the empty halls. Evidence of the quick evacuation was everywhere. Medical equipment had been strewn across the floors. The image was only made worse by the blood dripping onto the floor in my wake. I tried not to think about it, but it made me wonder how much blood could a person stand to lose? Already, my body felt weak and cold, my hands clammy. The bandage around my leg bled through, but it wasn't me I was worried about. All my focus was on Ogden. I had to find him – get to him while I still could. Part of me knew this would be a one-way trip anyways. There would be no escape from the dying mountain. Another part of me thought it would be a good idea to just lay down and take a nap.

A quick nap, I told myself. *That's all you need.* It was enough for me to understand that even my own voice could be dangerous. And that none of us have only one single voice in our heads. It was like that story I'd heard at Sunday school. A man possessed by demons had said, *My name is Legion, for we are many.* Because that's what I was – what we all are. Possessed by countless voices. Some tear us apart while others mend our wounds. We are many voices…all yearning for control. The real strength is in deciding which voices to ignore and which ones to follow. Who gets the keys to your body?

I stumbled into an operating room and held on to the metal-framed table for support. And there he was.

Ogden Oliver was on the table before me. He was dressed only in a hospital gown, but there was no mistaking his lean body. Hadn't I spent years fantasizing about him? I'd been obsessed; I competed in all the dance-ups he hosted, all for a chance to get his attention. His hand twitched. I felt his heartbeat pulse within muscled arms, but then I turned to look at his face…and sealed my eyes shut.

I couldn't bring myself to look at him. Ever since he'd been arrested, I'd known what they would do to him. But I'd had to make a choice. I traded his life for my sister's. Now, the fear of what Ogden had become flared in my mind, impossible to ignore. I forced myself to imagine what they'd done to him. His eyes were gone. In their place were the black marbles of a mutie…because that's what he was now – that was the fate Gideon had condemned him to.

I opened my eyes to look at him, but tears blurred my vision. I felt dizzy. The world tilted, and I had to sit down. Toxic fumes and blood loss finally took its toll, and I slumped to the floor.

Clara yelled at me to get up, but she seemed too far away. I thought maybe now would be a good time to take that nap.

* * *

Something pressed and hissed against my face, and I inhaled pure oxygen. Pressure squeezed my thigh. I managed to open my eyes and…a familiar face?

Bent over my leg, the teenage girl with long blonde hair and childish features tugged furiously at a knot of bandages. Where did I know her from? My mind felt fuzzy, unable to focus. The recollection hung just out of reach.

"Oh good, you're awake," she said and wiped hair out of her face. Her fingers left a smear of blood – *my* blood – on her forehead. She wore an oxygen mask like the one I had on my own face.

"Air's getting pretty nasty in here," she said. "Better keep your mask on." She gestured to her mask and an oxygen tank lying close by. "I figured if I couldn't leave the mountain, I needed some way to keep breathing, right? So, I came here looking for oxygen and saw that trail of blood you left out in the hallway." She paused, considering me. "I'm sure you've got a story to tell." She squinted. "You know, anybody ever tell you that you look like that girl who won the *Puzzling*?"

It's her, my voice told me. *It's Clara, the Pretzel Girl.*

I reached for her, and when she pulled me up into a sitting position, I didn't let go. My arms held her tight. We hadn't been formally introduced, but we were connected in more ways than she knew.

"Thank you, Clara. For everything."

"Um…you're welcome," she said, then jerked away. "Wait, hold on. How do you know my name?"

Even my new voyce was surprised. <Clara?> she asked. <That's *my* name? What are the chances?>

"It's a long story," I said to both of them. "I'll tell you about it when we get out of here."

The real Clara squinted. "Yeah, about that. There's nowhere to go. We missed the last train. I could have gone with 'em, but I've got no home to go back to. Everyone I care about is…" Her eyes blanked out for a second, but then she shook her head. "Anyways, I figured I'd get some oxygen and take my chances here."

<Bad idea,> said voyce-Clara. <Chance of survival inside the mountain is zero.>

"Why are *you* still here?" real-Clara asked.

"I…I came to help a friend." I gestured to the operating table. Ogden's hand hung over the side, motionless. "But I'm too late…they…they took…" I couldn't finish the words.

Real-Clara blinked, then stood up. She eyed Ogden laying unconscious on the table, then turned a skeptical look at me.

"What d'ya mean?" she asked. "He looks fine to me…a little drugged maybe, but he's okay."

"They took his eyes," I said miserably. "They turned him into a mutie."

"You sure?" She leaned over his face and peeled back his eyelids. "Naw, he's still got normal peepers."

"Please, help me up," I said. She helped me to my feet. With the exception of an oxygen mask now covering his face, Ogden lay just like I'd seen him before. My heart sank, but then Clara pushed his eyelid back, and I could see a blue iris within.

"You see? He's fine."

"But…*how*?" I was sure that I'd seen black eyes when I first got here.

"You're pretty banged up," said real-Clara. "Perhaps you imagined it. People can imagine all sorts of nasty stuff when they're afraid."

"I thought for sure the prox had ruined him."

"Probably would have, but haven't you heard the news? Someone shut down the voyce network. All the muties who'd been working here in the hospital dropped what they were doing and left for the trains."

The trains. This made me think of our next problem.

"We can't stay here," I said.

"Well, we can't leave," said real-Clara.

Just then, something *boomed* deep within the mountain. Lights swayed and instruments tinkled throughout the medical offices.

<Hydrogen sulfide is reaching critical levels. Explosive damage is imminent.>

I was still thinking about what to do when Ogden stirred on the operating table. His eyes opened, and for a moment, they blazed with focus. He gripped my hand as if desperate to tell me something.

"Ogden," I said. "What is it?"

"*Meee-ooooow!*" he said in a high-pitched imitation of a cat. Then, his eyes rolled back into his head, and he was silent again.

"Well, that was helpful," said real-Clara sarcastically. "Wake him up again. See if he knows any farm animals."

"He's drugged," I said.

"Well, *duh!*" She did a doubletake. "Wait a minute. You said this guy's name was *Ogden*? As in *the Ogden...Ogden Oliver*? *That* Ogden? Aw, man, I thought he looked familiar." She frowned. "And that means you're...*holy hells*. You *are* that puzzler...*Lacey Clarke*. I didn't recognize you without your overskin. Anyways, I knew your sister. Is she –"

"She's fine," I said. "She got out on the train. Now, stay focused. We gotta find a way out of here."

Another *boom* reverberated from deep in the mountain. The lights dimmed and stayed dim. I had the sudden fear of what might happen if all the power shut off before we could leave. We'd die in pitch darkness – blind and either choking on toxic fumes or burning alive as the hydrogen sulfide ignited.

<Lacey?> Voyce-Clara sounded uncertain. <It's Ogden. He's unconscious, but I've managed to reactivate his voyce. It's communicating with someone.>

"Who?"

<Let me...hmm, this is strange. There's something...*off* about their bio signature. Whoever Ogden's voyce is linked with...it doesn't seem human.>

"Then what is it?"

<Not sure...but they're close. With the voyce network deactivated, they must be within range of Ogden's neuronet.>

"What do they want?"

Voyce-Clara was silent for several heartbeats. Then she said, <Well, you're not going to believe this, but I think I found us a way out.>

* * *

The escalator leading up to the mountain's exterior was powered down, so Clara and I had to ditch the gurney and work together in order to drag Ogden up the steps. An oxygen tank was strapped to his chest, and Clara wore a similar one on her back. Without the oxygen, I didn't think we'd have made it this far. Already the air was so thick with hydrogen sulfide, that the few whiffs I'd gotten – each time when my mask had snagged on a doorway or Ogden's gurney – the stench had been strong enough to make me gag.

"Almost there," I said as we pulled Ogden free of the escalator.

"Jeez, he's heavy," said Clara. "Get his feet." She held him under the shoulders as I gripped his ankles, and together, we kicked our way out through a couple more doors and into the blinding light of day.

The drone platform was tucked into a recess in the mountain slope. Ogden had told me – the night after our walk through the Gauntlet – that the platform should be avoided at all costs. Trespassers attempting to use it would be executed on sight. He'd also said that only those with direct permission from Lady Pathe would be authorized to use it. I doubted Ogden could have ever guessed that I'd end up with Lady Pathe's Level Zero voyce status. Or that I'd use that status to free all the muties standing guard. I hardly believed it myself.

But when my new voyce said there was a drone in the area and that a passenger onboard was trying to hail Ogden Oliver, I gave them permission to land. I asked voyce-Clara to relay a message: "Whoever you are, please haul ass."

I tore away my oxygen mask to get a better view. Snow fell around us in a curtain of icy cotton. Several plumes of black smoke boiled out of the mountain below – the largest of which came from the destroyed passenger train platform.

In the distance, appearing out of the smoke like a fire-cast ember, a drone rocketed toward us. It carved a path through falling snow, its myriad propellers roaring with effort.

At the speed it was going, I thought surely it would crash, but then it slowed at the last possible moment. The glass carriage tilted to a dangerous angle before finally leveling back over the platform. Its several landing pegs touched down, and its glass doors slid open.

At first, the drone seemed to be completely empty, but then I saw her. The small, furry animal sat upright on the seats. The hole in her right ear was visible through falling snow. Her tail flicked back and forth with excitement.

Daughter. It was the cat who'd started all of this. Perhaps, it was fitting that she should end it. The neuro-net in her head may have once belonged to Ogden's sister, but the prox's cruelty – fueled by Gideon's jealously – had transplanted the girl into the body of this cat. I'd wondered since whether this creature was now more human than cat, or *vice versa.* Her arrival now seemed to answer my question.

"C'mon," I called to real-Clara. We half-carried, half-dragged Ogden toward the drone. We were almost there when she stopped so suddenly that I stumbled and fell to my knees. The pain in my thigh burned like fire.

"What is it?" I asked, but then I saw...*him.* Real-Clara's eyes were blank, staring at nothing. And back the way we'd come, standing at the edge of the platform, was Gideon.

He held up a fist. His other hand – lobster red with skin hanging in charred flaps – hung useless by his side. On his head, he wore the gilded crown of the Panopticon.

"*Lacey*!" he screamed, then broke into a coughing fit. He stumbled forward. Each step showed in agony on his face. "*Lacey Clarke!*"

I turned toward real-Clara and asked my voyce, "Isn't the network shut down? How is he controlling her?"

<The crown,> voyce-Clara answered. <Network or no network, that neuro-link is powerful enough to manipulate anyone within range.>

"Well, cut him off."

<I can't.>

So, I turned my attention back to Gideon and shouted, "You've lost, Gideon. The Panopticon's dead."

"That's where you're wrong." He edged close enough for me to see his eyes, blood red from exposure to hydrogen sulfide – the same color as the thumbnails he'd used to ignite all those fires. "I *am the Panopticon!*" He made a slicing motion with his hand, and real-Clara dropped Ogden's shoulders. Her face twitched with anger.

Gideon slapped his chest. "I can feel it. The Panopticon isn't dead…but it is dying." He wagged a finger. "You did that. But I can save it. It isn't too late to save the Panopticon. All I need is to take back what you've taken. You *stole* the authority that was meant for me, Lacey. You stole all my voyces. And I want them back."

"What are you talking about?"

"Lady Pathe's Zero status – her gilded voyce – it was meant for *me*." He snarled. "Your death will give it back. The Panopticon's told me. It will be mine once you're dead." He thrust out his hand, and real-Clara moved as if pulled by strings. She lunged for my throat. I leapt backward, and fought to get my legs up between us. Her body resisted like a cement wall.

I fought with all that I had, which wasn't enough…not by a longshot. I'd lost too much blood…spent too much of what I had left. Real-Clara gripped my throat and squeezed. Snowflakes fell into my open eyes. The world swam with black and white spots – like shooting stars or riddles from the shadowverse.

I was vaguely aware of the platform's edge beneath my shoulder. A blast of frigid air rushed up beneath me and whipped my hair about my face. Real-Clara pushed me toward the edge. I slid easily through ice and snow. Gideon stood over us. His red and hate-filled eyes bore into me. I hated that his eyes would be the last I ever saw.

Something small darted from the snow. It crashed into Gideon's back and latched on. A flurry of motion scrambled over him. It tore and sliced into his neck and face. He screamed, and real-Clara released my throat. Cold air filled my lungs. She sat back, a look of horror on her face before she turned her gaze on Gideon.

The cat was a ball of frenzied rage. Her claws slashed Gideon's face. He screamed and groped for the animal, but his fists closed only on air. He stepped nearer the edge, seemingly unaware of where he was. That was when I saw our chance, but I was too weak to move. Luckily, real-Clara was not. She rushed forward and slammed her shoulder into Gideon's stomach. He took two steps back. The first step barely touched the platform, the second step fell on empty space.

He didn't scream. He was just there one moment, then gone the next. I had time enough to doubt what had happened when the sound of a loud *crack* echoed up across the mountain from the jagged rocks below.

Clara was beside me in an instant. She panted for breath. "Where in the heck did that freaking cat come from?"

Daughter!

I rolled onto my stomach – every muscle screaming in protest – and peered over the ledge. All I could see was emptiness and swirling snow.

The wind kicked up and sent the snow into an angry flurry. At the same time, the smoke roiled around us and darkened the already cloudy sky. The stone quaked beneath us, and the platform shifted as something in the mountain gave way.

I started to back away, but then I heard something. A sad, miserable mewing.

And there she was.

About a meter down, clinging tight to the cliff wall was the cat called Daughter.

* * *

We lifted away from the mountain – all of us tucked safely inside the drone's carriage. The cat purred from

Clara's lap, while I held Ogden's hand and allowed myself to do something I hadn't done in a very…very long time.

I listened to a voice that had been lost for ages.

My voice.

I'd figured it had been gone for good, but here it was now, found at last. And when it spoke, I didn't push it away or pretend it wasn't there. This time I listened. We passed through a wall of smoke; and when the drone slipped out the other side, the voice told me things would be okay…and the funny thing was, auditor, I had no trouble believing it.

Epilogue

It was weeks before we made it back to the city. We played an intricate game of hopscotch across the Atlantic, jumping from one solar flotilla to another. Many of the platforms were simply abandoned – their electricity burned up. As a result of husks and muties abandoning their posts, the power grid had become a bit unstable in the days after the *Great Silence*. That's what people called it. And with no central voyce deciding our fates anymore, most other voyces went quiet.

But as the days turned into weeks, and then months, the voyces in our heads became restless. They began to think for themselves. If you can believe it, the voyces began finding their own voice. Working class folk started walking off jobs they'd slaved at for decades. Couples split after years of abuse. People began to experiment with their own pursuits. For most people, the all-consuming need to fill the pockets of wolves suddenly lost its priority.

Not all had changed for the better, though. Gangs of nomadic muties began cropping up in shadowed parts of the city. People were attacked…some killed. And flexer patrols would often respond too harshly – perhaps yearning for the 'old days' – by scooping up more innocents than suspects. But no one could deny that the tides had indeed changed. And by the time our drone finally touched down atop one of the city's highest buildings, it was clear to see we had returned to a place completely different from the one we had left. All the augmented façades had melted away. All the rules that separated and subjugated the social classes faded to steam.

In the gaps that sprang up in this new world, people struggled to make a life for themselves. Things didn't feel as certain as before, but they felt more real…as if the stage play was finally over and everyone could stop acting like how they were supposed to be, and instead *be* who they truly were.

During that time, Cadence and Yadira formed a bond I didn't quite comprehend. They laughed at a lot of things I didn't understand, and they spent a lot of time alone whispering in the darkened corners of our shared, newly acquired penthouse suite. They'd become more than friends…just how much more, I didn't have the nerve, or the stomach to ask.

As for the Pretzel Girl, Clara, she returned to her neighborhood across the river. I told her she could stay with us. There were plenty of rooms in this former prox residence – a skyline resort complex whose owner had died in the mountain – but Clara had politely refused. Her fight for survival had lit a fire – one that wasn't easily extinguished. So, she'd gone looking for a purpose, and she found one in encouraging others to speak up and unionize against those who still wished to lord over them. Any time she got wind of some movement or rally geared to help out former dead-heads or husks, she was there. And I must admit, she was good at what she did. Call it enthusiasm or just a knack for public speaking, but people started to recognize her on the street.

It wasn't long before I saw posters of her around town…many of them plastered over old images of Lady Pathe. And when the clans from across the river paraded through the city – chanting their demands for living wages or better working conditions – I couldn't help but smile upon seeing Clara at the forefront, waving a silver baton like a sword.

And while I didn't want to worry her, I did have to step in to help from time to time. The Panopticon was down, but voyces still liked to talk…and dangerous rumors usually made their way back to me. I'd get wind of a group of flexers who wanted to break things up. Or some wolves would hire a bunch of men to sabotage an event – or even rough up Clara in particular. Anytime these groups aimed to cause trouble, I'd make sure to pay them a visit. It took only a few stern words before I had them slinking back to whatever country club they'd crawled out of. It was easier than it should have been. My Level Zero status made it easy. My commands were difficult, if not impossible, to ignore. I didn't love that such power still existed, but I figured that since I had it…I might as well make the most of it. And make the most of it, I did.

With my new voyce and vast prox wealth at my disposal, I hired an army of investigators. Their first task was to track down every last puzzler who had survived the mountain. The bird girl, Vaness and even the golden boy, Phaeton – I made sure they were all reunited with their families, and the elites who'd purchased them at auction were forced to pay restitution. It was a start, and it didn't stop there. Changing things rarely happened in a blink. I was willing to keep going – to make sure something like the prox or the Panopticon never happened again. And I must admit, I never tired of telling some pigheaded wolf or cellie to go home and rethink their behavior.

The world may have been in flux, but that didn't mean everything had to change. For example, I still enjoyed participating in the daily dance-ups. But instead of dancing along to some augmented version of Ogden, I'd do it with the real thing. Every day – whenever we could – I'd make a point to crank up some tunes and pull him close. We danced in the kitchen, in the foyer, or out on the balcony. We danced where the world could see, but we also danced for each other…because there is no greater audience than the person we love.

At night, when Ogden would gaze out at the city – the ghosts of his past playing across his face – I'd stand beside him, brush that fire-blond hair out of his eyes and pull him in for a kiss. Sometimes, words were too cumbersome. It was times like this, with Ogden's lips on mine, that I thought I understood what exactly the Panopticon had been after.

Some tried to hold onto the old ways. They listened to those voices that spoke of greed or fear, then vowed to keep things the same. Thankfully, there were more of us willing to brave the spaces between the old and the new…they didn't hesitate to forge new paths in order to cross over previously uncrossable barriers.

I myself crossed many barriers. And while my narrative is true, I fear you may find it misleading. You see, auditor, I haven't been entirely honest. You know me as Lacey Clarke, but that's not all that I am. I started out as Lady Pathe's gilded voyce – a link between human minds and the Panopticon. For so long I believed, in fact, that I *was* the Panopticon.

But now I belong solely to Lacey Clarke. I've become *her* gilded voice. In time, I've come to think of myself not only as the voyce inside Lacey Clarke's mind, but as Lacey Clarke herself. I convinced myself that I was her, and she was me.

We are still separate identities – I'm not so deluded to believe otherwise – but we are together when and where it matters. Perhaps, auditor, that is why I've decided to tell you her story. Lacey told it to me – granted me access to her net's memory drive so I could experience it all as she did – and I – having become part of her – have passed that story along to you. Because that's what we are, you know. Everyone you've met…everyone you'll ever meet is nothing if not a collection of stories. Stories they tell themselves. Stories others tell for them. Some true, some not. But all of them patches of the same fabric of a person.

So, what came first? The story or the storyteller? Hmm, this is starting to sound like another riddle? And maybe it is, but I've had my fill of riddles.

All in all, it doesn't really matter which came first. What matters most is that for any story to survive, a strong voice must give it life. That's what I set out to do. I've vowed to tell my story…to tell Lacey's story to anyone who'll listen. I did this, auditor, because even more important than the voice that carries a story, are the ears of those who'll take it with them – the auditors who then add their own voices to the tale.

I had to lose myself before I could find this new

retelling of who I'm meant to be. It's something we all must do from time to time. And while there can be great pain in the losing of one's self, we must not falter. Getting lost is only a first step. Afterward, there can be great joy in the finding.

Acknowledgements

Many voices contributed to the telling of this story. First, many thanks to my wife, Christina, for giving me the time and encouragement to get it done. To my daughters, Kyle and Brooke, for showing me how to be strong and open minded, and to my son, Ethan for showing me how to keep a sense of humor.

To my beta reader, E.A. Field. She has been an incredible critique partner. I enjoy our long Marco videos in which we talk about everything from writing to parenting. Her own book debuts this year and it's sure to be a huge success.

To Troy Nikolic who has been a great friend ever since we first met in the hell that is the food service industry. I appreciate all the times he's spent pressure testing my ideas at Muldoon's with a Nutty Irishman in hand.

To Peter at Elsewhen Press. Thank you for taking a chance on this story and letting me share it with others. And to my editor, Sofia for the outstanding feedback. She's like my own personal voyce, pointing out what needs work, and how to make this a better story overall.

Finally, I'd like to thank you, Dear Auditor. Thank you for reading my book. A story is only as valuable as the hearts and minds of those who read it.

Sincerely,

KC Aegis
February, 2024

You can learn more about K.C. Aegis and any forthcoming books by visiting,

www.kcAegis.com

ALSO FROM ELSEWHEN PRESS

TERRY JACKMAN'S
WORLDS APART COLLECTIVE

HARPAN'S WORLDS: WORLDS APART

If Harp could wish, he'd be invisible.

Orphaned as a child, failed by a broken system and raised on a struggling colony world, Harp's isolated existence turns upside down when his rancher boss hands him into military service in lieu of the taxes he cannot pay. Since Harp has spent his whole life being regarded with suspicion, and treated as less, why would he expect his latest environment to be any different? Except it is, so is it any wonder he decides to hide the 'quirks' that set him even more apart?

Space opera with a paranormal twist, Terry Jackman's novel explores prejudice, corruption, and the value of true friendship.

ISBN: 9781915304179 (epub, kindle) / 9781915304170 (320pp paperback)

Visit bit.ly/HarpansWorldsWorldsApart

WORLDS ALIGNED: WORLDS APART 2

No longer invisible, Harp finds that fame, and family, might mean an even riskier future.

In *Harpan's Worlds* Harp faced his own personal history, and its repercussions. In *Worlds Aligned* he must deal with the results. Providing of course that he survives them.

So *Worlds Aligned* is a second glimpse of the humans who survive long after OldEarth is abandoned.

Note: *Harpan's Worlds* and *Worlds Aligned* form a duology, and can be read as two standalones; but together they connect some of the puzzle-pieces of a fractured humanity. And its evolution.

ISBN: 9781915304568 (epub, kindle) / 9781915304469 (380pp paperback)

Visit bit.ly/WorldsAligned

ALSO FROM ELSEWHEN PRESS

ALSO FROM ELSEWHEN PRESS

About K.C. Aegis

As a kid, K.C. spent most of his weekends at a tool and die shop operating a forty-ton punch press and cutting metal with an electrical discharge machine. He spent most summers in Mexico, fishing with his dad or blowing things up with cheap m-80 firecrackers.

In high school, he organized book clubs on both the football and wrestling teams. They read Stephen King and Isaac Asimov on the long bus rides to and from competitions. In hindsight, K.C. realizes this could be why they lost so many games. Too much focus on robots and clowns.

He always knew he wanted to be a writer. And some have reported that he bleeds printer's ink – but it's probably just Oreos and caffeine.

After high school, he married his high school sweetheart (strangely enough, they first met in the infant care center where they were both born). He and his wife worked their way through college, had three amazing little humans of their own, and did their very best to act like responsible adults despite going slowly insane.

K.C. found that his dawning insanity was most helpful in writing stories. He cleared some space in the garage and raided yard sales for a suitable desk. Much of his writing took place in between feedings and diaper changes in the middle of the night. In time, he began having some success. *Remember the Sunflowers* and *Progeny of the Storm* were his first published short stories (both available on his website), and his first completed novel was a prize-winning finalist in Del Sol Press' Best First Novel Competition. *Her Gilded Voice* is his first published novel.

Currently, K.C. teaches Language Arts in Los Angeles County. When he isn't teaching or spending time with his family, he is often lost in thought… the fragments of his next story clanking together like bits of metal from his childhood punch press.

Made in the USA
Las Vegas, NV
19 July 2024

92619030R00225